A NIGHTMARE ON ELM STREET™

THE DREAM DEALERS

BY

JEFFREY THOMAS

Based on characters from the motion
picture A Nightmare on Elm Street
created by Wes Craven

BLACK FLAME

To Hong, a dream come true.

A Black Flame Publication
www.blackflame.com
blackflame@games-workshop.co.uk

First published in 2006 by BL Publishing, Games Workshop Ltd., Willow Road, Nottingham NG7 2WS, UK.

Distributed in the US by Simon & Schuster, 1230 Avenue of the Americas, New York, NY 10020, USA.

10 9 8 7 6 5 4 3 2 1

ISBN 13: 978 1 84416 383 0
ISBN 10: 1 84416 383 0

A CIP record for this book is available from the British Library.

Printed in the UK by Bookmarque, Surrey, UK.

> "Dreams are true while they last, and do we not live in dreams?"
> —Tennyson, *The Higher Pantheism*

Welcome to the world of TranceBox!

As the new owner of this remarkable entertainment device, you are about to embark on adventures as limitless as the human imagination. Saxon Systems' TranceBox® utilizes the latest in CIT (Cerebral Interface Technology), making it possible for a user to experience the recorded memories of another human being (and even animals!), so that every sensation—from sound to taste to touch—is as vivid as it was for the person from whom the memories were derived.

Afraid to parachute for real? Experience it through TranceBox at no physical risk—but feel the same exhilaration the parachutist felt! Even a person confined to a wheelchair since birth can now know exactly what it feels like to scuba

7

dive through a coral reef, climb Mt Everest (if you can take a little cold), or even win a prize-fight (if you can handle a little pain)! Perform a concert for screaming fans, or perform delicate heart surgery. You guys can even know what it's like to deliver a baby, if you want to empathize a little more with your honey. Catch a pigeon, if you want to empathize a little more with your cat. Fight enemies in an assortment of pulse-pounding wars, or take to bed the lover of your dreams (providing you are eighteen or older).

During the time that you are interfacing with your TranceBox, your experience will seem no different from what the original subject experienced! But—you can bungee jump while safely sitting in your local coffee shop, or ride a rodeo horse while sitting in your classroom (just don't let teacher find out!). A timer can be set to control the duration of the experience, from mere minutes to hours (though in the latter case, it is best to be in the secure environment of your home and in the company of a person who could arouse you in the event of an important phone call, for instance, or an emergency such as a fire).

But TranceBox users are not limited to reliving the sensations/perceptions of actual events and actions. Just as vividly, a TranceBox user can experience dreams recorded from the memories of another person. Sure, we all have our own dreams, but that's just it—they're *ours*. Find out what it's like to experience someone else's dreams... *really* wild dreams, chosen especially for the intensity or strangeness of their content. It will feel as real for you as it did for the subject at the time, and like the memory recordings, you can replay the dreams again and again (talk about recurring dreams!). Any time of day, for as long as you desire, dream yourself into the ultimate escape. The wackiest nonsensical dreams... the hottest erotic dreams... or the scariest nightmares. No movie or video game can yet compete with the power of human dreams. Only the TranceBox can provide those kinds of thrills.

CIT technology goes beyond virtual reality. These recordings are another person's reality—but now their reality can be shared by *you!*

And TranceBox is so easy to use, even your mom can fly a jetliner or fight a bull! Its coin-sized software disks load and unload at the touch of a button. A single, wireless and self-adhesive receptor pad stuck to your right or left temple puts you in connection with your TranceBox. The signal is good for up to 30 feet—though as you can see, the unit will clip to a belt or fit nicely into a pocketbook. (See Page 7 for full Operating Instructions.)

TranceBox is enclosed in a durable plastic casing, but it's still a sensitive device. Avoid dropping, contact with water, or exposure to intense heat. Do not open the casing or modify the unit in any way. (See Page 2 for complete Safety Information.)

A small percentage of CIT users may experience seizures (even if they have not been diagnosed with epilepsy), severe headaches, hyperventilation, persisting hallucination, or interrupted cardiac function. If you have pre-existing health issues, consult your doctor before using TranceBox. (See Page 3 for complete Health Warnings.)

ONE

The air was full of static.

It fizzed soundlessly, a blizzard of swarming light particles. Everything was pixilated, grainy.

But more than that, Devon felt he had stepped inside a black and white movie. An ancient, silent movie—the film stock scratched with long flickering lines, flashing with specks and blips. A deteriorating black and white movie as seen through the static-filled screen of an old TV, before cable, a TV with poor reception, maybe receiving a broadcast bounced back years later—and much degraded in quality—from another planet.

Devon held his hand up in front of his face. He flipped it from front to back, staring at it through the pale luminous static, through the scoring and nicks in the scarred celluloid. So this wasn't a black and white world after all, but the tint of his flesh looked faded, bleached, as if colors here had been leeched of their lifeblood. He lowered his hand and turned slowly, taking in his surroundings.

There was almost nothing to take in. Everything seemed blank at first, just an empty canvas, a TV tuned to dead air. Just whiteness that the static and scratches could play across. But then he realized that he *was* seeing something—a thick, rolling fog illuminated weakly by an overcast sky. He could just barely perceive its churning movements if he gazed into those cloudy depths long enough.

A sudden sound made the teenager flinch. He had thought this was a silent movie.

It had been the caw of a crow. Now he heard the throaty croak of another one, from a different direction. The squawk of a third, behind him; involuntarily he whirled toward the sound. It made him uneasy, being surrounded by birds that he couldn't make out in all that muffling, blanketing fog. He flinched again when he saw a ghostly gray shape like an airborne rag flutter toward him out of the mist, piercing it in the abrupt black form of a large crow. He ducked, even though it flapped up over his head without really coming close. He lifted his eyes to watch it, and maybe he blinked, because the bird seemed to shoot ahead in the sky several yards in one quick lunge before it resumed its normal flapping, as if a few frames had gone missing from the film he was both watching and living in.

Though he felt no breeze on his face, Devon could tell that the fog was being pushed along slowly. Again, he was able detect its billowing movement if he watched it long enough. It was even beginning to thin off to his right, and so he pivoted his body to face that way.

He took a step forward, squinting into the vapors as they drew back gradually like a curtain. As he did so, his toe stubbed an object on the ground, and he looked down, squatted, rose with it in his fist. It was a short sword with a double-edged blade, and it reminded him both of an artifact he had seen many times in a museum in his town, and a plastic toy sword he had often played with as a boy. It was a Roman sword, called a gladius. Hmm... how did he know that name? Maybe he recalled it from the museum. Whatever the case, the weapon's weight in his hand gave him a sense of security in this shrouded world. But what was it even doing here?

And what was he doing here, himself? He had come into this world for a reason, and now he couldn't recall what that reason was, his mind as hazy and filled with static as the air around him.

A flapping, a whoosh over his head, but this time he couldn't see the crow responsible. He had felt the impulse to swing the sword at it but the unseen bird was gone before he could even lift his arm. As he twirled about in an attempt to catch sight of the taunting creature, he saw that the fog behind him had now thinned to a smoky haze. And in that haze, a dark shape had begun to coalesce.

What was it? A framework of some kind. A torture device? But why should he think that? He began walking toward it and stubbed his toe again, but this time the obstacle resisted and he pitched forward before he could stop himself. In falling, he let go of the sword and heard it clang on a hard surface and skitter away. His palms, when they impacted, found a granulated softness. He sank into it up to his wrists. Sand. The floor had become sand. It was as if it were these grains, swept up into the air, which were responsible for the sandstorm-like static. The air was as heavy and still as ever, like a moment fossilized in time.

The haze was ever clearing, however, and in pushing himself back to his feet, Devon could see that the floor of this place wasn't sand. There was only a square of sand, contained within a crudely-built wooden enclosure with diagonal planks at the four corners to accommodate small posteriors. There was even a rusted tin bucket resting in the sand, half full, with a matching shovel sticking up from it.

A child's sandbox.

Slapping the grit from his palms, Devon raised his eyes to that strange framework again. The supports for some tent-like structure, its fabric now stripped or burnt away? No. He could see chains hanging motionless from it, plastic seats suspended from the chains, a ladder and slide fitted to one end. A child's swing set.

Devon shuffled in a little circle, scanning more of his environment as the fog dissipated. He was beginning to make out a shadowy, looming perimeter. Its scale, as it became increasingly solid, made him feel increasingly dwarfed and vulnerable. He—and this miniature playground—must be standing at the center of some immense circular amphitheater; perhaps a football stadium.

Turning, he saw a hopscotch pattern chalked onto the stadium's floor, not far from the sandbox, a partially deflated ball and an abandoned jump rope. That was all the playground consisted of, besides a heap of junk piled beyond the swing set. It seemed to be a mass of wood scraps, maybe an old barrel lying on its side, loosely covered with some ratty-looking shag rug, striped in ugly green and red bands.

A crow alighted on top of the swing set with a caw. It cocked its head at Devon, and again he felt taunted. He glanced around him for his sword, but there were still coils of mist crawling along the floor of the stadium, obscuring his view.

The fog was ever receding, the circular wall of the stadium becoming ever more distinct. It reared darkly, and was apparently punctured with countless arched windows. There appeared to be four tiers of seats. Seats containing...

"Oh my God," Devon exhaled shakily.

So many, many seats. 50,000 of them. But how could he know that figure? 50,000 seats, and despite the quiet, punctuated only by a crow's croak here, another's squawk there, every one of those seats had been occupied all along. 50,000 spectators had been staring down at him, waiting for the mists to clear. He began to discern their forms. A few moments later, and he wished the fog had never cleared to reveal those rows and rows of avid faces.

Avid, fleshless faces.

They were an audience of skeletons. Some were more denuded than others, while some were still sheathed in parchment-like skin, resembling unwrapped mummies. Wisps of hair like cobwebs hung from the occasional skull. The skeletons were all garbed in robes, archaic clothing, but this attire was appropriate to the setting. For Devon understood where he was at last.

He stood in the center of an arena. More than that, it was the Colosseum of Rome itself. He saw now that the monumental enclosure was more elliptical than circular. Extending out from the third level was an immense canopy, shading the crowd from the sun, but the sky was still an overcast pearly gray and the canopy was tattered, hanging in ribbons. There was a private spectators' box on the first level, and though its interior was lost in gloom, he knew that the skeletons propped in those seats of honor must be wearing gold or other jewelry around the plucked bones of their necks and wrists. "Plucked" because he saw crows peppered throughout the vast audience, perched atop shoulders and skulls, occasionally snipping at a shred of scalp or thrusting inside a gaping eye socket with their quick beaks.

"No way," Devon heard himself saying, over and over, and he had probably been saying it for a while before he became aware of his own voice. "No... no way..."

Then there was a metallic creak behind him. It repeated itself. Again. A rhythmic squeaking sound, which he spun around to confront.

Where the gym set had stood unoccupied and motionless before, now one of its swings was rocking widely like a pendulum. A little girl rode upon it—a child of flesh and blood, not some grinning scarecrow of bones, and she was using her delicate weight to push her pointing, white-stockinged legs ever higher. She wore a frilly Sunday dress and matching headband straight out of the idyllic Fifties or early Sixties. She began singing, as though she had been waiting for him to look at her before she started, despite gazing into the sky as if unaware that he even existed.

"*Mori-tori te sal-ut-amus,*" she sang sweetly, drawing out the Latin words.

Not only did Devon recognize the words as Latin, but—although he had never studied the language—he realized that he understood exactly what they meant.

Moritori te salutamus: "We who are about to die, salute you."

Not far from the swings, a shroud of fog drew back to reveal another little girl, almost identical to the first, jumping rope. As she did so, her puffy dress bouncing, she sang, "*Ut quis quem vi-cer-it oc-ci-dat.*"

Ut quis quem vicerit occidat: "Kill the defeated, whoever he may be."

Gladiator mottos. Devon knew that. It was all he could really be sure of in the world at this moment. Wherever this world was.

"Hey," Devon called to the jump-roping child in a quavering voice. "Hey, little girl. Hey."

Their singing had stopped, but neither child took any notice of him.

A deep rumble. Was that a distant peal of thunder? He could believe a storm might not be far off, from that solemn sky. Still, it had sounded closer than that, and Devon revolved slowly where he stood. The rocking swing still squeaked behind him, but when he faced it again it swung empty, in slower and slower arcs. The jump rope once again lay abandoned on the arena's floor. For seconds only, Devon saw one of the girls standing rigidly, staring at him from across the vast arena floor, but she seemed to walk backwards very quickly and jerkily into the dregs of the fog, vanishing utterly.

That rumble. Deeper, clearer. Low to the ground, ominous—and right behind him. Devon swiveled warily.

Something was hiding under that heap of junk—the broken barrel, the odd pieces of wood, that ugly striped rug. Yes the rug was definitely moving. Slowly rising. Something four-legged, it appeared, was cloaked beneath it. A dog? If so, a *big* dog...

In one explosive burst, every crow scattered throughout the ancient stadium's skeletal audience flew into the air as if startled by a gunshot. Devon had not been able to appreciate how many of the birds there were until they were airborne. With an uncanny noise of countless beating wings, they made off in the same direction, and in dwindling they seemed to coalesce into a living black storm cloud. He had little time to focus on the birds' evacuation of the Colosseum. Devon's anxious attention snapped back to that rising shape covered with the ratty rug of green and red bands.

"Oh, wait, *wait*," was all he could utter, tremulously, rooted in place by a mounting terror.

Yes, a large four-legged body had risen from the arena floor. What he had taken for a broken barrel was the thing's chest. An emaciated chest with some of its ribs actually punctured through the creature's hide. What he'd assumed were scraps of wood were the thing's legs, the hide that covered them worn right through to bare bones, these bones somehow still joined together by leathery tendons. A long tail swished from side to side, like a whip lazily toyed with before a sadist lashes it at his victim—a whip of segmented bone.

A great, shaggy head twisted around to glare at him over one hunched shoulder, but there were no eyes to glare with. What Devon was seeing was the eyeless skull of a lion, unevenly covered in a layer of horribly scarred, raw, reddened skin. There were only enough muscles and tendons left on this desiccated head to work the jaw, which opened wide to show fangs all the longer for having no gums to root in. With the animal's mouth open beyond what seemed its natural limits, the lion let out more than just a rumbling growl this time.

A *roar*. Devon felt the vibration of the sound carried through the very floor of the arena. Up through the soles of his feet. Up, throughout his body, until it shook his heart inside him like a fruit ready to drop from its stem.

"No... no..." he whimpered.

Following its head, the lion shifted its entire body around slowly, as if stalking him though tall savannah grass, with a predator's unhurried patience. Its tangled mane was dark brown or black, but its body had that oddly striped green and red coloration like a mutant breed of tiger. And those claws at the ends of its forelegs seemed unbelievably long, much too long for the great cat to retract into its toes. Not only that, but the talons seemed to glint, to shimmer metallically as the lion moved...

Devon's first impulse was to flee, to try to outrun the thing, and get a head start *now* before it charged. But flee where? Was there a doorway here at the level of the arena's floor through which he could escape? And even if there were, would he have even a slight chance of reaching it before the lion reached him?

Then he remembered the sword he had dropped, the gladius' reassuring weight in his fist. His eyes flicked about for it desperately, the rest of his body paralyzed with fear, but he felt a lurch of hope when he saw the sword lying only several paces away, clearly exposed now with all but wisps of the fog having dispersed.

The lion seemed to have noticed him staring at the sword. It began to crouch closer to the ground, bunching up its muscles to spring.

Devon sprang first, sweeping his arm low and scooping up the sword in one fluid movement. His lunge brought him that much closer to the beast, and suddenly it was launching itself, bounding at him, roaring again with its mouth so huge, those powerful jaws perhaps unhinged like the jaws of a snake, stretched to swallow him whole.

With courage brought on by a jolt of adrenaline and the knowledge that he had no other option but to tuck in his head and let those razor claws slice into him, Devon hunched his weight low like a wrestler—like a gladiator—and held out the sword in front of him to meet the attack.

But something was wrong. The sword felt different from before. Lighter. Very much lighter.

He dared to drop his gaze to it for a fraction of a second. It looked the same as it had previously. Yet it was light enough to be hollow. Light enough to be plastic. Just another toy, dropped near the swing set.

Dear God—the swing set—his only remaining chance. If he could just get to it, climb up on top of it...

But the lion was running, running, then leaping into the air. Flying at him. It was as if he was flying toward it, though; falling, plummeting into the fanged tunnel of that gaping black mouth, growing so wide as if to swallow the entire world. Wherever this world was.

And then a waterfall of static crashed over him. A torrent of silently fizzing light particles so dense that their weight seemed to pound him into the ground like a stake where he stood, drowning out the lion's roar, drowning out his every sensation, then his every thought. Burying him. Snuffing him utterly out of existence.

"Oh my God, oh my God, oh my God!" Devon blurted, half scrambling up from his seat and only managing to sprawl onto his rear on the floor, limbs awry, as if he had woken to find that all his bones had been excised while he was unconscious.

Rising from his own chair nearby, Devon's older brother Alex sputtered a laugh, wagging his head. He bent over Devon, extending his hand. "You okay, there?"

Devon gaped up at his brother as if he didn't recognize him, his eyes bulging, chest heaving. In fact, for several moments he didn't quite recognize Alex. Later, when he was calmer, Devon would realize that the residual effects of experiencing someone else's memories had been what had contributed to that momentary lack of recognition. That and the blazing white panic that had flared in his head, blinding him to everything but his own gradually fading terror.

At last, however, Devon accepted his brother's help, and Alex hoisted him to his feet.

"Is that the most potent nightmare you've ever had, or what?" Alex beamed proudly.

"Man oh man. I don't know if I'd even call that fun," Devon managed to pant.

Alex took him by the arms and helped steer him back into his padded swivel chair. "Hey, some people have jaded tastes. That's what I have in mind for this. Something for people who seek the ultra-intense."

"That could give somebody a heart attack, man— I don't doubt it!"

Alex chuckled, wagging his head again as he removed the band he had placed around his brother's head a few minutes earlier. Wires connected the headgear to a console close at hand, glowing with lights. A keyboard and a monitor screen were adjacent to it. Alex rested the band on top of the monitor before he settled in his own seat again, rolling forward in it to clap a hand on his kid brother's knee. "Well, this definitely wouldn't be for grannies, I admit."

Still trying to regulate his breathing, Devon glanced over at the band atop the monitor, as if afraid the demonic halo would fling itself back on his head of its own accord. "Seriously, you think it's possible something like that could give you a heart attack?"

"Nah. Well, like, if you already had a serious heart condition, maybe. But then, a person with a serious heart condition could run into trouble doing just about anything."

Devon looked back at his brother earnestly. "I read in the TranceBox manual about possible cardiac malfunction."

"Hey, they gotta have their legal disclaimers. But yeah, TranceBox software designers do have certain safety guidelines to follow. You couldn't allow a program user to experience, for instance, the memory of a person actually having a heart attack. Or the memory of anybody being painfully injured or dying. There are limits they set for us to stay within so that nobody can get hurt using this stuff."

"Yeah, well, it can still happen. I saw this thing on the Web where they found a high school kid sitting on the john in a men's room stall. *Dead*. He had six TranceBox pads stuck all over his forehead. There were six TranceBoxes in his backpack—he had the five basic colors and the gold collectors' edition—and he was running a different program on every one of them simultaneously. Two were like wet dream things, one was the point of view of a leopard chasing down an antelope or something, one was a dive off a cliff into the ocean…"

"Was one a train going into a tunnel? A tree falling, played in reverse?"

"I'm not kidding. Whatever thrill he was going for gave him a massive aneurism or something and he died on the spot."

"Well, at least if he pooped in his pants, they didn't have to take him far to clean it up. Come on, man, you saw that on the web? That smells like urban legend to me."

"Why?" Devon persisted. "Why couldn't that happen?"

"You couldn't play six CIT programs all at once. It would just be… a jumble. A chaos."

"That's what I'm *saying*. This kaleidoscope of images and sensations just fried the poor guy's brain."

Alex rose from his chair again to pace the area in front of the equipment-heaped workstation. It was their long-standing habit to pace when their conversations grew animated, and Devon would have followed suit at some point had his legs not been still feeling so boneless.

Alex picked up a ridiculously large Styrofoam cup of coffee off the top of another piece of electronic equipment and sipped from it before he said, "The dream cut out on you just as the lion jumped, right?"

"Yeah, thank God! I don't care what you say—I would have had a heart attack for sure if I'd felt that thing land on me and start tearing into me."

Alex's tone became less mocking. More pensive. "The subject was a high school kid, himself. A kind of history buff. Into role-playing games, too. I figure he had an interest in ancient Rome; the reason he dreamed those things. How much did you feel like you were him—actually *him*, and not yourself?"

"Um, not too much. I still felt like me. Like, I knew I was Devon Carmack, not whoever that kid was. But then, I understood Latin. I knew the name of that stupid sword that went from metal to plastic."

"Yeah. That was the way it was for me, too. I find that in memories and dreams extracted from live people, the experience is more... solid. More whole. You really put that person's shoes on, you *are* that person, and lose your own identity. The sense of your own self is thoroughly replaced. But in these impressions we're reconstructing from dead people's brains, the results are more transparent. It's sketchier, less complete. You saw the interference, the imperfections in the visuals and whatnot. Not only that, you don't experience the full sense of the dead subject's identity. The dream or memory simply seems to be a template you place over your own identity."

"Okay, so will that flaw prevent you from selling this thing to Saxon, or what?"

"Shh." Alex stopped pacing to put a finger to his lips and glare at his brother meaningfully. He glanced around him to make certain no one else had wandered into the large, dimly-lit lab before he went on, in a lower voice, "No. See, that's what makes this so great! It's a different kind of experience. I think it's very valuable that you retain your own sense of self when you play these programs. I wouldn't want to change that. Sure, I'll work on cleaning it up, patching the more fragmented dreams into cohesive wholes, but this kind of effect is a very happy accident, in my opinion." Alex snorted, his humor returning.

"For a geek, this kid had a very tasty girlfriend. I've managed to pry out one memory of her, but what a memory. Man, getting it on with her is better than some of the real girls I've been with. And again, the cool thing is I'm not this kid getting it on with his girl—it's *me* getting it on with his girl. It's much more gratifying this way. It's where TranceBox programs need to go, I think. An experience just as vivid as the recordings from live donors, but more adaptable to whatever individual plays the software."

Devon was feeling more relaxed by the minute, and he began to swivel back and forth in his chair. He plucked up a monstrous action figure that one of the techs had placed upon another computer monitor in this work station, and began bending its limbs and posing it half-consciously. He glanced about the murky room, which except for the table lamp at this station was illuminated only by a constellation of colored lights both steady and fluttering, and the eerie bluish radiance cast from numerous monitor screens. There was an ever-present hum of electrical devices, the occasional mysterious chatter from one machine and moments later the muted chitter of another machine seemingly answering it back. Bundles of cables had been affixed to the walls here and there with brackets, climbing them like jungle vines, and even snaking openly across the floor in places. This was one of the series of labs belonging to Macrocosm Research, and its logo—consisting of a six-pointed star which Alex had explained to Devon on an earlier visit was a cabalistic symbol called "the seal of Solomon"—loomed on one of the gloom-enveloped walls. Macrocosm Research took on government contracts, such as the project Alex Carmack was currently working on: exhuming memories from the brains of dead people. They called this their Séance Project.

But working for Macrocosm Research was Alex's "day" job. He moonlighted for a smaller company—Mnemonic Designs—that created software for Saxon Systems. And Saxon Systems was the corporation made rich, in just two years, by the introduction of their TranceBox.

"Is your boss still here?" Devon asked in a near whisper.

"I don't know, maybe. Don't worry, Farhad's cool. He'll let you walk nine steps over the line, and then he'll come down on you hard on the tenth step. So I try to keep it at about seven or eight." He smirked, sipped his cooling hazelnut with cream and extra sugar.

"So, is this dead geek's girl better than Trisha?"

Devon ducked his head too late to avoid a hard swat across the back of it. "Hey, you ever mention that in front of her and I'll destroy you. No, she isn't better than Trisha. Okay?"

"Are you going to let me try *that* recording?"

"I wouldn't want to contribute to the delinquency of a minor."

"Uh, hello? I'm eighteen."

"I wouldn't want to corrupt you. I have to be a good role model for you."

"Oh jeesh." Devon set the monster figure back atop its former perch, bent into a wrestler's crouch with arms extended. "You gonna make a copy of that and try to develop it for Saxon, too?"

"Eventually, yeah. Like I say, these wet dreams experienced as a template over your own identity are much more rewarding, in my opinion. But I don't want to scatter my focus. Right now I want to stick to these weird nightmares we're collecting."

"Not to mention Trisha wouldn't be as likely to help you develop wet dreams as she would some spooky nightmares."

"It's not that, it's just that these nightmares are so unbelievable, so strong."

"And every one of these brains they come from... every one of them was a murder victim?"

"Yeah."

Devon felt his gaze drawn back to that ominous halo again, hooked up to the complex array of CIT gear. "How did the history buff die, then?"

"He was stabbed to death, I understand. Cut up pretty bad."

"I know it would be pretty horrific to relive, but... have you been tempted to experience his murder?"

"Me, resist any temptation? Yeah, all safety guidelines aside, I tried to access it. The closest I could get to it is that dream. I'm thinking maybe he was asleep, dreaming, when the murderer crept up on him and knifed him before he could fully wake up."

"What… what do you mean?"

"I think that's why the dream ends so abruptly, when the lion pounces. That's the last thing this brain experienced, apparently. That moment was the moment of this guy's death."

Devon stared up at his brother for several sound-less beats, and then hissed, "*Wow*."

"Yeah. I don't know much about this kid's death, or the deaths of the other people. We don't have access to the police reports, for whatever reason, even though we inquired about it. But I suspect it was a serial killer, because almost all of these vic-tims were teenagers, and all of them were from Springwood."

"What? So how come I never heard of a bunch of people murdered in my hometown?"

"Like I said, the police are tight-fisted with the records. Maybe it was some loony cop who went postal and they want to keep it covered up. Then again, these murders happened like twenty-five years ago—back in the mid-Eighties. I haven't tried digging it up on the web, but I'd like to when I have more time. It isn't so much the fact that they were murdered that made the government folks give us the contract on the Séance Project, though."

"No? So what is it that interests them?"

"Ahhh see, it's very intriguing. All of these dead people's brains were removed from the corpses—with or without their families' knowledge at the time, I don't know—and preserved. The reason is because every one of these brains we were given to work with had developed an odd tumor or growth in the inferior lingual gyrus in the occipital lobes."

"In the *whaty-what*?"

Alex grinned. "That's the area of the brain associated with dreams."

"Huh," Devon grunted.

"Now, memories are stored in different parts of the brain—there's no one memory locus. The occipital lobes are normally associated with vision, and lesions in the occipital lobes can cause visual hallucinations. But when we were scanning the brains, we detected that memories had been distributed to these occipital lobe tumors. And they were only memories of dreams, which made us think of the hallucinations that lesions in this area can cause, like I just said."

"But... wow. Yeah, that is pretty damn strange to find in a series of brains that are all murder victims from one town."

"Hence, our project." Alex clapped his hands together. "So, do you wanna see this guy's brain? History buff's?"

"Sure, Dr Frankenstein. Bring on the brains."

In a sepulchral, zombie-like voice, Alex moaned, "Let me give you... a piece... of my mind." He leaned forward into the work station, deftly tapped some keys, and then stood back with a sweep of his arm as if to say, "Voila!"

"Heh." Devon pouted, taking in the monitor's display, disappointed. "I expected you to bring out some faded old brain in a bottle of formaldehyde."

"Don't be so prehistoric. This is Macrocosm Research." Floating on the monitor in a void of black background was a very solid-looking human brain with light reflecting from its coiled tissues. It looked to Devon like a clenched, angry fist. Alex was able to rotate the brain on the screen, zoom in on it, zoom *into* it. He kept hitting keys, like a driver showing off what his brand new car could do. One moment the brain was in its ghastly natural colors, and a second later it was a mass of neon filaments, so that plunging through its depths was like swimming through a psychedelic coral reef.

Alex pulled them outside the organ again, to explain. "First the brains are scanned with neuroimaging, and these digital representations are produced. They're the brains of dead people, and long preserved, so obviously there's a lot of damage. Where cells are missing, we extrapolate. It's kinda like how a paleontologist might not find every piece of a dinosaur's fossil, so he has to sculpt a few missing bones here and there to connect everything up, except in our case, it's computer data filling those gaps. Once the entire organ is reconstructed, we can bring it to life, so to speak—make the brain perform as if it's a living organ again, with blood flowing through it and neural circuits operating, and so forth. We can simulate those processes in a way that gives the brain an even closer resemblance to what it was like, and what it was doing, when it was still in the skull of its living host."

"But you're, like, replicating solid matter. How do you get memories and dreams out of that? How can you put your finger on something that must have just been an electrical charge when it happened, here and gone in a blink?"

"Poor dense Igor." Alex wagged his head at his kid brother in grave sympathy. "The number of a brain's neurons, and their shape and their size—and that of their synaptic connections—actually become *changed* by the brain's experiences. That is, the brain has plasticity, and thoughts constantly *reshape* the brain. So the thoughts, the experiences of our history buff are essentially mapped in there in the very matter of which you so ignorantly speak." He patted Devon's cheek condescendingly. "Ultimately, though, in the computer it's all just numbers crunched up and waiting to be decoded. A puzzle waiting to be put together so you can see the picture on its pieces. From this chaos, we extract splinters of memory and tease out shreds of dreams. Sure, they're usually just fragments but to think we could someday get a real memory out of Einstein's preserved brain, for instance, or maybe even get a digital reproduction of Einstein's brain to stimulate original thought. *New* thought. Imagine Einstein formulating new theories from beyond the graaave."

"Whoa, wait. So... so... what you're saying now is, if you can make these brains function like they're still alive, and if experience is constantly reshaping the brain's structure... um..."

"Go on."

"My brain hurts just thinking about it, but couldn't you... couldn't you then teach the replica brains new things? Expose them to new stimuli, new experiences, which will shape them even more? Is it possible for the fake brains to *learn?*"

Alex leaned back from Devon a little bit to beam at him admiringly. "In a couple years, I have a feeling you're gonna be working right alongside me, my man. Anyway, that's an experiment for another day. For now," he gestured at the screen again. "We're reconstructing not just the murder victims' brains, but the tumors that all of them had." He dropped his voice to a tone both secretive and dramatic. "And it's the dreams stored in these weird tumors that I'm harvesting and putting together for my Mnemonic work, on the side."

As Devon watched, Alex zoomed into the digitally replicated tumor. Because of the way he had the image's colors turned to a lurid neon, to pick out in etched detail every root-like nerve, Devon felt as though he was whooshing at warp speed into sparkling constellations and nebulae... hurtling into an alien dimension. It brought back to him the vertiginous sensation of flying toward the blackness yawning between that mutant lion's wide, fanged jaws.

"Hello, boys," said a deep voice directly behind them.

Devon nearly ejected from the suit of his skin, and he noted that even cocky Alex spun around too quickly in his chair, splattering a few drops of coffee on his shirt front.

Oddly, the face Devon looked up into wasn't the one he had expected to see. But why had he thought he'd see a face covered in a web of yellow and red scar tissue, as moist and hot as the surface of a pizza thick with stringy cheese? The lion, still thinking about the lion. He had seen this man before, however. He was Alex's boss at Macrocosm Research, Farhad Azari. At thirty-six, Alex's supervisor in the Séance Project was a balding, soft-spoken Iranian, presently wearing a white lab smock over his street clothes. As he had only minutes earlier, Alex had repeatedly spoken of Farhad as being laid-back, mellow, but stern, if pushed over the limits of his patience. Seeing Alex go immediately on guard, grinning nervously, made Devon clench up inside as if he'd been caught doing something wrong by a strict parent.

"Hey, Farhad," Alex stammered, sounding too casual. "I was just treating my baby brother to a glimpse of the future. I think we have a Macrocosm man in the making here."

"I'm sure he's very bright, like his brother," Farhad said, smiling mildly at Devon.

"Though of course, his own brain is pretty saturated with girls right now."

"I think that makes us a lot alike, too," Devon said.

"Well… could be," Alex conceded.

"Just be careful, please, Alex," Farhad said, as both brothers had expected him to. "Remember that the work we're doing here is confidential, a government contract. The technology, and whatever findings we might establish."

"Oh yeah, of course, Farhad. I'm just demonstrating the, uh, basics. The concept of neuroimaging on this kind of level. He's a kid. To him it's like playing *Fantastic Voyage* through the brain, y'know?"

Neither Devon nor Farhad had heard of that old movie, but Alex's boss smiled indulgently again and drifted back a few steps. "I'm going home for the night. Are you two heading out, too?"

The brothers could take the hint, and practically sprang up out of their chairs. "Right behind you, Farhad," Alex chirped.

Devon followed Alex to his car through the parking lot of the looming, modern office structure that contained this branch of Macrocosm Research and other assorted businesses renting space. They heard Farhad's van starting up some distance away. It was nearly October, and a cool breeze through the lot caused Devon to shudder. He was anxious to get inside the car, and out of the chill and the strangely oppressive surrounding dark. Once snugly shut inside, he asked, "Will you get in trouble for having me in there?"

"Nah, I told you. I might get something like, 'You know, Alex, it might not be a good idea, in the future, to have guests in the building, and blah-blah-blah,' but two days later if he saw you in there again he'd just give me the same little warning like it was the first time. Don't sweat it."

"You heading over to Mnemonic now?"

"Yeah, after I drop you off. Trisha's already there, and I got some fresh work for us to huddle over tonight." He patted his jacket's pocket, obviously holding a disk of something or other filched from his conflicting research at Macrocosm. "Hey, so let me know how it goes with this girl tonight. First date, huh?"

"Yep."

"Is she cute?"

"She is fucking *gorgeous*, man."

"Yeah? We'll have to do a swap sometime. You can have Trisha, and I'll try out your girl."

"Cool with me. I've always had a crush on Trisha."

Alex glanced over at his brother as he drove them out of the gloomy parking lot. "You little shit! Lusting after my girlfriend!"

"And she lusts after me, too."

"Yeah, in your dreams."

TWO

"Graaace."

Grace Simmons raised her head from her pillow. She was petite, delicate, and those who had known her mother at that age said she had possessed the same wavy, long brunette hair, lustrous brown eyes and luminous porcelain skin. She looked more like fourteen than nearly eighteen, though it was a very lovely fourteen.

But at this moment, the dark brown hair was in tangled disarray around her face, and her eyes with their weighted lids were more bleary than glowing. She cocked her head in a pose of groggy confusion. She knew she had only lain down for a nap, rather than turned in for the night; she even remembered that she had a date tonight. A date with a boy who had apparently finally summoned the courage to ask her out, though she herself had had a crush on him since their freshman year—and now suspected the same had been true of him. Grace Simmons could at least get her mind wrapped around those concepts, though there was still a fog of confusion swaddling her. For one thing, she had been expecting her friend Ama to come to the house to pick her up, but it was not Ama's deep, husky voice that had just called out to her, called her awake.

Grace swung her legs over the side of the bed. She had lain down in her blue jeans and tight-fitting, striped polo shirt, removing only her shoes in order to doze. She had hoped the nap wouldn't mess up her hair too much for her date, but she had found herself ill-rested after last night. She hadn't had too many good nights of sleep for a number of years now, often preferring to sleep in the afternoon or early evening. On weekends and over summer vacations, she often stayed up all night, watching TV in her room or immersed in her computer, finally succumbing only when dawn limned her window shades with gold.

"Graaaace."

This time, hearing the voice more consciously, Grace shuddered. This time, she recognized it.

She stood, barefoot, and hugged her slender arms tightly across her slight chest. It was not possible that she could be hearing this voice. And yet, it wasn't the first time she had heard it. Though it was not possible that this person could be calling out to Grace, they had called her before. Too many times.

As always, despite her fear and the pain that now constricted her throat, Grace followed the voice as it cried out to her distantly, mournfully, for a third time.

"Graaace."

She left her bedroom and slowly descended the carpeted stairs to her house's first floor. It was pristine down here, pretty much uncluttered; her friends like Ama marveled at the home's cleanliness, its neatness, though Grace herself had always found this quality a bit sterile and uninviting. Her house was one of those that featured a room preserved behind a glass door like a museum display cordoned off with a velvet rope, its glossy and plush furniture more for the looking than the sitting. Her own bedroom was as much of a contrast to this general atmosphere as her parents had been able to tolerate over the years.

Without the voice having to cry out a fourth time, she knew from terrible programming to turn zombie-like into the kitchen with its presently subdued lighting. She knew to seek out the polished dark wood of the closed basement door.

She watched her small hand reach, trembling, to the knob, as if expecting its brass to be heated by a fire on the other side of the door, the metal hot enough to scorch her skin. When she finally closed her fingers around it, of course it was cool to the touch. Maybe even too cool. Just like always.

"Graaace."

Though her eyes were glassy now more with tears than bleariness, Grace did not hesitate very long in turning the knob. It was, after all, inevitable. She must obey the hollow and imploring voice, however much it frightened her.

A slight mustiness wafted into Grace's face upon cracking the door. Her father had a workshop down here, with his tools filed carefully in drawers and organized on the cork board above his bench, plus a small adjacent room in which he lifted weights. He even kept his own computer down here, on an obsolete metal desk he'd taken home from his job with the Transit Authority, rather than in the small ground floor den where he watched TV. The cellar was free of cobwebs, cool but not damp; Ama had joked it was neater than the living room of her own parents' house. Yet at this moment, Grace would have preferred opening the stone door of a crypt stacked with rotting coffins but this didn't stop her from drawing the door wide and flicking on the light switch to reveal the figure that patiently waited for her on the lowermost step.

It might have been a doppelganger of herself. Small, delicate, with matted hair hanging in its face to obscure it, cut shorter than her own but still wavy and dark. The figure wore a thin white summer nightgown, its arms just as white as they rose up, slowly, to reach toward Grace with crooked, splayed fingers. Several of the fingers were broken, bent at sickening angles, and the pallid flesh of the slim arms was slick with fresh blood that sluiced with nauseating slowness from ragged gashes and lacerations. Through the strands of hair masking the face, Grace could see the glint of light on hidden eyes, and the glisten of moist lips, open wide in a haunting, beseeching call:

"Graaace."

"Mom," Grace sobbed at last, wanting to reach down toward her mother, but unable to bring herself to do so, or to descend even one of the steps. As much as she loved her mother, at this moment she was even more afraid of her. It was the same every time her mother called her to the basement door and begged her to descend into her sorrowful, needy embrace.

"Mom," Grace wept harder now, shaking. "Mommy..."

With horrible suddenness, as if it had been precariously balanced upon her slender neck, the woman's head pitched to one side and hung there crookedly but the glinting eyes did not appear to blink.

"Grace? Grace?"

The voice was different this time. That of a man. A gentle hand took hold of Grace's shoulder and rocked it. At the touch, she bolted upright with a gasp, batting the hand away from her and barely restraining a scream.

Her father Neil withdrew his hand with a look of sad patience in his eyes. It was not the first time he had awoken her from this nightmare; not nearly the first. "Honey," was all he said, in sympathy. He straightened up by the side of her bed now, waiting for his daughter to compose herself.

"Oh, Dad," Grace moaned, rolling onto her back and covering her face with both hands.

"I know, baby. I know." Neil Simmons sighed heavily. "Honey, Ama is here. Downstairs. She's waiting to take you on your date."

"Okay, Dad. Please tell her I'll be right down."

"All right." Neil headed toward the door of his daughter's bedroom, but turned back in the threshold. "Are you okay, my love?"

"I'm okay, Dad. I'll be right down," Grace said from behind her wet hands.

"Baby… uh, this date. This guy. You know him well enough?"

"I've known him since freshman year, Dad. He's a very good kid. Not a trouble maker. Not a druggie."

"Good. Okay. Um, I'll go tell Ama."

"Thanks, Dad," Grace mumbled, waiting to sense his departure from the doorway before she uncovered her slick face. She sat up and immediately headed toward her bureau to check herself in the mirror. A date, her first date, at last, with Devon Carmack. She couldn't have puffy, bloodshot eyes for that, could she? Setting her face with determination, she picked up a brush to rake at her hair, as if each stroke was a flagellation to her own back to punish herself for weakness. Of course she loved her mother, missed her mother, but this pain, these dreams, were consuming her, even though it had been years now since the accident. Years since her mother had tripped and tumbled to her death down those treacherous cellar stairs.

Grace entered the kitchen (purposefully keeping her eyes off the dark wood of the closed basement door) to find her father there chatting amicably with her friend Ama from Springwood High School. Ama Oduro was eighteen, and had been born in Ghana, West Africa, though a number of years living in London before her parents had moved her to the US had left her with the vaguest of British accents and certain British expressions. She was tallish, rather heavyset in a solidly sensuous way, with a pretty face and hair currently braided into many thin braids. Though Grace was always a bit wary of arousing her moody best friend's hot temper, she found Ama to be generally jovial with her, and she was presently laughing heartily at her father's jokes.

Neil had just asked Ama who her date was for tonight, assuming this to be a double date. When she replied that Devon Carmack's friend Milton would be the fourth member of their band tonight, accompanying them to the movie but not as Ama's romantic partner in any sense, Neil said, "Hey, I can be your date tonight if you want, Ama."

She broke out in laughter again, and said, "If you were twenty years younger I'd say yes, but... I'm very sorry."

Neil exaggerated a big pout and said in a moping voice, "I understand." He hugged himself and cast his eyes off to the side with a forlorn sigh.

"We'd better get going, Dad," Grace told him, but he wiggled his right hand's index finger at her to come over and peck him on the cheek before she left. He wiggled the finger of his left hand at Ama next, and pointed at his other cheek. She only sputtered into laughter again as she led Grace out of the house.

"Not too late, girls! And be careful!" Neil called after them, watching them go.

Ama had found the Carmack home without much trouble, aided by directions Grace had acquired from Devon. When they'd rung the bell, they were admitted by Devon's mother, who let them in and promptly introduced them to Devon's father. Grace saw the resemblance to Devon in the older man and was pleased to speculate that Devon would be similarly attractive when he reached that age. She tried to listen to the parents' small talk—they related that they'd soon be embarking on a trip to Italy, hitting Florence, Venice and Rome, trusting their son to look after himself now that he was eighteen, but also knowing that his twenty-four year-old brother Alex would be looking in on him— but she found it hard to concentrate on their words when Devon appeared, smiling at her from across the living room while he waited for his parents to stop cutting in on his time with his date. Finally, he was able to usher Grace and Ama upstairs to see his bedroom, where his classmate Milton was already waiting for them.

"Did you find my place alright?" Devon asked Grace as they followed him upstairs.

"Well, I'm here, right?" Grace teased.

"Uh… yeah, I guess you found me, then."

"Nice ass on your boy," Ama whispered in Grace's ear.

"Shh!"

Grace found Devon to be quite attractive, posterior and all. He was tall and sensitive-looking, with shortish dark hair and large blue eyes that had a vaguely sad, hypnotic quality, complemented by pouty lips she had more than once imagined herself sucking on deliciously, one at a time. He was not strictly handsome in a conventional sense; he had a kind of quirkiness she couldn't express in words, but that humanness made him all the more endearing to her. In fact, this proximity to him—and now, the knowledge that she was entering into the very room where he slept each night—had her heart trotting at a good clip in her chest.

On the walls there were framed movie posters for odd, offbeat films, several of which she wasn't even familiar with, especially since a few of them were Japanese. *Tetsuo* and *Rubber's Lover* were two of the latter, both of which were apparently in black and white. The CDs and DVDs she saw stacked about were further testimony to his eclectic tastes, and he was an avid reader whose books overflowed their shelves and were piled on every available surface.

Milton Ferrara, Devon's best friend from Springwood High, sat at the computer. He too had already turned eighteen and was on the short side, though Grace found him attractive enough, with heavy-lidded eyes and the smudge of a mustache over extra-full lips even poutier than Devon's; his was a darker flavor of good-looking sensitivity. In one of his awkward preludes to asking her out, Devon had told Grace that Milton was a talented writer, with aspirations of becoming a published novelist. Grace knew it was no accident that when they'd come in, Milton just happened to be looking at a website that had accepted for virtual publication his first short story "sale," moneyless though it might be. She and Ama complimented him, at which he beamed shyly. Ama even scooted in beside him on a second chair to read his story then and there, if only perhaps to allow Devon and Grace to interact privately for a few minutes.

Casting her eyes further around his room, Grace spotted a TranceBox on Devon's bedside table, resting beside his alarm clock radio. She gestured toward it. "You've got one of those things, huh?"

"Huh? The TranceBox? Yeah, it's pretty wild. Ever try one?"

"No, I guess I'm not that interested."

"No? Really? Are you afraid?"

Grace gave him a bit of a look, but reined it in short of anger. Devon could not possibly know about the struggles she had with her own dreams, let alone inviting other people's psychic debris inside her skull space. "I guess I don't see the, um... allure."

"Well, it's just an amazing experience, seeing through other people's eyes, doing things that you might never otherwise do."

"But wouldn't it be better to try to, you know, stick to accumulating your own experiences. *Real* experiences? And seeing life through your *own* eyes?"

"I don't see it as a substitute for really living. Just, just something cool in *addition* to that. Anyway, I guess I'm biased. Did you know my brother Alex works as a TranceBox program designer? Well, he sort of moonlights as a designer, that is, for a little up-and-coming software company called Mnemonic Designs. His day job is for a place called Macrocosm Research, and they take on various government contracts, like the one he's working on now."

"Wow. You must be proud of him.

"You'll get to meet him sooner or later. He's a goof. I'm sure you'll like him, if you can handle a little teasing."

"I can dish it out, too, don't worry."

So, she would meet Devon's brother sooner or later? She liked the sound of that; it suggested that Devon was looking for a serious, ongoing relationship with her, and so far that was just fine by her. In his honest enthusiasm, he seemed totally innocent of what he had just implied.

"So... you don't want to give it a little try? Just something not too intense?"

"The TranceBox? No, really, no thanks."

"You're really not into it, huh?"

"It just seems like a big addiction with people all of a sudden. Like this big escape. Another technological drug."

Milton glanced over his shoulder at them, their words briefly distracting him from watching Ama read his story.

Devon replied, "Well, life is stressful for grownups and kids alike. The adults working their asses off to pay the mortgage, and kids like us pressured from too much homework, growing up too fast with our parents not always around. God knows my parents aren't always around."

"But your folks seemed pretty cool to me."

"Oh they are, they are. How about yours?"

"My dad is cool. My mom she, um, passed away some years back."

Devon looked stricken suddenly, horrified at having brought the subject up. "Oh my God, Grace, I'm so sorry."

"It's okay. You didn't know. Yeah, she fell down the basement steps in our house, carrying a box of Christmas decorations. The fall broke her neck."

"Oh Grace... Grace, that's so awful."

"Please, Devon." She smiled and touched his arm. "It's okay. But we can change the subject now."

"Sure, of course, of course. Actually, if you're ready, we can get going for the theater now. Personally, I like to get there early, to grab my snacks and settle in and all. I can't watch a movie if I miss even the first second of it."

"Are you kidding? A lot of times the previews are the best thing, anyway."

"Should we go in my car or yours?" Ama asked Devon, looking up from the computer.

Milton cut in, "I have a car, but Devon doesn't have his license yet. He's a little afraid to drive, huh man?"

Devon shot his friend a less than appreciative look. "I'm not afraid, I just haven't gotten around to it yet."

"See what I mean?" Grace said. "Instead of feeling what it's like to drive a race car through someone else's memories on a TranceBox, you could be driving a car in the real world."

"I don't have any race car TranceBox programs," Devon said a bit sourly.

Grace suddenly felt bad that she and Milton had teased Devon about something that was obviously a sore spot with him, a source of some embarrassment. She abruptly hooked his arm in her own. "We'll take Ama's car," she said brightly. "Right, Ama?"

"Sure, that's fine."

Grace smiled up at Devon, liking that he was nearly a head taller than herself. The smile gleaming from her lovely upturned face won a smile from him in return.

They grabbed various light jackets and sweaters, while Ama swiftly finished up Milton's story and again complimented him on having "sold" it.

Grace sidled up to Devon's friend and whispered to him, "You know, Milton, Ama doesn't have a boyfriend right now. Not that I brought her along as a sneaky way of hooking you two up, but you might want to bear it in mind."

Milton blushed a little and whispered back, "Um, she's very nice, but I'm kinda already seeing someone."

"Oh, really? Sorry, then."

"No problem. Thanks anyway."

The four teenagers exchanged cheery farewells with Devon's parents, and then they were off to the local movie complex in Ama's humble secondhand vehicle. During the drive through the crisp autumnal evening, seated in the back with Grace, Devon betrayed his excited mood by babbling. "I know you don't wanna hear this, Grace, but with the thrills the TranceBox has to offer, conventional movies could soon become obsolete! We might soon be watching movies where we experience aspects of the story—or maybe the entire thing—as if we're not just observing the action, but performing the action ourselves."

"But if actors record the action in a fictional movie, something based on a novel, for instance, and we experience it through their awareness, then we would know that we were just actors following roles, right? We wouldn't feel like the story's fictional *characters*."

"I'm sure they'll be able to block certain thoughts, filter or alter them, eventually. The roads are all wide open when it comes to this technology. Trust me, my brother hints at some really crazy stuff in the future."

"I dunno. I find it kind of depressing hearing a guy like you talk like this, you with all those cool movies and books in your house."

"Well, I don't really want to see conventional movies forgotten, any more than I'd want to see people stop reading. I guess I just get a little too enthusiastic about the technology sometimes, especially given my brother's line of work."

"Maybe I'm just old fashioned," Grace observed glumly. It was a simple enough way to dismiss the issue for now. The last thing she wanted to do, however close she already felt to Devon, was discuss her recurring nightmares...

That figure standing at the foot of the cellar stairs, patiently reappearing again and again, hoping for the day when it might finally coax Grace to descend and enter its blood-slick embrace.

THREE

Whereas Macrocosm Research's offices and laboratories were located inside an imposing office structure rising up like an island plateau from a sea of parking lots and landscaped fields of desolation, Mnemonic Designs rented its space inside a former brick factory building in the very heart of town. As elsewhere in the United States, Springwood's factories and mills had been largely transformed into such office complexes and even condos over the years, so that now a high-tech product like Saxon Systems' TranceBox was manufactured outside the country; in this case by Mexican laborers working for pennies in less than comfy environs. Such was progress in the modern Industrial Revolution.

Alex Carmack pulled into the ex-factory's lot with two jumbo coffees and a grease-stained, aromatic paper sack of Chinese food for himself and his girlfriend, Trisha Smith. He disembarked from his vehicle with a jaunty bounce to his step and elbowed himself into the building. He danced up the central staircase to the second floor, navigating the dimly-lit hallway to the frosted door behind which Mnemonic did its arcane work. With his arms laden, he kicked the base of the door, and one of the other Mnemonic software designers, Tim Finney, cracked it open to peek out.

"Hey, look, it's the delivery boy. Just hand me the stuff, kid, and I'll give you a buck for your trouble."

"Step aside, asshole, this stuff is hot and I'd hate to accidentally trip and hurl it in your face."

"Let him in, Tim," Alex heard Trisha yell. "I'm starving over here!"

Finney opened the door wide and let Alex pass by him to dump his load on a clear corner of the nearest work station. Finney was 31, small and wiry. He talked a mile-a-minute out of the side of his mouth, but when it came to his work, his mind was as quick as his consciously annoying verbal diarrhea. His eyes sparkling with mischief, a leprechaun in the flesh, Finney shifted closer to Trisha Smith where she sat before her computer. He began massaging her shoulders, round balls in her tight-fitting black T-shirt. "I like Chinese food, but Indian is my favorite dish. I bet you taste like curry, eh, beautiful?"

Trisha spun in her chair, forcing his hands off her, and glared up at him. "Knock it off, Tim." She was actually more concerned about Alex's reaction to Finney's pranking, however, knowing that despite his flirtations, Finney was a good husband and an even better father to his three young kids. But she knew Alex's jealousy, and Finney knew it too. He obviously liked to play Alex's keys. As expected, Alex's face had flushed red, making his eyes glow more blue behind his wire-rimmed glasses.

"Why don't you show a little respect, huh, fuckhead?" he growled in a voice shaking with rage.

"You sh-shouldn't be pa-pa-pawing her like that, ma-ma-man," David Schwartz, another Mnemonic employee, stammered to Finney angrily as he slipped on his windbreaker prior to leaving for the night.

"Oh, another of Trisha's many admirers jumps to her defense. Or stumbles to her defense, in your ca-ca-case, Dave."

"Fu-fu-fuck you, Finney."

"You're the most popular lady in the company, Trisha," Finney crowed loudly. "Then again, you are the *only* lady in the company."

"Chill out, everybody," growled the last member of Mnemonic Designs, its young founder, Shane Ryan. He too had his jacket and a backwards-facing baseball cap on in anticipation of taking off for home. "Fun is fun, Finney, but don't be manhandling your coworkers. And don't be hassling Dave, either."

"Hey, Shane, if these guys don't know me by now, they will never never never know me, oooh, oooh." He threw up his hands. "I love these guys, okay?" He winked at Alex and licked his lips. "Especially you, sexy. You get me hot when you're angry."

"Isn't it time for you to go home to your wife, Finney? And how would you like somebody talking shit to her, and grabbing her like that?"

"Huh? I'd make a video, put it on the Web and charge money, are you kidding? I'm getting hard just thinking about it."

Shane sighed and grabbed Finney by the arm, dragging him toward the door. "Let's go and leave Alex and Trisha alone to get some work done, okay?"

"Oh, I'm sure Alex and Trisha are gonna be getting *real* busy alone here tonight."

Shane shoved Finney out the door ahead of him. "Goodnight, guys."

Dave trailed after the boss, tossing a look back at Trisha on his way out. Alex stomped over to the door, still red in the face, and slammed it shut, then whirled to blaze his eyes at his girlfriend. "I don't know who makes me madder, Finney with that mouth of his or Dave with his frigging puppy-dog eyes."

"What do you mean about Dave?"

"I see the way he looks at you. Checks you out when he thinks you—and I—don't see him."

"Oh stop. You're being insane now. Let's crack open the food before it gets cold, huh?"

"Sometimes I can't take these losers."

"Sometimes you're too stressed out from working two jobs; that's the real problem."

Alex's hands froze in the middle of unpacking white cartons of lo mein and sesame crispy chicken. "Would you have me quit one of these two jobs, Trisha? And if so, which one would you suggest?"

"No, I would not have you quit either job, Alex. I would just have you mellow out a little, okay? Are we going to have a problem again tonight? Hours of exhausting arguing instead of hours of productive work?"

Alex sighed, dropped his gaze into the bag of food and breathed deeply of its mouth-watering scents. "No," he muttered. "Everything is fine. I'm just a little tired, that's all."

Trisha popped the tab on her coffee lid and took a sip. "That's what I thought." She came close to her boyfriend, ostensibly to peer into the food sack, but then she turned toward him, rising on the toes of her bare feet and smooching him on his goateed chin. "Better now?"

"Much better," he relented, smiling down at her a bit sheepishly. At twenty-three, Trisha Smith was short in height and voluptuously curvy, as made apparent by her snug T-shirt, riding high up in back when she sat at her computer, and thigh-clinging bell bottom jeans. Whatever shoes or sandals she wore to the office invariably spent their time off her feet and under her desk. Her hair was a thick curly mass, oil black, falling heavily down her back; her dusky skin betrayed her mixed ethnicity. Her wide-set eyes were huge and dark as chocolates, one of them turned slightly inward, giving her a look she derided as goofy and Alex considered achingly cute, just as the innocent sultriness of her eyes made him feel like hungry insects swarmed beneath his skin. Usually Trisha wore contacts, though tonight she had on her eyeglasses with their narrow dark frames. Trisha's mother was Anglo but her father was Indian. However, her father had abandoned his wife and child for another woman when Trisha was small, and she had felt as betrayed as her mother had. As a result, Trisha had legally taken her mother's last name and refused to acknowledge her Indian roots at all, despite Alex chiding her about this overreaction. He found her mixed heritage exotic, and embraced her neglected culture more than she did, but he couldn't sway her.

The two of them sat alone in the little lab and had their supper by the glow of numerous computer monitors in lieu of candlelight, while Alex explained to her exactly what he had acquired at Macrocosm that day, on the sly. He'd brought it here to Mnemonic for further work, with TranceBox software in mind.

"It's another chunk of dream," he told her, "and it's *intense*. I tell you, honey, when I edit all these fragments together into a single program, transitioning from one wild nightmare to the next, it will be the ultimate roller coaster ride through the skull, an absolute mind-fuck. TranceBox will be *begging* us to sell it to them once they sample it."

Trisha groaned tiredly and rolled her head. "I'm still a bit scared, though, if Macrocosm finds out. It's unethical use of their research. And if we sell the program to Saxon Systems, and it does get mass produced, it's very possible someone at Macrocosm will eventually read about it or try the program himself, recognize the source of the material, and come after you—and Mnemonic—with a titanic lawsuit."

"Honey, these dreams I'm sampling aren't copy-righted! And Macrocosm isn't really so much into the content of the dreams as they are those weird tumors and the question of why every one of these murder victims would have such a growth—whether they were the result of some toxin the killer exposed them to, or whether he was some freaky doctor who preyed only on his own patients, patients with brain tumors, and so on. Yeah, they wouldn't be thrilled if they ever caught on to what I've done but, honey, this could put our little company on the map big time, not to mention that I could retire from Macrocosm and only work here. And I know you'd like that, despite what you say. Hell, I'd really like working just one job, *this* job, too!"

Trisha sighed and forked more lo mein between her pretty, plush lips. Munching his own mouthful, Alex caught her eyes, smiled at her again, and on impulse leaned over to squeeze her knee. Trisha smiled a bit shyly in return. He was very ardent, very demonstrative in his affection for her. But her father had once been very affectionate toward her mother, too. Were Alex's feelings grounded enough, serious enough to last? Could she count on him to stand by her, or was this just an impul-sive romance for which he might soon lose his gushing enthusiasm, like a kid who wins an exciting video game only to move on to the next? As with their fledgling company, only time could tell how well they would weather the seas, whether or not they would make it to the firm ground of the far shore.

"So… do you want to try it? After we eat? The new dream?" He grinned.

"Did you let Devon try it tonight?"

"No, that was the gladiator thing. This one is brand spanking new. Hmmm?" He wiggled his eyebrows.

"Sure," Trisha said bravely, sitting up straighter. "Bring it on."

"Great!" Alex rushed a last couple of bites of chicken into his mouth and then got up to wheel a cart closer to where Trisha sat. Complex gear was stacked atop it, similar to some of that which Alex had used tonight when letting his brother sample the gladiator dream. Since Alex had not yet transferred the experimental dreams onto the sort of tiny disk that would play in a TranceBox, he didn't paste a TranceBox pad to one of Trisha's temples. Instead he fitted a metal band over the top of her head as Devon had worn, attached by wires to a unit on the wheeled cart. He then sat and commenced a flurry of key-punching, Trisha watching him work while she absent-mindedly adjusted the halo slightly for better comfort.

"Soon," he told her over his shoulder, in a corny hypnotist/showman's voice, "you will be feeling sleepy… *very* sleepy."

Despite his corniness, he was right.

Bells jingled when Trisha pushed the glass door inward, heralding her entrance into the convenience store, one of a chain sprinkled throughout this and neighboring states. It was night outside, and the transition from that pitch blackness into the fluorescent glare and the shelves' riot of colors made her squint for a moment. The light aggravated an imminent headache, a sudden throb of pain in the rear of her skull, and she paused near the counter for a moment to rub at the spot with her fingers before moving on into the convenience store's aisles.

Back in Mnemonic Designs, Alex watched with interest as his girlfriend, her face prettily composed while she slumbered upright in her chair, reached up languidly to dig her fingers into her hair and massage the back of her head. Her brow was now furrowed somewhat in concern or perhaps pain. It occurred to Alex that the area of her head she rubbed was the same general location where the tumor had been situated on the victim from whom this dream had been quarried.

Just into the first aisle, Trisha suddenly realized that she had seen no one behind the counter when she had paused there, and she glanced back that way. She saw only the unmanned register, the unattended rolls of lottery tickets and stacks of cigarette cartons behind the counter. The cashier was taking a risk that some punk might lean over the counter, snatch some cartons and bolt from the store before he or she could come back. Trisha turned and craned her neck, scanning the little store. Maybe the cashier was in the back room, working with the stock?

She resumed her shopping, cutting through the aisle she was in to the freezers at the rear of the store. Jugs of milk, bottles and cans of soda greeted her. She hesitated, staring through the glass doors at the array of chilled products. What she had come here for now escaped her. Damn! She always did this. When would she learn to make a simple shopping list?

Her eyes trailed over the jugs and bottles, hoping something would jog her memory. Maybe it was this pesky headache distracting her from the purpose of her errand, huh? Yes, it had to be the pulsing discomfort inside her skull interfering, because she couldn't even seem to make sense of the labels on the rows of drinks, cartons of eggs and cold sandwiches, let alone recall what she had come here to buy. The labels seemed blurred as if their ink had run, or faded from too much time exposed to the sun, or had even been splashed with indecipherable gibberish. It was as if she was shopping in a foreign country and couldn't make out the alphabet, let alone speak the language. It would be this way if I journeyed to India, she thought. She had never learned to speak her father's native language, and she sure as hell never intended to.

Perhaps it wasn't something from the freezer she was here for, after all, so she looked back down the short aisle she had just walked through. Cellophane-wrapped cupcakes, boxes of doughnuts and loaves of bread faced the opposite bank of shelves which overflowed with countless candy bars in glittering foil skins and bags of potato chips. But again, her eyes couldn't seem to focus on the words on the packaging. Even if one wasn't near enough to actually read the label on a popular product, its overall design could announce itself from a distance, owing to the endless bombardment of TV, magazine and billboard advertisements—and yet none of these products, not a single candy bar or bag of chips, looked familiar to Trisha. It was as if she was on a movie set, and the store's shelves had been filled with bogus products, there simply to fill the background and not to be scrutinized closely.

Okay, she knew she couldn't possibly be in another country, however sketchy her memory was at this moment, but was it possible her disorienting headache had caused her to walk into a foreign-owned market by mistake? These days, having become a melting pot like any other city or town in the United States, Springwood had an Asian market, a Brazilian shop, and even—she sneered inside—two little Indian stores. As unlikely as it was that she would walk somnambulantly into one of those, was that what had happened?

From the nearest shelf, she picked up a bag of round brown candies, maybe malted milk balls. The words emblazoned across the crinkly clear plastic looked like English, but looking at them too long made her eyes hurt. There was an odd aroma from the bag, and she brought it closer to her nose, sniffing at it tentatively. How long had this bag been sitting here past its expiration date? (*Twenty-five years*, said a voice in her head inexplicably.) Up close like this, she realized there was subtle movement inside the bag, and reversed it in her hands to look at the back, which was less obscured by writing. There, in amongst the spherical candies, as if those balls might be a mass of rotting eggs, squirmed dozens of tiny white grubs, their eyeless heads smeared with the decaying chocolate. Making an incoherent sound of disgust, Trisha flung the bag of candy onto the top shelf, where it almost tumbled off the edge before it came to a stop.

From the room in back of the store, Trisha heard the clink of bottles, followed by the muffled shattering of glass as something was bumped or dropped to the floor. She spun, startled, and stared at the closed door. "Hello?" she called, but it was unlikely that anyone would hear it, so softly did the word come out.

Several moments passed, in which Trisha stood rooted there expectantly, but still no one emerged from the back room. Should she leave, go to another store or maybe just go back home, since she couldn't recall what she wanted to buy anyway?

Suddenly, the lights in the store flickered and went out for a moment before they came fluttering back on, as if there had been a brief power outage. Trisha shuddered and hugged her soft, meaty arms that her boyfriend found so appealing to stroke and squeeze. She wished he was here beside her right now. Was it for Alex that she had come to the store? Yes, yes, that was it! Alex had sent her to the convenience store for some reason. She must remain here. She must force herself to recall what it was she was supposed to be doing here.

The chill brought on by nervousness hadn't left her. Chill. Maybe it was something in the freezer she needed to get, after all. An instinct, an intuition, or a half-glimpsed memory told her that she must go back there and take a closer look. Still hugging her goose-fleshed arms across her body, protectively squashed against breasts with their nipples gone hard, Trisha willed herself toward the ice-frosted doors of glass.

She peered through one freezer door, then another. Much of the glass was fogged, so she hadn't yet seen into the lower part of the freezer, but now she leaned down and narrowed her eyes intently. She couldn't make out what she was seeing. She took hold of the door's handle and began to pull. Just as she was starting to open it, letting out a wafting little mist of cold, she realized that she could see a human hand inside, glinting ring and all. It gave her a jolt, and she almost let go of the door. But surely it must be the store cashier on the other side of the freezer shelves. In the back room directly behind the freezer, he must be reaching into the shelves to place new bottles of soda, and rearranging the cartons of milk so that the newer expiration dates were in the back and the older dates up front. Getting a grip on herself, relieved that she had discovered the cashier at last, Trisha opened the door the rest of the way in one wide swing.

Cold washed over her, sank into her flesh, an arctic blast that seemed to freeze her where she stood, turning the blood in her veins to black ice. It wasn't really the cold that paralyzed her—it was the horror at what she was seeing, there in the freezer, on several of its lowermost shelves.

There was indeed a hand. And another hand, a leg and various other naked and frost-crusted parts of a human body, presumably the body of the missing cashier. However, none of these body parts were attached to one another. They had been dismembered and stacked in the freezer like just another product waiting to be purchased. Purchased before they expired and began to rot.

Trisha screamed, and the scream covered the happy little tinkling sound of the bells over the front door. When she whirled to flee toward the door, flee outside into the blackness of the parking lot, she saw that a man had just entered the convenience store, blocking her way out. And maybe it was the intervening aisles full of bright products that confused her aching eyes, but she just couldn't understand what she was seeing at first, until the terrible reality—this new, severely *wrong* reality—became undeniable.

The hideous figure standing at the front of the store, staring directly at her, was a man whose bald head was a mass of badly burned and badly healed scar tissue. He still retained an aquiline nose and malformed, almost pointed ears, features she knew were often lost when the burning was this severe. Perhaps to hide some of the wounding, he wore a battered brown fedora atop his head. Below that, he wore a ragged, oil-stained green and red striped sweater, dark brown pants, and work boots. Around the neck of the sweater was a bulky necklace of clearly authentic skulls, though the skulls were so small they must have been those of very young children. The oddest feature of all was that the striped sweater had four sleeves, seeing as the man had two pairs of arms, swimming in the air around him as if in some stylized dance as he began to stalk slowly toward her.

Most horrible of all was what she saw at the end of two of those swimming arms. On one of his right hands, the being wore a glove of leather and plated metal, the glove's four fingers supporting long, curved, single-edged knife blades. The fist was closed, just the index finger blade extended—slick with fresh blood, a drop running down its edge plopping onto the floor as Trisha watched.

In one of the double left hands, the scarred man held a human head by its hair. The head's eyes were half-closed, the mouth slack, its skin bluish and sparkling with frost. Though Trisha didn't recognize the young man or teenager to whom the head had belonged, she knew it was that of the store's cashier, the rest of his body preserved in the freezer behind her.

As he advanced, his tiny eyes glimmering with a hunger akin to madness, the man lashed out an impossibly long, wolfish tongue that reached down the front of his chest. He brandished his sword-like finger in the air with a flourish. The gesture's meaning was clear. And on he came, one sadistically slow, dance-like step at a time.

"No, please!" Trisha whined, as if such an unearthly apparition could possibly be reasoned with. She looked frantically left, then right, thinking to dart down one of the far aisles, circle behind the entity, and burst out into the parking lot before he could wheel around and slash at her. But she knew her own head movements were giving away her intent.

The man kept coming with a mocking show of ritual grace, savoring each moment of dread. Trisha leaped to the right and snatched a can of spaghetti and meatballs off the end of a shelf, then cocked her arm back to throw her meager weapon if the creature dared to come any closer.

But of course he dared.

As Trisha backed off, she felt the cold of the freezer door only inches behind her, reminding her only too well of how cornered she was. Then she remembered the back room; might she escape into there and bolt its door? But what if the door couldn't be locked from the inside? What if, in taking that route, she only trapped herself more gravely? No, the front door, the darkness beyond, the only way.

"Trisha!" a deep, distorted voice hissed from the thing, after the immense tongue had been sucked back up into the leering mouth. "Watch this!"

With that, the scarred man raised the frozen head a little higher and swiped at it with a flash of his razor-gloved hand. The blade expertly sliced the drooping mouth much wider, splitting its corners into a huge grin. The lower jaw dropped open, and from the mouth—like candy from a ghastly piñata—poured a torrent of those round brown candies she had examined. Of course, mixed in with the vomited candy was a swarm of those maggots or grubs, which squirmed in a blind frenzy when they hit the convenience store's floor.

"Oh God!" Trisha screamed, and she launched the metal can at the creature with all her strength. It missed the intended target of his head but solidly ticked his left shoulder, making him grunt. It would have to do. Trisha faked a lunge to the left, then dashed abruptly to the right, plummeting down one of the little aisles of products. Bursting from its end, she swept her arm across a shelf and cast a spray of potato chip bags in the scarred man's direction.

The man merely blinked as one of the bags of chips bounced lightly off his chest. He looked down at the mess Trisha had made. One of his four hands swept his fedora off his head, and he fanned himself with it as if he was winded from his slow-motion efforts. "You know," he rasped in that deep, oozing voice, "in the past I might have said, 'Clean-up in aisle four' right about now, but I've probably used that one already and frankly, I think I'm getting a little too old and cranky for that stuff."

Only half-hearing him, Trisha had fired herself out of the end of the aisle as if from a cannon and nearly collided with the store's front door. She grasped its handle and pulled. Of course, of course the door would not open, however much its little bells cheerfully tinkled from her heaving efforts.

The scarred man turned around with that same casual slowness. "Yes. No more fun and games, Trisha. Why don't I just get right down to business and gut you from your chin to your naughty place, *bitch.*"

"God, God, *please!*" Trisha wailed, giving the door one last yank before spinning and looking around feverishly for something heavy to hurl through its glass. A pounding on the other side of the front door made her look that way again, as much as she feared taking her eyes off the thing that crept her way.

A face close to the door caused her to gasp, but it was Alex's face, Alex out there slapping his palms against the glass. Calling in to her, "Trisha! Trisha! Wake up!"

"God, God, *please!*" Trisha wailed, batting the halo off her head even before Alex could finish disconnecting it. The metal band swung on its wires, dangling from the device to which it was hooked up.

"Easy, easy!" Alex told her, gathering up the halo and setting it aside more carefully. "Don't wreck the gear, honey…"

"Oh, Alex! Alex! Oh my God," Trisha panted, bending over her knees and holding her head in her hands, her long hair hanging down to hide her face. He reached across her to gather the curtain of hair to one side.

"You okay, baby?"

"I have the most killer headache."

"You do?" He knitted his brows in concern, remembering how she had rubbed her fingers in circles at the back of her head, and also recalling his thoughts of the tumor on the brain from which this latest dream had been culled.

Trisha sat up to look at him, flushed and droopy-eyed with pain. "You know, maybe this isn't what people are going to consider fun and games, Alex."

She realized she was echoing the words of that inexplicable being from the nightmare.

"Huh? Now you sound like Devon today. What is it with you guys? I experienced that dream, too, and I loved it! Talk about a rush!"

"It reminded me of riding the Rock n' Roller Coaster at Disney World for the first time. The moment that demonic thing started up, I thought, 'No way, oh no way, this is *not* fun.'"

"Now see, I *love* that ride! Zero to sixty in under three seconds!"

"Alex." Trisha frowned at him. "How did you get out of the dream, before that four-armed guy got to you? Who woke *you* up?"

"No one woke me up. I pitched a can of spaghetti through the front door with all my might, then ducked my head and jumped through." Now it was Alex's turn to frown. "What do you mean, four-armed?"

"That guy, with the scars. He had four arms."

"No he didn't."

"Alex," Trisha snapped, on edge from her virtual ordeal and the headache she'd awoken with, "I saw it quite clearly. He had four arms, and he was holding the severed head of the cashier."

Alex smiled morbidly. "Who, by the way, is the kid we got that brain from. I guess he worked late in that convenience store, and our serial killer, whoever that might be, came in and murdered the poor kid, apparently while he was dozed off behind the counter. Whether there was also a robbery involved, I don't know. I'm lucky my boss told me that much."

"But, when you experienced it, the scary guy only had two arms?"

"Yeah. What else? Describe him."

"Well, he had a fedora. A necklace of real skulls. And a giant tongue that might make him popular with the ladies if he wasn't such an evil asshole."

"What's all this? Fedora, yes, but I didn't see any necklace of skulls, or giant tongue, or…" Alex cut himself off, looked away sharply, and grinned in realization. He grasped Trisha by the knee. "Don't you get it, honey? It's Kali!"

"Huh?"

"Kali, Kali, the Indian goddess! These dreams from the dead have that important translucent quality, like a template—they lie over our brains and let our own thoughts and identity show through. You're half Indian, my love, whether you want to admit it or not. Subconsciously, you added aspects of Kali to that scary bastard. You had to have. Because I didn't see those Kali elements when I experienced the same dream."

"Wow," was all she could say, dazedly.

"And did he call you by name? Did he use your name?"

Alex saw his girlfriend and fellow designer give a violent shudder. "He sure did. Now that I think of it, that's the scariest thing of all."

"Me, too. He called me Alex. It was like he was really talking to me… like an actual person!"

"Did he tell you he'd gut you from your chin to your naughty place?"

Alex raised his eyebrows. "No, that came out of your own sick head, baby. What he said to me was something about feeding me my balls and washing them down with a Slurpee. Then he kind of apologized for the wisecrack and said he was going to take things more seriously from now on, or some shit like that. He said he's really irritable after going several years without killing anyone." Alex chuckled. "Crazy, crazy stuff, huh?"

"Yeah, he said something more or less like that to me, too. So who was he?"

"Some kind of boogeyman our poor cashier was dreaming of seconds before he got his head whacked off."

"And so, couldn't this boogeyman be a distortion of the guy who actually killed the kid?"

"Ah, I suppose. That's a provocative thought." He slapped her thigh. "Anyway it rocked, right? And did you see how sharp and clear this one is compared to the gladiator dream? I did some polishing in the imaging program, but it also came out a lot fresher-looking to begin with. I think our general technique is improving. I may go back and fish out that gladiator dream again from scratch, now that we're working out the kinks."

"It is incredibly impressive, I give you that. Maybe it's just not my cup of tea."

"My dear, when this thing hits the market we can afford to buy all the tea in China! Or India, for that matter." He gave her a nudge with his elbow.

"Kali," Trisha muttered.

"Goddess of creation... and *destruction*," Alex said in his favorite theatrical voice.

"Yeah," Trisha said, unconsciously rubbing the bony back of her head again. "The two often go hand in hand."

FOUR

"'The interpretation of dreams and symbols,'" Elizabeth Trice read to her class from the book in her hands, "'demands intelligence. It cannot be turned into a mechanical system and then be crammed into unimaginative brains.'" She closed the hefty volume with a thump and set it aside on her desk. "That was from Carl Gustav Jung's essay, *Approaching the Unconscious*, and it makes very clear that we can't trust the notion of the 'dream book.'"

Grace's notebook PC rested before her on her desk, its cover closed, her slender arms folded in front of it. Again, she glanced over at Milton Ferrara. She had never taken much notice of him before, during their freshman, sophomore, or junior years, but now his presence was a warm reminder of his best friend, Devon Carmack.

Devon. Might she consider him her boyfriend, or was that being premature, presumptuous, after a single movie date? She couldn't get him out of her head. It was all Grace could do to follow the psychology teacher's words as she continued on from the front of the classroom.

"As long ago as 2000 BC, the Egyptians were trying to develop a rigid system of interpreting dreams. This has continued on through the years, to today, with authors who are little more than pop charlatans and New Age quacks trying to convince us that if you dream of a red ball, it always means precisely this, and if you dream of a white goat, it always means precisely that. But these mechanical systems of dream interpretation are worthless, as Jung told us *years* ago. What a red ball means in a dream can be profoundly important but what it means in your dream and what it means in mine can be two radically different things, depending upon our own distinct identities."

Something made Grace glance at Milton yet again. She supposed it was how avidly he was listening to—or rather, *watching*—their psychology teacher. He was almost slack-jawed, and even vaguely smiling, as if in a daze. And because he was staring at the teacher so attentively, she too had seemed to be looking at him frequently throughout her talk, the way Grace had read some pop singers will single out a particular rapt face in an audience to play to. Grace now knew of Milton's interest in becoming a writer, and maybe this talk of dreams was stimulating his imagination, but she was beginning to think it was Mrs Trice herself who was stimulating the interest of Devon's buddy. After all, Liz Trice was an attractive woman. She was thirty-one, slim but shapely, her blond hair cut in a short bob with cute girlish bangs, her blue eyes lazy-lidded and her lips candy pink. In fact, Milton wasn't the only male student who was willing to show Mrs Trice attentiveness they might not be as likely to direct toward someone like smug biology teacher Mr Porter, or crabby chemistry teacher Mrs Mayer.

"There is a great difference," Liz Trice went on, pacing slowly in front of the blackboard as if strutting her admirable figure for the benefit of the aforementioned male students, "between these wrong-headed 'dream books' and the dream journals you will begin keeping as of today. And I'm not just talking about the technological medium here, as I know a good number of you will be using your notebook PCs for this purpose, which I strongly encourage, by the way, to make this more fun for you, hopefully. And no, I don't get a commission from the electronics industry for pushing their products." She laughed lightly, trying to keep her students engaged with humor. Milton chuckled appreciatively. "No, the difference with our approach is going to be more meaningful than that. In your dream journals you will be jotting down— every day, ideally—what you can recall of your dreams. You will not be attempting to analyze those dreams at this point, however. You will simply be recording their details; what occurs, what you see and experience in them. This exercise is in preparation for our study of the analysis of dreams, as Jung might approach it, and that will begin a month from now, when you've accumulated enough material in your dream journals for us to make use of. At the end of a month's time, when we're ready to begin that course of study, you will then be sharing your dreams with each other."

There were some soft moans, as certain students grew embarrassed in advance at the idea of having their peers examine the innermost workings of their unconscious minds.

"And you will be analyzing each other's dreams," Liz concluded with a pretty smile, pausing from her pacing to beam at Milton again in his front row seat. Grace thought he couldn't make his infatuation any clearer if he cupped his chin in his hand and gave a heavy sigh. Talk about daydreaming!

A student raised her hand. "Mrs Trice, I never remember my dreams!" she protested.

"Then make them up," whispered a boy behind her, but loudly enough for others to snigger and for Liz Trice to chide him.

"Now, now, there won't be any cheating here. This is important stuff, guys. Patricia, maybe I can help you with a few pointers on enhancing dream recollection. I'll talk to you a little toward the end of the class, okay?"

"Thanks, Mrs Trice."

Liz moved to her desk, and from it lifted a recent issue of the publication *Psychology Today* to hold up and show the class. The cover story was on the use of Cerebral Interface Technology—mainly, the TranceBox—as a form of entertainment. "Like I say, dreams are important stuff, guys. What we're going to be studying is very relevant to what's going on in current trends, so I feel this will be an interesting topic for you. According to *Psychology Today*, the number of people using CIT systems like the TranceBox to experience each other's thoughts, feelings, memories—and dreams—is just phenomenal, particularly among your age group, and spreading all the time. This technology is really affecting the world in so many ways, changing the way that we understand each other and ourselves. This is a time in which we may learn more about dreams and what they mean to us than at any time before. It's an exciting time for someone like me. And I want this dream journal project to be exciting for you." She grinned at Milton, as if this last comment had been meant specifically for him.

When Mrs Trice tossed the magazine back onto her desk, it almost slipped off the corner and fell to the floor. Grace was grateful that it didn't; she had a mental image of Milton flying up from his seat to gallantly retrieve the fallen magazine and present it to the teacher. Grace would have been too embarrassed for Milton to bear it.

"Okay, then," Liz Trice said, "why don't I talk to Patricia now while the rest of you open your notebooks, electronic or otherwise, and have a go at your first entry. Try to remember what you dreamt of last night. But keep your journal close by your bed from now on, so you can record your impressions immediately upon waking. That's the best way—before the memories disperse."

With that said, Liz slipped past Milton, brushing her hip against his elbow in the process, and approached Patricia's desk. Grace watched her, and thought it was a little funny for a mature woman to wear a top short enough to reveal a tease of midriff, however youthful her figure might be. The tightness of her blue jeans seemed a bit much for a psychology teacher, too, for that matter. But then, Grace liked Mrs Trice and didn't want to judge her prudishly, based upon appearances. She turned her attention to her notebook, opening its ash gray cover tentatively as if creaking open the lid of a coffin.

Last night, the dream had come again. Once more Grace's mother had stood at the foot of the basement stairs down which she had tumbled, her limbs gashed and bleeding, head lolling to one side on a broken neck, her hair mostly obscuring her face but eyes glittering with unnatural brightness through the dark locks. Extending her arms, straining them upwards toward her daughter.

"Graaace."

But last night, as with every instance of the dream, Grace had not been able to force herself down those steps to her persistent mother. She did not want to feel those cold, horribly broken fingers upon her own flesh. It felt like a kind of betrayal, however, not going to her mother. Not comforting her in her eternal torment.

Grace prodded a few keys half-heartedly. *Last night I dreamed*, she wrote, but then the words trailed off helplessly in her mind.

"...even if it's just a fraction of a dream," she heard Mrs Trice say, addressing the entire class again as she straightened beside Patricia's desk. "Even if it's just a single image, write it down."

Grace must write something. She couldn't bear to have the psychology teacher notice her hesitance, her repressed emotions, and come over to her desk next to pry herself with professional interest into Grace's vulnerable mind. So she found her fingers tapping, as if of their own accord:

> Last night I dreamed of a handsome young man with stunning blue eyes, who stood outside the door of my house, reaching his arms out to me, wanting to tell me something secret and important.

"Grace?" Devon called down the hallway.

Was she playing games with him? She knew he wanted to meet with her after school, so what was taking her so long? They'd end up getting locked in the high school for the night, if they weren't already. Not that the idea was without its appeal. They could go down and raid the cafeteria when they were hungry. And when they were sleepy, well, that could get downright cozy. But he knew he was letting his fantasies get on the far-fetched side.

A moment ago he had thought he'd heard someone behind him in the hallway, maybe a soft footstep or a body brushing against the wall, but when he'd looked back there'd been nobody there. Still, he began walking that way. He turned the corner and was faced with another long hallway lined on the right with metal lockers. On the left side, though, were a series of arched windows set rather high up in the brick wall of the old school. They looked more like the windows in an old factory or prison, being placed so high, there to admit light but not to encourage students to linger and gaze at the view below.

Nevertheless, Devon could plainly see that night had already fallen: it was pitch black out there. God—he had lost track of time! Maybe she wasn't coming after all. She might be having supper with her dad this very minute. He felt like a fool, and a little hurt, as he wondered if she'd stood him up. Then again, it could have been that she had never even received the e-mail he had sent to her notebook from one of the computers in the library, asking her to rendezvous with him after her last class.

Well, it was time to head home himself, then. He wished he had his cellphone with him to call her. He could still seek out a pay phone in the lobby for that, but at this point it was preferable to just wait until he got home to call. He was anxious to get there before his parents gave him hell for missing his own dinner. But what if he was locked in? Surely he must be. Did that mean that he would trip an alarm if he let himself out through one of the school's various exits?

As he stood there, a bit befuddled, Devon heard a screeching sound outside one of the arched windows, but without any moonlight or street lamps out there it was too dark to distinguish anything when he glanced up at it. No doubt it was only the branch of a tree, grown too close to the school. It had unnerved him for a second, but what did he expect—that someone had scaled the outside of the building, clinging to it like a human fly, to rake a knife across the pane?

He regarded the row of windows. It was funny, but he couldn't recall ever having seen them before. Granted, Springwood High School was large, a sprawling brick dinosaur with the feel of an obsolete mental institution, and he didn't frequent areas where he had no classes. Plus, the school would of course take on a different aspect at night with all its students and teachers wisely at home like he should be now but it perplexed him nonetheless.

The hallway seemed almost too long, and its lighting was subdued for these night time hours. Its end was lost in gloom, making the hall appear like it stretched into a shadowy infinity. So when Devon heard a deep rumbling sound from down the corridor, he couldn't see what its source was. But again, he wondered if Grace was still in the school after all, just tormenting him out of a sense of flirtatious fun.

"Grace?" he called. His voice echoed. "Come on, is that you?"

Perhaps it was the old maintenance man Mr Brown, whom the kids called Brownie. He looked like Popeye's great-grandfather and was nice enough... if you didn't piss him off in some way, like scuffing your heel on his freshly waxed floor or dropping crumbs from a snack you weren't supposed to be eating in the hallway. Devon tried to ease his nervous feeling by imagining an enraged Brownie running at him out of the murk, his mop upraised to smack Devon in the face with its soapy head. Actually, though, that image kind of unnerved him, too.

"Brownie?" he said uncertainly.

That deep rumble came again, almost like distant thunder, but it was more organic than that. And as Devon stood there, staring down the dark corridor, he began to make out a wavering light. It increased in intensity, becoming distinctly orange. He thought he could even hear the approaching crackle of flames. He could detect a smell too, like singed hair or burnt meat.

And then, from behind him, two hands came to rest on his shoulders. Close to his ear, another startling sound.

"Boo!"

"Oh my God," Grace whispered to herself, pausing some distance from Devon in the Springwood High library. She had found an e-mail from him on her notebook, sent from one of the computers in the library, asking her to rendezvous with him there after her last class. So here she was, almost out of breath from rushing, irrationally afraid that he might leave before she arrived, only to find his head down on top of his crossed arms, apparently having nodded off while scattered knots of students huddled over their homework at other tables around him.

Grace stole up on him, stealthy as a mischievous cat stalking a mouse. When she had reached him, she put her hands on his shoulders from behind (any excuse just to touch him), leaned over his back and hissed, "Boo!" in his ear.

Devon sat upright with such abruptness that the top of his head gave her chin a bit of a bump. She shot upright herself, though mostly from being startled. Devon half spun around in his seat, blurry-eyed and a bit frantic-looking. Oddly, it was more alarming to Grace than comical, and she felt immediately sorry for having jolted him. She reached out to touch his shoulder again, but this time to calm him.

"I'm sorry, Devon... I'm sorry..."

"Holy crap, Grace."

"I'm sorry... really. Are you okay?"

Devon let out a long sigh, his bearings coming back to him. "Yeah, I'm just... tired. I didn't sleep very well last night."

Grace came around the table to set down her backpack, her notebook stored inside it, and lowered herself into a chair opposite him. "You either, huh?"

"You had trouble last night, too?"

Grace regretted letting that slip; it might necessitate her having to elaborate. The recurring dreams of her mother were not something she wished to expand on in the least. She tried to dismiss her comment quickly. "I usually don't sleep well anyway. That's just the way I am, I guess. So what happened to you? Stay up too late chatting with sexy girls on the web?"

"I wish." He grinned. "Joking."

"Ha ha." But she grinned, too.

Devon ran a hand back through his disheveled short hair, making it spikier (and to Grace's mind, sexier). "I told you about my brother's design work for TranceBox software, right? Well, the other night he let me sample a program he was working on, a kind of gladiator thing; very freaky. There was this weird lion in it, with red and green stripes and metal claws. Anyway, I guess it really got under my skin, 'cause last night I dreamed of that lion again."

"Without using your TranceBox?"

"Right, just a regular dream. If you can call it regular. I was in the school, here, only the hallways were all different, like a maze, and every door I tried was locked for the night. There was no one around but me. But for some reason I was there looking for you."

Grace suppressed a smile. "Yeah?" she asked casually.

"I never actually *saw* the lion, though. I heard its claws on the floor, and I'd hear it growling, but the most I ever saw was its shadow on the wall, coming very slowly around the corners after me, taking its time. And its shadow was always flickering in this orange light, like there was this fire casting the light—a fire following the lion. Unless the lion was on fire himself."

"No wonder you didn't get much sleep."

"As a matter of fact, I was starting to dream the same thing right now, until you woke me up."

"Yikes. A recurring dream, huh?" He definitely had her sympathy. "Then I guess I'm not so sorry I woke you up, after all."

Again, Devon grinned. "I'm not sorry, either."

"You should join my psychology class; we just got this assignment where we have to write our dreams every day in a dream journal. I'll bet Mrs Trice would be really intrigued with yours."

"Sounds interesting. Milton will like that project... getting to use his writing abilities."

"Milton, ha. He made me laugh today. He's really got a crush on that Mrs Trice, huh?"

"Did he tell you that?"

"No, but it's as plain as day."

"I guess it must be, because I'm sure you're right. He talks about her all the time. Then again, she *is* pretty hot."

Grace swatted his arm. "Stop teasing me."

"Sorry."

"Well, I hope his girlfriend doesn't find out about his crush."

"Girlfriend? Milton doesn't have a girlfriend."

Grace looked bewildered. "No? The other night I sort of asked him if he'd consider asking Ama out and he said he already had a girlfriend."

"Not that I know of, he doesn't. Maybe... maybe he just doesn't care for Ama. Though I know he's not prejudiced."

"Maybe he's saving himself for Mrs Trice."

"Mrs Trice is married. Hence the 'Mrs' Not to mention she's old enough to be his, um, extremely young mother."

"Well, it could be he does have a girlfriend and you just don't know your friend as well as you think. Or maybe he met a girl recently, a new girlfriend that he's just begun dating." Grace's eyes twinkled with meaning.

"Uhh, could be."

"So did you have a reason for asking me to meet you, or did you just wanna talk about your freaky dream, or...?"

Devon shifted uncomfortably in his seat. "No, um, the reason I, ah... you know, asked you to meet me." He looked off toward some rowdy students laughing obnoxiously at another table as if they were distracting him, but actually to avert his eyes. "I was wondering if you might, you know, wanna think about going out somewhere this Friday night, just the two of us this time." When he returned his gaze to her, his face had taken on a decidedly redder hue. She saw his Adam's apple bob as he swallowed.

"Yeah, great, that'd be fantastic."

"Really? Excellent."

Really? Was he so surprised that she'd said yes? Wasn't he paying attention? She was *beaming.* "Okay, then but you'd better get some rest before Friday; I don't want you falling asleep on me, now." Oh my God, Grace thought, realizing how that had sounded. "I mean," she stammered, "I don't..."

Devon laughed, "Don't worry, I know what you meant. I promise not to fall asleep. I'll try to be well rested."

"Good. Me, too."

No more bad dreams for either of them this week, she hoped.

FIVE

Another moan from Patrick made Alex look up from the series of computer monitors arranged around him. As the anatomy specialist at this branch of Macrocosm Research, Patrick himself had helped Alex set up the gear that monitored his mental activity while he lay asleep and experienced this, the latest dream fragment that Alex had coaxed out of one of the digitally replicated brains. Patrick had won the coin toss to determine which of the two of them would experience the dream fragment first. Alex now wished he had insisted on being first; after all, wouldn't it have made more sense for Patrick to man the monitoring equipment, observing how the brain activity of one mind physically affected another's mind? Then again, all these findings were being recorded for Patrick to review and re-review later, at his leisure.

Alex watched Patrick's face. It was pinched and tense, the mouth frowning slightly. One of his hands was clutching the edge of the hospital gurney he reclined on. Alex couldn't help but smirk a little. Each and every dream they were salvaging from these brains, specifically from the odd but apparently nonmalignant tumors, was a nightmare. And this one must be a good one. Alex felt a twinge of guilt, however, at gloating over his friend's obvious discomfort. Patrick Tremblay was thirty, quite tall and gangly—an unlikely combination of geek and jock—a sports fanatic who had had no more luck getting Alex to attend sports events with him than he had inciting him to take up tennis. But battling each other in a video game, now that was a sport Alex and Patrick could agree upon.

Around his forehead, Patrick wore a halo like the one Trisha had worn the other night while trying out the convenience store dream, connected by wires to one of the units stacked around the wheeled stretcher. The impulses from the metal headband had put Patrick's brain into a sleep state only seconds before the dream recording had begun to roll. His brainwaves looked to Alex like the waves of a storm-tossed sea. Alex was itching to enter into this new dream himself, to see if it would fit nicely into the program he was putting together at Mnemonic Designs. From Patrick's reactions, however, he had little doubt of that.

"Uhh," Patrick moaned, more loudly this time. He even began to mutter, "Oh my God…"

His voice drew the attention of Julie Ip, another Macrocosm researcher, who had just a moment earlier removed her headphones. Julie was a music junkie, but Alex wondered if she immersed herself in her music while she worked because it helped her concentrate better, or as a way to avoid conversation with their coworker, Mr G. Alex tossed her a smile as she came wheeling closer in her chair. If he hadn't been so involved with Trisha, he knew he would have been pursuing Julie (to hell with that rock star wannabe boyfriend of hers). At twenty-six, Julie Ip was a couple years older than Alex, with a hip and funky style that he found very appealing, not to mention her extreme prettiness. She was the American-born daughter of Chinese-born parents, with very narrow eyes, very plush lips (their effect heightened by glossy red lipstick) and shoulder-length coal black hair. Right now she was wearing a black T-shirt for a band she liked, blue and white-striped men's pajama pants, and black canvas sneakers. Like Trisha, she was the only woman on her team, so she had to put up with a similar degree of flirtation, both playful and more than playful. Alex had to rein himself in on a daily basis.

"Whatcha listening to?" Alex pointed to her headphones.

"Just finished Nick Cave, *Murder Ballads*. Fucking unreal. I thought I heard someone having an orgasm, but then I realized it was string bean." She motioned toward Patrick. "He okay?"

"I'm babysitting him. He's fine. Though it looks like he might wet the bed any minute now."

Julie shot a glance over her shoulder, then scooted even closer to Alex and lowered her voice conspiratorially. "Alex, keep an eye out for Mr G, because he's definitely keeping an eye out for you. I can tell. I've got his creepy eyes stuck to me all the time so I know when it's happening."

"So now he wants to sleep with me?"

"It's not like that." She smiled. "He suspects you're into extracurricular activities, shall we say."

"Extracurricular activities?"

Julie couldn't help but laugh. "You almost pulled off looking innocent just now, Alex. Look, you don't have to tell me what you've got cooking on the side, but definitely don't let Mr G get a whiff of it. You know how he is."

Alex knew only too well, though it had taken him quite a while to see past Fotios Grigori's soft-spoken and amicable facade. Grigori, fifty-four years old, was the senior lab tech at Macrocosm, but Alex had the impression that the man felt he deserved to be more recognized for his achievements and should be farther along in his profession at this stage of his life. Under the smiles and pats on the back, Alex had finally come to sense the bitterly clenched fangs and barely retracted claws of envy and resentment. Alex had witnessed Grigori's machinations against himself, the other researchers and even their boss Farhad. Mr G was not above sabotaging the careers of his coworkers out of little more than petty spite.

But what infuriated Alex the most about Mr G was the way he focused both his maliciousness and his desire on Julie, these feelings walking hand in hand. Once it might have seemed mere harmless joking, when Mr G had told visiting researchers that Julie was his "girl," or when he had slipped his arm around her shoulders and asked Patrick and Alex if they thought he and Julie made a good couple. Ha ha, all in good fun. He would beckon to Julie with one finger, like a pervert sitting in his car luring a child, and when she approached him he would slip her a wrapped piece of hard candy, as if this gallant token should melt her young heart.

Julie had resisted Mr G's more serious advances—constant pestering to go out to lunch or coffee with him—as politely as she could, showing an admirable level of restraint. But these numerous declined offers had apparently inflamed Mr G's bitterness. Recently Farhad had reprimanded Julie for leaving the office, sans Mr G, for a two hour lunch on a day that Farhad was out, and for hiding her actions by not using her ID badge to scan out for that time as she should have. Who else but Mr G would have reported such a thing to Farhad the next day? Mr G had even crept over to Julie later, after she had been given the verbal warning, to advise her in a concerned and kindly whisper that she should watch her back around her coworkers from now on. Smiling tightly, Julie had assured him that she would certainly do so. Thanks a lot.

"I just don't want him to go to Farhad," Julie went on.

"Thanks. Believe me, I don't turn my back on the guy for long, anyway."

Patrick gave a deep groan, attracting their attention. "Ahhh… oh no."

This time, his moaning was loud enough to bring Farhad into the large work area from his small adjacent office. "Is he okay?" he called over.

"The recording is almost finished," Alex replied. Dreams, when they occurred naturally, of course actually took place in an extremely brief span of time, but for the purpose of recording and playback (especially where TranceBoxes were concerned), they were drawn out into "real time."

Farhad had worked his way across the room, leaning in to have a look at the monitors himself. His approach drew Mr G, who had been hovering around in the background, and who now frowned at the screens while rubbing his chin in the pose of a profound scientist.

"He's coming out," Alex announced, reaching out to start hitting pads on various keyboards.

Patrick's eyes flashed open and he sucked in a raspy breath that sounded like a dying man's death rattle. Before Julie could even jump up to remove the halo, he was already clawing the thing off his head and swinging his long body over the side of the stretcher, so that Farhad had to lunge forward and seize his arm to help hold him up.

"Oh *man!*" Patrick blurted.

"Easy, buddy," Julie told him, supporting his other arm. "Sit down."

Patrick waved them off, leaning his rear back against the edge of the gurney. "I'm okay but boy, that was just too much."

"Yeah?" Alex asked, practically salivating for details. "What did you see?"

"I'll tell you what I saw. I saw that fucking guy again. Just like the convenience store dream."

"What guy?" Julie asked.

Alex squinted. "The burned guy?"

"Yeah, him, in the red and green sweater," Patrick panted. "If I didn't know better I'd swear both dreams came from the same brain… but I do know better."

"This is really weird, Farhad," Julie said. "That lion too, in the arena dream, it has that scarred face, and red and green stripes. And those claws…"

"Why would these different individuals all be dreaming of the same person," Mr G said, "unless he was based on someone in real life, whom they all actually knew?"

"I doubt that guy was anyone they could have known in the real world," Patrick said. "I should hope not, anyway."

"Well, they definitely had to be sharing something in common," Alex said. "It sucks that we aren't being told more about them! They had to have been friends or fellow psych ward patients or fellow drug addicts. Some situation where they could stimulate each other's imagination in a profound way."

"The only two things we know for sure that they had in common," Julie said, "is that they all had a tumor in the same location and that they all got themselves murdered."

Alex recalled Trisha's theory—that the hideous dream man might be a distorted version of some real life individual who had ultimately slain these teenagers. "Farhad," he said, "it's very frustrating trying to do our job without having full access to these kids' files. What's the big cover-up with this? Can't we please ask the feds again if they'd reconsider giving us the full background history on the brains?"

Farhad raised a palm in the air in a clear and unyielding gesture. "No. If our sponsors wanted to give us those records, they would already have done so. Besides, I think mostly they're respecting the wishes of the local authorities, who may or may not have set certain conditions for the use of these brains. Anyway, don't ask me about this again. We just have to do the best we can with what we've got."

Mr G speculated, "I feel our sponsors simply don't want any of our findings to be influenced by our knowledge of the victims' personal histories or the circumstances of their deaths."

"I'd still like to poke around on the Web for info," Alex grumbled.

"I already have," Julie replied in a low voice. "Either there was nothing to be found in the first place, or it's all been systematically censored or suppressed."

"So what's the government so interested in here?" Alex asked, more loudly so the rest could hear.

Farhad sighed. "Well, my own belief is that they're interested in the ongoing evolution of the brain, its increase in mass and complexity. Perhaps they feel that this tissue growth, rather than being a tumor, might represent the emergence of a new genetic variant. A new haplogroup."

"Ahh, I dunno if their involvement is that benign," Alex said. "I think they're more interested in accessing people's memories remotely, mind-reading, mind control, or something of that nature. Whenever the government is involved in research,

I always automatically suspect there's a military application."

"Yeah," Julie joked, "maybe they're developing a weapon that will give people brain tumors that give them bad dreams."

Patrick mumbled, "Or maybe to give you bad dreams that give you brain tumors."

"That's not too rational a statement, coming from an anatomist," Mr G chided him in a gentle tone, "is it, Pat?"

"Well, something gave them all a similar tumor," he said. "And right now I don't have any rational answer for that. Like Alex says, when it comes to understanding the cause of these tumors, my hands are tied and my eyes are practically blindfolded if I can't run tests on actual organic tissues."

"As irrational as it sounds," Farhad said, "Patrick, I want you to scan each one of us who uses the CIT link-up, to keep an eye on any possible irregularities in our own brain tissues. Once a week, every one of us, okay?"

Alex felt a flicker of concern, recalling how Trisha had come out of her latest test session with a raging headache, but he tried to dismiss his worry. Look at all the kids who had fanatically embraced the TranceBox over the past two years. The rare instances of epileptic seizures and such aside, he had never heard of this kind of CIT software stimulating abnormal growth in the tissues of the brain.

He was still too intrigued by Patrick's talk of the scarred man to fret much about brain tumors right now, anyway so he spoke up. "Farhad... this thing about the guy with the burned face recurring in these kids' dreams. This is very important, one way or another. I suggest we all of us link up to the recording Patrick just tested, right now, at the same time, and then compare notes on what we experience. We know that our experiences will differ slightly, based on our own identities, but despite that—and *because* of that—I think it would be very compelling to see what each of us comes away with."

"Oh no, not me," Patrick said. "Count me out. I've had enough of that dream for one day."

"Come on," Alex teased, "are you a man or a mouse?"

"I'm a man, not a lab rat."

"Come *on*. We should be comparing notes on this. Seeing where things differ, where they remain the same. We could learn a lot from that," Alex persisted.

"Yeah, let's do it," Julie said. "The group sex method."

"A dream orgy," Mr G said, grinning. Yeah, Alex thought, that idea's got you sold, you slimy fuck.

"Patrick doesn't have to go in with us if he doesn't want to," Farhad said, motioning for Mr G to drag a few more chairs near. Already Julie was rearranging equipment carts and chairs to form a circle for them. "He can monitor the rest of us. When we're finished, we can compare our experiences with what he's already experienced."

Alex didn't push to have Patrick enter the dream again, grateful simply that Farhad had agreed to this much, and even to joining in the collective dream test himself. Alex could at least understand

Patrick's hesitance. Even though he could presently recall what he had dreamed about, should Patrick go back into that same dream again he would immediately forget what he had seen and re-experience everything all over again, fresh, as if it was the first time. Hence, he would not be able to shield himself with foreknowledge of whatever disturbing things awaited him.

There was some tuning and adjusting of the equipment, the hooking up of three more headsets. Then, as if in preparation for an actual séance, the five members of the Séance Project settled into their ring of chairs, Patrick being the only one of them without the metal halo upon his head. He tapped a few more keys, then looked around at the faces of each of his coworkers. They looked like four astronauts waiting for their shuttle to launch or four condemned murderers wired up for a mass electrocution.

"You guys sure you're ready for this?" he asked.

"Shut up and just hit the button, string bean," Julie said, sticking her tongue out to remind him she was only playing.

"Okay," Patrick said. "But remember, you asked for it…"

The air was full of static. It fizzed soundlessly, a blizzard of swarming light particles. Everything was pixilated, grainy. As he strolled down the path, Alex squinted through the tattered mists that obscured his surroundings. He had thought this weather had cleared up, but he saw now that it hadn't after all. Image: degraded, he thought vaguely, but then that line of thought eluded and abandoned him. He kept strolling, doing his best to ignore the long flickering lines scored through the air, the specks and blips in the deteriorated celluloid of reality.

There was a foul odor here, and it was familiar. It was the smell of animals, their waste and the musk of their very bodies, but with a strong undertone of road kill rotting in a highway's blazing sun. There was the sound of animals, too. He heard a peacock's distant cry, piercing through a muted jumble of other calls, grunts, screeches and rumbles. To his right, he saw a stone wall running parallel to the path, the earth beyond the wall set at a lower level. He diverted from the path, approached the wall and stared down into a misty enclosure. It was a large, open pen, he realized, now understanding that he had wandered into a zoo.

The shreds of fog cleared enough for him to see a rhino standing down in the pen, its bulky armor-plated body and great horned head making it imposing and prehistoric-looking. It was motionless and appeared to be gazing back at him impassively. Alex pushed himself away from the wall, continuing again along the path as it sloped gently downward. Near its bottom, it forked into several directions. For no particular reason, he chose the left-hand path; maybe to get a closer look at that rhino from another wall of its enclosure.

Alex started to rest both hands atop the wall, but a prick on his left palm caused him to give a yelp. He looked down to see that rusty nails poked up from the wall. Not only that, but the bases of broken bottles were set into the concrete. If they didn't want people leaning over or sitting on the wall so that they wouldn't tumble over the side into the rhino's pen, that was all well and good, but children could get hurt on these sharp deterrents, ending up with the need for a tetanus shot and maybe some stitches to boot. Thrusting his hands in the pockets of his jeans instead, Alex gazed into the rhino's pen again from this different angle. What he saw perplexed him, and he waited for the air to clear some more before he could believe what he was seeing.

The rhino was propped up with thick wooden sticks on its far side, like a two-dimensional cutout set into the ground; a mere facade. But it was still an actual rhino, not a life-size photograph. No, the rhino was in actuality *half* a rhino. The massive animal had been neatly sliced down the middle of its body, bisected, its other half nowhere to be seen (occupying its own pen elsewhere, maybe?). All its yellowish-gray organs could be seen, still slotted into their respective cavities, this side of the animal perhaps preserved and sealed by some chemical means to serve as a kind of educational cross-section but Alex found it only distasteful and grotesque. He withdrew from the wall and turned to venture further into the zoo's depths in search of living creatures instead.

Monkey screeches grew loud, but perhaps their cages lined another fork of the path; he couldn't quite get a sense of the direction in which those cages might lie. Still, their noises seemed oddly... scratchy to him. It was as if sound speakers amplified the monkeys' rowdy voices, but with a lot of warbling distortion and crackling interference. As he walked, the cries diminished behind him, blending into the background again.

To his left appeared a cage enclosing a gnarled hunk of tree for birds, in this case—not monkeys—to roost upon. There was no placard outside the metal cage (its bars caked in red rust) to identify the creatures inside, but it was plain that there were two crows perched on the bare, twisted branches. It was also plain to Alex, after studying the crows for only a couple of seconds, that they were dead; he even noticed how their feet had been wired to the branches. Suddenly, very close by, there was the sharp caw of a crow. A current of gooseflesh washed over his body. Looking above him, he spotted a speaker half-hidden in the boughs of a tree that grew alongside the crows' cage. Their sounds were a mere recording.

On he meandered, turning down yet another fork in the path, scuffing through the brown husks of fallen leaves. The fog kept him from seeing into most of the cages and pens along the paved trail, but the majority of them seemed vacant anyway.

There was a pen with a barnyard-like structure tucked into one corner, its cheery red paint flaking away. Straw was scattered about, and there was a gate in the fence through which people might enter the area. Alex recognized it as a petting zoo within the zoo. Maybe children could feed the animals here with pellets of food bought from machines like gum ball dispensers. Well, once upon a time that might have been the case, but Alex was appalled at what he saw within the petting area now.

Scattered about the enclosure were a dozen black goats of various ages, with fat bellies and those disturbing frog-like eyes of theirs, a few of them with impressive curling horns. A series of pipes—a network of plumbing better suited for a boiler room than a zoo—was rooted into the dirt floor of the pen, rising up, bending and piercing through the goats' preserved carcasses. These pipes wove in and out of their bodies, passing right through one beast's belly only to continue on through another goat's head, in one eye socket and out the other. A few rags had been wrapped around sections of the pipes, water leaking from these trouble spots in drips. Steam even hissed from around a red valve. This could not be meant as any educational display. What was the purpose of this ghastly arrangement? As a lover of animals of every stripe, Alex felt a boiling outrage. This was sadistic, barbaric, inhumane. Had the poor things been slaughtered for this obscene purpose?

His anger drove him onward. Alex knew he had a bit of a temper like his father Francis, whereas Devon was a bit more mellow like their mother Melinda. Well, sometimes you needed anger for fuel. Righteous anger at the injustice, the bullshit, seething all around you. Alex was not a violent man, but right now he wanted to stick a pipe through a human's head to see how *they* liked it. Whoever's sick head had orchestrated this abomination.

An animal bleated, and Alex thought it must be another recording until he whirled to see a white goat trotting along a different branch of the path, free from any cage, before it vanished into the mists. He also saw a red ball coming to a stop in a puddle of dead leaves at the base of a tree. He heard a child giggle, but this time the sound was crackly and he suspected it was a recording. He grimaced at the ball and the fog into which the goat had vanished. Why did he seem to glimpse a deeper meaning to the red ball and white goat, even have the impression it was a kind of secret joke meant to taunt him?

The wall to his right, maybe the high barrier of another pen, appeared to be riddled with bullet holes as if it had been strafed by a machine gun. Had they lined up and murdered those poor goats here? Coils of concertina wire were mounted atop the wall, making it resemble even more something from a war zone. There was a hole blasted right through the concrete further along, and Alex paused to peek through it. Already he had smelled the black smoke he saw rising above the top of the wall, and now he saw its source. It was coming from a pair of antelopes, propped up with sticks or pipes as the rhino had been, their charred corpses crackling with flames.

The length of wall veered off at a right angle, but Alex continued forward. He came to a chain-link fence with its gate standing wide open, dangling a loose chain and rusted padlock. Inside the sizable fenced area, several fires burned upon the bare dirt and Alex realized the fuel that fed them was large mounds of animal excrement. Flies buzzed in the air, angrily thwarted from their prize by those snapping, malodorous flames. Despite the growing stench, Alex felt weirdly compelled to enter through the gate. Ahead of him, at the pen's far end, was a structure made of corrugated metal with a curved roof like a small airplane hangar, all streaked with corrosion and punctured with strings of bullet holes. A creaking sound came from within the open structure, drawing Alex closer.

Standing in the threshold of the little hangar—a hand clamped over his nose and mouth against a stench even worse than that of the burning feces—Alex stared with disbelief into its gloomy interior.

The creaking was caused by a series of chains thick enough to moor a yacht, hanging down from the ceiling and swaying ever so subtly. At the ends of these chains were large hooks, and these hooks were pierced through the thick leathery hide of an elephant, which hung suspended in the air five feet off the hangar's floor. Its trunk drooped flaccidly and the open eyes were cloudy and greenish, pus having seeped out of their corners. Flies swarmed enthusiastically across the immense dusty carcass, which to them must have been like a planet floating in space, just waiting to be mined.

"You monsters," Alex seethed, not knowing just who these monsters were that he wished to curse.

And then he saw the elephant's belly move.

It was a bulge that came and went so quickly that Alex wasn't sure if he had truly seen it at all but even that slight movement had caused the huge corpse to swing slightly on its chains, a titan marionette.

He watched the belly, waiting to see if another bulge would surface. Instead, four silvery knife blades came poking out of the hide. With a terrible ripping sound, the blades tore their way downward, opening four long parallel wounds.

"Uhh…" Alex moaned in horror, backing off several steps, but too mesmerized to turn and flee. As if riveted in a waking trance, he began to mutter, "Uh… oh my God…"

The knife blades withdrew again, but a moment later two arms were thrust through one of the extensive incisions, pushing its lips outward. The widening of this wound had nauseating consequences. Immediately, a mass of rotting internal organs began to slide out in a semi-liquefied state. Mixed into this sludge of decomposing matter were countless white specks which Alex realized were maggots. Finally, the wound stretched to its limits, and with a sickening wet splash, disgorged a mountain of deliquescent intestines which slid away in all directions. In the midst of these heaped intestines was the body of a man, as if Jonah himself had been cut out of the belly of the whale. Or as if some monstrous birth had just taken place.

A slime-covered head rose up from the offal, looking at Alex and grinning. He recognized that burnt and scarred face, though he couldn't recall at this moment just where he had encountered it before. Alex could only watch, paralyzed by his terror, as the man extricated himself from the hill of guts, his sodden clothing dripping ooze. The last thing he did was reach into the entrails, pull out a soggy hat, and place it atop his head. Alex could see maggots like grains of rice resting on the fedora's brim.

The scarred man spread his arms and announced, "It's a boy!"

At last, Alex's paralysis was broken. At last, he spun about and bolted for the gate in the chain-link fence. He heard the scarred man lunge after him, right on his heels...

"Come back, Alex," the man's distorted voice hissed from behind. "It's time for *your* Caesarean section."

Alex hadn't heard the gate close behind him upon entering the enclosure. There was no wind to have blown it shut, and he certainly didn't recall having shut it himself. Nevertheless, as he ran toward the gate, he could see that not only was it closed, but the rusty chain and padlock had also been fastened into place.

Who had done that, behind his back, while he had been gaping in at the suspended elephant? Across from the chain-link fence, Alex spotted two monkeys up in the limbs of a tree. He hadn't seen them before, when he had first approached the pen. They were blackened by the flames that lapped at their crouching bodies, their faces reduced to fanged skulls, and yet Alex had the impression they were not merely stuffed cadavers wired to those branches like the dead crows. No, the monkeys seemed to be lurking there, their skull eyes gazing down at him with sentience, after having crept up to the gate and locking it to trap him inside with their master.

He flung his body shoulder-first against the gate. It rattled but didn't give. He knew the scarred man was directly behind him, so without sparing even a second to glance back he grasped the metal web of the fence and began to scramble up its side, in the hopes of throwing himself over the top before…

But a hand grasped his shirt and jerked him backwards violently. Alex's feet lost their purchase and his fingers were scraped against the corrosion coating the metal links. He fell to the dirt with a thud that drove the air out of him. The hand had not let go of his shirt, and it yanked him back to his feet. Alex was spun around helplessly, little more than a flop-limbed mannequin, helpless in his fear. His back was slammed up against the fence, and the hand switched from the back of his shirt to the front. He grasped the man's arm in its sleeve of green and red bands but before he could attempt to force it away, those four shimmering knife blades were pointing at his chest, only a millimeter away, poised to pluck the heart right out of him.

"Alex," the scarred man purred, his breath reeking of the elephant's decaying juices, "my talented friend. Don't you see I'm grateful to you?"

With one claw finger, he deftly cut away a button from Alex's shirt. The blade then peeled back the material, baring the skin beneath.

"Please!" Alex moaned, shaking. "What have I done to you?"

"What have you done to me? You've reconstructed me, Alex! Like the brain we're in right now." The scarred man looked all around him appreciatively. "That's why I have you to thank. You're helping to *remember* me out of the Hell I'm in. I'm like a genie, see? If no one remembers to rub the lamp, the genie has to sit inside, waiting and waiting and *waiting*." He clenched his discolored teeth. "Waiting in that... limbo. With no one to play with."

"Then you aren't going to hurt me?"

"Hmm... well let's see if I am, or I'm not." And with that, the scarred man pulled back his knife hand—then drove it squarely into the middle of Alex's chest.

He screamed. The impact of the hand against his sternum felt like a battering ram crashing into him, and yet Alex saw the four blade fingers bend and splay, as if made out of rubber. He was reminded of the way the gladiator sword had turned from solid metal to useless plastic in an arena he had visited once, in some other strange lifetime that he couldn't quite grasp at the moment.

"I guess I'm not strong enough to hurt you yet. I guess I still need some more reconstructing. But I can count on you for that, can't I, Alex? We're sort of a team, collaborators, aren't we?" Despite his words of camaraderie, the scarred man viciously tugged Alex away from the gate. He swiped his gloved hand at the securing chain, and even though the knives had turned to rubber against Alex's chest, they broke through the rusting links in a spray of sparks. The chain slithered to the ground and the gate swung open with a creak.

The scarred man extended his arm in a gesture of invitation. "Run along, Alex. Run along for now."

Alex needed no second invitation. He hurtled through the open gate, his sneakers pounding the dirt. Behind him, he heard the scarred man roar with laughter. Fog began to close in around Alex, a fog of more and more sizzling static. The laughter dwindled, and now it sounded crackly and scratchy like some old recording until the fog drowned out all sound, all sight, all sense.

SIX

"Come on, come on, so what's the big surprise?" Autumn Langevin asked her boyfriend Kent Lowe while they waited for Devon's brother Alex to arrive. She paced Devon's bedroom restlessly, like a caged leopard. He and Milton were currently downstairs chatting with Mr and Mrs Carmack.

Kent shrugged, distracted as he flipped through Devon's stack of TranceBox programs. One disk he wanted to borrow was called *Jolting Journeys*, and included the point of view of a scuba diver exploring a shipwreck; a professional skier shooting down frozen mountainsides; an astronaut floating outside his space shuttle. And he definitely had to borrow, again, *The Best of Battles* collection, with recorded recollections of soldiers both American and foreign, from various Middle East conflicts and even going back to the Vietnam

War—memories culled from both American and former Vietcong soldiers. These men might be old and gray today, but kids who were the same age now as the soldiers had been then could walk in their muddy boots, feel the adrenalin rush of navigating a jungle path or burning village and of cutting loose with an M-16 or AK-47 when the enemy made a sudden, shocking appearance. In an adult-rated program like this, you could actually know what it was like to *kill* a man, watch him die, look down at his decimated body—and of course, kids could find their way to acquire such hardcore disks easily enough. Programs like these were now even being used extensively in military training.

Kent finally set down his friend's disks and saw that Autumn, in her impatience, had begun fooling around with Devon's computer. "Hey," he said, "what are you doing? That could be private stuff, you know."

"If he wants to keep things private he should close the thing down, and not leave us bored up here while we wait for his brother's ass to finally show up."

Kent sighed, not wanting to push Autumn into one of her too-frequent surly moods. He had never had a girlfriend with whom he had had to choose his steps so carefully, for fear of setting off a land-mine (his mind was still on military matters, hence the analogy). As ever, Autumn's looks bought her a lot of leeway with him. She was seventeen, very short and very pale-skinned, her dirty-blonde hair long and straight, her squinty blue eyes defined by too much dark makeup. Her cat-like mouth curled naturally at the corners, which made for a great effect when she smirked or sneered, which was often. Kent found it sexy. Autumn's clothing tended toward the punky, with a lot of super-tight, under-sized T-shirts of white or black, baring a delectable expanse of midriff. Riding low on her bony hips would be tight jeans or oversized combat pants. Canvas sneakers or ugly, heavy boots would complete such an ensemble. She endlessly sketched the radical, often outlandish tattoos that she planned on getting just as soon as her parents stopped standing in the way of such an endeavor.

Kent was also seventeen, maybe a little too tall to be ideally matched to Autumn, and naturally muscular, though he had only flirted with sports since getting kicked off the basketball team in his freshman year. Despite still being a minor, he looked old enough that last year he had managed to get the artwork from the cover of a favorite music band's CD tattooed on his upper arm. His parents hadn't been happy about it, nor had he when he'd finally sobered up enough to realize what he had done. Incidents like these—the expulsion from the basketball team, and the tattoo—had finally added up to the point where his parents had managed to get him some help for his drinking, despite his initial resistance. Kent had successfully dried out over the summer, and luckily Autumn didn't drink—though she thought his tattoo was *very* sexy, and she sketched ideas for his future tattoos, too.

Kent heard footsteps and muffled voices coming up the stairs, so he shooed Autumn away from the computer. She sighed and turned her back on it, as Devon and Milton reentered the room.

"No brother yet?" Autumn noted sulkily.

Devon kept his tone as pleasant with Autumn as he could. "He just called, he's running late. His girlfriend is coming, too. Her name is Trisha; she's very cool."

Devon glanced past Autumn at his computer, recognizing right away that she'd been toying around on it. She was adept with computers, to say the least, and he didn't feel comfortable having her icy, lynx-like eyes burrowing into his machine. Afraid of the landmines, too, he simply gave a tolerant internal sigh.

Why had Kent gotten involved with this girl, of all the girls in Springwood High? Devon felt they were ill-matched. Still, at least Kent was a better match for Autumn than the more low-key Devon himself would have been. He still suspected sometimes, though he would never express such a theory to Kent, that Autumn had only begun dating Kent because of his friendship with Devon. Because she had wanted Devon, and he had not wanted her in turn. In his junior year, Devon had politely declined her obvious amorous overtures. But did she think that if she hung around with Devon's friend, attached herself to the periphery of Devon's world, he would finally change his mind about her? Begin to long for her, lust for her? Couldn't she tell that they were not suited for each other? And what was going on in her head lately, now that everyone at school must have learned that he and Grace Simmons were dating?

As if she had just read his mind, Autumn asked casually, "So when is Gracie getting here?"

"She and Ama are on the way, too. I just spoke to them a minute ago."

"Good. Let's get this party rolling."

Kent held up the *Jolting Journeys* and *The Best of Battles* disks for him to see. "Hey, man, okay if I take these home tonight?"

Devon didn't like to say no to his friend, especially since Kent wasn't one of those buddies who neglected to return borrowed items but lately he had begun to feel that Kent was using his TranceBox a bit too frequently, as if it had taken the place of alcohol as another form of addiction. He knew things weren't harmonious for Kent at home, and probably less than harmonious with Autumn too, and so it wasn't such a bad thing to have a form of stress release, but everything in moderation. Still, wasn't Devon being a hypocrite, given the secret reason for tonight's gathering? After a moment of mental stuttering, he finally said, "Why don't you hold off a few minutes until Alex gets here?"

Autumn nodded knowingly. "He's gonna give us a demonstration of something he's working on at that Mnemonic place, isn't he?"

"Something like that."

"Damn, that will be cool," Kent said, setting down the two disks. "I was hoping it was some freebie software, some old inventory they're cleaning out, something cool like that. So, is that it, then? A new test product?"

"He'll be here soon enough."

Before Alex arrived, Grace and Ama showed up. Grace gave Devon a big grin and impulsive hug. He hoped she didn't sense his discomfort, but he was a little self conscious about it in front of the others, especially Autumn. He saw the cold eyes behind Autumn's sneery smile when she greeted Grace. She even gave Grace a hug, too, as if to mock them. Grace didn't seem to catch the bitterness beneath the gesture; she merely seemed a little surprised by it.

Soon after Grace and Ama arrived, Alex and Trisha came up the stairs and into Devon's bedroom at last. Alex looked like he was beaming with enthusiasm, but Devon thought he appeared a little beat-up, too. He suspected his brother had been working very hard to get this project in a presentable state, getting too little sleep in the process.

Alex set down a backpack, and Devon quipped, "Shit, I thought it was a pizza delivery."

"I feel more like a drug dealer tonight," Alex said. "I hope everybody's ready for this… and by the way, thanks for coming."

Devon introduced Alex and Grace to each other. When Grace looked away, Alex wiggled his eyebrows at Devon meaningfully and gave a wink of approval.

Everyone had found a place to sit, whether on Devon's computer chair, the edge of his bed, or the floor. Trisha sat cross-legged and barefoot, having shed her sandals in the front hallway, but Alex remained standing. Triumphantly, he withdrew from his bag a handful of generic, clear plastic jewelboxes with hand-printed labels, and held them aloft for all to see.

"This, my friends, hot off the presses, is our latest project from Mnemonic Designs. And believe me, it's like no TranceBox software you've ever tried before…"

Sitting beside her on the edge of his bed, Devon looked at Grace from the corner of his eye, but he couldn't tell what might be going on in her head.

Alex continued, "With regular TranceBox programs, you experience things exactly the same as they felt to the person who lived those events at the time. They're pure memories, nothing more and nothing less. But with *this* program, you'll find your own thoughts, identity and personality will help shape what you experience, giving you a much more customized, personalized experience. No two people will experience exactly the same thing."

"Whoa!" said Kent.

"What kind of program is it, then?" Autumn asked. "I don't get it."

"It's dreams. Nightmares to be exact."

"Nightmares," Grace groaned softly.

"Yeah, why all nightmares and not all sexy dreams?" Ama asked. She kneaded Grace's shoulders in her strong hands. "Mmm, right, baby?"

The others laughed, and Devon said, "Wow, do that again, but let me get my camera first."

Alex grinned. "Maybe that will be the next disk. But for now, this is a nightmare program like no other. It will blow you away, trust me. I can't imagine a more intense thrill-ride than what you guys are going to be trying out here."

"So you want us to test this out for Mnemonic Designs?" asked Kent, excited.

"Yeah; I asked my boss if I could use my brother and his friends as a group of test subjects for the prototype, and he said sure, go for it. So here it is, pretty much edited and presented the way we'll take it to the public."

"How'd you like it, Trisha?" Devon asked her.

She waved her hand and shook her head, chuckling, "I've had my fill of that thing for the time being, trust me. It's you guys' turn to shit your pants now."

"Great," Grace mumbled.

"Yeah, I want you guys to try this out for a week or two," Alex said. "Then we'll get together again and you can give me your feedback. In return for your help, you can each keep the copy of the program I'm giving you." And with that, he started handing them out.

Grace hesitated in accepting her copy. "Um, I don't own a TranceBox."

"Me neither," said Ama.

"You guys don't get out of it that easily," Alex said, and he fished two TranceBoxes out of his backpack, handing them to the girls. "I come prepared."

"Thanks," Grace said unenthusiastically, lowering the little device into her lap. Again, Devon checked out her reaction to all this, but for now he said nothing. He hoped she wasn't angry at him for making her a part of this, but did she really object to TranceBoxes *that* much?

"So you guys are gonna make millions off of this, and we get paid for being guinea pigs with a free test copy?" Autumn teased Alex. "Wow. That's so big business of you."

"Hey, we're no major corporation here, just a little crew of geeks. For now, anyway."

Grace toyed with her jewelbox, opening its cover to reveal the coin-like iridescent disk resting inside like a pearl in its oyster. She couldn't hold in her personal feelings any longer. "Why should we watch other people's dreams when we have our own dreams—for free, too?"

"Well," Milton Ferrara said, "why watch a movie about another person's life when we have our own lives, you know? Or read a biography about someone else's experiences? We like to live through other people's eyes, but from a safe distance."

"Plus, of course, with this technology you can play any particular kind of dream, whenever you want and as many times as you want," Kent added. "Not to mention, my dreams *suck*, man. I guess I don't have the greatest imagination or something. And if I'm in a dream fight, my punches are like rubber and my swings are in slow motion. If it's a sexy dream, the girl and I always flirt around and agree to hook up later, but I never do find her again."

"And who exactly is it you're dreaming about, bubba?" Autumn asked him, elbowing him.

Kent said, "Nobody real, nobody real, don't worry. Anyway, have any of you tried the dream program *APEcalypse*? Man, you're on this pirate ship that gets stuck on some rocks near this tropical island, and these thousands of man-eating ape-things come running out of the jungle and try to get onto the ship. You gotta shoot your cannons at 'em, and fight them hand to hand with swords. And you even go to bed with this sexy pirate lady with a patch over one eye, at one point. Man, now *that's* a dream! The day I have dreams like that on my own, maybe I'll consider shelving my dream disks."

"I guess I need to buy a patch for my eye, huh?" Autumn told Kent. "Maybe you'd like me with a peg leg, too, you freak?"

Getting back to Grace's comment on experiencing one's own dreams, Alex informed her, "You know, Saxon Systems is working on a new kind of TranceBox that you'll be able to use to record your own memories and dreams as they occur. Imagine being able to play back a wedding or a vacation and experience it fresh again and again. Or play back a dream you really liked, a dream that came out of your own head to start with."

"Where did *these* dreams come from?" Autumn asked, holding up and shaking her jewelbox.

Alex tried not to grin as he said, "Just some very willing volunteers."

Grace returned the conversation to her own concerns. "Um, this technology affects how we interact with our own brains, so naturally it affects how people interact with each other. To me it's a kind of paradox. The TranceBox makes it so you can interact more intimately with another human being than was ever possible before, but at the same time, the person you're interacting with is anonymous to you. And it isn't *real* interaction, real give and take. It's more like peeking at someone's diary than having a conversation with them. People are getting inside someone else's head, but they go off by themselves to do it. It's this solitary process that cuts us off from each other more than it brings us together."

"A solitary process, like reading a book?" Milton the writer said. "We do that alone, but does that isolate us from each other? And isn't a novel's author anonymous to the person reading that book?"

"There's nothing wrong with a little fun— period," Kent proclaimed. "Whenever some new technology comes along, some people are always gonna be afraid, and look at only the negative aspects. No offense, Grace."

"Sure. No offense, Kent."

"So... Gracie," Autumn said, smirking, "are you gonna try this nightmare program out, or not?"

Devon finally spoke to her, leaning close and whispering, "You don't have to do it, Grace."

She looked at him hotly. "I know I don't have to do it," she said. Then she turned back toward Autumn. "Yeah, I'm going to try it. Alex needs our help."

"That's the spirit," Alex said. "I like your girl, Devon."

"Yeah, she's a real trooper, Devo," Autumn agreed.

Devon still looked concerned. "Are you sure you're really up for this, Grace?"

This time she made her reply more civil, not wanting him to think of her as bitchy. After all, it wasn't Devon who was responsible for her nightmares of the basement, was it? So she smiled and reassured him, "I'll be okay. Don't worry."

"No peer pressure here?"

"I'm doing it because I want to. Trust me."

Devon smiled and patted her thigh, then blushed a little at having done so. "How about the first time you try it, I stay there beside you, to watch over you? Will that make you feel a little better?"

"I don't know. I might feel self-conscious with you watching me sleep, in case I get really scared and act all stupid. I might prefer to have Ama watch over me."

His disappointment was apparent. "Oh. Well, whatever."

Grace laughed. He looked like a forlorn puppy. "Hey, okay, you can watch over me. That'd be great. You'll make me feel safe."

Devon beamed. "You'll do fine."

Trisha got up from the floor, swatting dust from her butt. "Let's celebrate and phone for some pizza like Devon said, huh? Treat's on me."

"I'm up for that," Alex said. "It's the least we big business types can do for you guinea pigs—right, Autumn?"

Autumn only looked at Alex and gave another of her patented, cat-mouthed sneering smiles.

SEVEN

"You see how Devon's asshole brother didn't like my innocent little comment?" Autumn Langevin said to Kent Lowe. This time they were seated in her bedroom, the nucleus of which was clearly her computer station. She had two computers and a plethora of attendant gear; so much that it looked like she could have started up her own software design company herself. She sat in front of the newer of her two computers now, tinkering, her back to Kent.

"I don't think Alex is an asshole," Kent said, a little bitter at Autumn's lack of attention. He had hoped that, with her parents out tonight, he and Autumn might be doing more up here than poking around on her computer and talking about Devon Carmack's brother. He sighed, rose from the edge of her bed where he'd been sitting hopefully, and swept his eyes across walls that Autumn had painted glossy black and stenciled with white Halloween skulls on an earlier weekend that her parents had been away.

Over her shoulder, Autumn said, "I'm just sick of how all these greedy corporations make fortunes off the meager pocket money of teenager like us."

"I'm pretty sure those sneakers you're wearing were made by a big corporation." Kent lifted one of her music CDs. "And these guys are making millions off kids like you and me, too."

Autumn wheeled around slowly in her chair, her black-outlined blue eyes feral. Kent knew right away he'd triggered one of those landmines before she even replied. "Yeah, I know they're taking my money. It's unavoidable for me to give it to them, unless I wanna live naked in some South American jungle, right? But do you or don't you see the point I'm making?"

Kent averted his eyes. "Yeah, yeah. I see it."

Autumn swiveled back to face her computer, tapping at keys. What was she doing, working on her website again? Couldn't she do that on her own time, when he wasn't here? But he wasn't about to put those thoughts into words; better to let her anger dissipate rather than throw more logs on the fire. Kent thought he'd take a stab at making the peace, and a last shot at coaxing Autumn toward the bed. He drifted up behind her and started playing with her long, fine hair, letting it sift through his hands. It was as if she didn't even notice, however. He let her hair fall one last time and sighed.

"It's eleven. My parents are gonna be pissed if I'm not home soon."

"So go. I'll see you tomorrow at school."

"Well, can I at least have a kiss goodnight?" he sulked.

Autumn leaned far back in her chair, tilting her head to look at him upside-down, and gave an exaggerated pout. Kent leaned over her, and while they kissed he slid his hand off her shoulder and onto her chest for a quick squeeze before she peeled his hand away and sat up straight again in her chair.

"You'd better go before you give me an erection," she told him.

He snickered. "Is there anything wrong with that?"

"Don't you know, Kent? I'm a *good* girl." She batted her eyes at him.

"If you say so." He shoved her head playfully and started toward her bedroom door.

"You can pleasure yourself while you think of these tonight." From across the room, she jerked up her T-shirt to give him a flash of black bra against white-white skin. Kent promptly started back toward her but she wagged a finger at him. "Uh-uh-uhhh."

"You're killing me, Autumn. You're a sadist."

"Maybe," she said sweetly.

Heaving another sigh, Kent let himself out of her room, closing the door a little too loudly after him.

Now it was Autumn's turn to sigh. She could only take so much of Kent at a time. He was easy on the eyes and good for a laugh, but she felt he was nowhere near her intellectual level. For a boyfriend like that, she would be better matched with someone like, oh, Devon Carmack.

With Kent finally gone, Autumn could get down to the business she really craved (not the business Kent had craved)—trying out this new TranceBox program that Devon's brother had hyped up so much. It had better be as good as he claimed, she thought, after all that build-up.

She saved the changes to her website, then kicked off her sneakers and reclined on her bed, where she opened the jewelbox she'd been given. She removed the shiny little disk and popped it into the TranceBox she kept on her bedside table. There were six colors to choose from, and her TranceBox was a dramatic blood red. The device had a compartment to store the adhesive receiver pad in, so she flipped its cover and took out the circular white patch, sticking it to her right temple.

Autumn watched a little screen on the TranceBox as she reviewed the disk's contents. She saw there were a series of "chapters" to the disk, as there were on most TranceBox disks. They had even been labeled. *Arena*, *Convenience Store* (ooh, that sounded scary, as in scared to be bored to death), *Zoo*, *Hospital*, and so on. She supposed she should play the disk in sequence, instead of jumping to a given chapter, but her father was a surgeon so ultimately she figured she'd have a look at the hospital dream. Maybe she could even get him to take a look at it himself sometime, if he were ever home long enough for her to ask him. For a moment, Autumn had recollections of her father sitting on the edge of this very bed, reading her much younger self storybooks so that she might have those "sweet dreams" that he wished her. But Autumn quickly chased away such maudlin reminiscences, as if even when alone she was afraid to seem vulnerable or weak. Anyway, enough of her own memories, it was time to relive those of another person.

Before starting the hospital dream, she programmed the device to wake her up when that chapter had come to its end, instead of automatically taking her along to the following chapter. She mustn't get greedy and try out every chapter in one night, she decided. After all, she had school in the morning.

Satisfied with her adjustments, Autumn depressed the PLAY button, then rested her head back on the several pillows that propped it up. She closed her eyes and waited for the machine to induce sleep. From there on, she entrusted herself to its care. It could do with her what it wished.

Autumn lifted her head and tried to blink away her grogginess. She must have dozed off. Looking around, she realized she was seated in a hospital waiting room, and it had to be the very early hours of the morning as it was absolutely empty except for herself. She had never seen an emergency room empty before, no matter what hour of the night it was. Children's noses were always running, accident victims were always bleeding. Human misery took no time off. Well, except for tonight. But then again, she was here, wasn't she?

She rubbed at her eyes again but couldn't seem to clear the blurriness from them; everything seemed dim and fuzzy. Not fuzzy as in out of focus, but gritty, grainy.

She looked herself over. No wounds were apparent, and she didn't feel sick except for her unclear vision. Might that be caused by a virus she was suffering, or by a drug she was taking for some ailment or other? Whatever it was, illness or medicine, it had obviously affected her memory even more than it had her vision.

There was a rumpled magazine in her lap, but she couldn't make sense of its cover no matter how long she stared at it. Some foreign medical journal? Words in a language she couldn't decipher were splashed above a picture of a human brain, partially dissected, with clamps holding open a section of its membranes. A bit strong for the cover of a magazine, she thought. Not that she was squeamish.

Rising from the hard plastic shape that passed for a chair, she looked up and down the ER waiting area. The fluorescent lighting was greenish and unhealthy, one of the tubes flickering in protracted death throes. The only sound came from a TV mounted near the ceiling, but the volume was lowered to a bare murmur. It looked like some kind of gladiator movie was playing; a man with a sword trying to defend himself from a snarling lion, but Autumn gave it only a glance.

She spotted a triage desk up front, but when she approached it Autumn found no one in attendance. There was a little room behind the counter, and

Autumn leaned over the desk to call, "Hello?" No answer. So what the hell was going on here? Was there a fire somewhere in the building and everyone had evacuated, forgetting to wake her up and take her with them?

Then, at last, Autumn remembered her father. Might she be here because of him? This was not the hospital he worked at, but could he have brought her here with him just for the company? It was the sort of thing he had done when she was little, showing her off to his colleagues, the doting nurses, the feeble older patients who sadly thought she was some grandchild come to visit them. Those had been nice days, before her dad's job had become so demanding that he spent more and more time there, and less at home. Her mother had taken that gradual turn of events even harder than Autumn had, as if it was a kind of betrayal, her husband's job the equivalent of a hated mistress. She had seemed to resent her daughter at times for not being a worthy enough substitute. At least, that was how Autumn had interpreted it. Of course, now that Autumn was nearly a woman and not so dependent on them, her parents had more time for each other again and, between that and her medication, Mom had mellowed out over the past couple of years. But all these memories were causing Autumn undue pain; the only thing she needed to remember right now was what she was doing in this place.

So, could it be a condemned hospital building, slated for destruction and reconstruction, that her father had been summoned to for some reason or other? Her mind raced through possible scenarios, but she couldn't be certain that her father truly figured into her reason for being here.

She must find someone, somewhere. She saw glass doors leading outside to where ambulances pulled up to unload their human cargo. The night was utterly black out there; the hospital might be floating in outer space itself, for all she could tell. She walked toward the glass doors, approached near enough for them to open automatically. They didn't.

"What the fuck?" Autumn whispered, growing more irritated by the second. She pushed at one of the manual doors, but it barely rattled in its frame. Locked. Okay, an abandoned and locked up hospital. She must indeed be here with her Dad on some special errand, but what could that be? And where had he gone off to, then? Should she remain in the waiting room until he came back from wherever?

"Fuck that," she muttered, and turned toward the nearest corridor she could see, pushing open a door to enter it. At least that door hadn't been locked.

Lining the corridor with its worn linoleum floor and ugly green paint job were doors to various darkened offices, which quick glances told her were also deserted. Several more corridors branched off from this one, and at the end there were elevators. Why not? Autumn stabbed at the buttons, and they lit, but nothing else happened—just one teasing squeak of machinery from the elevator shaft, and then nothing more. Letting out an exasperated sigh, Autumn headed for the metal door to the stairwell instead.

She tried the second floor first, but right away she could see there was no one at the nurses' station. Okay, then, if the hospital was slated for demolition, why did it look like people still worked here but had upped and left only recently, as in mere hours or even minutes ago? Autumn was tempted to use the phone system behind the counter to send her voice over the intercom, but that might be going too far; she didn't want to look like some panicky jerk. She'd find her Dad or someone, eventually. She decided to start checking in the patients' rooms next.

In the very first room, a private room with only one bed, Autumn found a person at last.

A man lay in the bed, his wall-mounted TV running that same gladiator movie she had seen on the set in the waiting area. He had the sound muted, and he certainly couldn't see the screen, either—not through the bandages that entirely covered his head. Red stains appeared in several spots as blood seeped through the layers of gauze. Maybe he didn't even realize the TV was on.

Autumn looked over her shoulder into the hall again. This man couldn't be here alone, surely. But how could they leave him unattended like this? In case she wasn't supposed to be in here and might get in trouble for it, she entered the room fully and gently closed the door behind her. She was afraid to wake the poor guy up if he was sleeping, but who else did she have to answer her questions?

"Hey, excuse me?" she said, slowly approaching the bed. "Hello?"

There was machinery arranged on a cart beside the bed, giving off a soft, rhythmic beeping. Various tubes snaked under the man's sheet, obviously plugged into his body, and a thick segmented hose penetrated his mummy-like mask to enable his breathing. Life support. Was he in critical condition? Was he dying?

"Hello? Sir?" A few steps nearer, gingerly. Even if he was cognizant of her, would he be able to talk around that breathing tube in his mouth?

She touched the man's arm through the sheet. No reaction, not even a change in the rhythm of his vital signs' beeping. So he was in a coma, then. What had happened to him?

A terrible thought occurred to Autumn then. Could this man be the reason she was here? Might this man be someone she knew? Kent, perhaps? Or even Dad?

She had to find out. No longer worrying about rousing the man, she pulled back his sheet to get a better look at his body. That was when she saw the bomb.

It looked crude, but very effective. There were multiple sticks of dynamite taped in a row, and wires affixed to a little electronic device, all of which was strapped around the man's bare chest. There was no ticking sound, so Autumn didn't know if the explosive device was already activated and if so, how long there might be before it went off.

Had someone sneaked into the hospital to strap this device to the man, in order to assassinate him? Why not just suffocate him instead, or disconnect his life support, something simple like that? No, Autumn felt that the man had come into the hospital this way. Maybe he was a terrorist, his face badly beaten by the soldiers who had captured him, and this was actually a military hospital. Maybe she wasn't even in the United States. The man's skin did look swarthy (which was a relief, since she could tell right away it wasn't Kent or her father). And his khaki trousers did look like they could be part of a military uniform. He was very young, little more than a teenager, but then soldiers usually were. Okay, so the big question—why wouldn't the staff have removed that bomb by now?

"Oh my God," Autumn breathed.

So this was why the hospital was abandoned. They didn't know how to remove the bomb. They had evacuated the building until specialists could arrive to defuse it.

"Oh shit," she whispered.

She had to get out of here, too. She rushed to the door, took one look back at the young man in the bed, and took hold of the knob. It wouldn't turn. She rattled it but the knob wouldn't budge. In shutting the patient's door, she had inadvertently locked herself in.

"Fuck!" she cried. She pounded on the wood and peered out through a small window at face level. "Hello out there! Hello! Let me out of here!"

The noise must have disturbed the man in the bed, for she heard him moan softly behind her. Autumn whirled around in time to see his right hand give a spasmodic jerk. The motion caused his

TV remote to slide off the side of the bed and clatter to the floor. Autumn hadn't noticed it until that moment.

The remote's striking the floor caused the TV channel to change. The gladiator movie was replaced with some kind of police drama or action flick. A masked robber in a liquor store— no, it was a convenience store—was menacing the proprietor with a knife. Autumn was too horrified to do more than take in the TV peripherally, because the bomb on the man's chest had just begun smoking. A thin black stream of smoke, winding up out of the electronic device.

Was it her imagination, or was the TV remote responsible for this change in the bomb's status? Could the electronic device be so sensitive that the remote's signal had affected it?

Autumn hammered at the door some more, yelled at the top of her lungs this time, shouted curses that ended up turning into an inarticulate shriek. If the young man moaned again, she didn't hear it over her own racket. When she looked back at the bed, she saw that smoke continued to pour out of the bomb, forming a haze in the air that smelled like burnt plastic.

"Oh my God, it's gonna go off, it's gonna go off," she babbled, close to sobbing. What could she do? There was no window in the room that she could smash and escape through. If she broke the window in the door, could she reach her arm down far enough to try the knob from the outside?

Or, should she pick up that remote, and hit some more buttons in an attempt to deactivate the bomb herself?

It was an absolutely crazy notion. She was more likely to set it off than shut it off. And yet her instincts, a strange intuition, told her this was the proper course of action. It was almost like another person's thoughts (the man in the bed?) telepathically invading her own mind.

Still, Autumn approached the remote tentatively, as if it was itself a bomb that would detonate at the slightest touch. She stood over it, contemplated it, and at last knelt down and took it in hand. She studied the numbered buttons, wondering which button had been struck to cause the bomb to smoke. She must not touch that button again! Was it the channel advance button? If so, should she depress the button that would reverse the sequence of channels?

It was worth a try. One button was as good as another. All she had to count on right now was her weird intuition, and since this button was the first one that had occurred to her mind...

When Autumn pressed the button, a spray of sparks burst out of the electronic device on the man's chest. She yelped, nearly dropping the remote. The channel on the TV was changed back to what should have been the gladiator movie, but maybe it had ended and a new program had begun—apparently a documentary about animals. An elephant was trotting across a dusty plain, its great ears bobbing with the motion.

Another spark or two shot out of the bomb, and if anything the stream of smoke had turned heavier and blacker. Had she shorted the thing out? Was it dead? Her instinct told her the bomb was far from dead. But how much could she trust these intuitions? They might be mere illusion, only causing her to worsen matters. She should have kept to her first instinct, she thought: trying to break out of this room, smashing the window in the door.

As delicately as she could, Autumn set the remote down on a table attached by a swinging arm to the side of the man's bed. Before she could turn back toward the door, however, she heard an awful squealing noise like fingernails on a blackboard. She whipped around to see that a face was framed in that little square window. A face gazing in at her.

If the young man in the bed had his bandages removed, this was what she might expect him to look like. And surely this new man had to be another patient here in the hospital! Because the face in the window was terribly, terribly scarred.

"Hello, Autumn," the disfigured man said.

"Who are you?" she blurted, almost falling back against the patient's table.

"Ah, how soon they forget, the people of Springwood. Then again, you're young. And they work very hard to scrub poor Freddy Krueger's name out of the records. Even out of the internet, I understand, but it looks like they can't scrub me out of people's minds altogether, can they?"

"I don't know what you're talking about!" Autumn whined. "Look, mister, please let me out of this place, okay?"

The doorknob rattled, but again it wouldn't budge. "Sorry, Autumn, but it looks like I can't do that. I'm still partly rubbed out, like I said, so I don't have all my strength back yet. It looks like *you* are going to have to open the door for *me*."

"I can't! I tried!"

"You haven't tried hard enough. This is your dream, Autumn. At least, partially. Think of it as lucid dreaming. Think that you can open this door very, very easily... simply by turning the knob."

"What do you mean, a dream?"

"This is all just a dream, little Autumn. Try to remember. A *dream*. So take control. Turn the knob. Trust me, you can do this." The thing that had called itself Freddy Krueger twisted its scarred lips in a sneering grin. "Let me out, Autumn. Don't you see? I'm the real prisoner, here, not you."

Right or wrong, Autumn's instinct was telling her to go nowhere near that doorknob, bomb or no bomb.

"Tell me how to deactivate *that* first," she demanded, gathering some of her cockiness back, pointing at the smoke rising up from the man in the bed. "Then I'll think about trying the door again."

"Let me in and I'll take care of it for you."

"Yeah?" she said dubiously. "I don't trust you."

"Why not?" He was trying to sound sweet but the words were more like a hiss.

"Because I think you *can* come in here, if you want. I think you want me to come out there, though, because you're afraid. Afraid of the bomb."

"I'll give you something to be afraid of if you don't open this door!" Krueger snarled, all niceties now forgotten.

"You are afraid of it, aren't you?" Autumn plucked up the TV remote and weighed it in her palm. "Do you think if the bomb went off with you out there, you'd still be close enough to get turned into hamburger?"

"You can't kill me, girlie. I'm just a dream man in a dream world." He blew at the fingers of his left hand as if sending dandelion spores into the air.

"Yeah? Well if this really is all just a dream, then this bomb is a dream weapon in a dream world. It's made out of the same stuff you are."

Krueger shook his bald head sadly. Through gritted teeth he said, "And to think I thought you and I might get along, for a minute there."

"I believe you're what they'd call in my history class, the classical mythological trickster."

"And I believe you're what they'd call in the school of hard knocks, dead meat."

Autumn heard the injured man groan softly behind her. She lowered her eyes to the remote. Could it be as simple as pressing the ON/OFF button? If she shut the TV off, would the bomb be shut off too? But if she shut the bomb down, would this Krueger person then be able to come right on in here as she feared might be the case? Still thinking in mythological terms, Autumn felt trapped between Scylla and Charybdis.

Another groan. Autumn looked over at the bed.

The person in the bed groaned a third time and turned their head towards her. Autumn found herself staring at the ceiling of her bedroom, which she had been meaning to paint black as well, but she hadn't gotten around to it yet.

She sat up in bed abruptly, remembering where she'd been and realizing that she was back, the TranceBox having released her from its spell at the point she had programmed. Autumn found her hair was sweaty, strands of it stuck to her forehead. She was almost hyperventilating, as if she'd been sprinting instead of lying inert.

"Oh... my... God," she gasped out loud, a feverish grin stealing over her face. "Devon's brother wasn't exaggerating after all!"

EIGHT

"Surprise," Alex said loudly, waving a Styrofoam cup of coffee back and forth under Julie Ip's nose.

Its aroma did the trick; she opened her eyes, lifted her head with a weary smile, and removed the headphones she'd been wearing. Alex heard a song playing through the earpieces, and before she switched it off recognized it as Todd Rundgren's *A Dream Goes On Forever*. When he'd come into Macrocosm Research's lab, he'd seen that Julie's forehead was resting in her palms, her elbows propped atop the work station in front of her. For a minute there he'd thought she was asleep.

"You are a saint." She accepted the cup. "No coffee for the rest of the team?"

"They aren't as pretty as you." Alex pulled up a chair beside her and opened the lid of his own coffee. "So, anybody say anything about me coming in so late?"

"Farhad didn't look happy after you called, but…" Julie shrugged.

"Crap. I was at Mnemonic past two AM, so I needed to catch some zees." Last week, Alex had confided in Julie at last about his extracurricular activities outside of Macrocosm.

"Catching some zees sounds pretty good right about now."

Alex finally noticed the redness of her eyes. "So… what's wrong?"

"Well, two kinds of headache. One is called Mr G, and the other is up here." She patted her skull with both hands.

Alex took a swallow of his drink, regarding her grimly. "First of all, what did he do this time?"

"Oh, let's see, I was standing on a stool to get some stuff off a shelf, and when I was ready to come down he asked me if I needed any help. He was about ready to put his hands on my waist. I told him—maybe a bit too sternly—that I was all set, thanks. Uh, then later when I told him I had a monstrous headache, he talked baby-talk to me and asked me if I needed a hug. Very politely, I assured him I was fine without a hug."

As icky as it all sounded to Alex, he couldn't help but laugh. Even Julie grinned. "God, I just can't get over it. As if you'd ever go out with this guy. Almost thirty years older than you, ugly as shit, and so skinny he'd probably get a hernia if he helped you off a stool."

"Excuse me—I'm not *that* fat!"

"You know I'm not saying that. Oh man, what a jerk he is. I guess he goes wild for you exotic Asian chicks; I know I do." Alex licked his lips. "Come on, say it, baby. Say, 'Me so horny, me love you long time.'"

"No way."

"Please! Just this once; make a guy happy." It was an ongoing joke between them. "Say, 'Me so horny, me love you too much.'"

"'Muck you!'" Julie said.

"Ohhh yeah, baby. Yeah."

"See, I don't mind that you sexually harass me, Alex, because I know you're just kidding. You *are* just kidding, right?"

"Uh yeah, just kidding. Right."

"Ha. You're cute today, but twenty-something years from now you'll be the creep offering a young girl a hug."

"You got a point." Alex smiled as Julie slurped some more coffee, but then the smile withered as he took in her reddened eyes again. "Headache, huh? Not the back of your head."

"Well, that's where it started." She touched the spot.

"Maybe we need to get Patrick to scan us all again."

"That might be a good idea," Julie said, her own mood growing solemn once more. "Mr G said he's had a pounding headache all day, too."

"Shit," Alex hissed, looking pensively at the equipment all around him. He prayed that nothing they were doing here was responsible for this. And he especially prayed that no headache-inducing influences were finding their way into the software he was still tweaking and fine-tuning at Mnemonic Designs. Not only might that shoot down his dreams of riches and fame but he had asked his own brother to test the program. If Farhad, a very rational man, felt sufficiently concerned to order Patrick to watch their own brains for the appearance of irregular tissue growth, then this was a matter to take seriously. Or was Farhad just being prudent, covering all bases, however unlikely? Alex told himself not to panic, not to jump to conclusions. All the data wasn't in yet.

"Mr G also said he's having nosebleeds," Julie added. "And nightmares."

"Yeah? Nightmares about the nightmares, huh?"

"Maybe. They are pretty harrowing, you have to admit."

"Damn it. I'm just afraid Farhad will get too worried about this, and put the brakes on the dream extractions." Alex glanced about but didn't spot Farhad—or Patrick or Mr G for that matter. Were they elsewhere in the labs, or maybe in Farhad's adjacent office?

Julie said, "I thought we'd pretty much milked all we could from those tumors. Dream-wise, anyway."

"Well, it doesn't hurt to keep squeezing."

Julie massaged her temples. "Maybe it does hurt."

Alex touched her arm. "Let's get Patrick to scan you right now."

"Can't."

"Why not?"

"Patrick didn't come in today; that's probably why Farhad was less than thrilled when you said you'd be in at noon. And Farhad hasn't been able to get Patrick on the phone, either."

"No?" Alex puffed up his cheeks, then released the air slowly. "That isn't like Patrick."

"I know. I don't like it either."

"Wanna try to call him again, ourselves?"

"The truth? I'd rather we drive over to his place, Alex. I'm afraid he might have a headache, too. Maybe one even worse than what me and Mr G are having."

Alex promptly rose from his chair, gathering up the car keys he'd just set down. "Let's tell Farhad we're going over there. You're sick, I'll drive."

"Thanks, Alex." Julie fetched her pocketbook, and brought her coffee along for the ride.

"So you haven't had any unusual headaches?" Julie asked, slouched across Alex's backseat with a hand clamped over her eyes.

"No, I've been fine," Alex said, looking in the rearview mirror.

"Maybe it's just a coincidence, then. Or maybe the experience affects different people in different ways."

"But Trisha—Trisha had an awful headache after I let her sample that convenience store dream."

He saw Julie peek from under her hand. "Yeah? I don't know, Alex. I realize you think you've got an oil field here, but personally I don't know what we've got going on."

"Our sponsors don't expect us—or want us—to tie it all together. They've probably got researchers spread all over, like blind men feeling different parts of the elephant. I'm sure they hope we never see the big picture." Alex sounded more than bitter. "They just want us to hand them the raw data. We'll never know what they do with it."

"Maybe that's just as well."

They were almost there. One more turn, and Alex entered tree-lined, blandly lovely Elm Street. It was like a suburban heaven where all the characters from Norman Rockwell's paintings would go when they died. Elm Street had an oddly untouched quality, as if its little neighborhood was enclosed in a giant time capsule. Its white-washed purity was almost eerie. Blue foliage shadows rippled restlessly across the neat sidewalks.

Patrick rented the top floor of a small house that had been converted into a two-family home. Patrick's landlord was his Uncle Ralph, and the two men found the arrangement mutually beneficial: Ralph Tremblay took comfort in Patrick's presence, since his wife Barbara had died of cancer several years earlier, and Patrick benefited from a more than reasonable rent. Alex had been over to play video games and knock back a few beers with Patrick a number of times, and had met Ralph more than once. Alex had teased the men about their "bachelor pad," speculating on what hedonistic activities took place there on weekends.

"His car is here," Julie noted, sitting up in her seat as Alex pulled in behind Patrick's vehicle in the driveway. Ralph's car was parked out front, on the curb. Alex got out quickly to open Julie's door for her, and as she dragged herself from the car she squinted her eyes almost entirely shut against the pain the sun caused her. "I hurt, Alex, I need a hug."

"I'll tell Mr G when we get back." Alex nodded toward the front door, then led the way up the walk.

Alex had to rap three times—each time louder than the last—until Uncle Ralph finally came shuffling to the front door. He was hard of hearing and ill of health, but Alex had always liked the mischievous twinkle in his blue eyes. He recognized Alex right away and pumped his hand. "Hey! Hey!" he said. "Long time no see."

"How's it going, Ralph?"

"Good, good. Is this your girlfriend?"

"Hi, I'm Julie." She stepped up beside Alex to shake the man's badly quivering hand. "I'm a coworker of Patrick's. He's in, right?"

"What? Oh yeah, yeah, he should be. I was just taking a nap." Ralph leaned out the doorway to glance at the driveway. "His car is here."

"We'll just go on up, Ralph," Alex said loudly, gesturing.

"Sure, sure, you do that." As Julie smiled and slipped past Ralph, his eyes twinkled and he put a shaky hand on the small of her back as if to help guide her along. When Ralph disappeared into his ground floor flat and Alex started up the carpeted front steps, Julie remarked, "I guess I really appeal to older men."

"Well, Ralph was in 'Nam, so maybe you remind him of a Vietnamese prostitute he once knew."

"Muck you, Alex."

The narrow steps ended right at Patrick's door, without even the courtesy of a landing. Alex perched on the top step and rapped his knuckles again. "Hey, wake up, you slacker!" he called.

After several long moments he looked down at Julie a few steps below him. "Again," she said. "He might have the TV on or something."

"I don't hear any TV," Alex muttered. He knocked as firmly as he had when summoning Ralph to the front door. "Hey, Patrick! Come on, man!"

"Alex. *Alex.*" He turned back to Julie, and she didn't look to be in the mood for any more playful banter. "We need to get the key from his uncle, if he has one."

"I'm sure he does," Alex said, equally serious, and the two of them descended.

Alex had to rap his sore knuckles several more times before Uncle Ralph reappeared, but he was able to produce a key to the upstairs flat. Armed with this, Alex led the way up a second time.

Uncle Ralph tagged along behind them, hauling his frail body up the staircase. Julie took his elbow to assist him and he flashed her a smile, but he had become too concerned to flirt. "You think something's wrong?"

"We have a, um, bug going around the office," Alex called over his shoulder. "We're just afraid Patrick might have it, too. He didn't come in to work today."

"Yeah… yeah… I thought I heard him up there, after he should have been to work."

"You did?" Julie said.

"He was yelling, swearing, saying he was gonna kill somebody. You know how he gets worked up playing those games, Alex."

"Yeah," Alex said gravely, as he slid the key into the doorknob. It turned freely, and he let himself into Patrick's apartment, Julie and Uncle Ralph close on his heels. It was a small apartment, just a few rooms, its slanted walls covered in sports posters and—to Julie's eyes—other god-awful sports memorabilia.

"Patrick? Yo!" she said, breaking off into the living room to the left. Alex turned right toward the bedroom, Ralph sticking with him.

Alex got no further than the bedroom's threshold before roaring, "Fuck! Fuck! Oh my God, no!"

"What is it? What's wrong?" Ralph cried, trying to squeeze around him, but Alex thrust his arms out to block him.

"No, Ralph, don't!"

But shaken as Alex was, he ultimately couldn't stop the older man from wedging himself into the doorway beside him. "Oh... oh no... oh *Patrick!*" Ralph wailed, breaking into sobs immediately. He hadn't seen this kind of carnage in over forty years. Not since the Vietnam War.

Julie came running. Alex had turned to embrace Ralph, both to comfort and restrain him. He was afraid the old man might have a heart attack, if he didn't have one first himself. Alex felt light-headed, surreal. He felt just as he did when testing his new nightmare software at Mnemonic.

Julie barged past the two men, and now it was her turn to wail. She fell back against the wall of the little hallway outside the bedroom, sinking down close to the floor to hug her knees. A moment later she had the presence of mind to reach into her pocketbook and dig out her cellphone. "I'm calling 911," she sobbed.

Alex eased Ralph back against the wall beside Julie. "You stay here, Ralph. Stay out here with Julie."

"Who did this? *Who?*" the old man blubbered.

"It may be a suicide," Alex said, grimacing toward the open doorway. He prayed it was so. As tragic as that would be, the alternative was too monstrous to assimilate. "You guys please, please stay out here. I'm going in to look."

At first, all Alex could register was the blood. It might have been thrown in his face from a bucket, so surely did it initially blind him to the other details of the scene. He forced himself to pay attention and forced his bile to stay down deep inside him where it belonged.

A suicide? Maybe a shotgun could have caused such a spray of blood. But then, as hard of hearing as he was, Ralph would have heard a gun discharge. After all, he had heard Patrick yelling, even if he had thought he was merely playing one of his video games at the time.

Alex crept close to the bed very timidly, as if afraid to wake his friend from his dreams.

Dreams. Alex spotted the TranceBox on the blood-splattered bedside table, at about the same moment he realized he was seeing four long, deep, parallel slash wounds running down Patrick's right cheek and across the edge of his jaw. Similar sets of wounds were carved into his chest, some of them criss-crossing, his sheet cut to ribbons and soaked with his life fluid. There were even defensive wounds hacked into his right wrist and hand from Patrick having raised his arm to futilely block the attack. Alex almost lost his mastery over his guts when he saw that one of Patrick's fingers was hanging half-severed as a result of these defensive gashes.

"Oh buddy," he whispered, wagging his head. "My buddy." He realized his eyes had turned wet. But then his eyes returned to the TranceBox again.

On some intuition, Alex reached out to Patrick's head, resting in profile on his saturated pillow. He took him delicately by the chin, hating to touch the still tacky blood and cooling flesh. Alex knew that rigor mortis took three hours to set in, and it had definitely set in; he winced as he had to use his other hand, too, in turning Patrick's head to point in the other direction. In so doing, he revealed the adhesive receptor patch for the TranceBox, still stuck to Patrick's left temple.

The same hunch that had told him the patch would be there commanded Alex to peel the thing off his coworker's skin and slip it into his jeans pocket. Fortunately, blood had already seeped under the patch, so when he removed it there was no stenciled circular outline left on the temple.

He moved around to the other side of the bed and lifted the gore-speckled TranceBox. It was still activated, he saw, though the disk inside it had completed its play an unknowable time ago. The device's little screen told him the disk's contents. As Alex read the information, he felt as though he stood on the deck of a yacht, and a large wave had just rocked the craft sickeningly beneath him. The screen revealed that the disk contained a number of the dreams they had extracted at Macrocosm Research. Not cleaned up and edited together as Alex had painstakingly done at Mnemonic Designs, but essentially the same material. Someone other than himself had burned the recordings onto this TranceBox-compatible disk. Patrick, or maybe even Mr G, Farhad, or Julie, must have done this at some point during the course of their studies. Was it all just part of the research, or did someone have the same idea he did—to make money off the dreams?

Alex felt ashamed for worrying about such a thing at this time but that didn't stop him from snatching up the disk's jewelbox and reading the handwritten label. He recognized the writing: it was, of course, Patrick's. So, video game afi-cionado that he was, had Patrick sniffed the money that could be made from this material, and decided to sell the raw data to another TranceBox design company? Or—dedicated worker that he also was—had he merely been doing some home research on his own, using the TranceBox because it was inexpensive but effective technology? Could it even be that, despite having been so unsettled by his recent exposure to the zoo dream, Patrick had taken the disk purely for his personal enter-tainment? Maybe Alex would never know but at least he didn't have to worry about Patrick cutting in on his idea now.

"Sorry, buddy," he murmured, pocketing the disk, then slipping the handwritten insert out of the jewelbox. He crumpled it up and tossed it in a trash bucket.

Alex looked up with a start when he realized Julie hovered in the threshold, making an effort not to look toward the bed. "The police are on the way," she told him in a strained voice.

"Good."

"Alex," she sniffled, "did he do this to himself?"

Alex gazed at his friend again. Thank God his eyes were closed. "No," he replied. "No, he definitely did not do this to himself."

Once more he contemplated those horrible wounds. When he had turned Patrick's face, he had uncovered another set of them—probably the ones that had killed him—sliced down the side of his neck, severing the left carotid artery. That would account for the jet of blood across the headboard and wall in that direction.

Four parallel wounds. Just like the incisions he had seen appear on the belly of the dead elephant in the zoo dream, just before the hideous scarred man had dropped out as if freshly born. Or *reborn*. The scarred man who, in one form or another, inexplicably haunted every nightmare salvaged from the preserved brains. The scarred man with his glove bearing four razored claws...

It wasn't long before the banshee laments of police sirens could be heard approaching Elm Street and though Alex didn't know it, over the years it had become quite a familiar sound around there.

"I know I shouldn't have tampered with a crime scene," Alex whispered into his cellphone, "but..." He stood just inside Ralph Tremblay's kitchen, watching as Julie sat down beside the old man on his living room sofa and took his hand. The detectives upstairs had just sent her down, done with their questioning of her.

She asked Ralph if he had anyone who could stay with him. Sniffling, Ralph told Julie that his sister and brother-in-law—Patrick's parents—were on their way over from another town right now. Despite their shock and grief at the news Ralph had had the sad duty to relate, they still had room for his welfare: his sister had assured Ralph they would take him out of there, lest Patrick's killer return.

On the other side of the phone, Farhad had been pausing for what was to Alex an excruciatingly long time. At any moment he expected his boss to chew his head off for what he had done. Finally Farhad gave a sigh and said, "It's a good idea you took it. Our sponsors have had some dialogue with the Springwood police, obviously, in setting up the Séance Project but I'm sure our government friends wouldn't want our work getting into the wrong hands—or to have the media find out about it—no matter what they ultimately hope to learn from or do with our research."

Alex was relieved that Farhad felt he'd done the right thing. At first, he hadn't even been sure if he would let Farhad know at all. "I'll bring the disk in tomorrow, but I think Julie and I need to go have a couple drinks right about now."

"Yes, of course. Take the rest of the day off."

"I might as well," Alex joked humorlessly, "since I took the beginning of it off. Um, Farhad…" He wanted to describe the wounds he'd seen on Patrick. The four parallel claw marks that each wound consisted of.

"Mm?"

"Ahh, nothing. I guess we'll talk more tomorrow."

"All right. Go take it easy now, Alex. Try to calm down. And take care of Julie, too."

"I will. See ya." Alex pocketed his cellphone, heaved a great sigh, then drifted into the living room and sat down on the other side of Ralph.

Ralph was only in his mid-sixties, but he looked much older from a lot of hard living and hard playing. Alex feared this day would put another ten years on the man. He was hunched forward over his knees as if his spirit had been surgically removed, leaving him hollow.

As Alex sat down, Ralph was wagging his head and saying, "If only I wasn't so damn deaf, I would have heard what was going on up there! I thought he was just playing his games, just playing, and all the time Patrick was fighting for his life." He broke into sobs and Julie rubbed his back, looking over at Alex morosely.

But Alex was distracted. Despite Patrick's defensive wounds to one hand, had he truly been fighting for his life? He lay in bed, still covered by a sheet, however slashed it was, and with his TranceBox activated. He had to have still been under the machine's spell, *asleep*, when attacked—and the raising of his arm for protection had simply been an instinctual reaction by his body. If what Ralph had heard was truly Patrick yelling in terror and rage at his assailant, Alex felt he still probably hadn't been fully conscious. He believed Patrick must have experienced his own death as part of whatever dream he was immersed in at that moment. Well, he didn't really know *what* to believe right now.

"Who would butcher him like that and why? *Why?*" Ralph groaned. "It's just like that Springwood Slasher thing…"

Alex turned his head sharply. "What's that, Ralph? What Springwood Slasher?"

Ralph looked up at him miserably. "Oh God, he murdered a bunch of children in Springwood back in the late Sixties, early Seventies. Barbara told me about it." He looked at Julie to explain, "My wife. This was her parents' house back then."

For a minute there, Alex had thought this "Springwood Slasher" could have been the serial killer responsible for the victims whose brains Macrocosm had replicated electronically but they had died in the mid-Eighties, from what he understood. Before he could ask Ralph if he'd ever heard about those killings, the old man beat him to it.

"Then around Eighty-four, another killer started murdering teens in Springwood, right here on Elm Street. One of the kids lived just across the street, over here." He gestured with his head. "He was carving kids up like the first guy. Maybe a, what do you call it, a copycat killer. And maybe this bastard is a copycat, too."

Alex heard a floorboard creak above him and lifted his eyes to the ceiling. The two plainclothes detectives who had responded to the call were still up there with the uniformed boys who had arrived first. Alex got up from the couch. "I'll be right back," he mumbled to Julie.

When Alex poked his head into Patrick's bedroom, the older of the two plainclothesmen waved him back and said, "Hey, we're all set with our questioning now, sir. You really need to stay downstairs."

"I had a question or two myself, detective, if that's okay."

The man narrowed his eyes a little, instantly wary. He and his partner were the classic seasoned-lifer-teamed-up-with-fresh-faced-rookie. The older detective was tall and lean with a silvery military haircut. The kid was short, good-looking, and had a kind of mascot vibe. He kept flicking his eyes to the older cop uncertainly for cues. This had to be his first murder scene. The older cop—Alex knew right away he'd seen more than one bloody body in his career.

"What is it?" he grumbled.

Alex watched as the coroner bent over Patrick, studying his lacerated neck. He prayed that he had left no bloody fingerprints to give away that he'd turned the corpse's head. He found himself surreptitiously slipping his red-stained fingers into the front pockets of his jeans.

"Um, I was wondering, sir, what you could tell me about the Springwood Slasher."

Again, the young cop's eyes jumped nervously to his senior partner. The older man's eyes went from wary to icy. One might have thought that Alex had spoken the secret name of the Devil.

"Look, kid." He stepped right up to Alex, imposingly. "Were you born in this town?"

"No, I—"

"If you were born here, and you were older, you might have a little more respect. We don't talk about that stuff anymore, all right?"

Alex swallowed, trying to hold his ground, but suddenly he felt like a child standing up to a stern school principal. "But did they ever catch that person? I mean, was the killer from the Seventies the same killer from the Eighties, and…"

"I told you," the older cop cut him off, hissing the words through his teeth. "That's all in the past now. Anyway, the Springwood Slasher is dead."

NINE

Devon Carmack picked a table near one of the school library's windows, squinting out into an afternoon suffused with golden light while he waited for the others to arrive. Grace, Milton, Ama, Kent and his unfortunate choice of girlfriend, Autumn. They had agreed to sit down together today after the last class and compare notes on their first few days of trying out Alex's nightmare program samples. Mostly it was just an excuse for some teenage socializing, but Devon was curious to see if anyone besides himself was having some serious nightmares *without* the help of their TranceBox.

Devon couldn't stay very long before heading home; that evening, he and Alex were supposed to go out to dinner with their parents, since they'd be departing on their trip to Europe the following day.

Rome, Florence, Venice. Huh? Rome, Devon thought. He wondered if they'd visit in reality the Colosseum that he had been visiting in TranceBox-induced fantasy. He felt a shiver, even in this warm bath of sunlight, at the memory of that dream arena.

Trisha would be joining them at the Italian restaurant they had chosen in honor of the trip, but to Devon's disappointment, Grace couldn't attend. Her father had told her he thought she was spending too many evenings out, and had insisted she spend the night in her own home, having dinner with him instead. Devon thought this was a bit extreme; Grace was hardly out with him every night, and never very late. She went to Ama's house several evenings a week in addition to seeing Devon, but Devon felt Ama wasn't the problem, since Grace's father had told her it was okay to have Ama over for dinner tonight—had even insisted on it. Devon was a bit concerned. He hoped this wasn't the start of a conflict with an overprotective parent. Maybe after having lost his wife, his daughter filled some of that empty space for him. If Devon was right, that neediness could put some unfair psychological weight on Grace's back. But he knew he shouldn't judge the man, as at this point he had only met him very briefly on two occasions.

If Grace's father seemed a bit too clingy, Devon occasionally wondered if his own parents had become a little too removed. Francis and Melinda Carmack traveled a lot, and when Devon and Alex had been younger they had usually gone along with their parents on these excursions. Repeated trips to the Disney theme parks on either coast, camping outside Maine's gorgeous Acadia National Park, even a trip to Seoul, South Korea when their Dad had had some business over there. But in more recent years—since Devon had entered his teens—they had been inclined to leave Devon in Alex's care, obviously figuring that the brothers were old enough to fend for themselves. Apparently they preferred their own company these days, enjoying a restored sense of freedom from their dependent children.

During one of his parents' vacations (a cruise that time), Devon had become self conscious about Alex having to essentially baby-sit him, and had asked him if he felt this arrangement was neglectful on their parents' part and, mainly, if he felt it was unfair to be saddled with his kid brother.

"Hey, man, don't worry," Alex had reassured him. "I've never minded it, trust me. And anyway, if this has made Fran and Lindy a closer couple, then I'm all for it. Look around. We're lucky they aren't divorced, like everybody else's parents are." He had patted Devon's shoulder then and grinned. "You can pay me back someday by baby-sitting our screaming quadruplets while Trisha and I spend a month in India, okay?"

Devon watched a squad of cheerleaders flounce by as they headed for practice, their hair awash in the gilded light, their short skirts white and radiant like the petals of flowers above the long stems of their smooth, delectable legs. He was hypnotized by the parade of young flesh, but then he felt guilty, knowing Grace would be marching her own lovely legs toward the library any minute now. Bad karma might make him lose her, and he still couldn't believe that he had her. Those remarkable eyes, doe-like and dreamy under long, straight brows. Those succulent lips that had both a little-girl quality and a sensuous allure at once. He ached to press his own lips to them. Did she find him weak, wimpy, for not already having done so? The most he had ventured thus far was a quick peck on her pretty cheekbone, last night when they'd parted after going out for burgers.

It wasn't that he was terribly old-fashioned in his morals; his head swam with countless erotic scenarios but, just as he hated discussing that he still didn't have his driver's license, Devon was afraid to admit to others that he hadn't yet been to bed with a girl. eighteen years old, a man by legal definition, and yet he was surrounded every day at school by sixteen year-olds more worldly than himself. He'd had the impression when Autumn Langevin had pursued him that he could have lost his virginity pretty quickly to her, and that fact alone had tempted his more animal nature, but good sense had prevailed. He wondered if Grace had figured out the embarrassing truth about him and naturally, he couldn't help but wonder about her own romantic history as well. His belief was that Grace was also inexperienced in this way. He hoped so; not just out of jealousy, but so that she would relate to him, wouldn't judge him as being immature or overly meek.

Well, if she was disappointed with him, he certainly hadn't sensed it. Last night at the burger place they had done their best not to drop gobs of food in their laps, since much of the time they had both been handicapped by using only one hand to eat. Grace had seemed unwilling to let go of his other hand, clenched beneath the table. No, he mustn't let his insecurities blind him to the fact that the girl really did seem enthusiastic about him. It was just that the thought of blowing it and losing her could drive him nuts if he let it.

He couldn't wait for her to arrive. He wondered if he'd have the guts to hold her hand again, right here in the middle of the library for all to see. Her absence tonight at dinner would make him feel desolate, especially when he saw Trisha beside Alex. But there he was getting negative again. Devon made himself smile. What was there to be so grim about all the time? He was a very lucky man. Life was good.

Grace was a dream come true.

Psychology was Milton's last class of the day, and he lingered after the bell so he could talk to Liz Trice alone. He was restless because he had promised to meet Devon and the others in the library, but Liz was still finishing up with another student. She kept throwing him little smiles across the room when the other student wasn't looking. Milton tried not to appear edgy, and smiled back. He cracked open the novel he'd been carrying along with his schoolbooks today.

It was *The Dream-Quest of Unknown Kadath*, by HP Lovecraft. Yes, the TranceBox could offer an amazing experience, but to Milton nothing beat immersing oneself in a book. He had become enthralled with Lovecraft's fantastical Dreamlands. The Vale of Pnath, the Peaks of Thok, the Vaults of Zin. The Tower of Koth, in the city of the terrifying Gugs, a race feared even by the dog-like ghouls who feasted on the corpses of humans in the waking world.

At last, the other student got up to leave. As she walked past Milton, he had the impression she gave him a knowing look. It embarrassed him. How truly secret was his and Liz's little secret? Milton often felt that he was more concerned about their being found out than she was, even though—with a husband and a professional career—she had much more to lose.

Liz came walking past the empty desks toward him, blue eyes sparkling and hips sashaying in her tight black skirt as if she was strutting down a modeling runway. When she reached him, she shifted around behind him as slinkily as a feline, leaning her breasts against his back to peer at his open book. "How is it, baby?" she cooed.

Milton threw a furtive glance toward the open door to her classroom. He saw a few students rush past on their way to go home, but no one looked in. Thankfully. "It's great," he replied. He was still shy with her closeness, her contact, even though they had shared much greater closeness and contact than this. "I've definitely gotta read more Lovecraft when I'm done."

"Maybe he'll stimulate some of your own work," she said. Liz was always encouraging him as a writer; more so, he told her, than even his English teacher Mrs Sullivan. Liz was pleased that he would say that. She didn't like the way Mrs Sullivan gushed about his writing. Let her find her own teacher's pet. Liz had once purposely come into Mrs Sullivan's room on a day when the English teacher had kept Milton late to talk more about his latest essay. After the icicles Liz's eyes had fired at him over Mrs Sullivan's shoulder, Milton had squirmed his way out of any further attempts on Mrs Sullivan's part to speak to him alone, though he thought Liz was misinterpreting the fifty year-old teacher's interest in him.

Looking up at Liz, heady with her generous dose of perfume, Milton went on, "And his Dreamland has gotten into *my* dreams, now. Or rather, it's gotten into the TranceBox dreams."

"And how is that thing going?"

"It's weird. In a few minutes I'm supposed to meet with Devon and the other kids his brother gave disks to, so we can discuss our experiences."

"Oh," Liz said dejectedly, pouting. "Okay."

"But I wrote about my latest dream in my journal already. Wanna give it a quick look?" He pulled his notebook out of his backpack, opened it and awoke the device. He deftly called up his writing program, followed by the dream journal Liz had assigned the class. She leaned against his back again to sample the latest entry. It read, in part:

I screamed, and the scream covered the happy little tinkling sound of the bells over the front door. When I whirled to flee toward the door, flee outside into the blackness of the parking lot, I saw that a man had just entered the convenience store, blocking my way out. And maybe it was the intervening aisles full of bright products that confused my aching eyes, but I just couldn't understand what I was seeing at first, until the terrible reality—this new, severely wrong reality—became undeniable.

The hideous figure standing at the front of the store, staring directly at me, was a man whose bald head was a mass of badly burned and badly healed scar tissue. More horrible than that, however, was the vertical mouth that split his head down the middle from top to bottom, open like a clam shell and full of hooked fangs, his merciless eyes pushed out to either side of this bear trap of bone and flesh. The man wore a ragged, oil-stained green and red striped sweater, dark brown pants and work boots. The oddest feature of all was that the striped sweater had four sleeves, and the man had two pairs of arms, one of the being's right hands tipped in long talons that flashed like steel…

"That's wonderful, sweetheart. Very vivid."

"That monster? It's a Gug," Milton explained.

"And what on earth is a Gug?"

"They're a kind of monster in Lovecraft's novel, with four arms and a vertical mouth. My brain put the Gug into a prerecorded TranceBox dream! Isn't that crazy? This dream belonged to another person's mind, but now it's changing according to things in *my* mind. It's like this bizarre dream collaboration."

"Vertical mouth full of fangs, huh?" Liz grinned. "Sounds like Freud's vagina dentata theory to me."

"Vagina *what?*"

"Vagina with teeth. Man's fear of emasculation, and so forth. But don't worry, *mine* doesn't have teeth."

Milton's face grew hot. Despite his fears of someone coming in on them and witnessing their coziness, a giddy feverishness got the better of him. He said, "That's good, 'cause I wouldn't want to lose a tongue or anything else important in there."

"Well, you haven't lost any of that stuff up here... where I *do* have teeth." She pointed to her mouth, then puckered her lips at him. He knew she would have kissed him next, and that it wouldn't have ended there, had they been at her house just then (as they often were, her husband being a second shift supervisor for a pharmaceutical manufacturer).

Milton glanced at the wall clock and grimaced apologetically. "I really oughta get going..."

Liz made a childish whining noise, and leaned harder against him as if to pin him into his seat with the sheer weight of her passion. She stalled him from leaving by reaching down to play with the notebook, scrolling through the dream journal entry to its end. There, she read the final words:

Ahh... a fellow predator of the young. I like that about you, Liz. You just need a little attention, don't you? And Milton, you need a little detention, you bad boy. It's a love story for the ages, like Romeo and Juliet, right Milton? But

then Romeo and Juliet both ended up dead,
didn't they? I think I could write a nice ending
like that for your story, too...

"Milton," Liz said, "why did you write this?"

He had thought she was only reading the conclusion of the convenience store dream. When he
realized there were new lines at the end of that
entry, and when he read those lines, his face
twisted in confusion. "What the fuck is this?"

"You didn't write this crap?" He could tell Liz was
less than amused by being called a predator in need
of attention. Icicle eyes, as in Mrs Sullivan's class.

"No, no way! I swear I didn't."

"Did you leave your backpack unattended long
enough for someone to sneak in your notebook and
do this?"

"I... I guess that could have happened. I don't
know when. But really, I swear, I didn't write this
stuff. You can see it doesn't fit into my dream at all,
Liz. And the person who wrote this... they wrote it
to the both of us. See?"

"Yes, I see that."

"Maybe... I don't know. Maybe someone hacked
into my computer when I was online, and once they
were inside snaked into my writing program. Shit—
maybe it's Autumn Langevin. She's one of the kids
Devon's brother gave a disk to. You know her? She's
a trouble maker and I hear she's a big time computer hacker."

"But why would she do that to you, unless she
had a big crush on you or something?" Liz narrowed her cold eyes.

"I don't know. Just that malicious hacker mentality. Look, I'm gonna see her in a few minutes, with the others. I won't hit her directly with it, but I'll feel her out to see if she gives off a suspicious vibe."

Liz nodded, still steaming. "Erase that shit," she said. She watched as Milton highlighted and deleted the mysterious paragraph.

So, if Milton was to be believed—and she found it unlikely that he was capable of such mean-spirited words—then that meant that someone knew about the two of them. Someone who had even threatened them. Could her husband have hacked into the computer somehow, when an internet link had left its door open? But her husband was no hacker, and if he suspected anything he'd be more likely to come at her face to face—raging at the top of his lungs, as he was inclined to do over far less serious matters than marital infidelity. In fact, she felt her husband was more likely to beat her to death than sneak a cryptic message into a notebook PC journal.

Milton muttered what was racing through her thoughts. "Somebody knows about us."

"Somebody *suspects*," she corrected him. "And they can suspect all they want. But no one knows anything." Still, her words rang false to her own ears. They were designed to keep him calm, keep him from bailing out of their relationship. Just as she had been afraid of scaring him off with reports of her husband's temper, having told Milton only enough about that to elicit his sympathy and tenderness. But as much as she always downplayed the risks of their relationship, so as to keep him blissfully content—and as much as she buried her own head in the sand, ostrich-like—there were times when the reality of what she was doing sprang out from the foliage and struck her like a booby-trap. This was one of those times. She was rigid with anxiety.

"I'd better get going," Milton said again, looking grave. "I'll keep an eye on that Autumn."

"It'll be okay, baby," Liz told him, forcing a tight smile. "This isn't anything. Just some asshole toying with us. They're jealous, that's all, because what we have is so beautiful." She squeezed his hand. "Right?"

He nodded and whispered, "I love you." He looked close to tears at that moment. Surely he knew there was no future for them. And the knowledge of that hopelessness just made his feelings even more poignant and powerful. Doomed love was the most potent brew of love, wasn't it?

"I love *you*, darling." Watching him leave her classroom, Liz almost got dewy-eyed herself.

Grace Simmons sat on one of the toilets in the girls' restroom right off the lobby of Springwood High, but not because she had to relieve herself. The relief she sought was a couple of minutes with her eyes closed. As eager as she was to meet Devon in the library, she half-wished she could head straight home and take a nap.

Under normal circumstances, she didn't sleep well anyway—those dreams of her mother, calling to her from down in the cellar. But now, since she'd begun testing out this program for Devon's brother, things were even worse. Yet could she blame herself? The dreams on that disk were terrifying. Last night, without even being hooked up to the TranceBox, she had had a nightmare about one of its sequences, imagining herself in an autumnal forest, while black-clad figures with swords—ninjas right out of a martial arts movie—flitted from tree to tree, drawing nearer and nearer but never coming directly into view. She had been dressed prettily enough, as a geisha, but her fan would have made a less than effective weapon had those ninjas ever come out at last from behind the crimson trees.

Grace propped her elbows on her knees and cupped her face in her hands. She shut her eyes, listening to other girls as they went in and out of the restroom. Catty gossip and toilets flushing. This wasn't exactly the coziest spot in which to seek a brief refuge, but at least the close metal walls of the toilet stall gave her a boxed-in sense of privacy that was otherwise hard to achieve in this place.

Other, more distant sounds. Lockers slamming. The cars of those kids that had them, starting up out in the parking lot.

"Grace? Grace?"

She jerked her head up, her eyes flicking nervously. No, it wasn't her mother's voice beckoning to her—it was Ama's. Grace was not standing at the top of her basement stairs; she had dozed off for a moment seated on the toilet, here in school. God, she hoped she wasn't late for her rendezvous with Devon and the rest in the library. She stood up, straightened her clothes, and pushed open the door of the stall.

The restroom was empty of its former traffic, most of the kids having no doubt headed home by now. Wanting to look good for Devon, Grace took a moment to check herself in the mirror. "I'll be right there!" she called out to Ama, whom she assumed must be outside the restroom door waiting for her.

Wow, when had this happened? A huge crack ran diagonally across one of the large mirrors over the sinks. She swore the girls in this school acted as wild as the boys, but she suspected that was a nationwide phenomenon these days. "Animals," she grumbled, shaking her head. Looking into the mirror made it appear that her head had been split in two and then the halves slightly misaligned when put back together.

In the mirror, behind her Grace saw one of the other stalls' doors crack open a little. She thought she glimpsed a shadowy face inside, and a glistening eye peeking out at her. Grace turned around to confront her sneaky voyeur—and it had better not have been a boy, stealing into the girls' room at the end of the day when he thought he could get away with such a disgusting scheme.

She saw the door ajar, but no shadowy face, and when Grace marched to it and flung it open she found no one inside. Thinking she might have the wrong stall, she opened the doors of those to the immediate left and right. Still she discovered no lurkers, male or female. She ended up opening the door of each stall in the row. Nothing. Huh—she definitely needed to get a good night's sleep.

"I'm sorry, Ama," she said loudly, moving to the door to let herself back out into the lobby.

When she emerged from the girls' room, three facts made Grace freeze in her tracks in utter bewilderment. For one thing, Ama wasn't waiting outside for her. Well, that could be explained easily enough. Ama had either grown impatient with waiting and irritably left for the library without her, or else she hadn't known Grace was asleep in the stall and had gone to seek her out elsewhere.

The other two things were harder to take in. For one, she found herself not in the high school's lobby, but in a corridor lined with metal lockers on the right and a series of arched windows set high in the brick wall on the left. For another thing, the sky outside those windows was pitch black. How long had she been asleep in the restroom? If night had fallen, did that mean she was locked in the school? Her father had insisted on her having dinner with him tonight; he'd be upset at her absence and might think she had defied his wishes and gone to spend the evening with Devon after all.

She could have sworn she had gone into a bath-room off the lobby. In fact, she didn't even recognize this particular corridor, at all.

Grace took a few uncertain steps down the hallway, still attempting to get her bearings. But she only became more disoriented as a harsh sound cut through the stillness. It had sounded like the caw of a crow, coming from the gloomy end of the long, long hallway. Grace craned her neck, as if that might help her see better into the murk, reluctant as she was now to take another step forward.

As she stood there, staring down the dark cor-ridor, she began to make out a wavering light. It increased in intensity, becoming distinctly orange.

She thought she could even hear the approaching crackle of flames. She could detect a smell, too. An awful, burnt smell...

Suddenly, there was an explosion of movement and fire. Grace's eyes widened in disbelief as a flock of crows began pouring down the hallway toward her like a train rushing through a tunnel. What made it all the more shocking was that the crows appeared to be on fire, cawing and squawking in agony, some of them crashing into the lockers on one side and the windows on the other, then dropping to the floor unconscious or dead, the flames enveloping their oily black bodies.

All Grace could do, in her horror, was spin around so that her back was to them, tuck in her head with her arms folded across the top of it, and brace herself. A second later they were all around her. Worse, they were crashing into her, buffeting her like a hurricane wind, their beaks tearing her clothing and gouging her flesh. She dropped to her knees with a cry, then coiled herself into as small a ball as she could manage, but still they pummeled her. Any moment, and their flaming bodies would catch her on fire, as well.

"Get up!" A familiar voice. A hand taking her hand, to help lift her out of her hunched position. "Get up, lazy ass!"

Grace stood, lifted her head and blinked up into the eyes of Ama, who grinned at her with amusement. "Oh God," Grace croaked.

"I recognized your shoes under the door," Ama explained. "Did you finish your business yet?" She gestured at the toilet she had lifted Grace from.

Grace glanced back at it numbly. "Um, yeah. What time is it? Is it nighttime?"

"Girl, wake up!" Ama patted her cheek. "We'd better go meet your boy now before he wonders where we are."

Grace looked past Ama at the mirrors over the sinks. No diagonal crack and no tatters in her clothing or gouges from bird beaks in her skin. She heaved a heavy sigh. She didn't know what was worse, some of these new nightmares she was suffering, or the one where her mother came to visit her, again and again, as if to impart some important knowledge to her.

Kent Lowe found Autumn waiting for him in front of her locker, sitting on the floor with her back resting against it, her notebook open on her crossed legs. She didn't seem to notice the kids inconvenienced by her presence as they had to step around her in the hallway, or lean across her to remove or replace books in their own lockers. Kent gave her a playful little kick in the sneaker with his own sneaker, and she grumbled, "Easy, ass-licker."

"Mm… I wish."

"You probably do, you pig." She grinned up at him. "Working on a new project for my site, and it's coming along great."

"Yeah? What is it?"

"A free download."

"Yeah, I could figure that much." Autumn's website was titled FALL LEAVES—THE FREE DOWNLOAD LADY. Fall Leaves was her online presence, not so subtly based on her actual name.

But of course, she couldn't use her actual name, since her website offered free downloads of illegally copied software. "What is it this time?"

Autumn shut the cover of her state-of-the-art notebook, like all her cutting edge gear made possible by her surgeon father's impressive salary. After she'd slipped it into her backpack, Kent held out a hand to help her to her feet. "Well," she said, "it's the disk Alex gave us. The nightmare program."

Kent just blinked down at his diminutive girlfriend, then managed, "What? The disk we're testing for Devon's brother? You're copying that onto your free download site?"

"Yeah. It's gonna be amazing! This is the first CIT program I've tried putting up there, but I know it will work. All the people who wanna download it have to do is write the file to a blank TranceBox disk, and voila! Stick on your patch and get ready for some nasty dreams!"

"Autumn, look, you can't do that!"

Her grin evaporated. "Why can't I do that, Kent?"

"Because, because, this is Devon's brother we're talking about here, not some company you have no connection to. Alex would go through the roof if he found out you were pirating his work as a free download, taking money out of his pocket!"

"That's just it, Kent—guys like him are taking money out of *our* pockets, all the time! These corporate assholes, these money-sucking big businesses..."

"He told you his design company is just starting out, they're not some big corporation!"

"But he has the same mentality. That's where him and his company want to be, and where they're going, by walking up a mountain of teenage allowance money. You heard Alex's bullshit. He's got that greed in his eyes, all the hype and slimy smooth talk."

"Autumn, it's *illegal*. Okay, your site was always illegal, but you've protected yourself with all kinds of shields and fake names and addresses, all this hacker armor. If you do this, though, and he discovers it... well, that crime is too close to home! You'll get busted, and then you'll be in a whole lotta shit. Lawsuits, maybe even jail!"

"Listen, I'm copying a rough prototype, not a copyrighted finished product."

"That doesn't mean much! It's still his work, his research."

"He'll still make his millions. How many people will find my little guerilla site?"

"It's the World Wide Web, Autumn."

She glared at him with a look of scorn that was on the verge of pure hatred. "Who are you really worried about here—Alex Carmack or me?"

Wilting in the blaze of her eyes, Kent could only squeeze out the last dregs of his strength. "I'm worried about my girlfriend but I'm also worried about my friendship with Devon."

"Devon? *Devon?* Sometimes I think that little yuppie tadpole *is* your girlfriend."

"What have you got against Devon, Autumn?"

Could her eyes become any more molten? "Why should I have anything against him? He means nothing to me. And you're starting to mean nothing to me, too, Kent. Is that what you want? Huh?"

He couldn't help himself from swallowing a lump of saliva. The click of his throat sounded gigantic to him, and he hated himself for letting her hear it, too. "No," he mumbled, shifting his eyes away. He saw a passing student glance at him, embarrassed by their noisy argument. "That isn't what I want."

"Could have fooled me. From now on, if you don't have anything good to say about my site, keep your opinions to yourself. You can ask Alex Carmack to design you a virtual girlfriend, if the stuff I do disgusts you so much."

"I didn't say that."

"What?"

"I said I didn't say that. Let's just drop it, okay?"

"Come on," she snapped, spinning away from him and moving so fast down the hall that even with his much longer legs he had to jog a little to catch up with her. "We're gonna be late for our meeting with your girlfriend Devon."

Kent and Autumn were the last to arrive, finding Devon, Grace, Ama and Milton already seated around two pushed-together library tables. "Nice of you guys to join us," Devon said, tapping his watch. That dinner with his folks was coming up fast.

Kent winced inside, expecting Autumn to bark, but she only smiled sweetly and said, "Sorry, we lovebirds just got so caught up in a romantic interlude."

"Oh yeah?" Ama laughed. "I wish I'd seen that."

"Now don't be a perv, Ama," Autumn said. "You guys can start without me; I've got a book to return." She held up the library book in question. Was it a secret joke, Kent wondered, showing Devon a book on website design? She walked briskly toward the counter.

Kent immediately leaned toward Devon and whispered, "I need to talk to you tonight. Can you come to my house?"

"I'm going out to dinner with my parents."

"Shit… when will you be back?"

"I don't know." Devon looked toward Autumn, standing at the counter, then returned his gaze to Kent. It wasn't hard to figure out the source of his friend's unease. "I can come over tomorrow. My folks will be gone on their trip by then. Can it wait?"

"Yeah, that'll work. Thanks." Kent sat back in his seat, just a second before Autumn turned from the counter and began striding in their direction.

Grace whispered to Devon, "Is everything okay?"

"Can you come to Kent's place with me tomorrow after school, or will your Dad be pissed?"

She squeezed his knee under the table. "Hey, just because he wants me to stay home tonight doesn't mean he's trying to keep you away from me."

"Are you sure he doesn't, like, hate me?"

"Nooo… my Dad is cool. And even if he did, I'm Daddy's little girl. I get my way."

Devon smiled and rested his hand atop hers, keeping it there on his knee.

"All right, where were we, bitches?" Autumn said, noisily scraping out a chair beside Kent and dropping into it.

"Well," Milton said, "while we were waiting for you two, I read these guys something I wrote about one of my dreams. It's part of the journal I'm keeping for psychology class. Actually it was a TranceBox dream, the convenience store segment. The way I experienced it, my subconscious mind incorporated a monster that I've read about in this novel." He showed them his copy of *The Dream-Quest of Unknown Kadath*.

"Yeah, but it was only partly that novel's monster," Devon noted. "It was still, at heart, the guy with the knife glove. The guy I've seen as a lion in the arena…"

"Me, too," Ama said.

"… and cutting himself out of that elephant in the zoo chapter…"

"Yeah," agreed Grace, who then shuddered.

"Not to mention the guy outside the hospital room's door," Autumn added. "And does he talk to you, even use your name? Taunt you personally?"

"Yeah," Ama answered, "he thinks he's real funny. In the zoo dream, he asked me if being with the animals made me feel close to my African roots."

"And then there's that Dracula dream," Grace muttered, more to herself than the others.

"Yeah, fuck, the Dracula one is the worst," Kent said. "And every time you use the disk again, it's like the first time. You don't remember being there before. And you don't remember *him*."

"He cornered me in the zoo dream and tried to stab me with his claws," Ama said, "but they broke and crumbled to pieces when they hit me, like they were just made out of sugar or something. He said he wasn't strong enough to hurt me yet, but he was 'almost there'."

"So who is this freak?" Autumn asked. "Why is he in every dream?"

"I've even had him in dreams *without* the TranceBox now," Milton said.

Kent turned to him. "You, too?"

"Come on, Devon," Autumn said, "tell us the truth. Is this guy..."

"Freddy Krueger," Grace broke in. "In one of the dreams he told me his name is Freddy Krueger."

"Okay," Autumn resumed. "Devon, is this Freddy Krueger some kind of virtual construct your brother inserted into the dream memories? Some kind of advanced AI?"

"If he did, he didn't tell me about it. I'm pretty sure Krueger was in all these dreams before my brother even extracted them."

"Well, did all the dreams come from one person, then?"

Devon didn't want to reveal that the brains had been those of people dead for several decades; that information was confidential. Not to mention that he didn't want to frighten Grace more than she already was. He only replied, "No. It was multiple donors."

"Okay, so how could *that* be? Why would different people all dream of this same, very distinct person?"

No one had an answer ready for that.

Kent was rolling Devon's pen back and forth thoughtfully between his hands. "What's with the guy with the bomb, in the hospital? The terrorist? He makes me as nervous as Krueger does. Why is he in there? It doesn't make any sense."

"Ah, hello," Autumn said, "it's a *dream*. It doesn't have to make sense."

"I hate terrorists," Kent said, still absorbed in his pen-rolling.

"Yeah," Autumn said with imitation gravity, "terrorists suck."

Kent looked up at her. He'd once had a computer hard drive ruined by a virus he received in an email, the mean-spirited prank of some faceless hacker. He thought of hackers as terrorists, of a kind but he did not say this to Autumn.

Grace cut into the conversation. "Devon, when will Alex want our feedback?"

Autumn smirked. "Already anxious to have this over with, Gracie?"

"Aren't you?"

"I think it's fascinating as all hell. What do you think, hubby?" She turned to Kent.

"Fascinating," he echoed hollowly.

Devon gave Grace a look both sympathetic and apologetic. "Like Alex said, he wants us to try this for a week. Maybe two. So we've still got maybe half a week, a week and a half to go."

Autumn gave a shrug and said, "Well, goodnight Gracie."

TEN

Devon was due to arrive in an hour, but Kent still wasn't sure whether he'd be able to go through with it or not—whether he could bring himself to tell Devon about Autumn's plan to make his brother's nightmare program available as a free download from her guerilla website. Autumn was still his girlfriend, and he felt loyalty to her no matter how much he disapproved of the pointless maliciousness that she called rebellion. It was her way of lashing out in anger. Well, better for her to lash out at big business than at him, but when the target was the brother of one of his best buddies...

And Kent especially didn't want to see Alex get any more upset than he already was. At school today, Devon had told Kent that one of Alex's friends and coworkers, Patrick Tremblay, had been murdered yesterday by an unknown assailant in his home.

Devon was bringing Grace along this afternoon. At first Kent hadn't been too comfortable with that, but he had come to know Grace lately and he felt she was cut of the same cloth as Devon: trustworthy, good-hearted. He envied Devon for that.

Outside, the late afternoon glowed with a mellow, nostalgic aura but inside his house, a demon was stalking Kent Lowe. It walked within his shadow, its talons slowly inserting themselves into his back. That demon was alcohol. Not since the summer, when his parents had enrolled him in a program to control his drinking, had the demon's whisper in his ear been so insistent. Why, why did it have to come hunting him, haunting him, today of all days, when he already had so much on his mind? But of course, it was the burden on his mind that had attracted the demon's attention. So, it hadn't been fully exorcized after all. It had been lurking, patiently waiting, all along.

His father had wanted Kent to stop drinking and so he had made sacrifices of his own, bringing no more beer into the house and emptying out the liquor cabinet. But one afternoon when mowing the lawn, Kent began searching for a funnel so he could pour more gasoline into the machine, and he had chanced upon the liquor cabinet's former contents stashed away in the garage. Bottles of vodka and scotch, rum and tequila, Greek ouzo and Turkish yeni raki, both tasting of licorice and both strong enough to burn the breath out of your lungs. Yes, the demon pointed its clawed finger toward Kent's bedroom window, down toward the roof of the garage. Its lair. The nest where it had been biding its time.

"No," Kent whispered aloud, staring at the window. "No way. Fuck that."

He turned toward his computer desk and spotted his TranceBox resting on the top shelf with stacks of software jewelboxes. Over the summer, when the demon had been steadily clawing at his back and his parents had been screaming at each other downstairs, like two more demons raging in a Hell beneath his feet, this innocuous-looking little machine had been a secret door into blissful escape, a portal to other dimensions, like a rift in time and space. He had been transported into the lives of other people in a kind of transmigration of souls. A temporary reincarnation. He had been able to forget his own life, to shed it like a snake skin so as to inhabit another person's flesh. And then there was the more fantastical brand of escapism that the dream programs provided. Dreams like morphine spreading through his mind, bringing him solace or at least a distraction so all-consuming that it eclipsed his own identity. Even when the dreams had been frightening, they had been *other* peoples' fears that he could sweep off his shoulders like dust when he awoke, feeling a brief catharsis. Until the TranceBox called to him again.

It was calling to him now.

Kent glanced at his watch. There was still time to kill before Devon got here. He could program the TranceBox to submerge him in its magic pool for just thirty minutes. He'd resurface, refreshed, in plenty of time to receive his guests.

So the question was simply, which of his disks to play? The first choice that occurred to him was a "wet dream" recording, whereby he could experience a sexual act through the eyes (ears, nose, mouth, hands and other parts) of another person. Once, just out of curiosity, he had tried a recording of a *woman's* point of view as a man made love to her, but he sure wouldn't want his friends to know that—especially that it had been, er, weirdly exciting. But he and Devon had discussed other wet dream disks they'd tried and swapped. Devon hadn't admitted to Kent that he was a virgin whose only sexual experiences to date had been virtual ones, but Kent had figured it out for himself and he didn't want to tease his friend about it. There had been times when Kent would have gladly given Autumn to Devon as a gift he could keep. Devon would have some for-real sex, and Kent would have some peace.

Thoughts of Autumn got his spirits down again. Damn. For whatever reason, he still loved her. He'd rather be in bed with her right now than reliving someone else's erotic encounter. He decided not to go with a wet dream, after all.

One jewelbox rested by itself, next to a high stack. It had a handwritten label. Alex Carmack's nightmare program, the one Autumn was probably, at that very moment, working to put onto her website.

He could understand her enthusiasm for it, at least; it was a real mind-fuck, especially the way he retained his own sense of identity while immersed in its world. He picked up the jewelbox, opened it, and contemplated the shiny little chip. Sure, why not a half hour's worth of crazy dreams in which he could totally lose himself? As when watching a horror movie, his fear would make him forget his real-life anxieties for a while.

Kent went over to his bed and lay back with the TranceBox in his hands, first inserting the disk and then programming in his commands. Yeah, just a single chapter would be enough thrills for one session. He set the machine beside him on the mattress and stuck the receiver pad to his right temple. He closed his eyes with a smile of nervous anticipation, like a kid waiting for a little train to bring him into the mouth of a carnival haunted house ride. Recorded screams echoed from inside, accompanied by the squeaking and flutter of bats. The double doors were opening inward now. Blackness loomed straight ahead. The train started creeping forward...

Screams echoing. The squeaking and flutter of bats.

Before he opened his eyes, Kent felt a strong, chilly wind crash against him like an ocean wave, almost knocking him back a step. His lids snapped open.

Screams. *Screams*.

Another gust of wind ruffled Kent's hair. It had a fine mist of almost-rain mixed into it. Tortured gray bundles of cloud clotted the sky, with only a pale yellowish light breaking through at the horizon. Kent found he was standing on the flat-roofed tower of a fortress or castle. Looking behind him, he saw taller pointed towers soaring high, stabbing at the bellies of the clouds as if to tear them open and release the rain they were pregnant with.

Screams An impossible chorus of screams. The throats from which they issued must have been uncountable.

Drawn by the screams, Kent walked across the flagstones of the turret's roof and placed his hands on its surrounding parapet but when he gazed down at the scene spread before him, he wished he had never taken a single step forward.

Below lay a gray and desolate plain, with a manmade forest to give the landscape a mocking semblance of fertility. It was a forest of high stakes, socketed into the earth. There must have been thousands of stakes, perhaps twenty thousand. *Thirty* thousand. They were arranged in concentric circles, as if in some kind of blasphemous offering to God, since only His eye looking down from above could appreciate the care given to the geometric formation. But only the Devil would accept an offering this staggering in its evil.

Because upon each tall stake was impaled a human being. For many, the stake entered through their bottoms and emerged from their mouths. Others were pinned like insect specimens through their chests or bellies. There were men, women and even babies could be seen skewered on the same stakes as their mothers.

"Oh my God," Kent hissed, his fingers hooked on the parapet as if they might dig right into the stone. *"Oh my God!"*

Many of the impaled were dead, some beginning to rot. Others, so many others, still moaned, wailed, *screamed*. Alive, somehow still alive. It was a mind-blasting choir of the damned, rising up to be carried on the wind in ghostly ululations.

"The trick," said a strange, distorted voice behind him, "is to oil the end of the stake, and not let them be too sharp. Otherwise, see, the impalee might die too quick, and we can't have that. How could we enjoy this music, otherwise?"

Kent whirled around so fast that he fell back against the parapet. For a vertiginous moment, he thought he might flip right over backwards and plummet to his death.

A figure dressed all in black spread his arms and smiled. "Listen to them—the children of the night. What sweet music they make."

The man wore a long black coat that flapped around him like a cape in the wind, its high collar turned up against his neck. He was monstrously burned, a half-melted effigy of a man, his bald head gleaming in the silvery light. There was a regal quality to him, however, as if he was some dark prince. The man's right hand wore a glove of black leather, and from each of the glove's four fingers sprouted an elegant blade of silver engraved with ornate designs.

Seeing Kent's eyes on them, he raised one dagger finger into the air. "But this is my preferred method of impalement."

"Who are you?" Kent got out in a strangled voice.

"I'm so sick of being asked that," the man snarled suddenly, losing his noble demeanor. "You've all forgotten me. That's the whole point!" He forced himself to become calm again. "History makes men like Vlad Tepes immortal, and fiction makes men like Count Dracula immortal but soon I'll make them both look like amateurs."

"Look, I just want to go," Kent said, desperately looking left and right like a cornered animal, but seeing no way to get down from the turret. There was no trapdoor in its floor. Tears began to fill his eyes. The screams were like stakes thrust into his ears, into his brain.

As if he hadn't heard him, the scarred man went on. "My name is Freddy Krueger. Remember that name, Kent. *Remember* me!"

"I will, I will. Please just don't hurt me!"

Still ignoring his sobs, Krueger turned to look down at the sea of impaled bodies. He drew in a deep breath of the stench carried by the wind—a miasma of blood and vomit, decay and excrement. He sighed blissfully. "Your girlfriend has my admiration, Kent. I'm glad I haven't killed her. What she's doing with that website of hers will make my world accessible to thousands, *millions* of people. Once, I was limited to one little town. One little street. Now, the whole wide world will be my playground."

"I don't understand. Autumn…"

"And Alex, wanting to mass-produce my nightmares. Both of them, doing my work and not even knowing it. Even Milton, writing his nightmares into that notebook of his, filling it with my essence. Opening another door for me to reach through into the waking world. The wonders of technology, huh Kent?"

"Since I'm Autumn's boyfriend, then you won't wanna hurt me, right?"

Krueger smirked at him over his shoulder. "Maybe I'm jealous. Maybe I want her for myself."

Kent babbled, "Okay, sure, she's yours then!"

"Now that's love for ya." Krueger returned his gaze to the vista of carnage. "These aren't real people now, of course, but they will be. This will be my reality. My crop of souls for the harvesting. My field of screams."

"I'm just dreaming all this... right?"

Krueger abruptly whirled around, his coat floating out from him like immense black wings. "How would you like to be the first *real* tree in the forest, Kent?"

"Please, please, I just want to wake up!"

Walking toward the cowering teenager, Krueger said, "If a man is impaled in the forest, and no one is there to hear his screams, did he really scream?"

Kent backed against the opposite parapet, quaking with sobs, too paralyzed to do more than watch Krueger come at him. But at the last moment, Kent did manage to do one thing...

He screamed.

"So your dad doesn't want you to have your own car?" Devon asked, sitting in the passenger's seat of Ama's borrowed car and looking over at Grace. She sat behind the wheel, a careful novice driver not taking her eyes off the road.

"No, well, he gets worried about me, but he's not as bad as you seem to think he is. He promised to help me get a car this year, so I can have it already when I start college."

"I didn't mean to suggest your father is bad, Grace. I like him, I do."

She smiled without looking his way. "I think he likes you now, too."

"Yeah? You think so?"

"Of course. Relax."

On the car radio, tuned to a soft rock channel playing mostly romantic oldies, Sade's song *Kiss of Life* came on. Devon spoke along to the opening lyrics: "'There must have been an angel by my side, something heavenly led me to you'."

Grace felt a shiver go through her. At this moment, she could believe those words; that their coming together was an act of divine providence. Preordained. But the matter at hand returned to her, and she nodded her head toward the windshield. "Is this it?"

Devon glanced outside. "Yeah, yeah, the gray house. Bluish-gray."

"Got it." Grace nosed the car up to the curb in front of Kent Lowe's neat-looking two-story house. Just home from work, his parents' two cars filled the driveway, and through the parted curtains of a first floor window Devon could see the flicker of a TV screen. The window of Kent's second floor bedroom was blinded by a drawn shade.

Devon turned back to face Grace. Neither had opened their door yet. "Well, here we are."

"Yep."

Like an angel herself, guiding their destinies, Sade sang, "You gave me the kiss of life..."

Devon leaned toward Grace, and she leaned toward him.

The kiss was a little awkward at first, their tongues fumbling over each other tentatively, but once they got their mouths settled the way they liked it the kiss was long and sweet, passionate but not frantic. Devon had slipped his right arm around Grace's waist, and she placed one hand on the back of his head. The song was their soundtrack, and Grace thought that whenever she heard it in the future, it would always pull this memory vivid and glittering out of her brain. Toward the end of their first kiss, Grace sucked on Devon's full lips—first the bottom, then the top—as she had fantasized about more than once. He was beginning to do the same to her lower lip when a car passed in the street close to their own, breaking the spell. Shyly they unlocked their mouths and extricated their arms from each other, though they switched to holding hands.

"That was nice," Grace said.

"Very nice," Devon sighed.

"I think we should go inside though, huh? Kent's waiting, and I'm afraid his folks will look out the window and see us."

"Yeah, let's go," Devon said, but he leaned toward her again for another quick taste of her lips before he cracked the passenger's door open.

They walked to the front door still holding hands.

Kent's mother answered the door for them, looking a bit frazzled and impatient. "You can go on up," she told the teenagers. As she hurried back in the direction of the kitchen, they heard her shout toward the living room, "Thanks for answering the door for me! I'm making supper, you know!"

"I'm watching something!" they heard Kent's father shout back from the living room.

"I hope that's not us in a few years," Devon whispered, leading Grace to the carpeted steps to the second floor.

"I promise not to be like that, if you promise."

Devon took hold of the handrail. He grinned foolishly, still intoxicated by what had occurred. "Promise."

From the second floor came a heart-stopping scream.

Grace seized Devon's arm, and he called up the stairwell, "Kent?" He started taking the steps two at a time, leaving Grace to follow at her own pace.

The scream trailed off into a loud, wet gurgling, just as Devon threw open Kent's door to see...

Kent hung in the air, as if invisible wires tethered him to the ceiling. His arms had flopped loosely to his sides, his legs pedaling slowly, his eyes wide and glazed with shock. He was still gargling the blood in his throat, still alive for a few moments more, as he floated down through the air. He resembled a man thrown off the side of a ship, drowning as he sank toward the ocean's bottom. Iit would be more accurate to say he resembled a man skewered on a stake, sliding down its shaft from the weight of his body and the lubrication of his blood, for there was a hole in his chest, just below his sternum. Blood ran from it in all directions, beginning to rain from his hovering body to the floor. There was a corresponding hole, from which more blood dripped abundantly, in his back.

"Oh shit! Oh shit!" Devon cried out, backing into Grace as she appeared in the doorway behind him. She clutched his arms, and now it was her turn to scream as they watched Kent's body continue to lower toward the floor. At last, it settled there, his arms giving one spasmodic convulsion and his gurgle fading away into his chest.

"Kent?" they heard his father yelling, pounding up the stairs. He pushed in past them roughly, and when he saw his seventeen year-old son lying on the carpet, the wound in his chest gaping as if something held it open for a few seconds more, he bellowed, "Kent! Kent! Oh God!"

"Devon," Grace sobbed, falling against his chest and tucking her face into his neck.

"Who did this?" Kent's father whirled at them, his bulging eyes crazed.

Devon almost expected to be attacked by him, as though the man believed they were the ones responsible. "I don't know," Devon's voice creaked, small and sickly.

But he thought he did know one contributing factor involved in his friend's death. Because he had seen the white patch on Kent's right temple. The receiver pad of his TranceBox.

ELEVEN

"You didn't have to come, man," Devon said to Alex as he slipped in through the Lowes' front door with Trisha close behind him. "Grace can drive me home."

"What was I supposed to do? Say, 'Huh? Your friend got murdered? Okay, well, see ya when you get here.'" Alex glanced past Devon at Grace and gave her a solemn nod. She just stared back at him with a face as white as a geisha's. "So his parents were home?"

"Yeah. They're in the kitchen talking to the cops. They're done with us... said we could go home for now." Devon dropped his voice. "It was scary, Alex. When they got here it looked like they thought we did it, Grace and me."

"They don't think that now, do they?" said Trisha.

"I don't think so. I should hope not."

"So, Alex Carmack," said a voice from down the front hallway.

The brothers and their girlfriends looked over to see two plainclothes detectives walking toward them from the kitchen. One was tall and lean, with a silvery military-style haircut, the other short and good-looking, with the appearance of being the older cop's nervous puppy-dog.

"Sir," Alex said.

"You guys are the bad luck twins, huh?" The senior detective stopped only inches from Alex's face, like an intimidating drill instructor trying to break him down. "Yesterday you find the mutilated body of your friend. Today, your brother finds the mutilated body of his friend. Crazy, huh? But maybe it's not so much that you guys have the bad luck. It looks like your friends are the ones with the bad luck. Right, Billy?" He smirked at his partner. "Would you want to be friends with these guys?"

Billy only shrugged, smiling sheepishly.

"It's very strange, I know," Alex said. "And if we can help you in any way, believe me we will."

"That's good, because I'm sure there are a lot of questions I still haven't formulated yet."

"Sir, it looks like there's a serial killer in Springwood. But this wouldn't be the first time, would it?"

The older detective narrowed his eyes. He didn't seem to like being challenged. "No, I guess it wouldn't. But like I told you, the Springwood Slasher is long dead. Even if he was still alive, he'd be too old to be cutting up young men like this. No, our killer has to be a younger man. You know, someone about, oh, your age. Or your brother's. Hell, I bet the two of you together would be more than strong enough to overpower a kid like Kent Lowe."

"What are you saying?" Trisha cut in, bugging her eyes at the man. "We can account for Alex's whereabouts when this happened, but I can't even believe what you're suggesting!"

"It's just a thought. I'm just doing a little mental doodling. Scribbling ideas out loud." He wrote his hand through the air. "I didn't mean to offend your boyfriend. Oh, he is your boyfriend, right? Or is the Chinese girl the lucky one?"

Restraining his temper, Alex said, "Julie is just my coworker. Sir, if you want to take us in, take us in. Print us, give us a lie detector test, knock yourself out. We have nothing to hide."

"I'm sorry if you find my mental doodling offensive, Mr Carmack. Maybe I'm out of my mind, thinking it's odd that you and your brother discovered the bodies of two of your friends in two days."

"I told you, I understand it's very, very weird. But my brother and I would not hurt these people."

"Maybe you didn't. But there has got to be some link between these events, wouldn't you think? I can't buy coincidence here."

"I'd like to know what the link is, too, believe me. So, like I say, we will be happy to assist in your investigation but unless you want to charge us, I don't think it's appropriate to be talking to us like that."

"Alex," Trisha warned.

"It's okay, young lady." The senior cop turned to head back to the kitchen, patting Billy on the shoulder to get him moving. "You kids can all go home now. But you can be assured, I *will* have some more questions to ask you. The both of you."

"Yes, sir," Devon said.

"Fucker," Alex hissed, watching the cops walk down the hallway, their shoes clacking importantly on the hardwood. They heard their voices join the muffled sobs coming from the kitchen.

"Well, it isn't really surprising the way they're acting," Trisha admitted, despite her misgivings.

Devon touched his brother's arm. "Alex, we need to get home and talk."

"Is she okay?" Alex gestured at the mannequin-like Grace.

"No, she is not okay. Let's go talk. Now."

With their parents having departed on their trip earlier that day, Alex had already been planning to spend the night at their house. Devon was eighteen now, so during the course of the vacation Alex had figured he would just check in on him either by phone or a quick visit daily, but he had also thought it would be nice to play the responsible big brother and sleep over for at least the first night. Then on the weekend, he was going to invite Devon to sleep over at his apartment. Now that two of their friends had been slaughtered, however, Alex had no intention of leaving Devon alone for a single night.

Devon helped Grace along as if she was an octogenarian and seated her at the kitchen table. Trisha poked around in cabinets to find what she needed to make a pot of coffee. "Mm, *Trung Nguyen*," she mumbled to herself, taking down a package of the Vietnamese coffee.

"Alex," Devon said, standing at the head of the table.

"Yeah?" He was gathering together four mugs for Trisha.

"Kent was still alive for a few seconds when Grace and I went in his room."

Alex faced his brother. "He was? Did he say anything?"

"No. But Alex... he was levitating in the air."

"What?" Trisha spun around.

"What are you talking about?" Alex asked.

"He was in the air, man! Just hovering there! And then he floated down, until he lay on the floor."

"Devon... you were upset, all right? You were seeing things. This shit is freaky enough without you hallucinating on me."

"I saw it, too!" Grace blurted suddenly, fresh tears trickling down her cheeks. "It's *true!*"

"It's impossible," Alex persisted.

"Well, it's what we saw," Devon told him. "I don't know what was happening, he had this big hole going right through his body but he was up in the air when we came in. And he lowered to the floor—slowly. It wasn't like something we saw for one second and misinterpreted."

"And he was hooked up to his TranceBox at the time," Grace added.

Alex's face went slack. He and Trisha exchanged looks. He had told her about stealing the disk from the crime scene. "He was playing his TranceBox while this happened?"

"Yeah," Devon said. "He had the patch on his head."

"Did you check out the disk he was playing?"

"No, I didn't think of it."

"You don't know if it was my nightmare program?"

"I told you, I don't know."

Alex tried to digest all this, but it just coiled around itself sickeningly in his guts. "Devon," he said at last, "let me tell you what I saw at Patrick's place."

He told Devon and Grace about having stolen the disk of Macrocosm research out of Patrick's TranceBox, and peeling the receptor patch off his temple. Lastly, he described the appalling state of Patrick's corpse.

"Claw marks? Like from a lion?" Devon said. That was the first thing that came to his head, for some reason. A *lion*...

"Claw marks, like from a glove with knife fingers," Grace muttered.

The other three all turned to stare at her.

She looked up at them and sobbed, "We've all seen him in our dreams. The man with the knife hand! *Krueger*!"

"Grace," Alex sighed, "let's not get dreams and reality mixed up here. I don't... I don't believe in the supernatural."

"But Alex," Devon said, "it obviously has something to do with the TranceBox and the nightmare disk. Both of these guys were playing the

TranceBox at the time they were killed. What does that mean?"

"I have no idea what it means. I know it's significant, I know but we can't talk crazy here. That guy in the dreams, he's an illusion."

"Well, why is he in *all* of the dreams, from all these different victims?"

"A shared hallucination. Mass hysteria. I don't know!"

"Look, you've seen him. You've talked to him. He's pure evil."

"He isn't *real*, damn it!"

"Maybe not out here. Maybe not in our world."

"So what is he, then? A ghost? A demon? Some kind of extra-dimensional being?"

"Maybe one of those things. I don't pretend to understand it."

Alex sighed, leaning back against the kitchen counter and pinching the bridge of his nose between his fingers. "I pray to God it isn't anything to do with the disk."

"If the disk had anything to do with it," Trisha pondered aloud, "then all of us who've tried it could be at risk."

Alex raised his head and snapped, "Don't you go jumping to conclusions, too, Trisha! We have to think *rational* here!"

"Well, I'm sorry if this threatens your dreams of glory, Alex, but we have to put our safety before that."

"What are you saying?" he shouted. "Do you think I don't care about people getting hurt? Is that what you're saying?"

They heard the front doorbell ring.

Alex pulled the largest knife out of a cutlery holder by the sink and strode out of the kitchen toward the front door. Before hurrying after him, Devon said to Trisha, "Now look who's acting all rational." What if it was the cops, with new questions to ask? What would they think of Alex brandishing a huge carving knife?

As he came up behind Alex, Devon saw that the person standing on the front step was a long-haired girl of short stature.

"Hey," Autumn Langevin said. "Can I come in?"

"Autumn," Alex said, recognizing her as one of the kids he had given a sample disk to. The one who'd had some smart-ass comments. "Yeah, come in."

When he shifted aside to let Autumn past him, she and Devon found themselves standing face to face.

"Autumn," Devon said, his eyes sincere in their pain, "did you hear?"

"I heard," she said. Her own eyes were red, puffy, but her tone was tough and solid.

"I'm so sorry. I'm so sorry."

"I wanna know what happened to him, Devon. His folks told me you're the one who found him. What did you see?"

Devon glanced over at his brother, then back at Autumn. "Come in the kitchen and I'll tell you everything."

"Devon," Alex cautioned, "a lot of this stuff is still confidential. What I'm doing at Macro-cosm…"

"I don't care. Her boyfriend was killed today, Alex, she deserves to know. Grace needs to hear everything, too. Macrocosm, where the brains came from, all of it. This concerns *all* of us now."

Alex sighed and gestured for them to return to the kitchen. "All right, all right. Let's go."

Over the span of an hour, their heated conversation had taken them from the kitchen to Devon's room on the second floor. Alex sat in front of his brother's computer, surfing the web. He sipped from his latest cup of coffee before relating his findings.

"Okay, it says here there have been tons of reported cases of levitation. A sixteen year-old named Clara Germana Cele, supposedly possessed by a devil, levitated five feet off the ground. That was in 1906. And a medium named Daniel Douglas Home levitated out a third floor window back in 1868." He scrolled down the screen. "But mostly it looks like it's been people caught up in a spiritual rapture. A Roman Catholic saint called Teresa of Avila levitated a foot and a half in the air. Jeez, that was for a half hour straight. And another saint, Joseph of Cupertino, levitated for *two hours* one time."

"Yeah, and didn't another guy feed five thousand people with, like, just two fishes and five loaves of bread?" Autumn remarked. "You don't believe that religious crap, do you?"

"If we're going to believe Devon and Grace, then there has to be a scientific explanation here! Maybe it's mind over matter. Maybe in the state they were in, Patrick and Kent were able to, I don't know, tap into some kind of psychokinetic power. Even some psychologists believe poltergeist activity is created by disturbed adolescents. And look at the religious zealots who manifest stigmata. They do that to themselves, maybe just through the power of their subconscious minds."

"Alex," Devon sighed, "I know you want to make sense out of this, but you're acting desperate now. What do you think? That Patrick made those claw marks appear on himself subconsciously, like stigmata?"

"He's right," Autumn said. "You just don't want to face the truth here. We've all met that bastard in our dreams now. The one time he really talked to me, I knew he would have hurt me if I'd been able to open that locked door."

Alex stared at the computer screen as if entranced. He muttered, "He tried to stab me with his claws in the zoo dream, but they were like rubber. He said he wasn't strong enough yet."

"Tell it to your friend Patrick," Autumn said. "And tell it to my boyfriend. Whatever he is, he's strong enough now."

Trisha was seated beside Grace on the edge of Devon's bed, rubbing the younger girl's back sympathetically. She looked up and said, "We can't any of us use the nightmare program again until we figure this out. We need to tell everyone at Mnemonic and Macrocosm, both."

"I told you," Alex groaned, "we need more information before we jump to conclusions! You want Macrocosm and Mnemonic to panic, act rash and abandon valuable projects when all the data isn't in yet?"

"We can't keep our theories to ourselves."

"What theories, Trisha? What theories do we really have yet, huh?"

Autumn interrupted them. "You said your friend at Macrocosm tried to find out about these Springwood Slasher murders online."

"Yeah, Julie Ip gave it a shot," Alex said. "She had no luck. Our boss Farhad let a few facts slip, like one victim being a history buff, another kid being into samurai flicks and martial arts—hence the subject matter of some of the dreams—so I think he knows more about the case than he's letting on but there's nothing to be found on the web."

Autumn gestured for Alex to vacate Devon's computer. "Get away from that thing before you give yourself an aneurism, and let me have a shot at it."

Alex complied, and watched as the little teenager plopped down in Devon's chair. Her fingers immediately began to fly over the keys like those of a piano virtuoso.

"What are you looking for?" Devon asked.

"Here we go." She sat back to wave a hand at the monitor. "This is the website for the Springwood police. But it's the *public* site. I'll bet they have a private intranet site like a lotta businesses do, so that only they themselves can access it. I'm just wondering if there's any way to hack into it off the public site, a hidden link or something, 'cause I know the public site won't tell us shit." She leaned in toward the screen again with a look of intensity.

"Okay, I think I know what might be happening here," Alex announced, nodding in satisfaction at his reasoning. He began pacing the room, as was his habit, as if the motion helped generate his thoughts. "Listen. The lead detective was very defensive about the Springwood Slasher, and the cops won't even let us researchers know about his victims. Maybe they're covering up the case because they never caught the guy, despite what the detective told me about the killer being dead. They're embarrassed that he got away. Or it could be he's a cop himself, whose identity they've been protecting for years."

"You've told me that theory before," Devon said. He had moved close to the bed and taken Grace's hand, rubbing his thumb across the top of it.

"There's more. What if somehow the killer found out we were digging memories out of his victims from back in the Eighties? And if he was a cop, he'd know that Macrocosm was doing this. He's afraid the memories will reveal his identity, see? So he's trying to stop the Séance Project, even if he has to come out of retirement and silence every one of us."

"That makes sense on the surface," Trisha said, "but how would this guy—even if he's a cop—know about the nightmare disks you handed out to Devon's friends? How would he know to come after Autumn's boyfriend? He shouldn't even know about Mnemonic at all."

"If he followed me one night, he could easily have seen me go to Mnemonic after I got out of Macrocosm. He might even have followed me the night I passed out those sample disks, then later followed Kent and found out where he lived. I didn't say I had every detail worked out yet, but doesn't that sound a lot more plausible than some monster killing people in their dreams?"

"That does sound more sane, I guess," Devon admitted. "But it doesn't make me feel any safer— the idea that a real life killer might be targeting us."

"You're forgetting the levitation, Devon," Grace said tersely.

"Maybe the two of you suffered a shared illusion," Alex replied. "Face it, all our brains could have been scrambled a bit by the nightmare program. It isn't like regular TranceBox programs, so it may have after-effects that we've never encountered before. Instead of stopping our testing, we should *boost* our testing to find out more."

"I don't know about that, Alex," Trisha said.

"This Krueger is a figment of our imaginations, Trisha! I don't know how he's been integrated into every dream from every one of those tumors, but isn't this the kind of thing that a research facility exists to find out? Our sponsors are paying us to unravel mysteries!"

"Speaking of unraveling mysteries," Autumn spoke up, "I'm in."

"In the intranet site?"

"Check it out," she said with smug pride, even as she continued to click through various pages of the website created for the local police force's private use.

"Damn, you're good," Devon told her, leaning over her shoulder to read from the screen.

"It gets better." On the monitor was a list of clickable links. One heading was CASE FILES. When Autumn clicked on this, it took her to a column of subcategories, such as ACTIVE CASES and CLOSED CASES.

Another link read: UNSOLVED.

"That one!" Devon exclaimed, pointing.

"Not so fast," Alex said. "If it's a cover up of some kind, they may have it filed as a 'closed' case. Supposedly the Slasher is dead. Look, they have a search engine. Type in 'Springwood Slasher' and see what happens."

Autumn did as Alex suggested. For a breathless moment, they waited for the search to come up empty-handed, all mention of the serial killer purged even from these secret files. Instead, a long series of links appeared on the screen.

"Whoa," Devon said. "Is every one of those a victim?"

Autumn clicked on one of the links, and a new page filled the computer screen. "Jackpot," she muttered.

Grace let out a whimper. Alex muttered something under his breath.

There were several photographs accompanying the case report that had come up. Autumn clicked on one of these to switch to a larger view of the image, but it really hadn't been necessary for her to do so. All of them could plainly see that the photo was of a right-handed glove made of leather and plates of metal, long curved knife blades affixed to the glove's four fingers.

* * *

"You see?" Alex said, triumphant, when they had read through much of the treasure chest of data Autumn had unlocked. "This is why the Macrocosm brains all had dreams featuring the same monster. By the Eighties, Freddy Krueger had become an urban legend, drilled into kids' heads! Springwood's own personal boogeyman, like New Jersey's Jersey Devil and the Mothman. Like Bigfoot and gray aliens. People always draw those aliens looking exactly the same, right? Here, too. The kids of Springwood, back then, all had this very distinct idea of what Freddy Krueger should look and act like, based on a distortion of the *real-life* serial killer, Freddy Krueger."

Through the use of the case reports of his crimes and the documents attending his ultimate arrest, the little group had formulated a biography of Freddy Krueger. He had been a murderer of young children, apparently committing the first of his killings in the summer of 1967. These murders had continued on into 1974, and the estimated number of victims was between twenty and thirty (all the bodies of his alleged victims had not been discovered, and certain killings couldn't be positively attributed to him).

But Krueger had been released from police custody on a legal technicality when it was realized that the warrant for his arrest had been improperly prepared. What had happened next stunned the Carmack brothers and the three young women. Evidently, some of the parents of Krueger's victims had banded together as vigilantes, trapped Krueger in a boiler room that he had been using as a hideout, and burnt him to death with Molotov cocktails.

That had been the end of Freddy Krueger's reign of terror. Until, apparently, 1984.

At that time, a series of Springwood teenagers had begun to be murdered, often clawed to death in the modus operandi of the Springwood Slasher, Freddy Krueger. As the body count mounted, it was suggested that these were copycat killings. Ultimately, no one was ever apprehended for these crimes, which had gradually tapered off as late as 2003.

"Copycat murders," Trisha said, reading through some of the pages they had printed out. "Or maybe Freddy Krueger never died in that fire."

"Exactly," Alex said. "He may have fled Springwood, terribly burned, then returned ten years later to seek revenge against the town."

"But if these new killings are Krueger come back for a third time, think about it, he was born in 1942. He'd be in his late sixties now."

"I know, honey, that's what the detective said. The Slasher would be too old to be killing people. But how do we know he couldn't still be dangerous? And even if Krueger truly did die in that fire in 1974, then there would have been a copycat killer, whoever that was. And it could be that the copycat killer is the one who murdered Patrick and Kent."

"It makes more sense, now that we've all calmed down a little," Devon said quietly, afraid to look over at Grace.

"I guess," Autumn mumbled, sounding reluctant to abandon their first conclusion, however wild it may have seemed. "I suppose there's no way to justify the idea of Krueger living on in the dreams of his victims but he sure did seem real to me when I was in them."

"*Everything* seems real in those dreams when we're in them," Alex reminded her.

"Kent's levitation," Devon continued. "I don't know what to say now. I suppose it could have been an illusion. Like you said, Alex, we don't know how the TranceBox might be affecting us, creating residual effects in our minds even when we're not using it."

"Bullshit, Devon!" Grace cried, taking his arm and turning him roughly to face her. "You know what you saw! It was real! How can I be the only one who still believes in the truth? You're all in denial because it's just too frightening for you to accept!"

"It's just too insane for us to accept," Alex corrected her.

"I'm sorry, Grace," Devon told her. "But maybe we—"

"Maybe nothing. I'm going home." She whipped around and started out of Devon's room.

"Grace, wait!" Devon cried. "No matter what's happening here, we're all in danger! Someone could be trying to hurt every one of us. You have to be careful, *please!*"

She glared at him from the doorway, eyes glistening moistly again. "Thanks for your concern."

"Let me walk you down to the car."

"Whatever," she said.

Devon went after her, and the others heard their combined footsteps thudding down the stairs.

Alex put his arm around Trisha's neck, drawing her closer until their bowed heads touched. "If only all this was just another nightmare," he sighed. "And I could wake up from it—right *now*."

TWELVE

Dr Peter Langevin lay back on his daughter's bed, his head and shoulders propped up against a mountain of mismatched pillows and a battered copy of the book *Oh, The Thinks You Can Think*, by another doctor—Seuss—resting on his lap. He had just finished reading it to his daughter Autumn, who lay beside him similarly propped up. "Been a long time since I read that to you, huh, honey?" he said to her, reaching over to give her hand a squeeze.

She had closed her eyes toward the end of the book (but she could still envision the mysterious "Stairs in the Night" very clearly), her lids acting as tightly sealed doors to keep the waters of her tears from flooding out. "Thanks, Daddy," she croaked.

"Look." He swung his legs off the bed and laced his sneakers back on. "I want you to be super-careful until they catch whoever it is who did this.

I don't want you going out at night, or anywhere alone. Stick close to groups of friends."

"I have been."

"I'm having a new security system put in on Saturday. For now, you know the drill on the old one." He stood up and checked his watch; almost 10:30. As a general surgeon, he was part of a rotating emergency room staff and was currently assigned to the graveyard shift. "Ahh, damn it. This is a terrible time for me to have to work these hours. I hate to leave you and your Mom alone like this. I wish they knew how the person who killed poor Kent got into his house like that."

"We'll stay locked up," Autumn assured him, trying to get rid of him quickly. She couldn't hold these tears in forever. She yawned and rolled onto her side, feigning sleepiness. "It's not like we're going anywhere this late, don't worry."

"It might be nice if you slept in your Mom's bed tonight. You could keep each other company."

"Sure. Then if the killer breaks in, he can kill both of us at once."

"Autumn!" her father snapped. "Don't even talk like that!"

"Just a little levity, Dad." She mock-yawned again. "I think I'm going to sleep now."

"You don't wanna sleep with Mom?"

"Frankly, Dad, I don't think either of us would be comfortable with that."

"You call my cell if you even hear a twig snap."

She saluted from the bed, her back facing him.

He rested the storybook on the edge of her bureau for her to put back amongst her more current piles of books later. "Not going to change into your pajamas before you drift off?"

"Later."

"Yeah right, later like when you wake up in the morning, huh?" He paused. "Baby? I'm proud that you're being so strong about Kent. But don't be *too* strong, you know what I mean? You talk to Mom or me if you need to."

"I will."

"I'm sure the police will find the monster who did this."

"Yeah, I saw them, they're all over it."

"You gonna be okay for now?"

"Uhhh goodnight, Dad."

He leaned over the bed to give Autumn a little slap on her blue-jeaned bottom. "Goodnight, moon," he quipped.

"Hardy-har."

Dr Langevin left her bedroom, and Autumn opened her eyes. Most of the tears must have dried up back there, after all; just one heavy drop rolled out, traveled along her nose, then poised at its end until she swiped it away with her wrist. When she heard her father's car pull out of the driveway, she sat up in bed and looked immediately toward the newer of her two computers. It stared back at her with its unblinking cyclopean eye, patiently awaiting her inevitable attention.

She settled into her chair in the midst of a fortress of electronic equipment. Within seconds, she was not only online but had called up the website construction program for her subversive domain, FALL LEAVES—THE FREE DOWNLOAD LADY. On the main page she had created a tumbling rain of animated fall leaves. A cheesy-sounding electronic version of the song *Forever Autumn* by Justin Hayward of the Moody Blues played in the background. Kent had never heard that lovely song before, so she had played him the original from her diverse music collection.

Kent. She couldn't really say she had loved him, but then love was a word that conjured in her mind vomit-inducing greeting cards with soft-focus photos of hand-holding couples—a bitter pill of deceit coated in a glossy shell of sugar. But Kent had made her laugh with stupid jokes, and had been a good listener when she needed to vent, and had been crudely effective in bed. Devon had said there was a gaping hole in Kent's chest when he saw him. Autumn felt like she had a gaping hole in her chest as well but to call it love? Admitting to love was like admitting to weakness.

And she found it odd that right now she was thinking more about Devon than about Kent. Talk about vomit-inducing; it had sickened her to see Devon holding hands with his whiny little girlfriend, poor fragile Grace, so shaken by Kent's death, as if he had been *her* boyfriend. Autumn could envision Devon's future with her, walking on eggshells so as not to nudge his brittle bride into another crying spell, another traumatized neurotic episode. What a waste of his intellect, having to pamper a wimpy prima donna, when he could be having stimulating conversations with someone more his equal.

"'My life will be forever autumn,'" she murmured as she tapped a few keys, quoting the song that played, "''cause you're not here...'"

She didn't know if those words were for Kent, or for Devon.

Autumn's hands froze above her keyboard, poised like twin spiders waiting to pounce. Tonight, she thought she could finish configuring the nightmare program into a web-based file. Tonight, she believed she could make the program go live, available to be downloaded by whoever out there might find their way to the site—her anonymous audience, of sorts—but bits of the conversation from Devon's house kept coming back to her.

Could the program be inciting hallucinations, such as Devon and Grace imagining that Kent had been hovering in the air? Or, as Alex himself had suggested at the height of his desperation for answers, might it even have put Kent into some kind of altered mental state, whereby he had actually caused his body to levitate through the use of telekinesis? Might the nightmare program be tainted with a virus, dangerous to the people who downloaded it off her site? Or had the more radical theories they'd discussed tonight been mere fantasies brought on by their panicky distress, until rationality had again prevailed? Devon and Grace had seen no levitation, then just Kent's wounded body collapsing to the floor from a standing position, perhaps. And the fiend from their nightmares was merely a carnival mirror reflection of a tangible, flesh and blood killer—lurking out there somewhere in Springwood's night even at that moment.

She had never put CIT software on her site before. She was certain it would work as intended, if she uploaded the program tonight. The program would be accessible for her visitors to burn onto a blank disk, and then use in their TranceBoxes like store-bought disks. The thought of it still made Autumn defiantly proud of her skills, her achievements.

But her hands continued to hover there, her fingertips resting so lightly on the keys that she barely felt them.

At last she sat back, as if released from some paralyzing force, removing her hands from the keyboard. She swiveled in her chair, her gaze trailing across the room's black-painted walls with their stenciled skull faces. Her audience, an audience of the dead, surrounding her, staring back at her. Could she really put countless people at risk when she couldn't be sure what effect the program might have on them?

The electronic music had played itself out, but a new sound came from the computer's speakers. A long, terrible, screeching sound, like fingernails on a blackboard. Like knife-points raked across glass.

Autumn jerked her head to look back at the screen. She saw only the front page of her website. THE FREE DOWNLOAD LADY. But wait. Where had the rest of the title gone, the words "FALL LEAVES"?

As she watched, the letters forming the word "THE" dropped from the title, tumbling away like the animated rain of leaves.

"What the fuck?" Autumn hissed.

The last "E" in the word "FREE" drifted away next. An "O," a "W," an "N" from the word "DOWNLOAD." More and more gaps formed as the title fragmented. Had she inadvertently screwed up her site somehow during tonight's tinkering?

"L," "O," "A," "D." Floating away gracefully like snowflakes.

"Oh my God," Autumn said with realization, as she watched two final letters flutter toward the bottom of the screen, an "L" and an "A" from the word "LADY". Now only six letters from her website's title remained.

An "F." An "R." An "E." A "D." Another "D." And a "Y."

"Freddy," Autumn whispered.

The name gradually faded into the black background, until that was all the monitor showed: blackness. The darkness began to lighten somewhat; enough for her to see the darker silhouette of a man's head within it. A man wearing a rumpled hat. Autumn was reminded of the hospital dream, that hideous scarred face outside the window in the door, peering through at her. Now, her computer's screen acted as the thin barrier separating them, a fragile membrane separating parallel worlds.

"Autumn," the familiar voice purred from the speakers. "You aren't having second thoughts, are you? All you have to do now is dot your Ts and cross your Is, and you'll show 'em all what a smart little girl you are. Maybe then they'll finally notice you, huh? Give you the recognition you deserve."

"This can't be real," Autumn said. "I'm not asleep! I'm not dreaming!"

"Exactly," the silhouette said. "That's the beauty of it! You're giving me another way into your world. I won't need people to be asleep anymore."

"And why the fuck would I want to help you do that?" she snarled. "So you can kill more people like you killed my *boyfriend?*"

"Killed... who? Now, why would I do that and hurt my priestess?"

"What do you mean, priestess?"

"If you help me, Autumn, and finish what you started, you could be giving me the power of a god. And I won't forget you. I'll give you power, too. You can stand right by my side."

"Like I could ever trust you! You would have killed me, too, if I'd been able to open that door in the hospital!"

"My word is gold. What else do you have to look forward to in your sorry little life? Marrying some boring clone of your late boyfriend, shitting out a few brats, watching hubby paint your white picket fence? I'm not in Hell; *Springwood* is Hell. Take a chance, Autumn. If you won't listen to me, listen to yourself. You know this is what you want."

"How do you know so much about what I want?"

"Because I'm the only one who understands you. You want immortality, to be young forever. Do you see any wrinkles on this pretty face?" He tilted up his chin, but thankfully it was too murky to make out his countenance. "You want the power of life and death. You want to be able to destroy all who oppose and offend you. Crush them in your fist." His gloved hand rose into view, its steel talons clashing together with a ringing sound. "You want to be like *me*, Autumn."

She looked behind her at the closed door to her room. Was her mother gaping at the TV downstairs, the cathode ray zombie she transformed into every night, or had she already turned in? Was the world beyond that closed door the same mundane world she knew, the world she ventured out into day after monotonous day? Was she truly awake, or had she dozed off while her father was reading to her? Or had she simply lost her mind?

"Autumn," the voice behind her insisted.

She swiveled around to face the monitor again. "For a god, you sure do grovel a lot."

The silhouetted head couldn't keep itself from giving an angry hiss.

"Maybe I'll get back to you," she said, and with that, Autumn reached out and shut off the computer's power. On the monitor of her older, secondary computer, the screensaver was suddenly replaced by sizzling static. Before anything could appear within that pixilated chaos, she quickly powered down that computer, too. Just to be on the safe side, she flipped the switch on the surge protector under her desk, cutting off the AC juice to her system altogether.

Exhausted by all she had experienced this day— the death of her boyfriend and promises of immortality—Autumn Langevin propped her elbows on the edge of her computer desk and dropped her face into her hands.

Several hours earlier, unaware that one of his friends had been killed that afternoon, Milton Ferrara had parked his car one street over from the house of his psychology teacher, Elizabeth Trice, and walked briskly the rest of the way, throwing furtive looks at ominous shrubbery and every passing vehicle that illuminated him in its headlights. He knew Liz's husband worked second shift, a supervisor at a pharmaceutical manufacturing company, but that didn't mean he might not come home early one night with a headache. Or with a suspicion of wrongdoing on the part of his attractive wife and while Liz had never really come right out and discussed it, Milton had read between the lines that Mr Trice had something of a temper.

Liz greeted him in a black satin dressing gown, looking sensually elegant, though he knew the tiny membranes of black lace that pretended to cover her femininity beneath that gown were a lot less subtle in their effect. She pulled him inside by the hand, and immediately into her embrace.

Just a short while later they lay tousle-haired and drained on Liz's bed, like two survivors of a shipwreck who had swum laboriously to shore. Milton looked happily dazed, both physically and emotionally. His expression had the quality of a dog's adoring stare, seeming almost pathetically grateful, so that even Liz found herself unable to face it. It made her feel embarrassed for him, and for herself. It made her feel like a ridiculous bimbo from a bad soft porn movie, greeting the pool cleaner in sexy lingerie. So instead she ignored him, lying naked on her belly with her ankles hooked in the air behind her and Milton's notebook PC open in front of her. Milton didn't mind. Her looking at his writing was as intimate to him as Liz gazing into his very soul.

"That was wonderful, baby," she told him when she'd finished, finally able to smile over at him and meet those vulnerable, smitten eyes. It was not his dream journal's latest entry, but a short story he had written for his English class. He had taken his inspiration from HP Lovecraft, as Liz had suggested to him, and she certainly didn't want to praise the story any less than Mrs Sullivan would. "What a wild imagination. You're so damn good." She reached over to give one of his strong calves a squeeze. "In every way."

"Yeah? You think I'm talented?"

"You're very talented. And very beautiful."

"You want to read something else?" He shifted closer to her and lay pressed up against her side, on his belly too. He closed the file for the short story and went on to access a new file, but all of a sudden he was looking shy.

"What's this one, sweetie?" she asked.

"It's a dream I had last night, but it's not for the dream journal. Let's just say it isn't suitable for class. It was a dream I had about you."

"Ohhh really? Well, I have to read this." Liz gave him a fast peck on the jaw, then engaged herself in his writing once more. She felt Milton's bashful, anxious eyes weighing heavily upon her. Wasn't his adoration what she craved? But in times of doubt, it lay on her chest like an anvil, so that she could barely get her lungs to fill. She almost resented him at times like this, and she surely resented herself. Still, she knew she could not do without the gift he gave her. The same gift she gave to him. Appreciation.

Milton took to caressing her back in long strokes, his index finger following the groove of her spine, but he got the impression she was feeling distracted and he stopped.

Actually Liz was confused by what she was reading. At last she said, "Honey? This isn't a sexy dream about me, it's another one of your horror stories."

"It's what?" He dragged the notebook closer to himself.

"Can you hold on a second, first? I have to use the ladies' room."

He looked up. "Need a hall pass?"

"Um, I'm all set, thanks."

"Can I watch?" he asked, naughty but blushing.

She only mussed his hair and threw on her satin robe before turning her back on him to leave the room. No matter how much he said he worshipped her bottom, she was ever self-conscious about its size, its smoothness, its resistance to gravity. After all, she wasn't his age anymore. She bounced out of the room lightly on bare feet, and Milton returned his attention to the file he'd opened. He began to read his own words.

There was more than just a smear of red underneath one eye. The lower half of her face was awash in sticky redness. It slickly coated her chin, and streams of it had even run from the corners of her mouth, down her cheeks and slender neck. Her mouth was open wide… too wide… its jaws forced apart like those of a snake swallowing a rat. For something large… too large… had been jammed inside her mouth. Something wet and glistening.

His eyes darted, stunned, to her chest. Between her breasts, a ragged-edged hole gave a glimpse of gaping darkness, like a narrow shaft leading straight to Hell. It was the cavity within which the object crammed into her mouth had formerly resided. Within which it had formerly pumped the blood through her veins… pumping to a faster rhythm each time they lay in each other's arms…

"Liz!" Milton screamed, as his stunned disbelief was replaced by an explosive combination of grief, revulsion and terror.

While reading, Milton's initial bafflement had turned to astonishment, and his astonishment had edged toward anger. What the hell was this? He hadn't written this stuff! He double-checked the name of the file, but it was still titled *Red Silk*, in reference to his dream in which he and Liz were amorously entangled on a bed covered by red silk sheets, surrounded by red silk curtains, with even the ceiling and floor masked by red silk. He had likened the effect to being enclosed within a gigantic human heart but that little erotic vignette was now gone, apparently deleted and this mysterious bit of writing left in its place.

The thing was, he could imagine himself writing it. It was in his style but he *hadn't*. And why would he write such a terrible thing about Liz? He was grateful she hadn't read enough of the piece to come across her name, or he was certain she would have been appalled instead of only confused. Milton was reminded of the earlier enigmatic writing Liz had discovered on his machine. The same person had to be responsible—but who? The earlier suspects flashed through his mind once more. Liz's husband? Again, why play games like this when he could just smash Milton in the face? Autumn Langevin, who had the skills to hack into his machine through an internet connection? But did she have the writing skills? Who else could have gotten their hands on his notebook to do this?

An odd thought came to him. Might it even be Liz, playing some kind of game with him? Was it just a coincidence that she had been the one to discover both these strange writings? On one occasion, he had in fact caught her toying with his computer. She had been talking to her sister on a cellphone and typing with her free hand, sitting nude and cross-legged on her bed (if only her sister could see *that*), and Milton had been the one using the bathroom that time. He had looked at the notebook's screen to see his name typed over and over, again and again. It had been charming but a bit weird, because she wasn't even looking at her fingers as they doodled, as if she wasn't even aware she was doing it. Another time she had written across his chest with lipstick: MINE, and then drawn an arrow to the spot where his heart beat inside him. With a laugh, she had then added another arrow, trailing down his hard belly to point at a lower organ of his body. Previously he had found such quirky behaviors endearing but now he wondered if these writings might be a more mean-spirited expression of that same quirkiness.

He heard the toilet flush, then the sink running. Quickly, before she could come back and see her name in the composition, Milton closed the file down for further inspection later. A moment later, Liz reappeared. She still wore her black robe but it was open down the front. Grinning, she ran the last few steps to the bed and pounced upon it, then spread out the sides of the robe like wings and closed them around Milton's face. Suddenly they were inside a little black tent of silk. It made him think of the red silk room of his dream.

The unease that had been haunting Liz, making her feel somewhat distant from her lover, had receded into its dark closet. She rained kisses across his face, each kiss chiseling away more of Milton's own tension. Her ardor made him doubt she could have been the one to write such nastiness about the two of them and he would worry about who was really responsible later. Right now, he had a beautiful woman straddling his chest.

"Hey, where's your story about me?" she said in a pause between kisses, lifting her head.

"You were right," he told her, "that wasn't it. I hope I didn't delete it by mistake."

Liz pouted, then cooed, "Well, I guess we'll just have to give you some inspiration for another sexy dream, huh?"

"Sounds good to me," Milton replied.

* * *

Milton awoke to find Liz spooned against his back. For a few moments he just lay there, luxuriating in the sensation. Finally, however, anxiety dispelled the fog of pleasure. They had dozed off! What time was it? He raised his head to get a better look at the clock radio on the bedside table.

10:40pm! Liz's husband's shift ended at 11:00, and his company wasn't even ten minutes away! Milton thanked God that he hadn't slept any later than this, but he needed to wake Liz up, get dressed and get out of her house right away.

He edged away from her and rolled over to face her. "Liz? *Liz!*" he said. He put his hand on her shoulder, covered by the blanket, and shook her gently. Her head, also partly covered by the edge of the blanket, loosely bobbed. "Liz, come on, wake up!"

Each passing second making him more frantic, putting them in more danger, Milton took hold of the teacher's shoulder again and pushed her with more force, until she flopped onto her back. The top half of her face showed above the blanket's satin border. Closed eyes and a red smear beneath one of them.

"Liz?" Milton said, gripping the end of the blanket and throwing it off his lover.

There was more than just a smear of red underneath one eye. The lower half of her face was awash in sticky redness. It slickly coated her chin, and streams of it had even run from the corners of her mouth, down her cheeks and slender neck. Her mouth was open wide, too wide, its jaws forced apart like those of a snake swallowing a rat. For something large, too large, had been jammed inside her mouth. Something wet and glistening.

His eyes darted, stunned, to her chest. Between her breasts, a ragged-edged hole gave a glimpse of gaping darkness, like a narrow shaft leading straight to Hell. It was the cavity within which the object crammed into her mouth had formerly resided. Within which it had formerly pumped the blood through her veins, pumping to a faster rhythm each time they lay in each other's arms.

"Liz!" Milton screamed, as his stunned disbelief was replaced by an explosive combination of grief, revulsion and terror. He sprang up from the mattress and scuttled back from the corpse in fear, even as he reached out to her arm and gripped it pointlessly, as if he might still be able to shake her awake. "Liz! Liz!" he wailed again.

Milton's notebook rested on the mattress on the opposite side of Liz, and its cover flipped open with the suddenness of a mousetrap being sprung. Milton let out an inarticulate little yelp, his eyes flicking toward the machine. A sputter of sparks jumped out of it like glowing insects, and then smoke began to pour forth. Instead of dispersing, the smoke seemed to coil in upon itself, boiling and churning thickly. In only seconds, a dense cloud had formed beside the bed. It quickly coalesced into a vaguely human shape.

That was all that Milton could endure. He leapt from the bed and flung his naked body at the bedroom door. His hand slipped off the knob. Looking down, he saw that his palm was slippery with his lover's blood.

Milton glanced behind him to see that the smoky figure had taken on a solid form. He recognized its features well, from many recent dreams and many different incarnations. Lion, Dark Prince, Gug, from HP Lovecraft's novel. But he knew that this was the creature's truest personification: a man in a green and red striped sweater and battered brown fedora, his raw red face looking like it had been flayed right down to the muscles. And one hand made of knives.

"Milton," the thing that had called itself Freddy Krueger in his dreams—both natural and TranceBox-induced—chuckled, taking a leisurely step toward him. "I thought maybe if I let you write a book about me, you'd spread my essence into thousands of innocent little brains. But I don't think reading books is going to affect people quite the way the TranceBox does. And anyway, I've read that shit in your journal, and well, I just don't think you have what it takes. Don't quit your day job."

Milton spun to face the door again and gripped the knob in both hands this time. He got it to turn, threw the door open and found himself gazing into a boiler room as spacious as a factory, lit only with red emergency lights, steam hissing from opened valves and ruptures in the snaking forest of pipes. Red-lit, dark and steamy as it was, Milton had the delirious impression that he was staring into that hole in Liz's chest, staring into her very interior. But there was no room of red silk here.

Yet the dreamstalker was stepping closer, so Milton could no longer afford to hesitate. He plunged through the doorway that should have led into the rest of Liz Trice's house.

Behind him, he heard Krueger look back at the corpse on the bed and growl, "He's MINE now, Liz. Eat your heart out."

Milton tore through the industrial maze, ducking down off-branching passages to throw his pursuer off his trail, hoping the steam clouds he ran through and the red-saturated murkiness would also cover his movements. In his recklessness, he collided with heavy chains hanging down from the ceiling, hooks at their ends, and gouged his unprotected flesh. He stubbed his bare toes, banged an elbow, slipped in a puddle of water that dripped from above and scraped his left knee raw. At one point, squatting behind an especially thick horizontal pipe to catch his breath, he rested his hand against its flank only to pull it away instantly, so painfully burned that it was all he could do to restrain himself from crying out.

He ran through a labyrinth of lockers with blistering paint, switch-boxes and banks of fuses, dangling cables and ladders leading up to catwalks which threw shadows like tightly-woven spider-webs across his naked, sweating, bleeding body. The further he ran, the vaster his surroundings seemed—a parallel world that consisted only of one interminable boiler room. What building or institution could such a limitless boiler room be servicing? Perhaps it was the boiler room of Hades itself, generating the heat for its lakes of boiling oil, the flames for its pits of flesh-lapping fire.

Milton smelled cigarette smoke ahead of him, cutting through the auto-repair scents of grease and oil. He squeezed between a hissing water heater and another massive pipe, to find himself in something like a clearing in the metallic woods. In a little open office there was a table with a lamp on it, the only bulb he had seen that didn't glow red. A cigarette burned in an ashtray. On a greasy blotter rested an old-fashioned scrapbook, and Milton crept over to examine it. He lifted its cover to find the pages filled with photographs of young children—everything from smiling school portraits to candid Polaroids that seemed to have been taken without the subjects' knowledge.

"You sick fuck," Milton whispered, understanding the meaning of what he saw.

"I don't smoke anymore, Milton," a voice said from the surrounding darkness. "That stuff will kill ya. That's more of a moment in time, you're seeing there. A snapshot. See, you're in *my* brain now."

Milton bolted again, panting and sobbing simultaneously. Were there no doors, no windows? There didn't even seem to be any *walls*.

Just as soon as he thought this, though, ahead of him he saw a bare red bulb enclosed in a little protective cage, its lurid light painting the surface of a cinder-block wall. A square-shaped bluish glow was set into this section of wall. A *window*...

With a sob of gratitude, Milton wove his way closer to the wall, the window. It looked small, but he would wriggle through it if he had to break every bone in his body to do so.

When he reached the window, he found it fogged over with condensation from the steamy air. He rubbed the mist from the glass with his bare forearm, then leaned close to the pane to peer through it. What he saw on the other side first perplexed, then shocked him.

He was looking into the room of someone's house. A woman was resting her face in her hands, perhaps nursing a headache, her long hair hanging down in curtains to hide her identity. There was a keyboard in front of her elbows. That was when Milton realized the truth. He was not looking out of a window. He was looking out of a computer screen.

And furthermore, he recognized this young woman. He had never been in her bedroom, but the black walls and stenciled skulls said it all.

"Autumn!" he cried, rapping his knuckles on the glass. "Autumn!" He glanced behind him, afraid to draw Krueger, but he had to take that chance. He rapped again, frantic. *"Autumn!"*

At last, the rapping and the use of her name caused the girl to raise her head from her palms groggily. She mumbled in irritation before she got her bearings. Then she squinted at Milton through the screen of her monitor, just as perplexed as he had been. Then, just as shocked.

"Milton?" he heard her say, her voice muffled through the glass.

He thumped the heel of his fist against the window. "I have to get out, Autumn! Please break the glass, or…"

"Break the glass?"

Impatient, near panicking, Milton looked all around him for a tool he might use to shatter the window on his end. With a lurch of his heart, he spotted a two-foot section of pipe leaning against the cinder-block wall. Right now, he might believe it was a more beautiful sight than Liz Trice had ever been.

Milton seized the pipe and hefted it over one shoulder like a baseball bat, pivoting toward the softly-glowing window.

"Shit, what are you doing?" he heard Autumn say, wheeling backwards in her chair.

A whoosh of the impromptu club through the air, and the end of the pipe crashed against the window. It left not a scratch on the glass. Cursing, Milton swung the pipe back over his shoulder for another mighty blow. He heard Autumn yelling at him—maybe yelling for him not to shatter the screen of her computer—but he ignored her.

The pipe was seized from behind in mid-swing.

"Oh God," Autumn Langevin whimpered, watching Milton being pulled backwards into the red-lit gloom, a soul-rending scream issuing from his cavernous mouth. She heard the clang of the pipe that dropped from his hands. Then she heard a sound like a bed sheet being torn down the middle, and Milton's screams were drowned by the blood bubbling in his throat. The darkness and the steam swallowed two obscure, struggling figures from sight, and then the screen began to fill with static until only the fizzing static remained.

Autumn looked down under her desk. The switch on her surge protector was still in the OFF position.

She lifted her eyes to the screen again. It was dark. Had she only imagined what she'd seen? Had she only been half-awake just now, still dreaming? Then she remembered the conversation, a short while earlier, with her seductive monster.

His power was *real*. He was an artist, shaping worlds, molding reality itself but once he had been a mortal man. How could he have come into possession of such power? And was he the only one who could wield it?

She should call Devon and Alex now, shouldn't she? Tell them what had happened to Milton Ferrara, tell them that their wildest speculations were true, after all?

Her cellphone rested close to her elbow. But she only dropped her eyes to it dispassionately.

Immortality. The power of life over death. Fuck being a priestess. She could be a *goddess*. And ultimately she might even trick the knife-handed trickster, so that he would have to worship at *her* feet.

THIRTEEN

"That's two of them," said Grace Simmons vehemently. She had already snipped Ama's sample nightmare disk into several sharp-edged pieces with a strong pair of shears. Now, she broke her own disk into fragments. "It's a beginning."

"Maybe it doesn't matter anymore," Ama fretted, sitting on the edge of Grace's bed with her. "That guy was in my regular dreams last night. I didn't go near the TranceBox."

Grace looked up at her friend. "What happened?"

"Well, I never saw him, but I knew it was him. I dreamed I was walking through the school, but I was the only one there. He kept following me through the halls. I heard him laughing, and he kept dragging his claws across the lockers. And I heard him say my name—calling to me."

Grace nodded somberly. "He's real, Ama. Trust me. He killed the guy who worked with Alex, then he killed Kent and last night, he killed Milton and Mrs Trice. I *know* it was him, no matter what they say."

They had both stayed home from school today, Grace feeling too sickened by what she had witnessed and Ama mostly to keep her company. A short while ago, Devon had called Grace from school to tell her the horrible news.

"Supposedly Mrs Trice's husband found the bodies," Devon had related at the time, "but the police have taken him into custody. They think he might've come home from work and found them in bed, and killed the both of them in a fit of rage."

"God, I can't believe this. I can't believe it," Grace had said. "How did they die? They weren't shot, were they?"

"No. I guess they got torn up pretty bad."

"And so now do they think her husband killed your brother's friend and Kent, too? Why would he do that? Or are we supposed to believe there are two people tearing people up in this town?"

"I don't know what to think anymore, Grace."

"You *do* know what to think, but you're afraid to think it. You know as well as I do that Mrs Trice's husband didn't kill her and Milton. Come on, Devon, wake up! Milton was your best friend!"

"I know that!" he snapped. He had never yelled at her before.

"We have to do something."

"Do what? Tell the police an undead serial killer is murdering people inside their dreams?"

"Not just any people. Our group, Devon. Anyone who's tried your brother's stupid nightmare software. Do you know what that means? It means I could be next. Or you. Is that okay, Devon? Should we just sit around and wait for that to happen?"

"Please, Grace, I can't even think anymore. Please stop hating me!"

"I don't hate you. I'm worried about you. And the rest of us, too."

"Okay look, I have to call my brother next and tell him about this, if he doesn't know already. Are you gonna be all right for now?"

"Ama is still here with me. I'm so tired. Devon, I was too afraid to sleep last night. I only slept for an hour, tops. I don't remember my dreams, but I don't think they were good."

"Try to take a nap. Tell Ama to watch over you, and wake you up if you start to look, I don't know, like something isn't right."

"I don't ever want to sleep again, Devon."

"Just... just don't use the TranceBox again, either of you."

Grace had chuckled bitterly at that advice. "Are you kidding? I'm never going near that thing again, and I won't let Ama do it, either but it might already be too late."

"I wonder if Milton had Mrs Trice try his copy of the disk. I wonder if they were using it last night."

"I don't think Krueger is confined to the program anymore. I think he's got the power back that he needed, and he can come and go in our dreams as he likes."

"Okay, look, I gotta talk to Alex now. I'll call back in a while, okay? And try to sleep?"

"We'll see," Grace had said but then she had blurted, "Devon—wait! Please tell me you believe in Krueger now. Please."

A few moments of silence had passed. Then: "I believe."

"You're not just saying that because I want you to?"

"Well, you did say 'please.'"

"Devon!"

"No, Grace, I'm serious. I believe it now."

Grace had sighed. "Thank you, Devon." And then she'd hung up.

Now, as Grace and Ama sat there with the snipped pieces of the two nightmare disks between them, there was a rap on the bedroom door. Cracking it open a bit, Grace's father Neil stuck his head into the room.

"You girls want some breakfast yet? How 'bout you, beautiful?" He smiled at Ama.

"It's almost 11 now, Dad," Grace said.

"Okay, then how 'bout some lunch?"

Last night when Grace had come home, her father had berated her for staying out so late. But when she'd broken into sobs and told him that she'd seen her friend Kent in the last seconds of his life, her father had taken her in his arms. This morning, when she'd told him she couldn't bring herself to go to school, he had called in sick at work himself, even though Ama was already here to keep her company. He'd explained that she might need him for moral support. And maybe even for protection.

"Ama?" Grace asked, deferring to her friend.

"Sure, I think I can eat now," Ama said, her grin bright in her pretty, chestnut-colored face.

Neil Simmons leaned into the room a little further, still holding the door knob. "Honey, last night you told me the police questioned you a bit at your friend Kent's house."

"Yeah."

"And did you tell them about those brains with the tumors that Devon's brother stole his program from?" Last night, in tearful gasps, Grace had managed to get the whole story out for her father. She had even babbled on about the Springwood Slasher, Freddy Krueger. Neil had seemed profoundly disturbed by her words, but he hadn't tried to talk her out of her convictions. Now she was self conscious about their discussion. Did her father think she had merely been acting hysterical at the time?

"We didn't tell the police," she said, "but Alex says they know about the tumors on the brains. His company tried to get information on the murder victims but apparently the police wouldn't cooperate much."

"No?" Neil nodded thoughtfully. Then he said, "So Alex doesn't know the history of the victims? Their identities?"

"No. The only really complete memories they've pulled out are dreams, from the tumors themselves."

"I see. And do you still have your copy of this program?"

She lifted the broken pieces and let them trickle through her fingers. "Right here."

"Why'd you do that?" he asked, sounding surprised, even dismayed.

"It could be dangerous, Dad! Nobody should be
using this thing. Why? You weren't thinking of
trying it yourself, were you? Please don't tell me you
thought of that."

"Well yes, I did think of that. After all the stuff you
told me last night, I thought I should look for
myself."

"No, Dad!" Grace cried. "What's the point? So you
can be targeted by Freddy Krueger, too? God, Dad,
don't be insane! I'm glad I broke these things before
you could do something so stupid."

Neil sighed heavily, gazing off into space for a
moment. When he looked back at the girls he
seemed to come back to himself, and he smiled at
Ama again. "Your burger, doll, how do you want it?
Bloody or burnt?"

"Somewhere in between."

"You got it." And he withdrew from the threshold,
snicking the door shut after him.

"Wow," Grace said, wagging her head as she
regarded the shards of the two nightmare disks,
"what was he thinking?"

As if it mesmerized him, Neil stared at the meat—
still raw and pink like striated muscle—hissing in
the frying pan. He teased the gleaming spatula blade
under the edge of the patty, then flipped it over.

He tried not to be angry at his daughter for ruining
her copy of the nightmare disk, and Ama's too. He
might still be able to coax her into getting another
copy from her boyfriend Devon.

So only dreams had been found like fossils in the surrounding stone of these dead brains? No intact waking memories had been extracted? Had the researchers been unable to extract such memories, he wondered, or were the dreams from the tumors their only area of interest? Even a dream memory might give clues to the identity of that brain's owner.

It frightened Neil Simmons. The idea that even a dream memory might betray important information about someone's life. About someone's death.

Victims of the Springwood Slasher, Grace had said. Whereas she and her friends had only recently become aware of that moniker, Neil knew it only too well. It extracted memories from his own mind.

It made Neil Simmons, who was forty-seven, remember being twenty-three years old, back in 1986. Those were years of terror. Parents in town had whispered of the Springwood Slasher again, just as they had in the late Sixties and early Seventies. Somehow, the Springwood Slasher had returned... claiming older children this time, teenagers, but using the same horrible methods.

There had been a teenage girl named Cassandra Wilcox living in Springwood then. What a name— Cassandra! She had been every bit as lovely as her name. Sixteen, but with such a full, voluptuous figure. Her ass had jutted out in a boastful sphere like an overripe fruit, and the twenty-three year-old Neil Simmons would groan softly to himself whenever he saw Cassandra walk past his house on the way to, or home from, Springwood High. She had lived only one street over from him. He hadn't been married to Grace's mother then—he met her the next year. No, in 1986 Neil's thoughts had been reserved for his neighbor Cassandra Wilcox with her beautiful chestnut-colored skin.

He would find excuses to be out in the yard at the times she would pass, so that he could wave to her. Soon he had the best-mowed lawn and the neatest-trimmed hedges in all of pretty Springwood. And with persistence, he even managed to exchange words with her on occasion. He began to greet her by name, that name like honey on his tongue, and one time as she passed he summoned her over and gave her a flower he had snipped from the blooms he'd planted in his yard to make it even prettier. She had giggled and shyly accepted it.

The weather had turned unpleasant one day. Through his curtains, Neil had seen Cassandra, beautiful Cassandra, walking to school with an umbrella open against a pounding rain. He had rushed to his door, hurled it open, and called her name again. He had told her he was on his way to work and could drop her off at school if she liked.

An hour later, like an angel fallen to the earth, like a flower crushed under a shoe, Cassandra Wilcox lay dead behind a little supermarket that had been shut down, to be replaced by a much larger version of itself closer to the highway. And Neil Simmons had sat in his warm car for a while, staring at the partially dressed body through his sweeping windshield wipers.

He could only pray that none of his neighbors had seen the girl enter his car. He prayed that if his fingerprints were on her body—around her crushed throat—that the rain would wash them away.

Then, as he regarded the spread-eagled body, a thought came to him and he stopped gnawing his thumb bloody. The thought that came to him was the Springwood Slasher.

But the Springwood Slasher didn't punch his victims, or strangle them when they were dazed into semiconsciousness. No. The Springwood Slasher slashed his victims.

That was when Neil Simmons had opened his glove-box and removed the handy utility knife that he always left in there with his flashlight and road maps. He then thumbed open the blade, and slowly, mechanically, got out of the car and approached the exquisite Cassandra Wilcox as if he once more had a flower in his hand to offer her.

Four deep slices in a row, they said the Slasher left on his victims. It had to be four deep, deep slices in a row.

Cassandra. Cassandra Wilcox.

Could one of the brains that these researchers had studied be the brain of Cassandra Wilcox? Mixed in with the brains of the Springwood Slasher's true victims?

If so, might there be a memory locked up in the vault of that brain? The memory of a man leaning over her in the rain, his hands around her neck, his thumbs pressing on the center of her throat? The grimacing, lustful face of a man rejected, angry like a jilted lover?

When people went unconscious, did they dream? And in a dying dream, might the face of twenty-three year-old Neil Simmons be preserved like a snapshot in a scrapbook?

He wanted to see that nightmare program. He ached to know if there was anything within those dream memories, anything at all—a man mowing his lawn and waving, a man offering a flower—that might shed light on things that were meant to remain buried. Buried. He had thought all this was buried forever. As much as he had loved her, he had hoped to never remember Cassandra Wilcox again. He had prayed for blissful amnesia.

As much as he wanted to experience the nightmare disk for himself, he dreaded the idea just as strongly. He did not want to look into her eyes again, living and sparkling or dead and glazed. He did not want to look through his *own* eyes again.

Neil gaped at the frying meat, hypnotized by the little pops of fat sizzling on its surface. Like drops of rain bursting on brown, dead flesh.

FOURTEEN

Bruce Simpson introduced himself to Alex as being from the Behavioral & Cognitive Sciences (BCS) division of the Social, Behavioral & Economic Sciences (SBE) division of the National Science Foundation (NSF). Alex noted that Mr Simpson's initials created the acronym BS. He was tall, with immaculately cut salt-and-pepper hair, a perfect tan and perfect teeth. He wasn't geeky enough to be a scientist; rather, he looked to Alex like what a team of real scientists would piece together Frankenstein-style in order to create the ultimate bureaucrat.

Farhad excused himself to return to some project he was working on today, leaving Alex and Simpson to speak alone. The two men stood in front of the large, six-pointed cabalistic symbol called "the seal of Solomon"—the logo for

Macrocosm Research—painted on one of the main laboratory's walls. Following his hand-shaking introduction, Simpson began complimenting Alex on the great work he had done thus far on the Séance Project.

Alex watched his supervisor walk away, unchar-acteristically meek in the presence of the government man. His mind raced like a hamster in a wheel, going nowhere fast, and for several min-utes he was speechless. Conflicted. On the one hand, he was desperate to defend and continue the hard work he was doing for Macrocosm, and even more desperate not to jeopardize the fruits of his labor at Mnemonic. On the other hand, there was Patrick, Kent, and now, he had learned during a call from Devon, Milton Ferrara, not to mention a teacher at Springwood High that Devon's friend had apparently been involved with. The husband was in custody, but Alex knew better. He had given Milton a sample of the nightmare disk.

Who next might fall victim to this curse?

When Simpson paused in his effusive accolades for Macrocosm in general and Alex in particular, Alex cut in. "Mr Simpson, I, ah, I have to tell you I'm pretty concerned about the safety of our crew here."

"Yes, Alex, I can tell you are. That's why I'm here now. We're concerned about the murder of Patrick Tremblay, too, and I wanted to offer you people our sympathy and our moral support."

Mr G walked close by the men, carrying a clip-board, but either he was trying to impress the government man by looking busy or else he truly was too involved in his activities to glance their way. Or maybe it was something else distracting him; Alex had noticed that Mr G's eyes were very red today, and that he'd been massaging the back of his head with a wincing expression of pain.

"Sir, it isn't just Patrick's murder. I have concerns about the brain-machine interfaces. The dreams we extracted from the brain models. I'm concerned..." His words trailed off. Without really being sure what was going on, how could he even frame his words?

"Alex," Simpson said in a soft voice, "I understand you've all had magnetic resonance imaging to check for the appearance of any brain tissue irregularities."

"Yes, sir, Patrick was doing the scans but we haven't done it since his death."

"And there have been no irregularities?"

"Not yet, no. But..."

Simpson smiled and put a hand on Alex's back, lowering his voice even further to a conspiratorial whisper. "Alex, see what I really don't want to do here is spook the troops, do you know what I mean? I know this is an emotional time, especially for you since you're the one who discovered poor Patrick."

"Julie Ip saw him, too."

"Yes, I know. I already spoke with her privately before you came in."

"Yeah, sorry I was so late. I didn't sleep well."

"Not a problem. Anyway, now I'd like to ask you what you saw, talk with you in depth about all your concerns, and answer whatever questions I'm in a position to answer."

Nicely phrased, thought Alex.

Simpson checked his watch, then continued, "I have to catch a flight to DC in a few hours, but what do you say we go down the street right now, sit in that doughnut shop I passed driving in here, have a coffee and chat for a little bit, huh? Out of earshot, so the rest of these guys can go about their work. This is such significant work being done here, and in the other Macrocosm branches; I can't stress that enough. How *important* you guys are! It's a delicate time, I realize that, of course I do. But anyway, let's go." A little more pressure from the hand on Alex's back. "What do you say?"

Alex glanced over at Julie Ip, sitting in front of one of the work stations busily typing at a keyboard. Heaps of gear were around her, and on top of one stack of equipment rested a halo-like interface headband. On her own head, however, she wore her usual headphones. Immersed in her work and her music, Julie nevertheless sensed Alex looking at her and smiled across the room at him. He smiled in return, making a mental note to bring back a cup of coffee to surprise her with.

"Okay, sir. I can never refuse a coffee."

Maybe Mr G hadn't been so oblivious about the government man pulling Alex aside, after all, because as soon as they had left he approached Julie and complained, "Why is he treating Alex like some kind of star? Taking him out to coffee. And why is he talking to him away from the rest of us? Does he think we don't all talk together about everything?"

With an effort of patience, displeased that he'd interrupted her in the middle of Nick Cave's ominous *Red Right Hand*, Julie removed her headphones and said, "I'm sure he isn't singling Alex out for praise, he just wants his take on Patrick."

"Or maybe he wants to question Alex about the secret activities he seems to be up to."

"What secret activities?" Julie asked innocently. "Anyway, how would he even know about something like that, unless somebody had emailed or called him to tip him off?"

Mr G seemed to squirm a little at that suggestion, and in disgust Julie realized it was probably true; maybe Mr G hadn't contacted this man in particular, but she bet that he had been spreading his suspicions to whomever would listen to them, both at the main office for Macrocosm Research and at the NSF.

She returned her attention to her computer screen in the hopes that Mr G would take his complaints elsewhere (and she was sure he would bitch to Farhad next), but a groan from the man made her look up at him again. He leaned forward over her station, supporting himself against the desk with one hand while the other was clamped over the back of his neck. His features were screwed into an expression of pain. "God," he groaned, "today is my worst headache yet."

"Did you take anything for it? Maybe you should just go home."

"Oh maybe. I'll try to hang in there a little bit longer." He shuffled back to his own work station and lowered himself into his seat. He then folded his arms across the edge of the desk and rested his forehead on them. Julie was torn between real sympathy and the sarcastic desire to ask him if he needed a hug, as he had recently asked her.

The pep talk the visiting Mr Simpson had given to Farhad, Mr G and Julie before Alex's arrival made it quite clear that the work at Macrocosm was not to fall into disarray with Patrick's death, and that instead, it should be tackled with a renewed sense of commitment. Toward that end, Julie applied herself now to squeezing more memories out of one of the reconstructed brains' golf ball-sized tumors. As Alex himself had once told her, it didn't hurt to keep squeezing, even if it appeared they had gotten all the coherent memory data they could wring from the brain models.

Julie had been running a fresh scan, and it had come to its end. So she took the halo down from atop the CIT unit where she had left it, and fitted it around her forehead. As she did so, she watched Farhad walk past and seat himself at yet another of the work stations. He, too, crowned his balding head with one of the cerebral interface bands. He looked over at Julie and asked, "Are you going under, too?"

"Yeah, I just finished a new scan."

Farhad called to Mr G, "Fotios, Julie and I are both interfacing now."

"Mm-hm," they heard the senior technician grunt, his head still lowered. It was their safety procedure that at least one of them should always refrain from interfacing in case there were problems and the subjects needed to be disconnected and roused. Sometimes this one person would monitor and record his coworkers' brain activity as they were exposed to the memory extractions. But Mr G didn't look too attentive at the moment.

Julie smiled back at Farhad and assured him, "I'm fine. I'm setting the timer at just five minutes. If I don't get any impressions from that, then I doubt I picked up anything anyway."

Farhad nodded, satisfied, and turned to his own work.

Having finished programming the CIT equipment to play back the scanner's results, Julie closed her eyes and reclined as much as her chair allowed, waiting for the unit to place her in a sleep-like state before commencing its playback.

The next thing she knew, her eyes were open again. It seemed she had done little more than blink. Had the five minutes passed already? A glance at the time on her computer screen's tool bar told her it had. She recalled experiencing only static, as if standing at the center of a raging, blinding snow storm. Maybe there had been vague, dark shapes shifting behind that nearly solid wall of interference, and vague distorted sounds just beyond the sizzle of white noise, but nothing more. The memory was so badly degraded that it was useless to her.

She removed the headband, wrapped its wires around it and set it aside, then began typing at her keyboard. All the gear in her station was linked into this one main keyboard, so her commands powered down the CIT unit. As she hit the last key-pads, she glanced over to see that Farhad was resting back in his chair with his eyes shut, still wearing his own halo. He hadn't told her what recording, new or old, he was accessing, or how long he would be under.

A deep moan caused her to swivel in her chair to face in Mr G's direction. He hadn't lifted his head from his crossed arms. Was he asleep, or just inca-pacitated by his pain? She was concerned for him now, however much she disliked him personally. She must awaken Farhad and ask him to help her run an MRI scan on the senior tech to see if there had been any abnormal tissue growth since the last time Patrick had scanned all of them.

Before she could rise from her chair, however, Mr G groaned again—a drawn-out, anguished sound that gradually changed into a garble of incompre-hensible words spouted by the tech in his sleep, as if he were speaking in tongues. His body began to tremble, and even jolted violently every few sec-onds with electrified spasms.

"Oh my God," Julie said, gripping the arms of her chair in horror. "Mr G? Fotios?"

As she watched, a lump rose on the back of his head, then seemed to shift to one side, like a mouse scurrying under a carpet. It shifted again in another direction, at least several inches. Then, in this loca-tion, it started to balloon.

"Farhad!" Julie shrieked, paralyzed in her chair. "Farhad!" She didn't dare take her eyes off Mr G, but she could tell that her supervisor didn't hear her; he was still too deeply interfaced with his gear.

The tumor had quickly swollen to the size of an orange—a grapefruit even—and now the skin of Mr G's head was stretched too taut to contain it. Julie heard the flesh rip, a spatter of blood speckling the tech's computer screen and paperwork. Mr G gave one last, especially violent convulsion, then went still. But his tumor hadn't finished growing yet. Next, Julie heard the terrible cracking sound of the plates of his skull coming apart at their sutures. Free of its prison of bone, a glistening red mass squeezed up into view. Was this the tumor, or Mr G's inflamed brain? Now, they seemed to be one and the same.

Julie sobbed, wanting to cover her eyes but unable to.

The mass was mostly shapeless, almost gelatinous, and it oozed out of the shattered egg that Mr G's head had become, slid out onto his shoulder, and then dropped with a heavy splat to the floor. Julie could barely make out the brain's convolutions due to its deformed state and a coating of slime-like mucous but—with an additional nauseating shock—Julie could see that in dislodging itself from his skull, Mr G's brain had dragged his eyes out of their orbits and pulled them along with it. They were still tethered to the brain by their muscles and the abducent and trochlear nerves.

Then, like the eye stalks of a snail, Mr G's eyes lifted on their connecting muscles to point at Julie. The optic nerves must still have been functioning, because she could tell the thing was *seeing* her.

Her paralysis was broken at last, and Julie launched herself out of her chair and dashed toward the sleeping Farhad. Screaming inarticulately, she practically collided with her supervisor and proceeded to shake him roughly. His features looked troubled, but he did not open his eyes.

Julie glanced back at the brain on the floor to witness yet another ghastly development. This time, she had to fight back the bile that rose in her throat.

Eight finger bones had sprouted—four to either side—from the misshapen, tumescent brain. They grew swiftly, until they became much longer than natural digits. The fingers bent at the joints, flexing. The brain rose up from the floor like the body of a giant spider on its eight armored legs and began scuttling at Julie, eyes wavering on their stalks.

Julie jerked the halo off Farhad's head and shook him again. "Wake up! Wake up!" But her supervisor would still not arouse from his artificially-induced sleep, and the mutant spider was drawing too close. Abandoning Farhad, Julie bolted.

The spider-like brain scrambled in pursuit, the tips of the finger-legs clicking against the floor like the nails of a dog.

Julie darted between two work stations in order to reach the nearest door. It would lead into the adjacent smaller labs, rather than take her from Macrocosm's suite into the corridor beyond, but she hoped to be able to shut the door and prevent the spider-thing from pursuing her further.

Behind her, the clattering sound of its legs drew closer and closer but she reached the door, turned the knob, and burst through. A moment after she had slammed the door shut again, she felt it thud as the disembodied brain hurled itself against the wood. There was no lock on the door, so Julie looked around frantically for something to barricade it with.

Julie was stunned to find she was not in the little hallway from which branched the other labs. It was a long carpeted corridor, like the one outside the space Macrocosm Research rented in the vast office structure. It seemed every other light in the corridor had failed, with more ailing bulbs flickering overhead. As a result, it was impossible for her to judge the length of the corridor.

In her panic, had she lost her bearings? Even if she had taken the wrong door, though, shouldn't this corridor be familiar to her? But there was no time to ponder. Julie began sprinting down the corridor, sobbing, until she came to the first of the doors that lined it. She tried the knob. Locked. She flung herself at the door opposite. Locked. Why should these doors be locked if the one she had shut against the brain-creature could not be locked?

This thought made her look back toward the door, just in time to see its knob turning. A second later, the door began to open and one eye stalk and the first of the eight legs poked into view.

Julie threw herself into motion again, almost bouncing off one wall to the other as she tried door after door. Not only were they all locked, but the more doors she tried, the more doors appeared ahead of her. How long could this corridor possibly be? It looked like a highway stretching off interminably into the night.

She whipped her head around to look rearward, and saw that the brain was moving less speedily. That was because it had gained in volume. The blob-like matter jerked itself along in horrible little flopping motions, like a flayed and crippled seal. The finger-legs didn't seem to be growing any longer, but they hooked into the carpet and did their best to help pull the glob along.

Julie continued on, breathless and lightheaded, trying more doors. Falling against one of them, she checked again on the thing's progress. It had grown even larger. Worse, she now saw that four crude limbs had coalesced from its bulk. These limbs dragged a roughly-shaped figure along on its belly. At the end of the front limbs were those claw-like finger bones and in the front a rudimentary head. When it lifted, Julie could see it had formed itself around Mr G's stolen eyes. The face, like the body, was that of a cadaver with all its flesh removed, leaving only the raw muscles beneath. But somehow, she still recognized that grinning face. It was the face of the man who had been haunting her nightmares lately.

He recognized her, too. "Julie," he crooned in an inhuman voice, his vocal cords not yet fully developed. "You look like you could use a hug."

Her legs propelled her on but they were losing their power and her aching lungs were constricted. She didn't try any more doors; it would only slow her pace further. She kept running for the end of the corridor, but it remained lost in gloom. It must have an end and an exit at that end. It must...

Behind her, with a grunt of effort, the still-forming figure managed to rise up onto its legs. It stumbled back one step, a little off-balance, but the grin on its face had not faltered.

Fog cloaked the floor of the forest, looking like a deep layer of snow, but overhead the leaves of the trees were an electric shade of red. The trunks of these trees were black up close but ghostly gray as they receded into the haze, resembling an army of soldiers at attention.

Beneath the swirling mist at his feet, Farhad crunched a layer of fallen leaves that he could barely even discern. He tried to make as little noise as possible, however, easing his weight into every step. He did not remember how he had come into these woods, what he might be seeking or what might be seeking him, but he knew intuitively that he was in grave danger.

There were two swords sheathed at his waist in lacquered scabbards; his long, curved katana and the shorter wakizashi. He paused and stared down at their braided handles as if he hadn't even realized he was carrying them until that moment. A strange impulse made him reach up and touch his balding head. He fingered a topknot of hair toward the rear of his skull.

From some distance off came the barest crunch of leaves. Farhad whirled toward the sound, his hand going to the katana's handle. He saw only the trunks of trees upholding the ceiling of leaves, like rows of columns vanishing into the cottony, slowly churning clouds of mist.

His heart was hammering now. If he should have to protect himself against a foe or some beast of the forest, he wasn't familiar with the proper use of a katana, however keen its blade might be. Still, it was a comfort to him that he had these weapons at all. Slowly, trying to minimize the hiss of the steel through its scabbard, he unsheathed the sword and held its long handle in two fists, the slender blade curving out in front of him.

Some warrior's instinct he hadn't known he possessed caused him to spin around just as a black-garbed man dropped down from the bough where he had been crouching. Farhad's blade whooshed through the air, cleaving the mist and sending it swirling in little eddies in its wake. He saw the flash of the other man's steel, but Farhad's blade was already hacking through the raised forearm. A greenish blood better suited for an insect's veins, but smelling of rot, spurted from the truncated limb. Farhad spun the blade around again, and in its second stroke he neatly beheaded his enemy. In the instant before the head toppled away, he saw only a black mask with a slit for the eyes. Headless, the ninja stood there a moment longer, gushing more of that green blood out of his neck stump, before his body crumpled to join his head in the carpet of fog.

Farhad swept the katana behind him without even turning his head, slashing open the chest of a second black-garbed ninja just as he lunged at his back. He was shocked at his own remarkable prowess. He faced this second man and found him stumbling back, clamping a hand over the deep gash in his chest. Foul green blood squirted between his fingers. This time, Farhad could see his enemy more clearly. What he had thought was a short ninja sword in the man's right hand was actually a glove with one long claw attached to the index finger. Again, all he saw of the man's face through his mask was the area around the eyes, but the skin around those hateful eyes appeared to be terribly scarred. Burned, perhaps.

The man made a sudden charge, whipping his steel talon at Farhad. There was a loud clang as Farhad's heavier blade bashed the ninja's claw aside. He followed through with a stroke that severed the scarred ninja's head from his neck. As before, the carcass fell away to disappear in the thick layer of mist.

A third ninja came leaping out of the haze like a black panther. He too had a long razor-edged talon affixed to his glove and he too had a face that appeared to be scarred beneath his mask. Was the scarring part of some ritual for a cult of fanatical assassins? Farhad had no time to ponder. He crouched low, the ninja's swishing blade just ticking his topknot, and with a powerful sweep cut through both his foe's legs. The man fell into the fog, and Farhad reversed the sword in his hands to stab it straight downwards. Though he couldn't see the ninja at his feet, he felt the blade plunge deep into his chest.

A fourth ninja was standing there, ready to attack, when Farhad looked up. Behind the black mask came a sadistic chuckle. This man also had the burnt flesh around his eyes. It was almost as if he hadn't been killing multiple warriors, but the same man over and over. Was he a ghost, then? A demon? Perhaps a little bit of both.

As if they had just read Farhad's thoughts, the first three ninjas he had killed shot up from the carpet of fog in unison. Two were decapitated, their necks still pumping out green blood, and the third wobbled awkwardly on his leg stumps. Despite their mortal wounds, all four looked ready to attack.

Farhad knew then that, even with his great swordsmanship, he could not win against his supernatural enemies. So he turned swiftly and fled, racing straight into the heart of the forest. Into the heart of the mist. Let them do their best to pursue him without eyes to see or feet to run on.

Still, he immediately heard the crackling of leaves underfoot as the four ninjas burst into pursuit.

Farhad wove to the right, then back to the left, hoping to throw them off his trail, but it was difficult to lose them when he was making so much noise across the bed of leaves himself. Then, ahead, he saw something that made him halt in his tracks for a moment.

A door hovered slightly off the ground. A wooden door, with a brass knob. It was not set into a wall; it simply floated there in space with more of the crimson forest spreading behind it. Was this some doorway to Hell that the demons had come through or a way out of the Hell he was in?

The door was strangely familiar to him, though it was featureless enough. The word "Macrocosm" hovered in his mind the way the door hovered in the air. Yes, it was an exit! He intuitively recognized that the floating door was his way out of this world.

Leaves crunching behind him. He had no time to lose. Farhad threw himself toward the door.

Just a few last yards before he reached it, the door swung open and a figure appeared on the threshold. A figure poised to leap out toward him.

Without breaking his stride, Farhad leveled his samurai sword at the new figure, another ninja, dressed entirely in black. Through the slit in the mask, Farhad saw dark eyes with Asian eyelids. No scars on this one.

Before the fifth ninja could pounce from the doorway, he drove his sword straight into its guts. The blade all but punched through his enemy's back. He heard a cry. A cry in the voice of a woman. The blood that sprayed from the wound when he jerked his blade free was red, not greenish.

The ninja dropped forward into the bed of fog, but managed to stay on its hands and knees. Farhad realized he had seen no sword talon on the figure's right hand. He took his left hand off the katana's handle, reached down for the ninja's mask and tore it away. Longish black hair spilled out.

Julie raised her head, her face anguished and blood trickling from one corner of her mouth. "Farhad," she rasped.

"Oh no, no... Julie!" Farhad cried.

The undead ninjas circled him like a pack of hyenas, just deep enough in the mist to remain unseen, those that still possessed heads chuckling maliciously.

He sheathed his sword and took Julie under the arms, dragging her to her feet. She groaned in misery, trying to staunch the flow of her blood with both hands. Farhad pushed her toward the open doorway. Impossibly, through it he saw a corridor stretching into gloom. "Hurry," he said. "Go back!"

"No," she whimpered, "he's in there chasing me!"

"You have to go back—hurry!"

She was too weak to resist. Farhad shoved Julie through the doorway and saw her collapse on her side on the corridor's carpeted floor.

"Forgive me," he sobbed, as he slammed the door closed. The portal disappeared immediately, swallowed up in the fog. He turned to face his opponents, then again drawing his sword from its scabbard, but with a hopeless tear spilling down his cheek. A moment later, the four ninjas came for him from four different directions, finger swords slashing through the veils of mist.

Alex opened the door to the Macrocosm Research suite—Simpson having dropped him off in front of the building before heading on to the airport—and the moment he stepped through it Julie fell against him, so heavily that the large hazelnut coffee he had brought back with him from the coffee shop to surprise her with dropped to the floor, darkly staining the carpet.

He held her away from him by her arms, his eyes dropping from the blood running out of her mouth to the greater amount of blood spreading across her mid-section and the front of her pants.

"Oh my God. Oh my God," he gasped.

Julie dug her fingers into his arms. "Help me, Alex," she croaked. "Help me erase everything."

He looked past her into the main laboratory. In just that quick glimpse he saw smashed computer monitors, stacks of equipment toppled off their carts, empty software jewelboxes strewn on the floor, patterns of blood squiggling here and there across the carpet.

She sank toward the floor and he eased her the rest of the way down, pressing her hands over the wound in her belly. "Don't move, Julie. You just stay there, I'm going to call 911."

"I already did," she whispered. When she said that, Alex realized he'd already been hearing sirens wailing in the distance.

"Don't move," he warned her sternly, fighting back tears. "Don't you move."

Alex looked up and dashed over to Mr G's side. The senior tech's head was down on his arms, blood having flowed copiously out of his ears. When Alex pushed him upright, he saw that blood had also run out of the man's nose and mouth, and his eyes stared into oblivion. He left him there and hurried over to Farhad, who reclined in a chair at one of the work stations, still wearing a cerebral interface headband. "Farhad. Farhad!" he shouted. He took hold of the metal halo, but as he pulled it free the motion caused Farhad's head to flop to one side and drop off his shoulders to the floor.

The headless corpse sat there still gripping the armrests of its chair. Its flesh was pale as wax, the neck stump all but bloodless, as if the man had

done all his bleeding somewhere else. Somewhere
very far away.

Alex fell back against the edge of a desk, spun
away and vomited onto the carpet.

By the time the emergency vehicles pulled up
outside, and by the time Alex managed to crawl
over to Julie Ip, covered in her blood and his vomit.
He found her lovely Asian eyes open but unseeing,
as if she was wearing her headphones, entranced
by some secret music only she could hear.

When the paramedics and the policemen hustled
into Macrocosm Research, they found Alex Carmack smashing equipment in a mad rampage. It
took several men to subdue him and lock the handcuffs around his blood-smeared wrists.

FIFTEEN

Like her boyfriend Alex, Trisha Smith arrived at work very late that day, having had a rough night. Sleeping over at another person's house—in this case, Alex's parents'—had always been rather uncomfortable for her, let alone the heavy discussion they had had about the death of Devon's friend Kent.

When she entered the workspace for Mnemonic Designs, it was to find her three coworkers (sans the moonlighter Alex, who wouldn't come by until he'd gotten out of his day job) clustered around one computer terminal toward the back of the room. David Schwartz was in the pilot's seat, so to speak. At twenty-seven, Dave was the main sales/marketing force behind Mnemonic. Despite his stutter, he did an exemplary job courting Saxon Systems and other companies with their software, and advertising their services and products. Mnemonic was ever trying to expand and diversify, and Dave's efforts did as much to turn their goals to reality as the work of the design team itself.

Trisha played down Dave's crush on her whenever Alex grumbled about it, telling him that he was exaggerating the situation, but in reality she thought Alex had it right. As soon as she came in, Dave practically broke his neck looking over at her. He smiled hugely.

Shane Ryan looked up at her more casually. Only twenty-eight years-old, Shane was the founder and owner of Mnemonic Designs. He was generally quiet, driven and intense, hot-headed on occasion, but certainly not without a capacity for fun. His crew was loyal to him. They knew he had good marketing sense, and a kind of vision. He was prepared to take risks, hence his willingness to accept the materials that Alex had surreptitiously imported from Macrocosm Research. Shane lived with his girlfriend and two sons, and was known to be good to them. As usual, he had on a backwards-facing baseball cap.

"Look who decided to show up," he teased mildly.

"Sorry, Shane."

"Hey there, my Kama Sutra cutie," said Tim Finney, the other worker huddled over Dave's shoulder. "Come check this out, hurry."

Trisha came over and took in the computer screen. She almost gasped. It was a still image taken from one of the sequences of the nightmare disk— a shot of the audience of skeletons overlooking the arena. Dave had been experimenting with laying type on top of the image. He had skills as a graphic artist as well but he still wasn't satisfied with the graininess of the picture, and was trying to tweak it in the art program he had moved the image into.

"Come on," Finney goaded him, "use the Schwartz, spaceballs."

A bit dismayed on some gut level, Trisha murmured, "So you were able to get the recording transferred to a strictly visual format?"

"Yep, that would be me," Finney boasted. "Welcome to primetime, bitch! Good old 2D. Now a person could play through the entire disk like they were just watching a movie but what fun would that be? That'd be like watching a porno instead of doing the deed yourself. Anyway, now we can get screen shots for advertising. Damn, I'm good."

"Dave's mocking up some cover art," Shane said. "If we don't have to pay an outsider to do that, we'll save some major bucks."

"There," Dave said, sitting back, satisfied that he'd done the best he could with the rough image. "Tha-tha-that will have t-t-to do."

"Fucking guy's stutter gets worse when you're around," Finney said, grinning devilishly. "Stop making him so nervous, Trisha. Get your boobs out of his face." He waved her away from Dave.

"Shut your pie hole, Tim," Trisha said dryly. She looked back at the image on the screen and fidgeted. "Guys, you know Alex and I talked a lot about the program last night and, uh, I think he needs to do some more tests at Macrocosm to really ensure that it's safe."

"What do you mean?" Shane said, frowning.

"I don't know. Look, when he comes in this evening let's all stay late and go over it in depth, all right? It's very important that we do that." The unsettling picture on the screen magnetized her eyes to it once more. "Alex's brother called us this morning. A friend of his was murdered last night. The boy's teacher, too."

"I heard that!" Finney blurted, eating up the scandalous nature of the incident. "Her hubby came in and caught them doing a little home tutoring, and carved 'em up six ways of bad. Poor bastard, I'd have done the same thing if it was my wife."

"That was his brother's friend?" Shane asked.

"Yeah," Trisha said, "and that's not all. Another friend of Devon's, named Kent Lowe, got murdered last night, too. And the thing is, Alex gave *both* of those kids samples of our disk. Isn't it weird that these two kids and that teacher got murdered just like Alex's coworker Patrick? Last night we didn't know about the boy and the teacher but we were talking about Kent and Patrick, trying to figure out a connection."

"Wa-wa-wow," Dave said, gaping up at her.

"So what are you saying?" Shane asked, looking displeased by the pall this seemed to cast over his big project. Maybe his biggest project yet. "Yeah, that's fucking scary, and I don't like murders going on in the town where I live, but what does that have to do with the nightmare disk?"

"Hey," Finney said, "you think the government guys backing Macrocosm found out what Alex did, and they're putting a hit on everybody who has one of our disks?"

Trisha sighed. "Look, I'd rather hold off discussing it until Alex gets here tonight. If I talk about it alone, well, I just don't want to do that. It all sounds crazy. All our theories."

"Okay, sure, we'll talk," Shane assured her. "Of course I want to hear what Alex has to say. This is some crazy shit going on in town."

"Thanks, Shane."

The little cluster broke up, Dave saving his mock-up of the jewelbox cover art. "Well, anyway," Shane said, "you're in time for us to test the program again. We tightened some screws this morning. I hate to tamper with it any more without Alex being here, but I'm sure he'll approve of what we did. If all went well, we got the image clearer on the zoo sequence and the sound crisper on the samurai dream."

"You're going to test it *now*?"

"Why not? Every time we tweak it, we have to check on how everything plays."

"Can't we please wait for Alex, Shane?"

"He can try it out for himself later. If we're going to have this big powwow you want this evening, and we also have to wait until he gets here to test the improvements, we'll be here all night."

Trisha looked at the screen where the arena shot had been, as if she could still see it—but now there was only an innocuous desktop of the Mnemonic Designs logo. "I really don't feel comfortable testing it now, Shane, and I wish you guys wouldn't do it, either."

Now Shane's patience was showing stress cracks. "Trisha—why are you acting so spooked? How can those murders possibly be connected to our disk? It's a coincidence. The teacher didn't have a copy of the disk, did she?"

"No, but she was with a boy who did. It isn't just the murders, Shane. I'm afraid the program itself might be dangerous."

"What? How, dangerous?"

Dave cut in, siding with Trisha. "I don't nee-need to tr-tr-try it right na-na-now, either."

"Stop brown-nosing her, Dave," Finney said. "Not that I would mind putting my nose up that heavenly ass myself." He laughed and made squeezing motions with both hands.

"Ugh," Trisha said.

"Come on, Dave," Shane sighed, reining in his annoyance, "the three of us are going to try it out. Trisha can baby-sit us, that's fine." He gathered up three jewelboxes containing freshly burned disks of the fine-tuned nightmare program, compatible for playing directly on the TranceBox system. "Pick your favorite chair and let's take it for a test drive."

Alex Carmack's polo shirt still reeked of his vomit, and the blood soaked into it was turning stiff and brownish as it dried, but at least they had removed his handcuffs and put a Styrofoam cup of coffee in front of him. His hand trembled badly as he lifted it for a sip.

"And you don't know this Simpson's first name?" asked the tall, lean detective with silvery hair cut in a severe military style. His young partner, Billy, just gaped at Alex as if mesmerized by seeing his very first major criminal.

"No, I don't recall it but look, can't you just page him at the airport? Maybe his flight hasn't taken off yet…"

"Even if this Simpson exists," the senior detective said, "and we did catch him before he left. Yes, he might be able to vouch for you that he dropped you off at Macrocosm Research, but that doesn't mean you were with him at the times the murders took place. We haven't established the exact time of the killings yet. Maybe you killed your coworkers right *after* Simpson dropped you off."

"Well, you keep doing your tests, and you'll establish the time! And try to find this Simpson, whether he's already in flight or even if you have to get him through the NSF offices because he can tell you I was with him when this was happening!"

"And can he tell us," the detective said, rising from his chair to pace the interview room slowly, "why everyone around you seems to be getting slashed to pieces, Mr Carmack? You with your interest in the old Springwood Slasher case?"

Alex gave the man a long look. "I admit," he said slowly, "it doesn't look good. And I don't know how to explain it to you in a way that would keep me out of the local asylum."

"Try me," the detective said, leaning both hands on the table. "I've heard some wild stuff in my time, believe me."

Alex stared at him longer, his blue eyes intense through his wire-framed glasses. But finally he said, "I get one phone call, right?"

The detective sighed. "You've seen the movies. So are you going to call the National Science Foundation about this elusive Mr Simpson?"

"No. I'm going to call my girlfriend."

"Suit yourself." From his pocket the detective pulled his own cellphone. Alex's cell had been confiscated upon his arrest. "I'll be right outside." He motioned with his head for Billy to get up and follow him. Pausing in the threshold, the senior detective pointed at the phone in Alex's hand. "Just one call. That thing will tell me if you make more than that."

Alex nodded. "Got ya."

The detective held his gaze for a moment, then stepped out into the hall. The door locked shut after him.

For a moment, Alex had been tempted to unburden himself to the man and tell him everything. Was it possible that the police force of Springwood already knew something of the truth behind Freddy Krueger, and his survival in another dimension or plane of existence—the world of dreams? Was that why they had entombed and jealously guarded all files related to the Springwood Slasher killings in the sixties and seventies, and those that came later?

Well, right now Alex didn't feel like trusting anything but a sure bet, and that was Trisha. First things first. He had to let her know what had happened at Macrocosm, and then she could take on the effort to get in contact with Simpson, wherever the man might be.

The phone rang only once before Trisha flicked her own cellphone on. "Alex?" she blurted.

"Yeah, baby. I'm—"

"Where the *fuck* have you been?" she all but screamed in his ear. "I've called you a hundred times!"

"I'm at the police station. I'm under arrest, honey."

"What?"

"I went out for coffee with an NSF guy named Simpson, who came down to put some pressure on us to keep the Séance Project going strong. When I came back to the lab... honey... Julie, Mr G and Farhad are dead." His voice broke. "They were mutilated. Farhad was even beheaded."

"Oh God, Alex! Oh God!"

"And they think I did it. Julie called 911 before she died. The police came and found me covered in blood." He lowered his voice and hissed into the phone, "Trisha, it's *him*. It's Krueger. What we were talking about the other night? It's true. I don't know how, but it is. He's real. And he's killing us when we cross over into whatever parallel universe he lives in. Somehow, we go there when we dream and if he kills us there, then we die out here."

"But... but we have to tell them it isn't you! We have to show them, somehow."

"Well, I obviously don't wanna go to jail for killing all these people, but I don't know how to even begin telling them..."

"Alex, listen." He could tell Trisha had already been close to tears before he called. "Shane, Tim, Dave—they all hooked up to TranceBoxes to test some adjustments they made to the nightmare disk."

"For God's sake, wake 'em up!"

"That just it—that's why I've been looking for you! I *can't* wake them up, Alex! When the time had passed that they should have woken up, when the program timed out, they didn't wake up! I disconnected their receiver patches, I shut off the three TranceBoxes, I even took the disks out of them. They're alive but it's like they're in a coma! I've tried shaking them, slapping them…"

"Oh man, oh man, oh man," Alex was chanting to himself.

"What should I do now, Alex?" She sounded close to panic. "Should I call an ambulance?"

Alex bent over the table, resting his forehead against its cool edge. His free hand was clenched in a fist on his leg. Just on the other side of the door were the police. He could send them right over to Mnemonic this minute but what would they do when they got there? Might they, or paramedics, only make matters worse by disturbing or moving the three dreamers? If Krueger wanted to kill them in the dream realm, what could the cops do to protect them, short of going into that world themselves?

"I don't know," he moaned, "I don't know, I can't think anymore. You have to try to stay calm, Trisha, try to think of something else you can come up with to wake them. Look, power all the gear down. All of it. And start erasing all our data. Wipe the hard drives clean. Destroy every prototype disk you can get your hands on. Every file." He couldn't believe he was even hearing these words come out of his mouth. "Everything. Judging from what Krueger himself has said to us, it looks like he was forgotten for a while. We've been sort of remembering him back to life. We're the source of his power. Maybe if we destroy the memories of him we've restored from the brain models, it might weaken him. Sap his energy."

God, he thought then, recalling an earlier project the NSF had contracted Macrocosm Research to take on—with very impressive results. Alex and the rest of the crew had worked on a means by which to delicately erase memories from the human brain—everything from scrubbing it entirely clean to removing just a single hour from its logbooks. At that time, Julie had read Alex an excerpt from Shakespeare that she had found relevant to their work:

"Canst thou not minister to a mind diseased,
Pluck from the memory a rooted sorrow,
Raze out the written troubles of the brain…"

The tissues of the hippocampus—the portion of the brain controlling the laying down of new memories—withered naturally with age, reducing memory. The technique Macrocosm had developed was something like this; a controlled brain injury. An imposed amnesia. It involved blocking protein synthesis, memory reconsolidation, altering neurons, synapses and their relationship, minutely remolding the plasticity of the brain. Subtracting instead of adding memories, experiences. Censoring the individual's personal history. Long-term memory, short-term memory, it could all be manipulated.

God only knew what the government might want with this technology, but theirs was not to question why—theirs was to cash their paychecks.

They had even experienced the procedure them-selves. Wearing a neuromodulation halo—something very like the headband they would later wear to experience the memories unearthed from the recon-structed brains—at one point in their studies Alex had had an entire day of his life excised from his memory. Trisha had found it quite amusing, filling him in on what he'd forgotten.

If Alex could only use that technique now, and erase the memories of Krueger from everyone who had been exposed to his "virus."

How far back would he need to go? Well, for the surviving kids who had sampled the prototype disk, not too far. For himself—the only survivor now of the Séance Project—he'd need to go back to the very first dream memory excavated from the brain models and experienced by him through CIT hook up.

But it could be done. Their own biological hard drives could be reconfigured. The equipment and the software still existed at Macrocosm; Alex thanked God it wasn't amongst the gear he had managed to damage before the police had restrained him.

There were two questions, however. How could he get to that gear when he had been apprehended as a serial killer? And would "unremembering" Krueger truly rob him of his power or was it too late now for that?

"Alex?" Trisha said, pulling him out of his thoughts. "Are you listening to me?"

"Baby, just do like I said. Erase what you can of our data. And keep trying to rouse them. Try *everything.* If you can't wake them up in, say, a half hour, then call 911. Okay?"

"Okay but…"

"And honey, please call Devon. He won't know where I am. You have to tell him."

She sighed. "I will." A pause. "Alex, I'm so scared. I'm so afraid that any minute now, I'm going to see terrible things start happening to these three guys."

"I wish I was there with you. I'm so sorry." Alex squeezed his eyes tightly shut. If he let a single tear escape, he felt like he would lose all his strength along with it. Maybe even his sanity, too. "I'm so, so sorry for all of this."

Springwood High School had just let out for the day, but Autumn Langevin had managed to escape fifteen minutes early. She leaned her back against a tree trunk, watching the students as the old brick building disgorged them. She stood in a pile of fallen leaves so orange they seemed to glow. Around town there were already cardboard skulls grinning out of windowpanes, pumpkins on doorsteps, scarecrows in yards, and of course the stores had been overflowing with Halloween candy, decorations and costumes since August. Needless to say, it was her favorite time of year but it was also the most melancholy time of year, in a romantic kind of way (not melancholy in an exasperating way, like Christmas). It was the time of year when she communed the most with her melancholy, with the acidic kind of rage that bubbled in her deeply and mysteriously. It was a rage she couldn't understand. It seemed out of proportion to anything that might inspire it. It went beyond feelings of abandonment by fathers, mothers, would-be boyfriends. It was a rage at being human, and thinking, and feeling. A rage at being alive.

Only toward the end of the day had she heard that Grace had been absent today. On impulse, Autumn had decided to wait outside for Devon to appear. She was still torn about what she had seen and experienced last night. Torn as to how to act upon what she knew. If she could talk to Devon, alone, it might decide her course of action.

She stood up straighter as she saw him emerge from the building. She felt her heart take one step ahead of her feet. Before she could move in his direction, she heard a horn beeping, and turned to see Ama waving out the driver's window of her secondhand car. There was a silhouetted head in the passenger's seat, but Autumn didn't need to make out the person's features to know who it was.

Devon jogged over to the car, and without waiting to see him get in, Autumn turned her back and swished her feet away through a sea of leaves, glowing like a molten lava that sought to drown the world.

Climbing into Ama's car, Devon teased, "Well, if it isn't those crazy school skippers, Thelma and Louise." His humor was anything but heartfelt, but at the same time he was immensely grateful that Grace was no longer angry at him: she'd greeted him with a radiant smile. He sat leaning forward in the backseat, reaching over the passenger's seat backrest to stroke her hair as they rode along. She took his caressing hand and gave it a quick squeeze.

Ama drove them back to Grace's house. They sought comfort in each other's company after learning what had happened to Milton and Mrs Trice. They needed to talk about that some more, about the danger they were *all* facing now. As Grace and Ama had speculated earlier, what if Krueger no longer needed the TranceBoxes to invade their nightmares? After all, the victims he'd started claiming back in the eightie's, after his first mysterious resurrection, certainly hadn't been using TranceBoxes. So how could they protect themselves, short of never closing their eyes again?

Despite Grace's recent assurance that her father Neil liked him, Devon thought it was more of a strained politeness. Still, Devon and Neil smiled at each other and exchanged a few obligatory niceties in the kitchen. Watching them, Grace had a sudden inspiration, and cut in, "Dad, we're pretty shaken up about our friend. Can Devon sleep over tonight?"

If Neil's smile had been strained before, it looked positively painted on now. "Honey, you know I really don't think it's appropriate for a boy to be sleeping over here. No offense to you, Devon."

"Well," Grace said sweetly, trying to make her tone light and humorous, "I am almost eighteen, you know."

"And what do you mean to suggest? That anything goes now?"

"Daddy, we wouldn't be doing anything! It's just... it's just we're not safe with this killer going around. Devon's parents are away on vacation!"

"I thought you told me his brother is staying there with him. Isn't that right, Devon?"

"Yes, sir."

"Daddy..."

"I'm sorry, honey. Look, you can have Ama sleep over." He turned and smiled at Ama warmly. Ama with her pretty face and chestnut-colored skin. She was no Cassandra Wilcox but there could be only one Cassandra Wilcox in any man's life, right? "You're very welcome to stay here tonight, my love."

"Thanks, Mr Simmons," Ama said in her musical Ghanian accent.

He wagged a finger at her with mock sternness. "When are you going to start calling me Neil?" He turned back toward Grace. "Ama's gonna have to do, honey."

"All right," Grace sighed, throwing Devon an apologetic look.

A few moments later they proceeded upstairs to Grace's room. Just as they crossed its threshold, Devon's cellphone rang.

It was Trisha. Grace and Ama saw the blanched look come over Devon's face as they watched him listen to Trisha's words. "What is it?" Grace whispered, gripping his arm but he raised his index finger, indicating that she should wait.

"I'm coming over," they heard him say into the phone. "No, Trisha, I'm coming over. You need someone to help you. If Alex can't be there, then I will. Okay. Okay. Good. I'm on my way." He pocketed the phone. Practically trembling now with his intensity, Devon locked his striking blue eyes onto Grace's.

"What's wrong, Devon?"

"A lot but I can't take the time to explain. In a couple minutes I'll call you on my cell, and fill you in while I'm on the way."

"On the way where?"

He switched his gaze to Grace's best friend. "Ama, I need a favor. I need you to drive me to Mnemonic Designs—right now."

SIXTEEN

From behind the steering wheel of her used car, Ama looked out dubiously at the rambling old factory building, now converted into office space for small companies like Mnemonic Designs. With the afternoon sun glowing warmly across the red scales of the factory's brick skin, and making the leaves of the trees along the downtown sidewalk glitter as if their ends had been dipped in molten gold, it was hard to imagine that inside that building at this moment a trio of men had dreamed their way into another world.

"Maybe you guys could use my help, too," Ama told Devon as he got out of the passenger's seat.

He slammed the door, then leaned in the window. "No, Ama, you better stay with Grace. Take turns sleeping tonight. If the other person looks like they're having a nightmare, wake them up right away."

"And what if we can't wake up like these guys?" She motioned with her head toward the building. "Somebody has to stop this Krueger, Devon! We can't live the rest of our lives in danger like this."

Devon nodded slowly, his expression determined. It was the expression of a person with an immense weight on his back, but a grave responsibility to fulfill, like a boy turned man by his decision to go off to war.

"You're right," he said, straightening. "We can't."

Trisha was right there to open the door upon his first knock. Devon's heart immediately went out to his brother's girlfriend. Her eyes were reddened from crying, her face pale and puffy, her thick mane of long black hair wild around her face like Shakespeare's Ophelia gone mad. She looked ready to burst into fresh tears—but of gratitude—as she grabbed onto one of Devon's arms and squeezed it. "Oh, Devon, I'm so glad you talked me into letting you come over. I don't know how Alex would feel about that, but I can't stand another minute alone here."

Devon stepped in and she closed and locked the door after him. He looked off toward the lab area. "Krueger's killed two of my best friends in the world. Now my brother is arrested for murder because of him. I want to do everything I can to stop this, Trisha."

She took his hand. "Come on, you can look at them for yourself."

Shane Ryan, with his baseball cap removed, Tim Finney and Dave Schwartz had wheeled their chairs into a little circle. Thanks to Trisha, their respective TranceBoxes no longer rested in their laps and they no longer wore a receptor pad on their temples, but they couldn't have been slumbering deeper had they been cryogenically frozen. It was disconcerting seeing these men this way, since Devon had met them all through Alex before. Shane doted over his girlfriend's two little kids, and Finney was a devoted father of three. It made Devon's blood percolate inside him.

"The last thing I tried," Trisha explained, "was pinching Dave's nose shut and covering his mouth, to see if the lack of oxygen would snap him out of it. He only turned red and coughed a little. Earlier, I burned Finney's thumb with a cigarette lighter. Not that I haven't wanted to do that anyway, from time to time." She attempted a chuckle but it came out tattered.

Devon bent close over Dave and watched his eyes dart back and forth beneath his lids as if they followed a hypnotist's bauble. "They're in REM sleep," he noted.

"And they're atonic—gripped in REM paralysis. In other words, they're dreaming."

"At least they're still alive. For the moment."

"I don't know how long it takes for Krueger to attack a person, they've been out of it for a couple hours already!"

"Maybe," Devon said, "maybe he's holding them somehow. For bait, to lure us in after them."

"Well, he can forget about luring any more of us in there, too."

Devon looked up at her. "That's why I'm here, Trisha. I'm going in."

"What?" she cried, her eyes going frantic. "Are you crazy? So the four of you can get sliced up? No way, Devon. Alex would never let you do that and I won't let you do it, either."

"Trisha, who's left to fight him? At least I know what we're up against now, where these guys didn't. We can't let him go on and on, killing more people. He'll kill every one of us who used the nightmare program, sooner or later, TranceBox or no TranceBox. He's infected us now. Who else can fight him at this point but us?"

"If you did go in, what would you do? Try to kill him? Could he be vulnerable that way, in there?"

"I don't know. I'd kill him if I could. At least, maybe I could find these guys," he gestured toward the three sleepers, "and lead them out of there somehow."

"But think about how the program works, Devon. These dreams originally belonged to other people. When we go in, our identities get blurred because of theirs. And we aren't really aware that we're dreaming, or what we're doing there. It would be like you didn't know about Krueger until he struck, and then it would be too late."

"Maybe. It might go that way. Or maybe what I know now will stick with me. Think of it. At first Krueger himself was limited to reliving these memories the way they were recorded, trapped in their parameters with little room for changing the details. We've seen variations of the same scenarios played over and over. But if he's stronger now, maybe he has more freedom and flexibility to shape his environment. The dreams will lose their walls, their limits. So if he can shake off the rigidness of the original dreams, then maybe we can, too. Step out of our dream roles, like the gladiator, the samurai, and be more ourselves in that world."

"This is all just assumption. Risky assumption."

"Could be. Or it could be intuition. We've been in this world and we've come out alive before. My body, my brain, my soul, whatever had a taste of it, and so now I think I've got some instincts about it. How the game works."

"I've had a sense of gut instinct today, myself," Trisha admitted. "But we came out alive before because Krueger was weaker before. He had only recently been resurrected. I think... I think the more powerful he becomes, the more easily he can kill. And the more he kills, the more powerful he becomes. That's what my instincts are telling me."

"Well, I'll find out soon enough. I'm going in. I'm sorry." He glanced around him. "Tell me you didn't trash the TranceBoxes yet, and the sample disks."

"I've got them in a tote for now. I was erasing hard drives when you came in."

Devon followed Trisha to where she had placed a cardboard tote atop a desk. In it were heaped a number of variously-colored TranceBoxes and clear software jewelboxes. He picked out one of the portable CIT units and popped one of the prototype nightmare disks inside it. Then he looked at Trisha meaningfully. "I had another idea on how to fight Krueger, or rescue these guys, but I feel almost too guilty to even say it."

"What is it?"

"I was wondering if you'd go in there with me."

Trisha's eyes widened. "Oh Devon, oh no."

"It was just a thought. Strength in numbers. I thought it might be possible for us to team up, pool our resources."

"Devon, you're showing me what a brave guy you are. I never knew you had this strength before. But me... I just don't think I have that in me."

He nodded. "I understand." Then he forced a smile. "Anyway, I'd be more afraid of Alex than I am of Krueger, if anything happened to you because of me."

Trisha looked back across the room at her three unconscious friends. Devon held his breath as he watched her. He could see the gears turning, her sense of self preservation arm-wrestling with her concern for others—her fear wrestling with her courage. At last, more to herself than to him, she said, "I worked on this program, too. I'm as much at fault as Alex is. People are dying because of something I had my hand in and you're right." She looked back at him. "We're all going to die from it, sooner or later, anyway. My instincts tell me that, too."

"So we might as well go down swinging, huh?" Devon said.

Into Trisha's eyes came the same fire-forged hardness that had transformed and aged his own boyish features. She said, "Let's just use one box, and we'll program it to transmit to two receiver patches. I don't know, but maybe it will keep us close together, instead of separating us in there. God knows I want you holding my hand through this, if at all possible."

"Okay, that's a good idea." Devon smiled again, as proud of her as she was of him. "I'm not as brave as you think. That's why I want you to hold my hand, too, if at all possible." He reached for her hand now. "Come on. I always did want to sleep with my brother's girlfriend."

"Brat," she said.

Since waking in the waiting room, Devon hadn't met a single soul in the hospital. Was it no longer in service, decommissioned? If so, why was the power on, and what was he doing in here? If it had been evacuated due to a dangerous gas leak, or some other kind of natural or man-made disaster, how had he been overlooked? He touched his head, feeling for wounds that he had been waiting for the ER doctors to tend to. Nothing. So why this maddening amnesia? He was forgetting some very important things, here... he knew that much, at least.

When he had no luck looking for *who?* Who was it he was looking for? His father? Was his father a surgeon here? No, that was ridiculous; his Dad was not a doctor. His Dad was on vacation now, he remembered. He and Devon's Mom were in Italy right now. So who was it he had come here looking for, then? A patient? Anyway, when he had no luck looking for whoever it was he was looking for, he tried the elevators. When he found those were not functioning, he took the stairs to the second floor instead.

The nurse's station was abandoned. For some reason, he had expected to see a woman there with hair that was a thick curly mass, oil black, falling heavily down her back, her dusky skin betraying mixed ethnicity; wide-set eyes as huge and dark as chocolates. A woman who could help him, offer him support. Together, she could help him find the person—persons?—he was looking for but the nurse's station was empty, so reluctantly he went on alone to the first of the patient rooms ahead of him.

There was a man in the room's one bed, hooked up to some softly beeping life support gear on carts. A muted TV on a wall bracket was playing the same gladiator movie that Devon had seen playing on a TV in the ER waiting room downstairs. Was this the person he had come here for? He closed the door behind him—gently, in case the patient was asleep—and heard it click. As he took a step closer to the bed, his toe stubbed something and made it skitter across the floor a little. He saw that it was the TV remote, fallen from the man's hand perhaps. Devon stooped to retrieve it. He then glanced again at the TV, and what he saw there made him jump. The camera was trained on the arena's vast audience, and it was an audience comprised entirely of human skeletons. A crow flew past the camera, startling him. Impossibly, as Devon watched, the right arm of each and every skeleton rose in unison, the hands formed into fists with the thumbs pointing up. Then, every bony hand rotated so that the countless thumbs all pointed downwards.

Devon had to banish this unsettling image. He jabbed the remote toward the TV and pushed the channel advance button. The gladiator movie was replaced with what appeared to be a nature documentary. A vividly green praying mantis had caught another, smaller insect in its serrated front claws and was chewing into its still-living body.

A sound from the bed made Devon glance that way sharply, in time to witness a brief spray of sparks into the air. A puff of black smoke followed, coiling out of the chest of the man who lay there. Concerned, Devon rushed to his side. Had the man's life support system shorted out? But when Devon looked down at the patient, he saw something far more alarming.

A bomb was strapped to the man's chest, under his open pajama top.

It looked crude, but very effective. There were multiple sticks of dynamite taped in a row, and wires affixed to a little electronic device. It was from this electronic component that the black smoke continued to rise. There was no ticking sound, so Devon didn't know if the explosive device was already activated and if so, how long there might be before it went off.

He returned his attention to the remote in his hand. Had his changing of the channels affected the electronic device? The thought terrified him. One wrong button touch might detonate the bomb! Delicately, he set the remote down on the man's bedside table before returning his attention to the patient.

Was he a terrorist? A hijacker? A desperate bank robber who had threatened to blow the place up if it didn't empty its drawers for him? The last thing Devon expected to see, at this point, was the face of Shane Ryan—his brother Alex's boss at Mnemonic Designs. Despite the fact that Shane's face was swollen and bruised from some accident or savage beating, the top of his head swathed in bandages and a breathing tube snaking through one nostril, Devon recognized him immediately. He realized then that Shane was the person he had come here looking for.

No, not just Shane. Dave Schwartz, too. And Tim Finney. Alex's and Trisha's other Mnemonic coworkers.

Trisha!

Trisha was supposed to be here with him, somewhere close by. That had been the plan, anyway. He rushed to the door, hoping to call out for his brother's girlfriend, but he found that the doorknob would not turn. He had inadvertently locked himself in.

All this time Shane's life support system had gone on beeping in the background, but suddenly the sound changed. Devon whirled around. Shane had just flat-lined. "Oh my God!" he cried, and he began pounding on the door desperately. He shouted, "Hey out there! Trisha! Somebody! Hey! Help!"

Devon darted back to Shane's side, looking around for a call button with which to summon a nurse, but he saw none. Helplessly, he stared down at the young man's battered but peaceful face. He had suffered no final convulsion, gone into no death throes. He'd simply succumbed while in his coma. Apparently his head wounds, no doubt damaging his brain, had been too much for him. He was dead.

Devon felt a crushing despair, a sense of failure. A more frantic feeling arose then. He must get out of this room. He might still find Dave and Finney before it was too late. And Trisha. He had to join forces with Trisha.

An awful squealing noise, like fingernails on a blackboard, caused Devon to spin around and stare at the locked door. His eyes were drawn to the window set into it. The hallway out there was dark now, as if the lights had been shut off since he had come in here. Devon could not see who it was who had made the clawing sound on the other side of the glass but through it, muffled, he heard a deep and sinister chuckle.

"Krueger," he whispered, then remembered everything.

Bells jingled when Trisha pushed the glass door inward, heralding her entrance into the convenience store, one of a chain sprinkled throughout this and neighboring states. It was night outside, and the transition from that pitch blackness into the fluorescent glare and the shelves' riot of colors made her squint for a moment. The light aggravated an imminent headache, a sudden throb of pain in the rear of her skull, and she paused near the counter for a moment to rub at the spot with her fingers before moving on into the convenience store's aisles.

"Devon?" she called, but in a subdued voice, as if she didn't belong here and was afraid to attract the attention of anyone other than her boyfriend's brother. She felt Devon should be in the store, but at the moment her mind was blank as to what he would be doing here, and the reason why she was looking for him at all. Maybe it was this abrupt headache that distracted her, hid her thoughts behind the glare of pain?

Halfway down the aisle, she glanced back at the register. No one was behind the counter, but was that where Devon was supposed to be? Had he found himself an after-school job here?

She decided to check the back room. It could be that Devon was putting away some new stock, or bringing out stock to replenish the shelves. In fact, as she started walking toward the rear of the store, she thought she heard a muffled sound from behind the swinging door. On her way, however, something in the freezer drew her eyes. Frowning, she stepped closer to the misted glass doors for a clearer look.

At first she couldn't quite accept what she was seeing in there. Was that a human hand? Steeling herself, Trisha opened the door in one wide swing.

Cold washed over her, sank into her flesh, an arctic blast that seemed to freeze her where she stood. It wasn't really the cold that paralyzed her— it was the horror at what she was seeing, there in the freezer, on several of its lowermost shelves.

There was indeed a hand. And another hand, a leg and various other naked and frost-crusted parts of a human body. They had been dismembered and stacked in the freezer like just another product waiting to be purchased.

Trisha wanted to scream, but she restrained herself. Somehow, she wasn't as surprised about this discovery as she should have been. Somehow, she felt like she had even been expecting it. And when she heard the happy little tinkling sound of the bells over the front door, she turned toward the sound with a dreadful kind of inevitability.

The hideous figure standing at the front of the store was a man whose bald head was a mass of badly burned and badly healed scar tissue. Perhaps to hide some of the wounding, he wore a battered brown fedora atop his head. Below that, the man wore a ragged, oil-stained green and red striped sweater, dark brown pants and work boots. Around the neck of the sweater was a bulky necklace of clearly authentic skulls, though the skulls were so small they must have been those of very young children. The oddest feature of all was that the striped sweater had four sleeves, seeing as the man had two pairs of arms, swimming in the air around him as if in some stylized dance as he began to stalk slowly toward her.

"Krueger," Trisha said in a tremulous voice. She was beginning to remember things now.

As she watched him come, a third eye—vertical in orientation—opened in the middle of Krueger's scarred forehead. "I see you've found your way back to my store again," he said, smirking. "You can run—but you can't hide from what you are, my little Indian princess."

On one of his right hands, the entity called Krueger wore a glove of leather and plated metal, the glove's four fingers supporting long, curved, single-edged knife blades. The fist was closed, just the index finger blade extended—and this blade was slick with fresh blood.

In one of the double left hands, Krueger held a human head by its hair. The head's eyes were half-closed, the mouth slack, its skin bluish and sparkling with frost. Despite this, Trisha recognized its features. Along with the body parts stacked in the freezer, this was all that remained of her Mnemonic Designs coworker, David Schwartz. Poor Dave who had clearly had such a powerful crush on her. She emitted a loud sob, and at last tears started filling her eyes, her newly fire-forged exterior beginning to crack and crumble.

Krueger placed the point of his index finger-knife under the decapitated head's bottom jaw and worked it up and down like the mouth of a ventriloquist's dummy. Krueger taunted her, "Tha-tha-that's all, folks!"

As Krueger danced ever nearer, Trisha had been unconsciously shuffling backwards, until at last her shoulder-blades contacted the cold glass of the freezer. She whimpered and suddenly whipped her head to the left and right in search of a weapon, but she saw nothing promising within reach. Facing forward again, at the top of her lungs she screamed, "Devon!"

The door at the rear of the store burst open. A figure came charging through it, holding aloft a crowbar used to open crates. Tim Finney let out an inarticulate bellow like a war cry.

"There you are!" Krueger snarled, looking less amused now as he switched his attention from Trisha to her coworker. He hurled Dave's severed head at Finney, but without losing his momentum Finney dodged it like a quick little boxer ducking under a slower boxer's wild swing. Trisha heard the flung head slam sickeningly into the wall to her left. A moment after he had thrown the head, Krueger was lunging with his knife glove, its one extended finger like a thrusting sword blade, but Finney swung the crowbar and it struck Krueger hard on the wrist. The impact slapped his arm out to one side. Trisha thought she had even heard the sharp crack of splintered bone.

Krueger howled. It was the first time in all the dreams that Trisha had seen or sensed him in, that she had heard him utter a cry of dismay. Of *pain*. Such was the price he had to pay for becoming *real* again.

"Run, Trisha!" Finney yelled, flailing madly with the crowbar so as to give the creature no opening for its remaining three hands. The sheer tornado-like intensity of his attack was making Krueger back off a reluctant step at a time. *"Go!"* Finney ordered her.

Trisha dashed to her right to plunge down another aisle, away from the two opponents. She made it to the front of the store, past the register, and seized hold of the door handle. The bells above the door jingled a little when she pulled but the door would not open. She jerked at it again and again but it would not budge. *Locked!*

She looked back and realized that Krueger was drawing closer, Finney on the opposite side of him. With her trapped at the front of the store, Finney was inadvertently driving Krueger right in her direction. Krueger realized this, too. Suddenly he whirled, latching his three hateful eyes onto her—and rushed at her.

Maybe he intended to seize her and use her as a human shield to get Finney to relent in his berserker-like assault. But Finney wasn't going to let Krueger get his three unwounded hands on her. He tore after the monster with a frantic burst of speed and sprang like a leopard, hurling himself onto the dream-stalker's back.

Trisha fell back against the door, as if staring down an out-of-control locomotive. For several delirious moments, Finney rode upon the killer's back. He managed to swing the crowbar around in front of Krueger, then pulled it back across his throat and held it there in both fists in an effort to crush his Adam's apple. One of Krueger's frenzied hands clawed at Finney's head, trying to snatch onto his hair, but it was cut too short.

Suddenly, the sheer forward motion of the two grappling men hurtled them straight into the convenience store's front window, only a couple of feet to Trisha's left. She instinctively covered her face with both arms, so she didn't see it, but the sound was explosive as the plate glass window shattered. She heard a rain of tinkling ice, each tiny crash a receding echo of the first ear-splitting crystalline burst.

Trisha uncovered her eyes and observed the damage—the gaping black portal, like a hole smashed into the very fabric of reality. Through it she saw only a lightless void. She couldn't hear whether the two men still tangled in the parking lot, rolling together on the ground or perhaps back on their feet to square off again. Going through this hole seemed to be her only avenue of escape from this world. It was the direction she had come from when she'd entered the store in the first place.

She swept aside some merchandise on display in front of the window, then stepped up onto its low ledge. Glittering shards crackled under her sandals. Trisha ducked into the large opening carefully, afraid to gash herself on the threatening icicles of glass. She made it safely through, dropping to the floor of the parking lot outside.

Still she heard no noises from the two men. Still she saw nothing at all ahead of her in the darkness, so utter that it seemed to swallow up all light and sound like a black hole in space. But she started jogging forward, blindly, into the heart of that black hole until it swallowed her up, too.

Trisha's eyes flew open. She sat up abruptly in her chair, ripping the adhesive patch off her right temple.

Opposite her, also wearing a TranceBox receptor pad, was Devon. He was reclining in his own chair, his eyes still closed.

Trisha flew to his side and began shaking him. "Devon!" she pleaded. "Wake up, please wake up!" She peeled off his white patch, then scooped up the TranceBox they had both been tuned into. So much for teaming up in their dreams! She powered the device down, removed the disk, and was about to resume her efforts to awaken Devon when her eyes fell on her three Mnemonic Designs coworkers, their chairs clustered in a little circle a short distance away.

For the moment, Trisha abandoned Devon to rush to Shane's side. She was shocked to see how battered he was, his eyes purple and swollen shut, blood running from his smashed nose. She felt his wrist for a pulse, and found none. Next, she switched her attention to Tim Finney. His face and hands were terribly lacerated, and there was an especially deep gash across his throat. Blood still ran freely from this gaping wound, pattering to the floor to form a spreading pool. He was clearly dead, but whether he had sustained these injuries from the glass he had smashed through or whether they had been inflicted by Krueger's knife hand, she did not know. She hoped it was the former. She hoped he had died as a result of his own sacrifice, and not at the hands of that monster.

Lastly, she turned to Dave and began reaching for his shoulder, but then stopped herself. His face was unnaturally white, almost blue, and still sparkled subtly with thawing ice crystals. She saw the bloodless line of severance at his neck, and was afraid that if she touched him even lightly, his entire body would tumble to pieces like a house of cards.

"Oh God," she wailed, letting out all of her anguish and fear at once. "Oh *God!*"

A hand alighted on her shoulder, and Trisha spun around to see Devon standing there, looking weary but awake. Thank God, awake.

She threw himself into his arms and sobbed, "Oh, Devon! I thought you were trapped in there, too!"

Over her shoulder, Devon took in her three slain coworkers. He could only look at them for several moments before he closed his eyes and buried his face in Trisha's hair. All his hard-won strength seemed to drain out of him then. He felt crushed, completely helpless, just another pig waiting for its appointment with the butcher.

SEVENTEEN

The girls had been very quiet for a while now, and peeking into his daughter's room, Neil Simmons discovered why. Grace and her best friend Ama were curled up asleep in bed, back pressed to back, dressed in their clothes except for their shoes. A subdued glow of late afternoon sun through the curtains seemed to preserve them in a moment of frozen time, likes two flies embedded in amber. Grace's radio still played softly, like a lullaby.

A while back, Ama had briefly left to give Devon a lift somewhere. Watching her sleeping form from the doorway, Neil was glad she had returned. His eyes drifted very slowly, like a lingering caress, across the contours of her body. The lush hill of her hip, in profile. Her full thighs, gripped in tight blue jeans. Down to the pale soles of her bare feet. His gaze dwelt on her toes, which he imagined taking into his lips and sucking, savoring, one by one by one.

He nearly groaned with his longing. It had been so long since he had been intimate with a woman. In fact, not since his wife had died in her tumble down the basement stairs. Much, much too long. And now, because of what Grace had told him about the brains used by Devon's brother at Macrocosm Research, Cassandra Wilcox had returned from the dead to haunt his own brain, a ghost who could be locked away for a time but never exorcized. She was both his dearest and most dreaded memory.

Neil took one stealthy step into his daughter's room. At any moment he was afraid that the barest ripples of the air, displaced by his body, would awaken one or the other of the sleeping teenagers. With another step, and another, their faces remained passive and their breathing soft and even until at last, Neil stood by the edge of the bed, directly over Ama.

As if it willed its own movement, he watched his hand float toward her neck. Lightly, ever so lightly, his fingertips came into contact with the beautiful dark skin there. They trailed along its curve in a whisper.

A flutter came over Ama's features; she knitted her brows and muttered in her sleep. Swiftly, Neil withdrew to the doorway. He slipped around the corner out of sight just as he heard the bedsprings squeak, Ama propping herself up to gaze groggily around her.

"Oh dear," Neil heard her say in that charming Ghanian accent of hers, keeping her voice low so as not to wake Grace, "we *both* fell asleep."

The bedsprings squeaked again. She was getting up from the bed. Neil withdrew further, ducking into his own bedroom just a little further down the upstairs hallway. From the darkness there, he heard Ama pad barefoot from Grace's room and let herself into the bathroom. He emerged from his bedroom again, inching closer to the bathroom door, which Ama had left ajar.

He could hear a subtle liquid tinkling. The sound gave him a strong mental image, alluring in its crude earthiness. He closed his eyes, rested his head back against the wall of the hallway, and shuddered. He had tried, all these years. He had tried to keep things buried.

The toilet flushed, and there came the sound of water running in the sink. Neil opened his eyes and followed the sound like a dark river to its source.

"Graaace."

Grace Simmons raised her head from her pillow and swung her legs over the side of the bed. As always, despite her fear and the pain that now constricted her throat, she followed the voice as it cried out to her distantly, mournfully.

"Graaace."

She left her bedroom and slowly descended the carpeted stairs to her house's first floor. Without the voice having to cry out a third time, she knew from terrible programming to turn zombie-like into the kitchen. She knew to seek out the polished dark wood of the closed basement door.

She watched her small hand reach, trembling, to the knob as if expecting its brass to be heated by a fire on the other side of the door, the metal hot enough to scorch her skin but when she finally closed her fingers around it, of course it was cool to the touch. Maybe even too cool. Just like always.

"Graaace."

Grace did not hesitate very long in turning the knob. It was, after all, inevitable. She must obey the hollow and imploring voice, however much it frightened her. At this moment, she would have preferred opening the stone door of a crypt stacked with rotting coffins but this didn't stop her from drawing the door wide and flicking on the light switch to reveal the figure that patiently waited for her on the lowermost step.

It might have been a doppelganger of herself. Small, delicate, with matted hair hanging in the face to obscure it, cut shorter than her own but still wavy and dark. The figure wore a thin white summer nightgown, its arms just as white as they rose up, slowly, to reach toward Grace with crooked, splayed fingers. Several of the fingers were broken, bent at sickening angles, and the pallid flesh of the slim arms was slick with fresh blood than sluiced with nauseating slowness from ragged gashes and lacerations. Through the strands of hair masking the face, Grace could see the glint of light on hidden eyes, and the glisten of moist lips, open wide in a haunting, beseeching call:

"Graaace."

"Mom," Grace sobbed.

With horrible suddenness, as if it had been precariously balanced upon her slender neck, the woman's head pitched to one side and hung there crookedly. But the glinting eyes did not appear to blink.

Never before had her mother's energy seemed so urgent, so magnetic, her will seeming to overpower Grace's own. For the very first time, Grace took one shaky step downward. Then another. A third. A fourth. She reached across herself to grip the handrail in both fists in an attempt to halt her descent. The mother and daughter seemed locked in a silent tug-of-war.

Now, for the first time, Grace's mother spoke words other than her daughter's name but these words came out muddled, garbled, impossible to distinguish, as if her broken neck choked them off halfway up her throat. It was a sound that caused gooseflesh to crawl across Grace's body.

Her mother gave up on trying to say whatever it was she had attempted to get across. Instead, she touched her left elbow with her right hand, dabbing her fingers into a wound gouged there in her basement fall. With her blood-slick fingers, Grace's mother reached to the wall beside her and began to paint in sluggish, laborious strokes. She had to dip her fingers in the blood several times more in order to complete the message but Grace could understand it even before the second word was complete. Two words that simply read: YOUR FATHER.

Grace understood the words, but she didn't understand their meaning. Her father? Did she want Grace to go fetch her father now? If she wanted to see her dad, why had she come into her dreams instead?

Was her mom trying to warn Grace of some danger Dad was in, or some danger that he represented?

And then, intuitively—as if her mother was finally able to convey the knowledge to her telepathically—Grace understood all. The mind-blasting, heart-breaking truth that her mother had returned again and again in her dreams to tell her.

Her father. *Her father...*

Grace's mom had not tripped down the basement stairs in an accident. She had been *pushed*. Shoved, no doubt in a fit of anger. An impulsive act of hatred.

Grace's father had murdered her mother.

"Mom," Grace sobbed again, almost hysterical with grief. "Oh no... no... Mommy..."

She was so filled with aching sympathy for her mother that Grace let go of her double grip on the handrail. Following her own will now, she continued descending the stairs as her mother had been beckoning her to do through all the many recurring dreams. Grace would close her eyes and take her mother into her arms. Maybe that act of compassion would fulfill the spirit and allow it to finally move on.

When Grace was two-thirds of the way down, her mother abruptly pivoted and stepped out of view— deeper into the basement.

"Mom?" Grace cried, quickening her pace down the rest of the steps. "Mom?" When she touched the concrete floor, cold under her bare feet, she too turned into the basement itself.

The basement was huge. Vast. Pipes criss-crossed the ceiling and communicated between ceiling and floor like the roots of titanic trees soaring above this cavern. Machinery of unknown purpose hunched within the web-like networks of plumbing. Steam hissed out of ruptures in the pipes and out from around valves on boiler tanks, here and there. The only light came from red emergency bulbs protected inside little wire cages.

In the distance, Grace saw her mother's back for a moment as she disappeared into a cloud of steam, which in the scarlet light looked like a huge hemorrhaged brain. Grace hurried after her. "Mom!" she called again.

Chains hung from the ceiling, tinkling. Water dripped down from above in places. Grace flinched when a fresh spurt of steam hissed to life beside her as she passed. Pushing one of the vine-like chains out of her path, Grace saw her mother take another turn ahead of her. She broke into a little trot to catch up.

This was not her basement; she knew that now. That was okay because she also knew this was a dream.

When Grace emerged from another boiling mass of steam, it was to find her mother waiting for her a little farther on. Grace came to a stop. She still ached to embrace her, but the apparition's terrifying appearance gave her a moment's pause. She had to gather her strength before she approached.

Before Grace could do that, another figure appeared from behind a bank of circuitry and stood beside her mother. A man in a green and red striped sweater with a fedora on his head, who seized Grace's mother by the throat with his left hand and plunged his gloved right hand's knife-fingers deep into her mid-section.

"Mommy!" Grace shrieked.

More horrible than Grace's mother making some tortured sound was the fact that she made no sound at all. She just went limp in Krueger's hands as he jerked the knife blades out of her gushing stomach. Then he flung her slack body to one side, out of sight, like a puppet whose purpose in the play had been served and who was no longer needed.

"Oh," Krueger rasped in that mocking, distorted voice of his, "Grace wants her Mommy? I know how you feel—my own Mom was a saint."

"You bastard!" Grace screamed at him, red-faced and impotent in her rage.

"I am a bastard, I admit. You know, you should consider yourself lucky, Grace." He took a menacing step forward. "You have only one maniac for a father. I've got a hundred of them!" And with that, he spread his arms out like wings and charged at her, laughing.

Grace spun on her bare heels and took to flight, diving blindly into the red-glowing fog of steam.

Neil pushed the ajar bathroom door open, startling Ama as she was drying her hands on a towel

She laughed, embarrassed. "Mr Simmons, you scared me!"

He smiled. "Neil."

"Neil," she corrected. "I'm all done in here now." She moved forward as if to let him have his turn in the bathroom, but he didn't step out of her way, so that her movement only brought them closer together in the little room.

"Did you have a good nap?" he asked, putting both his hands on the eighteen year-old girl's shoulders, squeezing them and rubbing his thumbs under her collarbone to massage her. "Feeling better now?"

Ama's bright grin looked nervous, uncomfortable. "Yeah, but I didn't mean to doze off. I was supposed to watch Grace while she slept."

"Oh yeah? Why?" Still rubbing. Squeezing.

"Well," Ama replied evasively, "she's just upset after everything that's happened. She's afraid to have nightmares."

"I see. You're such a good friend, Ama. Such a sweet, sweet girl." Neil's hands ran down the outsides of Ama's arms as he stepped even closer to her, his body only inches away. He leaned in to kiss her lingeringly on the cheek near her ear. "A very sweet and lovely girl."

Ama chuckled and lightly tried to push him back. "Thank you, Neil."

Neil's heart was at full gallop in his chest. He withdrew his lips from her cheek, only to reapply them a few inches lower, on the tight skin of her neck. He pressed his nose against it to inhale its warm smell, as his arms began to encircle her back in an embrace.

"Neil!" Ama whispered, twisting more urgently in his arms now. "Please!"

"Please," he echoed her, his embrace tightening as his lips shifted to another spot on her neck. One hand slid up under the back of her shirt, across the smooth expanse of skin there. The other drifted lower to cup one of her bottom's full cheeks through the snug casing of her jeans. "Ama, please come to my room with me. I'll make you feel good, baby, so good."

"No!" Ama said, more loudly and more forcefully. Though generally good-natured and cheerful, Grace had known Ama to have a hot temper. That temper flared up in her now.

"Please, baby," Neil cooed huskily.

"Stop it!" Ama shouted, not caring if Grace heard them anymore. She was a solid girl, strong, and she shoved at Neil with all the power she could put into it. Taken by surprise, he flew back from her, and the little bathroom rug he stood upon slipped out from under his feet. Neil went toppling backwards and Ama heard the back of his head crack hard against the edge of the shower stall as he thudded to the floor.

"Oh God! Oh my God!" Ama gushed, regretting her actions. She dropped to her knees beside the man and shook him. "Neil! Neil!"

He did not respond. The blow to his head had rendered him unconscious. His eyes were closed and his mouth was open slightly, as if he was only peacefully asleep.

Grace was running, running, bashing her shoulders against dangling chains and almost tripping over pipes rooted into the floor. She ducked down this aisle of the maze, then that, but the industrial labyrinth was of seemingly limitless proportions. Which was the way back to her basement steps—or had they ceased to exist altogether?

She was turning down another narrow passage, hoping to keep Krueger off her trail, when a figure stepped directly into her path and grabbed her by the arms.

"Grace!" her father blurted, his eyes wild. "Oh dear God, where is this place? How did we get in here?"

With a cry of revulsion, Grace shoved her father away from her. Now her own eyes went wide, but with fury rather than fear. "*You!* You killed my mother!"

"Wha... what?" Neil Simmons looked helplessly around him. "Grace... please... I don't understand any of this! What's happening?"

"Why, Daddy? Why did you kill her—*why?*"

"Who said that? Who told you I did that?"

"*She* did, you bastard!"

"She did? That's impossible. She..."

"I hate to break up this little family reunion," croaked a self-amused, sadistic voice as another figure stepped out of the churning steam. Freddy Krueger wagged his index knife-finger at Neil as if scolding a naughty boy. "Well, well, well, if it isn't the Springwood Slasher."

"Who are you?" Neil demanded, trying to sound firm despite the tremor in his voice.

"Well, I thought *I* was the Springwood Slasher, but then you started taking over my job for me. I would have been more than happy to cut up that

Cassandra Wilcox bitch myself, Neil. You shouldn't have assumed to sign my name to your own sloppy handiwork."

"I don't know what you're talking about!" Neil roared.

"What did you do, Daddy?" Grace demanded.

"I didn't do anything!" he cried like a petulant child. "I didn't do anything!" Then he shoved past his daughter and bolted, before either of his accusers could torment him any more. From around the corner of a bulky machine a white arm emerged, close to the floor, and its gnarled hand seized him by the ankle. Caught off balance, Neil dropped heavily onto his chest. Grace saw him kicking out at whoever had gripped his ankle, but they would not release him. He blubbered hysterically and tried dragging himself away on his belly. In doing so, he also dragged along the person who had grasped onto his leg.

It was his wife. Grace's mother. Bleeding though she was, she had managed to pull herself along through the hellish boiler room on her belly. Her eyes gleamed vengefully through the mask of her dark hair.

"Thanks, Mom," Krueger said, calmly walking over to Neil and planting a boot in the small of his back. His reached down and knotted the fingers of his left hand in Neil's hair, lifting his head up. Then he curled the blades of his right hand around the front of Neil's throat.

For a terrible moment, Grace and her father locked eyes. His were crazed and desperate, still pleading. For a fraction of that second she felt a stab of pity for him. Then that pity was gone, and she seized the opportunity by sprinting off into the red-lit gloom.

Behind her, she heard a man's long, gurgling scream.

"Please wake up, please!" Ama begged, shaking Grace. Why couldn't she rouse her? Ama was close to tears now. But just as she was going to shake her again, Grace's eyelids snapped open. She grabbed onto Ama's arms.

"Ama," Grace slurred, the mists in her mind dispersing.

"Grace, something happened to your father. I, oh… we have to call an ambulance—hurry!" Ama pulled her smaller friend out of bed, dragging her by the hand into the hall and on to the bathroom. But when the two of them looked in, its white floor tiles glowed blankly. "Where is he?" Ama panted, looking about frantically. "Where did he go? We have to find him, Grace!"

Grace knew where to look. "This way," she muttered, and this time she dragged Ama along by the hand. Downstairs, and on into the kitchen. There, Grace opened the dark wooden door leading down into their basement, and reached out to flick on the wall switch.

When the light came on, it illuminated Neil Simmons lying below them at the base of the cellar stairs, sprawled on the floor with his head at the center of a widening pond of blood.

EIGHTEEN

"I destroyed everything I could think of," Trisha said to Devon as she drove them toward the police station, "but I'm not thinking straight and I may have forgotten something. Alex can help me remember." She gestured with her head toward the cardboard tote full of TranceBoxes and jewelboxes containing the prototype disk in the backseat. "And then there's that stuff."

"We still need to gather up Grace's and Ama's disks, and Autumn's," Devon said, "to account for everything." He glanced out the window as they rode along, noting that evening was stealthily encroaching on the town of Springwood, and said, "Trisha, why don't you drop me off at Autumn's place before you go on to the police station. I know I could just call her and tell her to destroy it, but I want to see her disk in my hand. Also, I was thinking, now that Shane, Dave and Tim are dead, the cops will know the killer is still on the loose, and they'll let Alex go. With my luck, they'll think *I'm* the one who killed those guys, 'cause I was at the scene. You know?"

"Yeah, that's a thought. You have a connection to all the victims, either directly or through Alex. Okay, then, I'll go on to the police alone, tell them I found my coworkers slaughtered at Mnemonic and hopefully get Alex out of there as quickly as possible. Presumably they won't think I'm the murderer! So which way to Autumn's house?"

He told her. While they headed in that direction, Devon called Grace on his cellphone. She picked up right away. "Devon!" she said, having seen his number appear on her cell's screen.

In a mad flurry of words, he told her what he and Trisha had experienced and about the three dead men they'd left behind at Mnemonic.

Her tone somber, Grace told him, "My father is dead, too."

"What?" Devon exclaimed.

"I'll tell you later. I can't talk about it now."

"But…"

"I'm okay, Devon." She sounded calm, in a burnt-out and fatalistic way. "Don't worry about me right now. Anyway, Ama and I already destroyed our sample disks, snipped them to pieces. Just go get Autumn's disk and call me back when you can. Meanwhile, I'm going to call the police about my Dad. Well, I'll call them as soon as I can get myself to talk to them about it."

"Oh, Grace, I'm so sorry!"

"Yeah," she said. "Okay, I love you, Devon."

These beautiful words, on top of the shocking news she had just related, blanked his mind for several seconds, but Devon eventually got out, "I love you, too." Then Grace disconnected.

Before arriving at Autumn's, Devon thought it couldn't hurt to call first to be sure she was home, let her know he was coming, but the phone rang and rang unanswered. He gave up trying; they would be there soon enough anyway.

When Trisha did pull up in front of Autumn's house, Devon noticed there was only a single car in the driveway. One of her parents must not have been at home, or else the two of them had taken one car together. Maybe Autumn had even gone with them, hence the unanswered phone. Devon looked up at the second floor windows, frowning. The windows regarded him coldly, too, like the eyes of a gigantic skull. An odd sense of intuition tickled his brain again. He felt very strongly that Autumn was home—up there, behind one of those veiled windows. With a grim sense of purpose, he reached around in back to pluck one of the TranceBoxes out of the tote. Next he took a prototype disk from its jewelbox—the disk shimmering like the steel of a knife blade—and inserted it into the TranceBox. With that intense look on his face, he resembled a soldier slotting a magazine of bullets into his gun.

"What are you doing?" Trisha asked, horrified.

"We can't destroy all of these yet. Look how we needed to go in after Shane, Tim and Dave."

"And it didn't do them any good, did it?" Trisha reminded him. "All it did was almost get you and me killed. You leave that here, Devon."

He ignored her and let himself out of the car. "Go get my brother out of jail, Trisha."

She glared out at him. "Don't you do anything cocky! It was reckless of us to go in before. We can't risk it again."

"This is just an 'in case of emergency break glass' measure," he reassured her, holding the device up.

"Oh yeah? Well, you'd be better off with a fire axe instead of that thing."

Without another word, Devon started up the front walk to the house, but he did glance back to give a brief wave before he began knocking on the front door. Trisha continued watching, in case no one was home and he still needed a ride. Devon knocked again. No answer. He looked at Trisha, shrugged, and tried the knob. Locked.

Trisha saw Devon kneel down and inspect the series of water-rounded stones that bordered flower beds to either side of the front step. He weighed each rock in his hand. What was he going to do—hurl one through the front window? But then Trisha saw him crack one of these rocks open into two halves in his hands. A hollow plastic replica. She couldn't help but smile. Smart kid, just like his brother. Devon held up the key to show her, grinning triumphantly, then fitted it into the door knob. He let himself inside the house, then shut the door behind him.

With a reluctant sigh, Trisha continued on toward the police station.

Stand there, baulked and dumb, stuttering and stammering, hissed and hooted, stand

and strive, until, at last, rage draws out of thee
that dream-power which every night shows
thee is thine own; a power transcending all
limit and privacy, and by virtue of which a man
is the conductor of the whole river of electricity.

— Ralph Waldo Emerson, *The Poet.*

These were the words—in red letters against a
black background—that Devon read off Autumn's
computer screen as he leaned over her shoulder.

He could smell the shampoo of her freshly-
washed, long and straight blonde hair. He could
also smell a pizza scent from her slightly parted
lips. Downstairs he had seen a greasy pizza box on
the kitchen table, a few crust ends still inside it.
Her parents had probably bought it for her before
heading off to wherever it was they had gone.
Devon was relieved that when they had gone, they
hadn't activated the security system that he'd seen
next to the door upon letting himself into the
house—though maybe it was Autumn who had
neglected to turn it on.

She wore a black, long-sleeved top that clung to
her slender frame, making inviting bumps of her
breasts that a primitive part of Devon's mind kept
dragging his eyes back to, despite all the serious
matters at hand. Baggy black pants, black combat
boots, like a commando ready to be parachuted
into dangerous territory. Her eyes were heavily out-
lined in black, too. Her makeup-shaded lids were
closed. And, like a bandage over a wound, a
wound penetrating straight through her skull and

into her brain, there was a white adhesive patch stuck to her right temple.

Devon had set down his own TranceBox upon entering her room, and had immediately picked hers up instead. He had shut it off and removed the disk from it. Now, he even peeled the receptor pad from her temple and shook her by the shoulders. "Autumn!" he commanded. "Autumn, wake up now!" But like a hypnotist who had lost control of his subject, he could not arouse her from her trance. She was a tainted Snow White, enchanted by a poisoned apple. A flawed Sleeping Beauty.

His gaze returned to the computer monitor, as he once more tried to make sense of what he was seeing there. It appeared to be the front page of a website called FALL LEAVES—THE FREE DOWNLOAD LADY. Instead of viewing the page live on the internet, it looked like the page had been called up into a website construction program. Animated fall leaves continuously floated down from the top of the screen to the bottom. A cheesy-sounding electronic version of the lovely song *Forever Autumn* by Justin Hayward of the Moody Blues played in the background. And there was a photo of a man centered on the screen, above that Emerson quote.

Devon's eyes lingered on the man. He looked increasingly familiar. Blondish curly hair, a rather prominent nose. An unsettling sort of sneering grin as the man stared directly, defiantly, at the camera that had captured this image.

"Oh my God!" Devon muttered, finally realizing who the man was. It was a photo he had seen of

Freddy Krueger in one of the police files Autumn had broken into on the Springwood police's private intranet site. A photo taken of the man when he had been apprehended for his crimes—shortly before being released due to that faulty arrest warrant. Devon hadn't recognized him at first, associating Krueger only with his scar-faced, undead manifestation. "Don't tell me she's in love with this bastard," Devon said then, thinking of the disturbed and pathetically needy women who fell in love with serial killers like the so-called Night Stalker and the Gainesville Ripper. He prayed the image of the mortal Freddy Krueger was only there to shock, instead.

What was the purpose of the site? Well... "free download;" Devon guessed that pretty much said it all. Obviously, the site belonged to Autumn. But what did Krueger have to do with it? Devon looked around the page some more, then took hold of Autumn's mouse. When he moved the cursor over the image of Krueger, it turned into a hand symbol. Not a little white hand with one finger pointing, it was a tiny leather and metal glove with a pointing knife blade for a finger. The picture of Krueger was a clickable link. Not only that, but when the cursor changed to that tiny razored glove, a text box also materialized. It read: "To download the NIGHTMARE PROGRAM, click here."

"Oh no," Devon said. "Oh fuck no."

He saw that in the tool bar at the bottom of the screen there was a collapsed window. He clicked on it and brought the window up. It was a progress box, monitoring the rate at which a file was being transferred. And the text in the window read:

Import of NIGHTMARE PROGRAM to FALL LEAVES SITE 76% complete.

"Fuck," Devon chanted, "fuck, fuck, fuck! Autumn, what the hell are you *doing?*" There was an option to cancel the transfer, and he immediately clicked on it.

The slow transfer of the huge, complex file continued. Now 77% complete.

Devon reached over to the computer's tower and punched the power button but its green light remained on. He then hunkered down under the desk and flipped the orange-glowing switch on the surge protector. That should have killed all power to her system, with its two interconnected computers.

78% complete.

Gritting his teeth, Devon crawled further under the desk, brushing past Autumn's boots, and took hold of the surge protector's plug where it was slotted into the wall socket. When he closed his hand on it, a current of raw electricity flowed through his hand, up his arm, and seemed to punch him right in the heart. Devon was thrown back onto the carpet, stunned, his hand zapped numb and his eyes wide.

But his eyes were wide because the face on the screen was moving. Speaking. And it was no longer the face of the mortal Freddy Krueger, but his horribly burnt alter ego.

"You can look, Devon, but you'd better not touch. Something important is happening here and you don't want to meddle."

"Let Autumn go, leave her alone!" Devon blurted, hardly believing he could speak with Krueger while awake. Had the blast of electricity knocked him unconscious?

"Autumn's finally come to her senses, so I think it's *you* who should leave her alone, little boy. A person has to side with the winning team. And you, you're definitely a loser."

"She can't be helping you!" Devon snarled, slowly regaining his feet.

"Why shouldn't she? What else has she got? Two parents who leave her alone in the house with a psycho killer on the loose? A killer who made a shish kabob out of her own boyfriend?"

"No, no, I don't believe it. You must be manipulating her!"

"People manipulate themselves, kid, and blame it on fall guys like me. I'm just a patsy!"

"She's a smart girl—she'd know better than to trust you. She'd know that whatever you said you'd do for her, it'd just be a trick."

Krueger pressed his index knife-finger to his lips. "Shhh... she'll hear you. Anyway, Devon, maybe our little Fall Leaves has a death wish. Unfortunately, she wants to drag everyone else along with her. Hey, a drowning man loves company." A burst of static cut through the image framed against the web page's black background. For a moment, Devon had a glimpse of the original photo of the mortal Krueger. "Well," he said, "it's been nice chatting, and we'll definitely get together again *very* soon but the upload is almost finished, so it's time to go chat with my girlfriend." He blew a kiss toward the slumbering Autumn. "Scratch ya later."

Another crackle of static, but this time when the picture reverted to Freddy Krueger as he had appeared in life, it remained that way.

"Fuck you," Devon hissed. He looked all around him, not so much searching for a weapon with which to bash these conjoined computers to bits (though of course, that was his first impulse), but searching his mind for the weapon of strategy.

To hell with it—strategy would have to wait. When all else failed, there was blind brute force. Leaning in the corner of the room by Autumn's bed, Devon had spotted a baseball bat—no doubt put there before she'd decided to align herself with Krueger. Devon rushed to it, picked it up, and turned in time to see a flash of light like a photographer's strobe going off. A twisting branch of lightning shot from the center of the computer screen, right out of the forehead of the leering mortal Freddy Krueger. Its end seemed to pierce Devon's chest like the prongs of a pitchfork, actually lifting him off his feet and slamming his back into the wall. It riveted him there, several feet off the floor, like a butterfly stuck on a pin

"I warned you not to meddle, fucker!" growled a familiar voice from the speakers.

Devon opened his mouth in agony, but couldn't even get a sound to pass through his jaws. He was quaking all over as the current raced along every nerve, through every vessel in place of his blood, traced the knotted convolutions of his brain. His vision was blackening, and a detached part of him wondered if that meant his eyeballs were literally being seared a carbon black.

Yet Devon still held the handle of the baseball bat in his right fist. With all the strength his charged muscles could summon, he threw it toward the computer station, hoping it wouldn't strike Autumn's head instead. Maybe that would be for the best, too.

The screen was not shattered, but the monitor was rocked back by the blow. It was enough to disrupt the flow of electricity. The rippling light-ning bolt withdrew, letting Devon drop with a gasp. Before it could seek him out again, he bounded forward onto the bed, then off it, using its springs to propel him. He landed just to the right of the computer, scooped up the bat from the floor, and cocked it back across his shoulder.

A hand reached directly out of the screen. Though it was bluish, as if formed from some ethereal matter like plasma or ectoplasm, it was clearly a right hand wearing a glove with four blades along the fingers, elongating them into talons. It grasped at Devon, but already the base-ball bat was whooshing into motion. Again and again Devon pounded the monitor, both its screen and its casing. He finally managed to put some indented spider-webs into the glass. Then, afraid to touch the machine with his bare hands again, he used the bat as a lever to topple the monitor to the floor in a burst of glass and a spray of sparks. Devon shoved its tower to the floor next, followed by the other computer's monitor.

"Nooo!" he heard an outraged voice bellow through the speakers, the sound like ice-picks puncturing his eardrums. Before the volume could increase further and be used as a weapon against him, Devon attacked the speakers, bashing them repeatedly until pieces of them spiraled through the air.

At last he leaned on the bat, panting, listening to the angry sizzle and crackle of the dead and dying computer components. He raised his eyes to Autumn. She was still sleeping, oblivious.

He felt he had stopped the transfer of Alex's nightmare program to Autumn's website in time. But she was still in there, in the dreamworld, with Krueger and if her website offering Krueger's nightmares to the whole of the internet had been Autumn's bargaining chip with him, well, that bargaining chip was gone now. Devon had shattered it himself. He was still convinced that Autumn would have been betrayed by Krueger sooner or later, no matter what Devil's deal they had struck between them, but now she would be at risk immediately and Devon felt responsible for that, however misguided the girl was.

He had to go in after her.

If he kept the baseball bat in his hands while he let the TranceBox put him under its spell, would he then bring it with him into the dreamworld through the influence of his unconscious mind, through the sheer force of his will? He hated to go in there empty-handed again, without a weapon. He needed *something* to go up against Krueger with. Did Autumn's father keep a gun in the house? Could he bring that with him? Or was there something already within the dreamworld that...

Yeah, Devon thought. He smiled. *Yeah.*

But there were obstacles he would have to overcome to put to use the weapon he had in mind. Then again, Devon possessed scientific impulses, like his brother. Experimental leanings.

Devon thought of the story he had related to his brother (and which Alex had dismissed as an urban legend at the time)—the kid allegedly found dead in a high school lavatory, hooked up to six TranceBoxes simultaneously, overlapping and combining their respective programs.

If the story was true, the experience had overloaded him. Fatally.

Could Devon overlap just two programs? Combine them, and hope that in this combination, he could better manipulate their features and attributes to his own purpose?

It was worth a try.

Devon scooped Autumn out of her chair, into his arms, like a bride to be carried over the threshold and then to their wedding bed. Her small body was slack and light, a human scarecrow. He stretched her out on the bed, then pulled the computer chair up beside her and sat in it himself as if he might read her a bedtime story. He placed two TranceBoxes before him on the edge of the mattress—the black one he had taken from Trisha's car, looking like a sinister giant beetle, and

Autumn's blood red one. Next, he advanced the two disks in them to two different chapters of the nightmare program.

Finally, Devon pressed two adhesive receiver patches to his temples—one on the left, and one on the right.

He reclined in the chair, waiting for the fog of artificially-induced sleep to descend on him like an anesthetizing drug. He watched Autumn's face, feeling a mixture of worry, pity and anger. His eyes played across the spill of her long, fine hair over the pillows, her parted cat-curled lips, and again, the contours of her torso in her snugly-fitting black top, riding up to show a pale stripe of midriff. What a time for him to finally find her attractive—him now with lovely Grace, and Autumn's guerilla warfare with the world come to *this*. Was it just the distorting influence of encroaching sleep, or perhaps he was confusing his concern for her with something else? Whatever the case, it was too late for these quirky feelings.

That drugged fog rolled in now, and all his thoughts—however inexplicable—were buoyed away to the domain of dreams.

NINETEEN

Another gust of wind ruffled Autumn's hair. It had a fine mist of almost-rain mixed into it. Tortured gray bundles of cloud clotted the sky, with only a pale yellowish light breaking through at the horizon.

When she had become conscious of her surroundings, Autumn had found she was standing on the flat-roofed tower of a fortress or castle. From below the tower had risen an impossible chorus of screams. The throats from which they issued must have been uncountable.

Drawn by the screams, Autumn had walked to a heavy wooden trapdoor set into the flagstones of the turret. With some effort she had raised it and descended a stone spiral staircase, ultimately emerging into the open air.

Before her stretched a gray and desolate plain, with a manmade forest to give the landscape a mocking semblance of fertility. It was a forest of high stakes, socketed into the earth. There must have been thousands of stakes. Upon each one was impaled a human being. For many, the stake entered through their bottoms and emerged from their mouths. Others were pinned like insect specimens through their chests or bellies. There were men, women and even babies could be seen skewered on the same stakes as their mothers.

Autumn had been here before, repeatedly, but previously there had been no trapdoor by which to descend. It was as though she had *willed* it into existence and though she vaguely recalled having witnessed this mind-boggling atrocity on earlier occasions, the horror of it scorched her soul as if for the first time.

The reason for this might have been the fact that, because she was so much closer to the victims this time, she realized that she *knew* some of them.

Milton Ferrara and Elizabeth Trice were skewered on the same tall stake, facing each other in a perverse embrace, ribbons of blood flowing down their naked sides and twining around their dangling limbs. Mrs Trice was wailing at the sky, but when Milton spotted Autumn his crazed eyes beseeched her and he stretched out a hand toward her. She did not take it. She turned her eyes away.

There were others whom she didn't recognize, however, squirming on their stakes in unfathomable agony, their running gore twirling around the shafts of the stakes like the stripes on a barber pole. She did not know Shane Ryan (incongruously, wearing his backwards baseball cap), Tim Finney, or David Schwartz of Mnemonic Designs. She did not know the Macrocosm Research team of Julie Ip, Mr G, Patrick Tremblay and their boss Farhad Azari but in scanning these tormented faces, her gaze ultimately fell upon the face of Kent Lowe. Her boyfriend.

And Kent saw her, too, at that moment. "Autumn!" he sobbed. "Autumn!" He tried to lift his arms to reach for her imploringly, but weak as he was from pain and blood loss, they flopped back down to hang by his sides.

Tears began to fill Autumn's eyes as she stared up at Kent, raised like a scarecrow—or a martyr—against that murky sky. She took an impulsive step closer to him. "Kent," she croaked.

"Don't do it, Autumn!" Kent pleaded. "He won't give you power! After you help him with what he needs, he'll just kill you, too! You can't trust him..."

Autumn nodded. "I know," she murmured, as if entering into this dream had awoken her from another one. "I know." She fought back a ragged sob. "I'm sorry, Kent. Okay? I'm sorry."

"Ohh, I can't believe this," said a voice behind Autumn. "I turn my back on you for one minute, and here you are cheating with your old boyfriend."

Autumn turned slowly around to face the owner of that voice.

Before opening his eyes, Devon heard a subdued, electronic beeping noise close beside him. When he opened his lids, he saw a cart of life support systems resting beside him. He patted at his body urgently and sat up in bed to examine himself, but he found no tubes running into and out of his body, and he wasn't even wearing a hospital gown—just the regular clothes he had been wearing upon entering Autumn's house, and...

Autumn's house. Autumn's room. The two TranceBoxes...

This was a dream.

He scanned his surroundings more warily. What he could see of them, anyway. A thick fog enclosed the bed like the walls of a room; impenetrable. The only other thing he could really see was a television resting on the small table that was connected to his bed by a pivoting arm. The TV was playing what appeared to be a nature documentary. A vividly green praying mantis had caught another, smaller insect in its serrated front claws and was chewing into its still-living body.

As his mind sharpened and became less groggy, so did the fog around him begin to quickly break up and become less opaque. He saw that he had a roommate, lying in a bed identical to his, but this person's life support system's screens, and his TV screen, were blank. That was because his roommate was dead. A human skeleton lay in the second bed, stripped of its clothing and its flesh. The only thing the skeleton still possessed was the bomb strapped to its rib cage.

It looked crude, but very effective. There were multiple sticks of dynamite taped in a row, and wires affixed to a little electronic device.

He was not alarmed, as another person surely would have been. This was what he had been *hoping* for.

With the fog continuing to clear, Devon swung his legs out of bed and stood. He found a remote resting by his TV. Just to be sure he had the correct remote, he checked the skeleton's bedside table, too, but didn't find a second one. He flipped the remote over and withdrew its battery for the moment, as if removing the clip of bullets from a handgun lest it accidentally go off before he needed it.

After pocketing the remote, he then set about the task of delicately unstrapping the bomb from the skeleton's chest. He was careful not to bump the electronic device that was the bomb's brain, for fear that a wire might loosen and detonate the thing. Or, almost as bad, render the bomb useless to him.

A loud caw make him look up, startled. A large crow made ghostly gray by the dissipating fog flapped low over his head. A crow? He followed it with his eyes, and realized that now he could make out the barest outlines of his environment. It was a *vast* environment, no hospital room. The mists continued to recede, like gauzy veils drawn back to reveal an audience of thousands upon thousands of skeletons just like the one lying under his hands.

Of course. It came back to him. He had programmed this in himself. The gladiator chapter. Devon smiled. This time he was not locked into that one little hospital room with the bomb; overlapping the two nightmare chapters had placed him into a much more open location.

Finished unstrapping the bomb, he gently draped it over his shoulder by its straps. He turned in a slow circle, studying the distant perimeter of the Colosseum, looking for a means by which to exit it. He must go in search of Autumn, now that he had the weapon he'd wanted. She was in one of these dream chapters somewhere. He would walk across the borders from one to the next to the next, if he had to, until he found her.

With more crows occasionally circling and cawing above his head, Devon began walking across the arena's floor.

Krueger wore a long black coat that flapped around him like a cape in the wind, its high collar turned up against his neck. His monstrously burned bald head gleamed in the silvery light. There was a regal quality to him, as if he was some dark prince. As Autumn watched, he shed the heavy coat and tossed it behind him onto a pile of long stakes stacked up like logs, waiting for fresh victims to impale. "I guess I'm not gonna be king of the world, after all," Krueger sighed. Under the coat he wore his green and red striped sweater, and from behind his back in a cheap magician's trick he produced his worn fedora, fitting it onto his head. "And I have your friend Devon to thank for that." His tone became a lot less jovial with this last statement.

"Devon?" Autumn said.

"He interrupted that work you were doing for me." Krueger tilted up his chin and squinted into the distance, as if trying to make out something approaching from far away. "And now your Prince Charming's come looking for you. How romantic."

"Devon is coming to rescue me?" Autumn laughed and sobbed at the same time.

Krueger returned his malevolent gaze to her. "Looks like our partnership has to become... severed, sweetcheeks."

Through her streaming tears, Autumn again took in the immense forest of suffering that spread before them, gesturing toward it inadequately. "Look what you did to these people. Look what you did to Kent!"

"Mm," Krueger grunted, stroking his knotty chin, "Yeah. Well, I've always had a flair for decorating." He chuckled, wagging his head. "I thought you had more guts, kid. I thought you were more like me. But I guess there's no one quite like me, huh?"

"I sure hope not," Autumn said, grinning, "you fucking pathetic child molester. You're not a god. You aren't even enough of a worm to eat my shit."

"Bitch!" Krueger growled, stooping down and snatching up one of the heavy stakes from the pile of them. Holding it in front of him like a thick spear, he charged at Autumn before she could flee or even throw herself out of his way.

The oiled, blunt point of the stake entered her chest just below the breastbone and punched out of her back. Her eyes bulged and the breath was driven from her, so that she couldn't even cry out. With his unnatural strength, Krueger then angled the stake up so that Autumn was lifted above him into the air, her legs pedaling helplessly. Grunting, Krueger carried her that way for a few steps until he came to a hole waiting in the ground. He socketed the end of the stake into it, then stepped back and looked up to admire his handiwork. Some of Autumn's blood had sprinkled down onto his face, and a long wolfish tongue lashed out to lick it off his cheeks and chin.

"Sorry to break your cherry," he told her. "I tried to be gentle."

Autumn could only mutely glance over at Kent, his eyes fastened on her in sympathetic anguish, and then back down at Krueger's upturned face. She knew that in her own world, her mortal body was dying, if not already dead. She realized that here, her soul would remain damned in this Hell of Krueger's making, at least for as long as he continued to wield his mysterious, infernal power.

"If you like your pal Devon so much," Krueger said to her, "I'll be a nice guy and put him right there beside you." He pointed his left hand at another hole in the earth. As Autumn watched, that hand began to morph into another kind of limb. His gloved right hand was undergoing the same transformation. The two new limbs extended out of his splitting sweater sleeves, long and oddly jointed. Serrated, saw-like teeth—as silvery as rows of little steel knife blades—emerged along the inner surface of bent, hooked claws.

They were the forelegs of a gigantic praying mantis.

TWENTY

"Oh no. Oh no," Alex whispered to himself, watching the face of the silvery-haired detective as he took Trisha's call on his cellphone. Detective-in-training Billy gaped up at his mentor with similar dread, but at least Alex had a better idea of what had happened.

"Okay," the senior detective said tersely. "Okay. We're on our way. But you sit outside in your car and keep the doors locked, just in case the person who did this is still inside the building."

It's worse than that, Alex thought. The person who did this was still inside their *heads*.

The detective pocketed his cellphone and glared down at Alex, still seated at the interrogation table, as if he couldn't quite believe that Alex had had no hand in the crimes that were taking place. He said, "Now all of your coworkers at Mnemonic Designs are dead. Your girlfriend said she was off to pick up some coffee, and when she came back she found three individuals slaughtered. Seems like you and her have your coffee habit to thank for your lives."

"I can't believe it. Shane… Tim… Dave…"

"Someone's killing all the people around you. You're connected to all this somehow, but that somehow I can't figure."

"All that means is I'm at risk, too. And Trisha. Thank God she's okay, at least." Alex spread his hands. "Well, I obviously didn't murder these people, sir, so am I free to go now?"

The detective narrowed his eyes suspiciously but what could he say at this point? "You're free to go, for now, but I'm sure we have a lot more to discuss, once I have one fucking clue about what is going on here."

Alex rose and extended his hand. "Can I have my phone back then?"

Still the detective looked reluctant, as if it was a gun that Alex had asked to have returned. But the man fished it out of an inner pocket of his jacket and handed it over. "I suggest you go home and sit tight. Keep your eyes peeled. Just in case someone might want you next, like you say. In fact, maybe I should put a guard on you."

"That isn't necessary, sir." It wouldn't really help, and would only make Alex feel like he was still something of a prisoner. "Sir, you and I both know a lot has been suppressed about the Springwood Slasher…"

"Let's not get into that again.

"Freddy Krueger…"

"He's dead!"

"Yeah, I know he's dead. But that doesn't seem to matter, does it?"

The cop shook his head. "I've heard some crazy bullshit about Krueger. A lot of crazy bullshit. And I've kept my mouth shut about it like I was told. I suggest you do the same. Now, you want to go home? So go. I have to meet your girl at Mnemonic now."

"I guess I'll be calling a cab," Alex muttered. He watched the two detectives walk briskly from the room, leaving the door open behind them for him to pass through unchallenged but Alex wasn't ready to leave just yet. He quickly punched up Trisha's number.

"Alex?" she said urgently. "Are they letting you go?"

"Yeah," he said. "Thank God you're safe, baby!"

"I told them I'm meeting them at Mnemonic, but I'm really parked just down the street from you. At the last minute I wasn't sure if I should let them tie me up in questioning right now. What do you want me to do?"

"Good thinking. Honey come and get me and we'll go over to Macrocosm. Remember the targeted memory-erasure project I worked on? We have to undergo that procedure. You, me, Devon and whoever of his friends are still alive. If we can wipe Krueger out of our memories, I think it will siphon off all his power, break his connection to us."

"That's a great idea. But will Macrocosm be off limits to us, as a crime scene?"

"I think they've got what they need from there. I still have my key card."

"So you should call Devon, I dropped him off at Autumn's house. He was going to check in on her."

"All right. I'll try rounding up him and the others, so I can get them over to Macrocosm, too. We need to do this thing as quickly as possible, first all of you, and then me last."

"Okay, then. Wait for me out front, I'm coming to get you."

The silvery-haired detective was named Larry Barnes, and while he'd been a cop for a good long while, he had only moved to Springwood in 2000, long after the Springwood Slasher—Fred Krueger—had murdered perhaps dozens of adolescent children, and long after he had been punished for his sins by a vigilante party of grieving parents. Still, since his arrival in Springwood, Barnes had seen some very odd crimes occur, vicious murders that seemed out of place for an otherwise innocuous little Ohio town. More mysterious than the murders themselves, it seemed to him, had been the efforts of his comrades to suppress the details of the crimes. He had even been personally warned by his superiors not to discuss certain details of these murders with anyone. Not with the family of the victims, not with the press, not with his wife, not with God if he was a praying man.

He had been in the Marines, and he knew how to take orders and stick to them, how to enforce those orders himself. He didn't question them verbally, and he barely even did so mentally but this latest series of killings was just too much for him to passively swallow, especially since he had been personally assigned to the case, the recent retirement of some of the older boys having left him as the department's senior investigator. He wasn't about to believe the irrational urban legends regarding an undead child murderer who could attack you in your dreams. He had to rein in his impatience when he heard those whispers at the station, and wondered at such times if a kind of mass hysteria had hit the Springwood police force in the Eighties and hadn't let go since. All local myths aside, though, he had to concede that there was definitely something about these killings that wasn't right. Well, no murders were right, but these killings *really* weren't right.

Barnes had good instincts; they'd served him well throughout his career as both soldier and cop. And while Alex Carmack's closeness to this case certainly justified viewing him as the prime suspect, Barnes' own gut feeling was that the guy was no killer. Not that he was ready to exonerate Carmack altogether; Barnes was reluctant to heed his own intuition. Nevertheless, that intuition told him that things were more complex, and more bizarre, than this young man slaughtering all his coworkers from two companies, plus his brother's friends besides.

Yet, if Carmack—and/or his kid brother—had nothing directly to do with these homicides, what kind of game were they playing by Trisha Smith not being here at Mnemonic Designs, as she'd said she would be when she'd called to report the murder of her three coworkers?

Barnes' cold eyes took in his partner Billy, green around the gills and presently green in the face, seated in a computer chair with his head between his knees to keep from puking. His eyes shifted next to one of the trio of victims, zippered up in a black plastic body bag and laid on a collapsed gurney, waiting for removal while the coroner's team continued their work with the other two victims, making sure all photos were taken that needed to be taken, all evidence collected that could be collected. At least that body, Timothy Finney's, could go out in one bag. Hell, it would almost be possible to put that David Schwartz guy in a series of sandwich bags.

Yeah, as if he wasn't pissed off enough already in his frustration, now Barnes had to wonder where Carmack's girlfriend was at. She hadn't been waiting outside in her car as he'd instructed her. At first he'd thought maybe she'd returned inside the building, but she wasn't in here, either. Had she become too spooked and gone home? Or had the killer found her, and taken her off to chop into pieces, too? Barnes had dispatched a man to go check her apartment and he himself had been trying to call Carmack, but either the man didn't want to answer his phone or something had happened to him, too. Maybe it hadn't been such a good idea to let him go, after all—now he couldn't be sure where the guy was. Hopefully, he would also be found at the apartment he shared with Trisha Smith.

Barnes came out of his reverie to wander about the lab again, frowning down at this piece of equipment and that. He saw a few open and empty jewelbox cases on the floor. He saw clutter that looked a bit too extreme to be simply sloppy work habits. "This place was trashed, too," he said more to himself than to the uniformed cop standing next to him. "Not like Macrocosm, but it was still trashed. And why is that?"

At the far end of the lab he encountered a computer with a blank screen, but a flashing green light on the tower told him it was not shut off, had simply lapsed into sleep mode. He nudged the mouse an inch, and the screen came back to life with a little hiss of static. On the desk beside the keyboard were some printouts that appeared to be still shots captured from some computer program. Barnes picked them up and shuffled through them, grimacing. Grotesque. They were all the same image but with different styles of type laid over them; prototypes for software cover art, obviously. The image was of an audience of countless human skeletons overlooking what appeared to be an arena.

Nothing seemed too disorderly at this work station. Because it was here at the back of the large room, facing a wall of brick and partially blocked by other gear, had this computer been missed by whomever had ransacked the place? Barnes leaned in closer and played with the mouse. He studied the many icons clustered to the left of the monitor's desktop. One of these icons was in the shape of a human skull, and was labeled: 2D NIGHT. PROG.

Barnes double-clicked on the skull.

On the screen a sort of movie began, but so far it was simply a static camera angle peering into a churning void of fog or steam. There was sound coming over the speakers, though; the distant caw of crows. Then, even further away, the voice of a little girl singing. The language didn't sound like English, however. Barnes leaned in even closer, cocking his head. That wasn't... Latin, was it?

Barnes' head was only inches away from the screen when he saw the man emerge from the fog.

He jolted back, startled. That face. A mass of hideous scars. And the grin on that face. And the eyes, locked ferally on his own. A hand rising up, with knives for fingers. He came walking toward the camera. Walking fast. Closer and closer.

Over the speakers came a new voice: "2D is no fun, is it, Officer Barnes?"

The detective still had the reflexes of a good Marine, and jumped back in time to avoid those razor-edged claws as the burn-faced man reached his arm right out through the computer monitor's screen.

Detective-in-training Billy sat up abruptly in his chair at the deafening roar of three shots being fired from Larry Barnes' semi-automatic pistol.

Billy and the uniformed cops came running, drawing their own weapons, thinking that the murderer must have been hiding in the room and had suddenly lunged out at Barnes. All they saw, when they reached him, was the senior investigator gaping numbly at the shattered screen of a computer monitor, sparks spitting out of its exploded shell. He had fired a round into the computer's tower as well. His smoking handgun dangled heavily at his side.

"It's true," he was mumbling to himself. "It was all true."

"Larry," Billy said, nervous now, his eyes lingering on his partner's pistol. "Are you okay?"

Barnes seemed to collect himself then. His eyes refocused. He turned slowly toward the others, slipping his gun back into its creaking leather holster. "I want someone who knows computers to start erasing all these hard drives, if they aren't already. I want all the data in this room destroyed, right down to the last Solitaire game."

"But we can't do that, Larry," Billy protested meekly.

"Do it!" Barnes bellowed, and the others drifted back from him, cowed.

With the recent retirement of some of the older boys, he was the ranking detective in Springwood now. And now, at last, he understood the weight of responsibility that role brought with it.

Grace Simmons was more than a little worried about her boyfriend, Devon.

At Macrocosm Research with Trisha, priming the equipment there for the memory-expunging process, Alex had called Grace to say that he had been trying to reach his brother for twenty minutes but he wasn't answering his phone. He had asked Grace if she could get over to Autumn's house to check on the both of them, and if Devon were still there, to bring them and Ama over to Macrocosm. Then all of them would be present to undergo the procedure.

"Trisha told me he brought a TranceBox with him," Alex informed Grace. "If he did something stupid, and is hooked up to that thing, you call me back right away."

"Okay, Alex," Grace had replied, her heart thudding at the very suggestion.

Now Ama was driving Grace over to Autumn's house through the blue gloom of early evening. Grace felt surreal, disjointed from reality, as she pictured her father's body still lying in the basement of her locked house, left behind them, strangely *alone*—but she couldn't afford to call the police about a dead man just yet, with living people to worry about. She would just as soon forget about him altogether at the moment. In fact, when she underwent this memory-purging experience, wouldn't it also erase the truth she had found out about her Dad? After the procedure, she might never again learn what he had done to her mother. She might end up mourning his death forever, thinking him just another innocent victim in a series of strange murders that she would no longer have any personal knowledge about.

Maybe it would be better this way. Blissful, merciful amnesia. Yes, she could write a note to herself, tuck it in her pocketbook. "You had your memory of the past few weeks wiped out," the message to her future self could read, "and you must know this: Dad murdered Mom." Despite the horrendous and unforgivable thing he had done, she had still loved her father and she didn't doubt that he had loved her. That was all she chose to remember of him. Yes, she would be an orphan now, miserable about having lost her other parent but better that than living the rest of her life filled with hatred and betrayal.

Ama pulled her car over to the curb in front of Autumn's house. As she and Grace climbed out, Grace glanced up at the windows on the second floor with a heavy sense of foreboding.

Ama rang the bell and pounded the door, but they didn't wait long for an answer. Grace tried the knob, which turned freely. The two friends hurried inside, directly to the stairs leading to the second story. "Devon?" Grace called as she pounded up the steps. "Autumn?"

It was she who let herself into Autumn's room first. So it was she who was the first to scream.

Devon reclined in an office-style swivel chair beside the bed, like a psychiatrist who had dozed off while listening to his patient's troubled confessions. A white TranceBox patch was stuck to either side of his head, and two of these devices—red and black—rested on the edge of the bed in front of him. The floor was strewn with shorted-out computer equipment, still smelling of smoke and burnt plastic, and a baseball bat lay on the carpet. Adding to the hallucinatory nature of the scene, the white skull faces stenciled on the glossy back walls leered from all sides like a taunting audience of skeletons.

Autumn lay on the bed, her limbs splayed out to the sides. There was a yawning hole gouged into her chest, the blankets and mattress beneath her having become a dark bog of gore.

"No, no, no!" Ama sobbed, tearing her eyes away.

Grace forced herself to become all business. Hysteria wouldn't help Devon. She saw that he had programmed both TranceBoxes to play two different chapters of the nightmare disk, but he had also programmed them to awaken him in a half hour. That time had just elapsed, and the disks were no longer spinning inside the machines, but Devon was clearly still locked in his spell. She peeled away both adhesive patches, shook him, lightly slapped his face. "Devon!" she shouted. "Devon, please, you have to wake up now! Listen to my voice, Devon. Can you follow it? Can you find your way out of there?" She stifled a sob. *"Devon!"*

"We have to get him to his brother," Ama said huskily, avoiding looking at Autumn again, "so he can clean out his memory."

Grace nodded. "You get his arms; you're stronger than me. I'll take his feet. We need to carry him down to the car."

"We have to take those, too, so they can be destroyed." Ama pointed to the two TranceBoxes.

"Right." Grace opened Devon's shirt a little and tucked the pair of devices inside it, against his bare skin, like two parasitic creatures feeding off his blood. Then she and Ama took opposite ends of his slack body and hoisted it out of the chair.

Somehow they got him down the stairs without breaking his or their own necks. Carrying him to the car, Grace dreaded someone seeing them and calling the police to report two teenage girls hefting what appeared to be a dead body. But soon enough they had Devon in the backseat. Grace sat beside him, while up front Ama got her car into motion again.

"Hang in there, Devon," Grace whispered to him. His head rested against her shoulder and she stroked his short hair. "Don't you let him get you. Don't you let him." She saw a tear drop from her face onto his cheek.

At any moment, she expected to see some terrible wound open up in him. Four deep, parallel slash marks, as if plowed into his flesh by an invisible hand.

She pressed her lips to his temple, where one of the patches had been. In her head, the song *Kiss of Life* by Sade surfaced. She realized that soon, the memory of their first kiss would be deleted from her mind as if it had never occurred. That was a kind of death in itself. This thought was just too much for her. Her efforts to remain calm were crumbling. To herself as much as to Ama she blurted, "He's just a shell! His body is here but his soul is somewhere else!"

"We'll be there soon," Ama reassured her.

"He's all I have, Ama! He's all I have left now!"

"Don't lose it, Grace," Ama warned her.

But Grace was already reaching into Devon's shirt and pulling out Autumn's red TranceBox as if extracting a faulty mechanical heart.

She activated it, and saw its little screen light up. One device had been set to *Arena*. The other, to *Hospital*. Why two TranceBoxes, and why these two separate chapters? She would only try one chapter, but which? Purely at random, Grace selected *Arena*. Should she set the timer to automatically wake her up? Well, that hadn't done Devon much good, had it?

In Autumn's bedroom she had shoved the two receiver patches, removed from Devon's head, into her jeans pocket with their sticky sides pressed together. She dug them out and peeled them apart. Then, after glancing at Ama's rearview mirror to be sure she wasn't watching, Grace stuck one of the pads to her left temple, hidden under the fall of her hair.

Grace leaned her cheek against the top of Devon's head, pressed the start button of the crimson-colored TranceBox, and closed her eyes.

With her eyes closed, Grace couldn't see the chapter title change by itself on the TranceBox's tiny readout screen. The word *Arena* was replaced with a chapter that didn't even exist on the sample disks.

This new chapter was called: *Boiler Room*.

TWENTY-ONE

Grace floated in the womb, waiting to be born.

Her eyes opened, and she could see nothing in the liquid darkness. Her instinct was to gasp in surprise, in shock, at finding herself awake and alert before it was time to be delivered into the world—but if she did so, she would suck this surrounding amniotic fluid into her lungs and drown on it. Trying to remain calm, she uncoiled herself from her fetal position and reached out around her, feeling for the womb's walls. She touched them, and they were hard and cold. In feeling them more, searching for an opening, she realized that the walls were actually one circular wall, like that of a cylinder. Above her head and below her feet, however, she came into contact with nothing but more water.

Her chest was already beginning to burn, clenched like a fist on its last few molecules of oxygen. She had to find a way out without delay. Grace kicked her legs, propelling herself upward, also walking her palms along the curved wall to aid in the motion. Just as it seemed she must draw in a breath at last—and fill her lungs with killing black water—her hands found a circular opening in the side of the cylinder. She pulled herself into this, squeezing inside a narrower horizontal cylinder or off-branching tunnel. It was not very long, ending in another vertical section. When she stood up here, her head broke through the surface of the water and at last she drew in great greedy mouthfuls of air between spluttering, hacking coughs.

Grace tried to pull herself up through the top of this vertical section, but bumped her head on a ceiling only several inches above her. She was trapped here, with just enough of a pocket of air to breathe in. So should she descend again, work her way back into the main tank or metal womb or whatever it was? Maybe there were other openings, other off-branching arteries in this gigantic circulatory system that she could explore. Yet she was reluctant to leave this tiny sanctuary. She could easily become lost in a lightless maze, dead-end herself in some tunnel with no pocket of air to breathe at all.

Grace's extended hands encountered a flaw in the cylinder's smooth inner surface. She fingered a raised seam like a scar that ran entirely around her in a circle. This was a point where two sections of the cylinder had been joined together somehow. Welded, she realized. She pressed both hands against the wall directly below this sealed lip and pushed, desperate to break the segments apart from each other. She hadn't really expected to win much of a result, but in fact she did detect just the faintest give between the two joined lengths.

Encouraged, Grace braced her back against the curved wall behind her, and her feet against the opposite side. She pushed outward with her legs, straining, grunting. She felt more give. Then, she heard a metallic rasp, and immediately the water level began to drop as it leaked out of the split she had opened. Crying out triumphantly, Grace drew back her legs and then stamped them powerfully against the compromised seam. She repeated the attack, again and again, like a baby kicking the inside of its mother's womb.

Suddenly, the section she floated in tilted forward from the strain of rupture and the weight of the water inside it. It swung down like a falling tower, and from its end vomited out not only the liquid contained within it, but Grace along with it.

She thudded to a concrete floor with a grunt, painfully banging an elbow and a hip. She clenched her eyes and mouth shut as the separated section of pipe continued to gush gallons upon gallons of water upon her but soon enough, the flow diminished and she could open her lids again.

She saw the broken length of pipe, slanted down toward the floor, just a trickle coming from the black hole at its end now. The outside of the pipe was scabbed in rust but what really seized her attention was the color of the liquid dribbling out of it. Red. And not red with rust.

Grace looked down at her body, lifting her hands. She was entirely painted with a coat of blood, lying in a wide pool of the scarlet life fluid, slowly emptying into a recessed drain in the concrete floor. She scrambled to her feet and instantly began spitting out the residue of gore in her mouth. Its taste made her want to throw up, but she wrestled for control of her stomach.

Wringing the blood out of her hair, she blinked around her at her surroundings.

Billowing clouds of steam obscured most of her environment, making its scope undeterminable. Red emergency bulbs inside little wire cages saturated the steamy fog, adding to the scene's bloody color. Through the haze she could make out more twisted, interweaving pipes both great and small. She felt like she was inside some gargantuan, and dangerously diseased, human body.

Then, as she began to get her bearings, a name came back to her.

Devon.

She looked around her again, but more fervently this time. She had been so busy fighting for her life, she had forgotten that it was his life she had come here to save.

She also recalled that she had planned on searching for him in an arena. This was no arena. Well, not literally. Maybe in a figurative sense.

From behind her came a weird bleating sound. Grace whirled to see a white goat trotting out of the fog, negotiating a path between two hulking factory machines of some kind before vanishing back into the mists. Before she had even digested this image, a child's red ball came bouncing out of the fog from another direction, went into a roll, and came to a stop in the draining puddle of blood.

Krueger was close. Toying with her.

Hesitantly, Grace started forward, allowing intuition to choose the direction. She dreaded venturing into those obscuring masses of steam, but she could not dawdle in one place. Devon's very life might depend upon her course of action. Devon. He was the only thing she had left in any world, real or imagined.

She felt her way between two other huge factory machines, the functions of which she couldn't fathom from their appearance. Coming to the end of the corridor created by their flanks, she heard two sounds in the distance. One was the faint tinkling sound of dangling chains stirring. The other sound was the crying of a baby.

Biological programming sprang to life inside Grace; the infant's bawling grabbed her right at the base of her maternal instincts. She let the sound guide her through the swirling haze. It grew steadily louder, but not much clearer; there was a muffled quality to it.

Ahead of her, she began to make out a white form that floated in the air as if levitating. Drawing gingerly nearer to this specter, Grace realized it was either the same goat she had seen only minutes earlier, or a close relative. Its unsettling eyes with their frog-like pupils stared fixedly, unblinking. It had old blood crusted in its nostrils. The thing's belly was immense, but she had noticed this feature on goats seen at zoos and farms and didn't know if it meant this animal had been pregnant in life. Well, it certainly wasn't alive anymore. Two chains were hooked deeply into the animal's hide, so that it hung suspended in the air, swaying very subtly as if someone might have bumped into it not so long ago.

The baby's squalling came from the goat, from *inside* its bloated belly. To further demonstrate the fact, Grace saw a bulge shift across the animal's abdomen and disappear again. Then, another squirming motion. Had the infant been sewn inside the animal carcass? Was it suffocating to death?

Grace glanced around her for a tool of some kind. She must find a way to cut the belly open! Before she could make such an attempt, the belly began to cut *itself* open.

A small, single blade poked out of the animal's swollen gut, slitting it wide in one clean motion. The internal pressure of rotting entrails and the gases of decomposition caused the animal to burst open like a pinata. Downwards splashed a torrent of blackish blood and a liquefying intestinal tract. Mixed in with this deluge fell the body of a naked child. But he was no infant, more of a toddler, and even as he lay there beneath the opened goat, he continued to age at an astonishing rate.

Grace took a step back, transfixed with horror.

The boy, now a teenager, managed to rise to his feet and stare at her. He was naked, and in his right hand he held the razor-sharp box cutter he had used to free himself from inside the goat's carcass.

Still, he aged, gradually becoming familiar to her, until, at last, seeing that his daughter was afraid of the box cutter he gripped in his hand, Neil Simmons tossed it aside and held both hands out to her.

"Grace," he said. "Honey…"

"No!" Grace cried. "You're dead! You're dead now!"

"I'm not dead, baby. I live forever in you. In your genes. In your head."

"I don't want your genes!" she shouted. "I don't want you in my head!"

"It was an accident, sweetheart. Both times. I loved them. Both of them. I didn't mean to be bad. I didn't mean to hurt them." He took a step forward.

"You stay away from me!

"But I love you, Grace. I love you… even more than I loved Mommy. Even more than I loved Cassandra." His imploring expression changed into a seductive smile, and the tip of his tongue moistened his upper lip. "Maybe they were just filling in for the girl I really wanted…"

"No!" Grace shrieked, clamping her hands over her ears to blot out this insanity.

Neil's finger traced a heart shape on his chest, using the foul black blood his naked body was smeared with. "Forget about that little Devon and I'll show you what a *real* man can do." Neil extended his arms, inviting her into his embrace but even as he reached for her, his arms were altering, distorting, rippling with strange bulges. Suddenly, the flesh of his palms split open and two long blade-like appendages tore out of them. Then the flesh of his arms began sloughing off around these new arms like the skin shed from a snake. Neil's new arms were long and oddly jointed. Serrated, saw-like teeth—as silvery as rows of little steel knife blades—emerged along the inner surface of bent, hooked claws.

They were the forelegs of a gigantic praying mantis.

Grace screamed, spun away and fled headlong into the wall of steam that had been roiling behind her.

"Where are you going?" called a familiar voice after her. Not her father's. It belonged, of course, to Krueger. "Daddy wants some sugar!"

Since Trisha was the only one of their group available to Alex—at least until the others got there—she was the first to undergo the memory-eradication process.

Whereas Alex had submitted to this procedure himself, in the midst of its development, this was Trisha's first experience and her nervousness was apparent. "You haven't done this in a while," she joked weakly as he fitted the neuromodulation halo onto her head. "Don't regress me to a toddler or something, okay?"

"I wish I could just specifically target anything to do with Krueger, and leave the rest of your recent memory intact, but we didn't take the process that far at Macrocosm. I know others are doing that kind of work, either using the technology we developed or alternative methods." He leaned back and keyed in a few last commands. "Okay, baby, just close your eyes, make yourself comfortable. It will first put you into a sleep-like state, like the TranceBox does."

Trisha looked more nervous than ever at the comparison. "I won't dream while I'm going through this, will I? I'm afraid that—"

Alex squeezed her hand and cut her off before she could finish. "You won't dream. I won't let him near you again. After you go through this, I'm pretty sure you'll be free of his taint. One by one, we're gonna purge Krueger out of our heads the same way the cops have purged him out of their public files, and wherever else a person might have learned about him. I really can't blame them for that now, can I?"

"Mm," Trisha grunted, her eyelids fluttering slowly closed.

Watching her, Alex still held on to her hand, rubbing his thumb across the top of it. This reverie was broken when his cellphone began to ring. He slipped it out of his shirt pocket and brought it to his ear. "Hello?"

"Alex!" He recognized the accent as Ama's. Her deep voice was breathless. "I'm on my way there now but I have to tell you, when Grace and I got to Autumn's house, Autumn was dead..."

"Oh, fuck!"

"And Devon... he was playing two TranceBoxes at the same time. We disconnected him, but we can't wake him up!"

"What?" Alex flew out of his chair and began to pace frantically. His loud voice and frenzied pacing had not so much as raised a flicker in Trisha's eyelids. "Get him here, Ama, as fast as you can!"

"I just pulled over for a few seconds to call you."

"Well, get moving again, please—Krueger could catch up with him at any time!"

"There's another thing to tell you! Grace was sitting in the back with him, and I didn't realize it until a minute ago: she connected herself to a TranceBox, too. I think she went in to try to find Devon but now," she let out a sob, "now I can't wake Grace up, either!"

"Okay, okay, keep it together, Ama... their lives depend on you and me now. Get moving, get them here. Hurry!"

"Okay. Okay." Then the line went dead.

"Fuck!" Alex roared, still marching back and forth, clenching the cellphone in his fist. "Devon... what the hell are you thinking, man?"

Fighting for composure, he stopped in one spot long enough to check on the progress level of his girlfriend's memory erasure. He had estimated the date that he'd first allowed Trisha to sample one of the dreams stolen from Macrocosm Research, and gone back several weeks further than that estimation, just in case. Even with his conservative approach, it didn't really amount to a significant portion of time that Trisha had to sacrifice, thank God, so the process was already 61% finished. He watched the progress bar steadily fill, like a syringe slowly drawing in the lethal solution that would be injected into the IV of a condemned murderer.

The thing that had once been a man named Fred Krueger followed the scent of Grace Simmons's fear the way a shark can smell a single drop of blood in twenty-five gallons of sea water. Though he couldn't see her ahead of him, her terror was a palpable thing—displacing the air, sending out ripples of disturbed energy like waves of sonar. It was a homing beacon by which he tracked her patiently through the steam and the darkness. Anyway, he relished drawing out the apprehension, the dread. A good lover knows that foreplay is the key to pleasure.

As infinite as the boiler room limbo appeared to be, he knew its corridors, its nooks and crannies, only too well. Until recently, he had been wandering here restlessly—in want of some prey—for hours beyond counting, for days, for years. He had paced like a lion in its cage, ravenous between feedings. The lonely Hell he was imprisoned in was a Hell of his own making.

Yes, he had visitors only too seldom, so why rush the experience now? A starving man might be inclined to wolf down his food, but Krueger wanted to savor every bite, especially when his present guest was as luscious a morsel as this young woman, who actually looked like an even younger girl. A delicate flower, fresh for the plucking.

As if using them to burrow through the clouds of hissing steam, Krueger flexed his new mantis-like limbs with their steel barbs, imagining how it would be to tear the girl's clothing away with them, once he had her cornered. Imagining how it would feel to run the side of the chitinous claws teasingly across her fragile exposed flesh... before he tore that away, too.

Grace was near now, very near. He *willed* a wall to materialize out of the fog ahead of her. These were his building blocks to play with, after all, and he could shuffle them around as he wished. She would encounter a dead end, and when she turned—he would be there. As much as he had wanted to draw out the experience, his fantasies of touching her flesh with his claws had made his belly growl too insistently with its hunger. Time for the lion to feed.

Suddenly he paused and tilted his chin up, as if to sniff out another scent that only he could detect, or listen to some distant sound that only his acute hearing could discern. He knew the taste of this soul from having relished its distinct brand of terror before.

Trisha Smith. A little older than what he usually favored, though still a succulent morsel. He narrowed his small, inhuman eyes in confusion. Trisha was asleep, yet also in some way not asleep. He tried to sense her more clearly, pushing his faculties to their limit. No, he couldn't focus in on her. She wasn't dreaming. Something was off here. Something wasn't right.

And then, Trisha was gone. Completely and utterly gone. Even when his prey were wide awake, Krueger still felt a connection to them. A thread of some kind that linked them, once he had first tasted their souls but Trisha's thread had been severed. It was even as if it had never existed at all.

Not only that, but something like a dizzy spell washed through his system, making him light-headed. He even stumbled backwards a step before he caught himself.

Krueger growled in impotent rage. Something definitely wasn't right. What was going on? How had Trisha escaped him in this way? He couldn't even remember the taste of her soul anymore. It was as though he had suddenly been stricken with amnesia.

Worse than that was this sudden weakness, this inexplicable fatigue. What was going on out there, in the waking world? If they were doing this to him somehow, they would regret it. Oh, would they regret it.

He returned his attention to Grace. She had reached the dead end but then, abruptly, she was gone, too.

With Grace it was different, however. In his brief dizzy spell, he had let down his guard. She had found a crack in the wall, so to speak, and slipped through it but Krueger sensed her on the other side of the wall. She had only escaped into another chamber of the dreamscape. It was a crack he could follow her through.

Flexing his mantis arms again, Krueger gave another growl and surged ahead after her.

TWENTY-TWO

Alex heard a car horn beep outside in the parking lot of Macrocosm Research. Before he could run to a window, however, his cellphone rang and he brought it to his ear. It was Ama.

"Alex, can you come out and help me get them inside? I think I can carry Grace if you can carry Devon."

"I'll be right down." Lowering the phone, Alex glanced at Trisha, whom he had just disconnected from the memory-erasing apparatus. She blinked up at him groggily. He was reluctant to leave her alone just yet. "Honey, do you remember who I am?"

Trisha sat up straighter and gave him a look like he was the one who had lost his memory. "Um, yeah, I should hope so." She glanced around her, recognizing that she was in Macrocosm but also taking in the equipment that Alex had smashed in his rampage. "What's going on, Alex?"

"I'll have to explain it later. Trust me. Just sit tight a few minutes, baby, I have to run downstairs. Devon needs me." Alex ran his hand over her cheek and bolted for the door before his befuddled girlfriend could protest.

By now Devon had come close to walking the entire circumference of the huge arena, very close to its wall, and he hadn't found any kind of doorway by which to exit it. How had the gladiators entered the arena to fight, then? He reminded himself this was only a dream Colosseum and did not have to exactly correspond to its earthly counterpart, did not have to follow lines of logic.

He finally came to the point he believed he had started at, and stood gazing up the high wall. If he went back to the twin hospital beds at the center of the arena and tore their sheets into strips, knotted them together, could he then tie a weight at one end and hurl the makeshift rope up over the side to haul himself into the seats? Would there be a way out up there, at least?

Behind him—so close that the small hairs rose on the back of his neck just like he had read about in countless stories, without ever truly believing that such a sensation was possible—Devon heard a little girl's voice sing sweetly, "One, two, Freddy's coming for you..."

He spun and saw the child standing just a few yards away from him. She wore a frilly Sunday dress and matching headband straight out of the idyllic Fifties or early Sixties. She must have been wearing a blond wig, too, unless the crows had decided to leave her scalp intact while they pecked all the flesh from her. For the little girl was nothing but an empty-eyed skeleton inside that pretty dress. Her white tights hung baggy around her leg bones like an ectoplasmic layer of flesh. She was impaled on a metal rod stuck in the ground, running through the core of her body to prop her erect—a ghastly scarecrow.

Devon flicked his eyes about the arena warily. Krueger was close, then. He was beginning the game.

The fog had entirely cleared from the Colosseum by now. Though the sky overhead was still an overcast pearly gray, the arena itself was picked out in sharp relief, a crystalline quality almost more defined than reality itself. Distantly, Devon saw that the two beds still rested at the center of the fighting floor. He began walking briskly toward them, dismissing the skeleton child as he passed her.

"Three, four, better lock the door," he heard a sweet voice lilting behind him.

"I'd lock it if I could find one," Devon said aloud, defiantly, refusing to look back as he continued walking.

Then, there was a kind of one-second earthquake. Devon froze in his tracks, thrusting out his free arm as if to balance himself while his other hand squeezed the straps of the bomb more tightly. The child's singing was cut off as if a button had been punched to stop a recording's playback and now the arena was subtly murkier. It wasn't really that the sky had grown any darker, it was something else:

The air was full of static.

It fizzed soundlessly, a blizzard of swarming light particles. Everything was pixilated, grainy.

More than that, Devon felt he had stepped inside an ancient silent movie, the film stock scratched with long flickering lines, flashing with specks and blips.

Just like that, the arena had lost its sharply etched quality. Devon assumed this was another trick of Krueger's, designed to unnerve him. He didn't realize the truth—that this was none of Krueger's doing. Devon didn't know that this deterioration in the quality of the nightmare corresponded with Trisha Smith's memory erasure and Krueger's subsequent deterioration in strength.

For lack of a better plan, Devon resumed walking toward the hospital beds, afraid that they would dematerialize at any moment. Who knew what trick Krueger might throw at him next, to disorient him? That was the coward's main strength anyway, wasn't it? Feinting before he threw the razor-tipped sucker punch.

"Looking for me, Devon?" said another voice behind him. While it was still female and young, it was not the singing child's voice. "Too little, too late. But it's the thought that counts."

Devon allowed the distraction to win his attention, if only because he recognized this voice. He turned.

It was another skeletal scarecrow, though this one was impaled through its rib-cage on a tall wooden stake. Instead of a Sunday dress, the female skeleton wore a black, long-sleeved top but it was no longer tight on her body, no longer made inviting bumps of her breasts that he couldn't drag his eyes away from. Baggy black pants, black combat boots. Though her face was a grinning skull with black wells for eyes, the long and straight blonde hair still flowed in the breeze, and Devon thought he could even detect a freshly-washed shampoo scent.

"Autumn," he whispered and he knew then that he was indeed too late to rescue her, just as her voice had said.

With his eyes on it, her skeleton had nothing more to say. Her face just leered at him enigmatically like those skull faces stenciled on her bedroom walls.

As if to purposely mock him, a crow fluttered down out of the air and alighted on one of the scarecrow's shoulders. "Get off her!" Devon snarled, lunging forward, so angry he had to catch himself before he swung the bomb off his shoulder like a club. Fortunately, the crow burst into flight again with a petulant squawk.

He was almost reluctant to leave her, if this thing could truly be thought of as Autumn, but he had no choice. There was nothing he could do for her now, real or illusion. Devon turned his back on her and headed on toward the stadium's center. It was close now.

His "roommate" lay there just as before, his life support read-outs and TV set blank and soundless. The TV for Devon's bed, however, was still playing that nature documentary about praying mantises. It looked like the same vivid green mantis he had seen on the screen when he'd awakened but instead of munching on a smaller insect, it now appeared to be holding a human finger bone in its serrated forelimbs, and gnawing on it busily with its mandibles. More of Krueger's mind-screwing. Devon didn't have time for it.

He set down the bomb between the bones of his roommate's legs in order to free his hands to work on knotting together a rope. He was just pulling the top sheet off his own empty bed when he heard a scratching sound behind him, like knife blades against glass. Devon turned in time to see the TV's screen spider-web as if a hammer had struck the glass—from the inside.

A second blow and the glass shattered. The arm of an impossibly large mantis emerged, scrabbling at the air as if blindly feeling for something to slash with its metallic barbs. The limb's exoskeleton was green striped with red.

"Shit!" Devon hissed, watching as the head of the mantis pushed through the screen, its blank globular eyes fixed on him, and mandibles working as if in anticipation of chewing his flesh. The immense insect continued pressing its striped body through the frame of the broken TV. The second forearm followed, and then the first of the slender hind legs. As big as it was, the insect appeared to be growing even larger before Devon's stunned eyes. Its long abdomen was so thick by the time it squeezed through the TV that the set's plastic casing itself suddenly cracked wide into two pieces, spitting out a brief cascade of sparks. Then the mantis—as big as a man—dropped to the floor of the arena like a new cicada having crawled out of its shed husk.

The mantis reared up and cocked its head to one side, contemplating him. The bent front claws that gave the creature its name scissored languidly as if to tease him, their jagged rows of spurs gleaming like steel shark's teeth. Devon thought he could understand why Krueger had selected this manifestation. It was the pure, mindless embodiment of a predator.

Devon had backed against the edge of his roommate's hospital bed, and he groped behind him for the bomb he had left there. To distract Krueger from his actions, he put on a show of mock bravado, trying to keep his voice from quavering. "Aren't you going to say something like, 'You really *bug* me, Devon?'"

No words came from between the mantis's mandibles. Its muteness was more eerie than if it had said something to him. Instead, it simply began stalking toward him slowly on its stilt-like, green and red banded legs.

In the boiler room limbo, Grace had almost plunged head-on into a wall that appeared out of the steam as if dropped down in front of her that very second but instead of blocking her, it actually offered her a means of escape. She blinked, and after the blink there was a door in the wall that she swore hadn't been there at first. It was metal, and streaked with rust, and when she tried the handle, she discovered that it was unlocked, as well.

She went through the door and slammed it behind her with a ringing metallic clang. There was no bolt on the other side, or any other means to lock it, so she just resumed running to put as much distance between Krueger and herself as she could.

As she ran, Grace noted that she was in a corridor made from stone, its ceiling arched. It was extremely dark, but ahead of her she saw flickering orange illumination that she recognized as firelight. There seemed to be a number of evenly spaced flames, and she let them guide her. When she reached the first of them, she saw that it was a burning torch fitted into a wall sconce. Thinking that the torch might be useful as a weapon (maybe she could burn that burnt demon again), she carefully brought the torch down and held it out in front of her as she continued on through the tunnel, now at a brisk walk instead of a run. She kept throwing furtive glances over her shoulder.

The corridor curved, she realized, as if it traced a gigantic circle. She followed this curve, and as she did so a window or doorway appeared at the end of the tunnel. The light through this opening was a flat pearly gray, but it was daylight nonetheless. Something else was revealed, however.

There had been sounds to prepare her to some extent, but seeing the birds was worse than hearing their many little croaks and mutterings had been. Because of these subdued noises, she had guessed that there were crows roosting inside the tunnel for its final stretch, but she froze in her tracks when she saw how *many* of them filled the end of the stone corridor.

Hundreds of quick, glossy black heads jerked to look in her direction. The wavering orange glow from her torch glittered in their seemingly countless, bead-like eyes. Her sudden appearance made the birds restless. They rustled nervously, shifting around each other, many even hopping a little into the air, fluttering their wings briefly.

Grace took a few tentative steps forward. She was terrified that once she was in their midst, surrounded by them, the crows would abruptly lunge at her from all sides, nipping at her flesh, pecking the meat right off her bones like a school of airborne piranha. She was more afraid of what might be *behind* her in the tunnel so she advanced a few steps more and again, testing the waters. Slowly, so slowly...

She was amongst them now, shuffling along gingerly. One crow hopped onto her foot and then off; she wanted to scream. Their feathers brushed her ankles as she waded through them but at least the opening was close now; it was an arched doorway, and she could see outside. The horrible vision out there told her where she was.

Skeletons. Thousands upon thousands of human skeletons that sat and watched some drama, some battle, taking place in the arena below.

Just as Devon's hand closed around the straps of the bomb, the mantis scrambled at him with a startling burst of speed, its long legs carrying it across the space between them in a heartbeat.

Instinctively, Devon swung the home-made bomb around in front of him like a shield. Let the monster lash out with its claws and strike it—ignite it. If the two of them went up in a ball of flames together, so be it.

At the sight of the bomb, the praying mantis recoiled warily, retracting its vicious claws.

"Oh you don't like this, huh?" Devon taunted it, side-stepping now so that he wasn't boxed in by the hospital beds. He thrust the bomb out at the mantis with both hands. "You afraid of this, Krueger? Who's the terrorist now, huh? You or me?"

The mantis side-stepped too, and made a menacing chittering sound with its mandibles. It wanted to strike out with those claws so badly that Devon could taste its rage. He knew that if he let down his guard for a second…

"Krueger!" screamed a distant voice, which the amphitheater's vastness caused to echo.

The scream ignited another kind of explosion. A black cloud blasted out of an arched doorway in one of the arena's tiered walls, up amongst the rows and rows of seats. It was a cloud that broke into hundreds of cawing and squawking crows, excitedly beating their oily-black wings.

The mantis's head swiveled on its neck, and Devon looked up as well. He gaped at what he saw. Grace had emerged from that doorway, and she was being roughly buffeted by the startled crows as they streamed out into the air. In doing so, a good many of the birds passed through the lapping flames of a torch Grace held in one fist. As a result, these crows caught flame and flapped above the arena madly, circling and swooping, seeming to almost tumble through the air in their pain and panic. It was a surreal image that even transfixed the mantis. As much as the creature was distracted by the explosion of crows, it was even more focused on the beautiful young girl who had stepped out of that dark passageway.

Devon was distracted as well. *Grace!* What was Grace doing here? At the same instant, he also knew that he must use this opportunity—must take advantage of the monster's distraction. It was obvious to him that Grace was purposely creating a diversion, with the intention of luring Krueger away from him. She was stumbling down a stone flight of steps, as much to get away from the last of the escaping crows as to get closer to the edge of the viewing area. As she came, she again screamed, "Krueger!"

Devon made his move. He dashed to the right, as if to simply run away from the mantis, but his intention was to then cut sharply left and circle around in back of it, to seize onto its body from behind. Not only would he be away from those claws up front, but he could then strap the bomb around its middle and fasten it onto its back.

But as much as Grace presently commanded the predator's attention, it still caught Devon's sudden movement peripherally. It whirled around with terrible speed and grace, its folded claws like straight razors ready to open for the slashing.

Trisha Smith watched in mounting confusion—and the beginning of frustrated anger—as Alex hovered above the body of a lovely young teenage girl, drooped limply in the chair where a few minutes earlier she herself had awoken. He had placed the neuromodulation halo on the unconscious girl's head, and was now reaching over to punch in a command on a keyboard.

"Why are you doing this, Alex? Why can't you tell me?" Trisha persisted in questioning him.

Alex was so absorbed in his actions that he didn't even glance at her. Instead, he flashed over to where Devon slumped in another chair, to check on his condition and observe him for signs of distress. "Devon! Devon!" Once again he shook him forcefully, but once again Devon wouldn't come out of his slumber. Alex had wanted to erase his brother's memory first, and apparently Devon had been in the dream realm longer so he might be more at risk, but Alex had to concede that Devon was physically stronger than Grace and theoretically better able to protect himself from Krueger if he came under attack. If only he could subject them both to the erasing process at the same time!

"Alex, do you hear me?" Trisha said, following behind him. "God, you'd better have a really good reason for erasing my memory, that's all I can say."

Ama was standing beside Grace's chair, holding her hand. She looked over and said, "Trust us, Trisha."

Trisha looked back at her, exasperated. "Who are you?

"I'm Grace's friend, Ama."

"And who is Grace?"

"*She's* Grace." Ama nodded down at the girl in the chair.

"Devon's girlfriend," Alex said, now checking Grace's progress meter.

"Devon has a girlfriend?"

Alex finally looked up at her. "Trisha, will you *please* just sit down?"

"All right, okay, fine." Trisha raised her hands as she backed off, and then muttered, "I'm going to make a pot of coffee."

"Good idea," Alex said.

"At least I can still remember how to do that," she huffed, walking across the lab.

In swinging around, the mantis caught Devon with the side of one of its front claws, rather than the serrated metal blades, but the impact smashed into his left wrist with an agonizing crack of breaking bone. The bomb he had been holding in both hands was flung out of his grip, struck the arena floor and tumbled away. The blow had thrown Devon onto his side, and from his low angle he saw the bomb come to rest under the hospital bed he had been lying in when he entered the dreamscape. For a breathless moment, he expected this rough handling to detonate the explosive device. Did Krueger expect it, too? Maybe belatedly realizing the risk it had run in striking at Devon blindly, the mantis kept back from charging him.

But the bomb did not go off.

"Get away from him!" Grace was shrieking from the stands, waving the torch as a further bid for Krueger's attention. "Come and get me! You want me, not him!"

The mantis's extraterrestrial-like head pivoted to gaze her way again. Meanwhile, Devon scurried to his feet as quickly as he could with the use of only one hand. He dug his right hand into his pocket for the TV remote. He had to get the battery back into it or it was useless! Then, he had to reach under the bed and retrieve that bomb. Whether a weapon or merely a shield, it was all that stood between him and Krueger. Maybe he couldn't get close enough to actually attach the explosive to him, but if he could just throw it at him or slide it across the ground, under the mantis's body, and hit enough buttons to cause the device to go off.

The mantis's head rotated his way again and saw Devon awkwardly trying to stick the battery back into the remote with just one hand, pinning the remote against his thigh to do. Devon lifted his gaze to see that the monster was no longer engaged by Grace's diversion. It started stamping toward him once more on those long, green and red-striped legs, intent on reaching him before he could attempt to reach the bomb.

Startled, Devon fumbled the battery. It dropped to his feet.

"No!" Grace yelled but then her voice began to taper away, like the shout of someone falling down a deep, deep well. This odd change in her tone caused both the mantis and Devon to look her way again.

It was more a ghost of Grace they saw, a translucent phantom image of her. It was so insubstantial, in fact, that the torch had fallen through a fist no longer able to hold it. Then, a second later, even the phantom was gone. Grace had vanished.

There was another one of those one-second earthquakes that Devon had experienced before. This one jolted the arena more violently. He heard blocks of masonry tumble here and there, but there was a more profound disruption. All those seated skeletons were not wired together like the one in his biology class at Springwood High. Whatever force had been holding them intact was withdrawn now. All at once, 50,000 skeletons fell into pieces in their seats. The crashing sound was ear-splitting, like nothing Devon could have imagined. Falling bones collided with each other, so that the skulls and limbs of the skeletons closest to the Colosseum's edge actually began raining down into the arena itself.

There were other changes. Every crow that had not already dropped cooked from the sky now plummeted dead as if shot. A thumping rain of hundreds of dead crows. And the static in the air had become more grainy, too, making the grayish light all the murkier.

Perhaps most striking of all, however—within one blink of his eyes, Devon saw the giant mantis replaced with the familiar form of a crouching, grimacing Freddy Krueger.

Krueger was still glaring at the place where Grace had been standing before she so mysteriously disappeared. "Bitch!" he snarled. "What are they doing out there?"

Devon backed off a little, bumping the edge of the hospital bed his skeletal roommate lay on. Its form, too, had fallen into loose pieces, the jaw even having separated from the skull. Devon reached behind him, fingers scrambling.

Krueger spun around, his eyes more enraged than Devon had ever seen them. Then, the dreamstalker was spreading the knives of his gloved hand and hurtling toward him.

As soon as Grace's progress meter read 100%, Alex was tearing the neuromodulation halo's metal band off her head and transferring it to his younger brother's. Ama leaned over Grace to lightly pat her cheek and call her name.

Trisha watched her boyfriend work frantically to get Devon prepped for the memory-scrubbing procedure. "You act like it's a matter of life and death, Alex."

"It is, Trisha, believe me. And at the end, I have to go through it myself. I'll do Ama first, and then it's my turn. I'll set everything up. All you should have to do when I'm finished is take the halo off my head."

"And when it's finished, you won't know any more about all this than I know right now?"

He glanced up at her. "With any luck—no. I won't."

Devon closed his fist around his roommate's femur, and swung it with enough force to drive a baseball right out of the stadium. At the same time, he lifted his already damaged left arm like a shield as Krueger slashed with his knife fingers. They sliced deep, in four parallel rows, cutting almost to the bone but the bone in Devon's fist smashed into the side of Krueger's head with tremendous force, sending the fedora off his head.

The dreamstalker went stumbling back, knocked into a daze, and collapsed onto the empty hospital bed.

Doing his best to ignore the vividly red blood flowing out of his lacerated arm, Devon knelt down and retrieved the battery he had dropped. He then sat down heavily on the edge of his room-mate's bed to try again to insert the battery into the remote. Whether from blood loss or simply queasiness from seeing so much of it run out of his plowed flesh, Devon felt close to unconsciousness. The static all around him was in his head now. He fell back amongst his roommate's scattered bones, and they dug uncomfortably into him. In lying down this way, staring across at his new room-mate, Krueger, Devon could see the crude bomb lying under Krueger's bed.

He was so near, Devon knew the blast would kill him, too. But then, he was bleeding to death anyway and Krueger had to be stopped. He must not reach into the waking world again and he must not be here, waiting, should anyone again blunder into *his* domain.

Devon thumbed one button. A burst of sparks lit up the shadows under the bed. Randomly, his thumb pressed another button. Black smoke began to billow out from beneath the bed now.

Krueger groaned and lifted his head from his pillow groggily, like an ill-rested dreamer who'd suffered a sleep haunted with nightmares. Seeing the remote control pointed in Devon's hand, his eyes went wide.

"Shit!" he rasped.

Devon felt himself blacking out. He thumbed another button, then another but the bomb did not detonate.

His vision was failing him. He could barely see his own arm anymore. Krueger could barely see Devon's arm anymore, either. The boy was becoming translucent, just like the girl had.

Krueger began propping himself up in the bed and reaching across for that extended remote but the apparition of the boy grew even more intangible, and the remote dropped right out of his phantasmal hand.

Krueger's eyes followed the remote's descent to the arena's stone floor, glued to it until it struck that hard floor, the top side with its control keys facing downward.

The makeshift bomb detonated, just as the last ghostly outline of Devon Carmack disappeared altogether.

The fiery explosion obliterated the bed Krueger lay on and hurled him high into the air. When he struck the ground again, he bounced and rolled before coming to a stop. He felt the knotted scars on his face glowing red with fresh burns, fresh pain. And he could tell by looking down at a body that was no longer there, that he had been torn asunder in the blast.

He opened his mouth wide to howl in outrage and agony, but he had no lungs to force air up his neck, and not much in the way of a neck, either. The best he could produce was a series of bursting blood bubbles.

And then, the real earthquake hit. The ground shook, huge cracks zigzagging open in the arena's

floor. Its walls split and began to thunderously dis-
integrate, spilling more and more bones onto the
fighting floor. The sky had darkened, going black,
and lightning bolts crackled in its depths. And the
static. More and more static. Making it hard to see.
The world was drowning in static, a signal breaking
up...

A chasm-like crack in the floor of the arena
yawned even wider. Krueger's severed head went
over its edge. It plummeted down, down, still
trying to howl all the way.

TWENTY-THREE

The thing that had once been a man named Fred Krueger floated in the womb, waiting to be born.

His eyes opened, and he could see nothing in the liquid darkness. He uncoiled himself from his fetal position and reached out around him, feeling for the womb's walls. He touched them, and they were hard and cold. In feeling them more, searching for an opening, he realized that the walls were actually one circular wall, like that of a cylinder.

Krueger braced his back against the curved wall behind him, and his feet against the opposite side. Then, he pushed outward with his legs. He heard a metallic rasp, and immediately the water level began to drop as it leaked out of the split he had opened. Growling triumphantly, Krueger drew back his legs and stamped them powerfully against the compromised seam.

Suddenly, the section of pipe he floated in tilted forward from the strain of rupture and the weight of the water inside it. It swung down like a falling tower, and from its end vomited out not only the liquid contained within it, but Krueger along with it.

He thudded onto a concrete floor with a grunt, the separated section of pipe continuing to gush gallons upon gallons of water upon him but soon enough, the flow diminished and he opened his eyes.

Krueger saw the broken length of pipe, slanted down toward the floor, just a trickle now coming from the black hole at its end. The outside of the pipe was scabbed in rust but what really seized his attention was the color of the liquid dribbling out of it. Red. And not red with rust.

As he rose to his feet, Krueger looked down at his body. He was entirely painted with a coat of blood. Out of his mouth slipped an unnaturally long tongue, which swished over his cheeks and chin. He swallowed, then sighed with something like bliss. Flexing the knife-tipped fingers of his glove, he turned in a little circle, taking in his surroundings. They were only too familiar but even this monotonous limbo was better than being a scorched head on an arena floor.

He was surrounded by a dense fog of hissing, churning steam, like wall-to-wall cotton soaked with the bloody light from red emergency bulbs in little wire cages. Chains hanging from the ceiling clinked softly as they swayed. There was the drip of water from above.

Then, a less familiar sound. A harsh young voice that called out of the steam clouds.

"Yo—motherfucker."

Krueger whipped around with a startled growl.

A teenage girl emerged from the swirling mist. She was very short and very pale-skinned, her dirty-blonde hair long and straight, her squinty blue eyes defined by too much dark makeup. Her cat-like mouth curled naturally at the corners, which made for a great effect when she smirked or sneered. She was doing a little of both now. She wore a long-sleeved black top, baggy black pants, black combat boots. There was a hole in the front of her snug-fitting top through which her skin showed, but whatever wound might have corresponded with that hole had already healed.

In her right hand, she carried a screwdriver with a long blade.

Behind her, a teenage boy stepped out of the fog. Kent Lowe was tall and naturally muscular. He looked old enough that he had managed to get the artwork from the cover of a favorite music band's CD tattooed on his upper arm. In his fist he carried a large, rusty wrench.

Milton Ferrara appeared, Elizabeth Trice alongside him. Their flesh had also healed after its former, horrendous wounding. He carried a length of pipe in both fists like a bat. Liz Trice had simply found a pencil, but she gripped it like a knife.

Footsteps behind Krueger made him whirl around the other way again. Standing before him were Shane Ryan, Tim Finney and Dave Schwartz. They hadn't found any improvised weapons in the boiler room limbo, but they clenched and unclenched their bare fists.

From another side, out of the steam came Julie Ip, her lovely Asian eyes hard and narrowed. Along with her were Patrick Tremblay and Fotios Grigori, whom in life had been nicknamed Mr G And Farhad Azari carried a flat strip of metal in both hands as if it was a samurai sword.

Krueger desperately spun toward his last avenue of escape, but Neil Simmons stood there. He had found a box opener, and he had thumbed out its razor-sharp blade.

"Wait. No, you wait," Krueger snarled, facing Autumn Langevin again.

She grinned. "Your worlds are gone, so we're leaving now," she told him. "But we thought we'd stop by and pay our respects before we go."

"Stop!" Krueger howled, trying to scare them back by raising his knife glove, but the circle of his victims began to close around him.

"No funny little quips for us, Krueger?" asked Julie Ip.

"How about, 'Ready for a group hug?'" said Autumn Langevin in an imitated raspy tone, as she lifted her long-bladed screwdriver.

EPILOGUE

Bruce Simpson introduced himself to Devon as being from the Behavioral & Cognitive Sciences (BCS) division of the Social, Behavioral & Economic Sciences (SBE) division of the National Science Foundation (NSF). He was tall, with immaculately cut salt-and-pepper hair, a perfect tan and perfect teeth. He wasn't geeky enough to be a scientist; rather, he looked to Devon like what a team of real scientists would piece together Frankenstein-style in order to create the ultimate bureaucrat.

He was friendly enough, though, in his maybe-or-maybe-not-sincere way, and pumped Devon's hand. "So, this is the young guy I've heard so much about."

"Well, I didn't think that I was exactly ancient," Alex kidded, seated beside Devon at a work station within Macrocosm Research's main lab area.

"Oh, you're both quite the bright young men," Simpson assured him. "You guys are what we always need in the research field—fresh blood. A fresh perspective." As he let go of Devon's hand, Simpson frowned and pointed at his other arm. Devon was wearing a T-shirt, and so the four raised white scars on his forearm showed very plainly. "Wow, you did get cut very badly then, didn't you?"

Devon lifted his arm to inspect it himself. "Yeah, I guess."

"Of course, he doesn't remember anything about it," Alex explained. "When I carried him in here, my girlfriend Trisha swore she didn't see him bleeding. When she noticed it, though, she bandaged him up right away."

"So apparently the person who killed your colleagues is the same one who attacked Devon."

"That's what the police think but they still haven't apprehended a suspect. I guess you've heard that they even suspected me for a while there—and they weren't happy when they found out I'd erased my memory. That looked very suspicious to them and rightly so, I have to admit. But what can I say? I took a lie detector test for them afterwards. At least it convinced them that I didn't remember why I erased my memories. Who knows," he joked, grinning, "maybe I did kill everyone and just wanted to hide the evidence the best way I could—by destroying my recollection of it, not to mention the memories of my evil accomplices like Devon and my girlfriend."

Simpson smiled oddly, almost with a knowing kind of expression, his eyes seeming to twinkle as he studied Alex's face. "Well, I hardly think that was the case. I'm sure you had your reasons for undergoing that procedure."

"And it looks like the killer had his reasons for trashing the lab, here, and all our hard-earned data. The police suggested I did that, too, but that's even more crazy than accusing me of murder. My work is precious to me!"

"That's why I value you so much, Alex. And your brother here is cast from the same mold. I'm very pleased that young Devon will be working with us, too." He patted Devon's shoulder. "Part time, as soon as he graduates high school. And when you get out of college, Devon, you're guaranteed quite a career with Macrocosm Research. I don't work for Macrocosm myself, of course, as you know but I will certainly be pulling some strings." He winked.

"I appreciate it, Mr Simpson," said Devon earnestly.

Simpson went on, "After the tragic events that took the lives of your colleagues, your involvement in the work here at Macrocosm is more vital than ever, Alex. We need you. We need the both of you, to make a new beginning."

Devon spread his hands. "Here I am. I'm in for the long haul, sir."

"Good man," said Simpson. "Look, let me run back to my hotel, take a little nap and a quick shower, and I'll meet you boys back here when you get out. I'll treat you to a nice steak dinner, what do you say?"

"Sounds great," Alex told him.

Simpson shook hands with both brothers. "Later, then." He gave a little salute and let himself out of the rented Macrocosm suite.

"Well." Alex swiveled in his chair to beam at his kid brother. "Looks like you made a good impression. Of course, I pimped you like crazy, so you can cut me in for a percentage of your future wages if you'd like."

"Ha, keep dreaming."

Alex pivoted the monitor in front of him so that its screen faced him. Floating in a void of black background was a very solid-looking human brain, with light even reflecting on its coiled tissues. It looked to Devon like a clenched, angry fist. Alex was able to rotate the brain on the screen, which he did idly as he spoke. "Sometimes I wonder if the killer is the one who told me to erase our memories, or else he'd kill us too, and that's why I was too afraid to let Trisha know what was going on. She said I told her it was a matter of life and death."

"Mm," Devon grunted, also staring into the screen. The brain pictured there was a digital replica, produced from neuroimaging scans of one of the killer's victims. When a forensic pathologist had discovered that each of the victims' brains exhibited a strange tumor-like growth in the inferior lingual gyrus in the occipital lobes, the brains had been requested for study by Macrocosm Research. At first there had been some resistance from family members, and—oddly enough—even more resistance from the Springwood police. In the end, however, the government people from the NSF, headed by Bruce Simpson, had persisted and succeeded in at least obtaining the brains temporarily—long enough to scan them before returning them to the corpses prior to burial.

Devon read the name of the victim, as it appeared at the bottom of the screen. LANGEVIN, AUTUMN. It unnerved him to think that the organ on the monitor represented her personality, embodied her essence, contained all her loves and hates. Autumn had been his friend Kent's girl, but Devon had suspected that Autumn was still attracted to him after having pursued him unsuccessfully in their junior year.

Alex switched to the scan of another victim. IP, JULIE. Devon saw him wag his head in disbelief and deep regret. "She was a great girl, Julie. If I didn't know Trisha, I'd have been all over her."

Devon knew how he felt. He had lost close friends, too. Kent Lowe. Milton Ferrara. Why had the murderer chosen them? And why should they all have that same mysterious tumor, in various stages of progression? What had they experienced or been exposed to that could affect their brains in such a way?

Alex settled on the scan of a subject named SIMMONS, NEIL. To an untrained eye, each brain in itself would appear indistinguishable from the others, but who knew what secrets might lurk in this one anonymous-looking organ, for instance? Alex gestured at the image. "So you're gonna date this guy's daughter tomorrow night?"

"Yep. She could use a little cheering up, that's for sure. I've had a crush on her for ages. As far as we're concerned it's our first date, but the kids in school say we were already dating right before all this stuff happened." He chuckled. "It's crazy, huh?"

"That explains why she was here with us, anyway. God, who knows what was going on, though." Alex sighed. "Well, when I've got these models acting like fully functioning organic brains, I'll be going in there and digging out all the memories I can. We may have lost ours, but theirs' will probably be intact. Then hopefully we'll have some answers to what happened. Hopefully we can piece it all together."

"And put a face to this killer," Devon said grimly.

"Yeah. Whoever this bastard is," Alex Carmack promised vengefully, "we'll drag him out of the shadows—into the light."

ABOUT THE AUTHOR

Jeffrey Thomas is the author of the acclaimed collection *Punktown*, which features an introduction by Michael Marshall Smith. It has been translated into Russian and German editions, the latter with artwork by HR Giger. His novels include *Letters from Hades, Boneland, Everybody Scream!* and *Monstrocity*, which was nominated for a Bram Stoker Award. His short fiction has appeared in St. Martin's *The Year's Best Fantasy and Horror*, Daw's *The Year's Best Horror Stories, A Walk on the Darkside*, and the *Thackery T Lambshead Pocket Guide to Eccentric and Discredited Diseases*. He lives in Massachusetts. *A Nightmare on Elm Street: The Dream Dealers* is his first novel for Black Flame.

Also available from Black Flame

FINAL DESTINATION
AN ORIGINAL NOVEL™

DEATH OF THE SENSES

An orginal novel by Andy McDermott

Thirteen stories up, Manhattan was noticeably quieter than down on the street. Jack could still hear car horns below, but the constant rumble of street noise had faded, giving them an odd, distant quality.

Just as Beriev had said, there were two other cops on the roof on the tenement building, but they were keeping well back from the edge, standing near the entrance to the stairs. Looking past them, Jack could see Lonnie, or at least his top half, his back to them. His lower body was hidden behind the parapet.

"Hey, Pete. Who's this?" asked one of the cops with a dubious look at Jack as he and Beriev walked over to join them.

"Reckons he knows our guy over there," Beriev told them. Jack wasn't the least bit surprised that he didn't bother to tell the cops his name, or mention the small fact that he was also the person who'd saved his partner's life the night before. "Thinks he might be able to talk him down. What's he like at the moment?"

"Seems to have quietened down at the moment," said the cop. "Problem is, every time we try to get close he sets off again."

"What kind of things has he been saying?" Jack asked. Both cops looked at him as if waiting for Beriev's permission before deigning to reply. Beriev nodded slightly.

"Crying, mostly," said the second cop, speaking for the first time. "Lot of stuff about how he can't take any more, how he's got nothing to live for. Not very coherent, it usually turns into a screaming rant after a minute or so. I don't think he really cares whether we can make out what he's saying or not, he just wants to get it off his chest."

Beriev regarded Lonnie for a long moment. "You think he's serious about jumping, or he just wants attention?"

"Hard to tell," said the first cop. "There's been a few times when he's let go of the roof completely—puff of wind is all it'd take to send him over."

"Good job it's not windy, I guess," Beriev said, still watching Lonnie. "Okay then, Curtis. See if you can get through to him."

Jack took a deep breath, then walked slowly across the roof.

* * *

Amy wasn't quite sure how she'd got suckered into it, but she was now standing on the edge of the top step with a microphone jammed into her face and telling that over-made-up harpy Chelsea Cox everything she knew about Jack. Whatever the blonde's power of persuasion was based on, she was very adept at it.

"A real-life hero despite being homeless," gushed Chelsea, turning to face the camera and at the same time subtly moving across to push Amy towards the edge of the frame, "who follows up saving the life of a police officer one day by attempting to talk a potential suicide down from the roof of a tall building the next. An inspiration to us all. We'll bring you more on this story as it develops. This is Chelsea Cox for WNYK news." She gave the camera her trademark sign-off look, a hint of a pout and a suggestive narrowing of the eyes as she tipped her head slightly, held the pose for a few moments, then clicked her fingers. "And clear. George, you get that?"

"Got it," said George though her earpiece.

"Think you might use it?"

"We could drop it in as a breaking story during the next commercial break—if they guy's still up on the roof, that is."

"Yeah, I know it's not much, but you can cut in some footage of the leaper as well." Chelsea turned and blinked in surprise as she realised Amy was still standing next to her. "Oh, sorry. We're done now, thanks." She turned back to Brad.

"I, uh… oh." Amy felt oddly disappointed at being dismissed so suddenly, and even a little embarrassed about the fact she was still standing there like a dummy. A sudden change in the noise from the crowd made her turn.

"Hey, he's moving," said Brad, quickly aiming the camera skyward.

"Get back! Get back! I warned you, don't come any closer or I'll jump, I'll do it, I'll really do it!"

"Lonnie?" Jack called, cautiously. "Lonnie, it's me."

Lonnie stopped twitching, peering warily back over his shoulder. "Jack?" he asked in a slightly less agitated voice.

"Yeah, it's me."

"What do you want?"

Jack took another couple of careful steps, then came to a stop about six feet from the ice-covered parapet, his hands held up to show Lonnie he wasn't trying to grab him. "I was... I was kind of hoping to get you back onto this roof."

"Don't waste your time, Jack," said Lonnie, starting to twitch again. "I told you last night! I just can't take any more of this, I just can't..." His voice tailed off and he closed his eyes, slowly lowering his head. Jack thought he saw the bead of a tear grow in the corner of his eye. "I went to the shelter last night after I left you, Jack. It was full. So I went to another one. It was full too. And another, and another. You know where I slept last night, Jack?" He opened his eyes again, the tear breaking free and rushing down his cheek. "A kennel. A God-damn kennel! I slept inside a busted-up old doghouse that somebody had put out with the garbage!" His voice cracked as he started to shake, sobbing. "I had to sleep somewhere that people didn't even think was fit for an animal!"

"Lonnie," said Jack, very carefully moving a step closer to him, "listen to me. I know things are pretty bad, but that's no reason to just give up. There's always a chance, there's always hope."

"No, no, you're wrong," Lonnie said, taking one hand off the edge of the parapet to wipe his eyes. Jack winced, freezing in place. "There's no point. This is it, Jack, this is the bottom. There's nowhere else I can go."

"Except up."

"You really believe that?" Lonnie asked, looking over his shoulder at Jack again. "Look at me! Look at what I've turned into—what I'm doin' right now! No, there *is* no chance, there *is* no hope. Not for me, anyway. If all that I've got to look forward to for the rest of my life is more of the same *shit*," he suddenly yelled the word, "that I've had for the last few years, then... then what's the fuckin' point?" He looked away, staring out across the city.

Jack took the opportunity to move another small step closer to him.

"I can see him," Brad suddenly announced. Chelsea and Amy both looked at the monitor. Even at the sharp angle from which they were looking up at the roof, Jack's head was now visible above its edge. That meant he must only be a couple of feet from Lonnie, Amy realized.

"Keep the camera on him," Chelsea ordered. "George, you watching this?"

"I'm not even blinking," the reply crackled through her earpiece.

"Ready to go live if we need to?"

"My finger's on the button."

Jack could now see enough of the street below to give him a slight feeling of vertigo. He had no idea whether Lonnie was prone to it or not, but he was close enough to see that even in the cold, his friend was sweating.

"A cop told me something this morning," he said, trying to keep his voice as level as possible. "She said that even if people really do mean to kill themselves by jumping, they always scream on the way down. The second they do it, they regret it."

Lonnie said nothing, but Jack could tell by his expression that he was listening.

"It's no way to go out," Jack continued. "Screaming in terror because you realize you've just made the worst mistake of your life and there's nothing you can do to change it." He hoped he wasn't overdoing it, but he was running out of options.

"I've made other mistakes," Lonnie sobbed.

"But there's still a chance you might be able to do something to fix them! I mean, come on, look at how much you helped me. I wouldn't have survived my first couple of months on the streets if I hadn't met you, if you hadn't told me how to keep going. Lonnie, please, let me help you." He made a deliberate move forward, now only one step away from being able to reach out and touch Lonnie. Or grab him.

"Jesus, he's almost there," said Brad, barely breathing.

Chelsea put down the monitor and moved back in front of the camera. Whatever happened, it was going to take place in the next few seconds, and she wanted to be ready.

"Get back on the roof," Jack begged.

"What about them?" Lonnie asked, shooting a look in the direction of the cops. "What'll they do to me?"

"I don't know. They'll probably arrest you, but—" he quickly continued, seeing fear cross Lonnie's face, "believe me, a night in a cell's not so bad. I was in one last night."

"What did you do?" Lonnie asked through his tears.

"I'll tell you... if you get back on the roof. Here." He held out his hand.

Amy tensed, one hand to her mouth. She didn't have to watch the monitor now to see Jack reaching out for Lonnie.

Slowly, shakily, Lonnie took one hand off the parapet... and reached back over it, his trembling fingers touching Jack's.

Jack closed his grip. The two men looked at each other for a moment. Lonnie managed to smile for the first time in days.

"He's got him!" Brad gasped.

Chelsea frowned. A leaper being talked down from a roof as opposed to jumping from it was a third or fourth story, at best.

"Okay, Lonnie," said Jack, "now, really slowly, really carefully, turn around. I've got you. Just turn around and let me pull you back up."

From nowhere, a cold wind sprang up. It wasn't like a normal wind, Jack thought, a continuous force of moving air; this somehow felt more like a snake circling around them, looking for the place to strike...

Lonnie shifted slightly as the wind hit him, one foot on the ledge, the other raised just above it as he prepared to turn around.

Ice cracked under his toes.

Lonnie's foot shot out from the ledge, his unsupported weight instantly dragging Jack forward and slamming him hard against the unforgiving brick of the parapet. Pain ripped across his chest.

But he still had Lonnie's hand—

"Whoa!" Chelsea gasped. Even anticipating the fall hadn't prepared her for it.

But the man wasn't falling, not just yet...

* * *

"Help me!" Jack screamed over his shoulder at the cops, as Lonnie kicked and thrashed in panic on the other side of the parapet. "Help!"

He could hear them charging across the roof, but he couldn't keep his grip. Lonnie's fingers were slipping...

Amy made an indistinct sound of horror somewhere deep in her throat as the struggling man broke free of Jack's grip and plummeted downwards with terrifying speed, his coat caught by the wind and flapping open like wings—wings that could never fly.

"Shit!" exclaimed Chelsea involuntarily, not caring if she was now on a live feed. She watched him drop, whipping past the windows behind him. Whatever happened, however messy things were, she had to be ready to turn to camera and deliver her report...

"No!" Jack yelled, the cops crashing against the parapet, against him, just a fraction of a second too late.

Amy watched, unable to look away, as Lonnie fell and started to scream. Nine floors up, eight, seven-six...

Lonnie's flapping coat snagged on one of the phone wires stretching across the street. It should have either torn under his weight or simply slid off as he fell past.

It didn't.

Instead, it wrapped around the cable, not once, but twice. Impossibly.

But impossible or not, it held. Lonnie was jolted to an abrupt, rib-breaking halt just two stories above the ground.

Tracking Lonnie's fall, Brad was caught by surprise when the plunging figure suddenly stopped, continuing to tilt the camera all the way down to the ground before he realized something had happened. Reacting on cameraman's instinct, he snapped the zoom lens in to cover as wide an area as possible, Chelsea flashing into view as the picture pulled back. The guy was caught on something at the top of the frame...

Lonnie's coat finally ripped and he started to fall again.

Chelsea snapped her head round to look into the camera in amazement. "Did you get that?" she gasped.

The phone wire, freed of the sudden weight that had pulled it down, cracked like a whip, a wave motion rushing along its length towards the other side of the street.
Lonnie hit the ground, injured but still alive.

Amy barely had enough time to register what had just happened when something passed above her, a strange serpentine movement. The phone line…

The wave reached the end of the phone wire where it connected to the building where Amy, Brad and Chelsea were standing on the steps.

Ice had built up on the wall from a leaking pipe, growing one freezing drip at a time to spread like tentacles along the half-dozen lines running into the building. Hanging down below the cold mass were long, pointed icicles, melted and refrozen together over days into top-heavy masses with claw-like points.

The wave hit the heavy ice. Part of the motion was sent back along the wire; the rest was transmitted into the ice as a vibration.

The ice shattered with a sound like breaking glass.

Chelsea instinctively looked up at the unexpected noise directly above her.

It was the last living thing she ever did.

A chunk of ice, two huge icicles melded together with foot-long tips sharp as daggers, hit her in the face. The jagged spikes plunged right through both of her eyes in a wet spray of ruptured eyeball and spurting blood and brain matter. The sheer weight of the ice rammed the tips of the icicles right through the back of her skull before the shock of the impact sheared most of the frozen mass away. It crashed to the ground between Brad and Chelsea's still-standing corpse and exploded into jagged fragments.

* * *

Amy turned when she heard the noise, just in time to see the back of Chelsea's head burst open in a slurry of red and gray. The body somehow stayed balanced for a moment, hands twitching, before its knees slowly buckled and it toppled backwards down the steps, long shards of ice still protruding from its gushing eye sockets. Somebody behind Amy shrieked. She would have done so herself if she'd been able to catch her breath.

A voice was yelling in Brad's ear. It took him some time to work out that it was George back at the studio frantically telling him that they were still live and asking him what had happened. The face in his viewfinder wasn't Chelsea but the young Asian cop they'd just interviewed, staring at him in horror.

Had what he'd just seen through his camera been real? He cautiously pulled his head back from the viewfinder and looked down.

It *had* been real.

"Did you get *that?*" he asked, of nobody in particular, before throwing up.

The story continues in

DEATH OF THE SENSES

1-84416-385-7

An orginal novel by Andy McDermott

Available from Black Flame
www.blackflame.com